KOUSBAWI

A Story of love

By Lynda Chehade

Published by New Generation Publishing in 2015

www.newgeneration-publishing.com

 New Generation Publishing

Dedication

For my dear husband Nicolas Fouad Chehade, a
unique and wonderful man and the inspiration
behind the story of Kousbawi. Written as a tribute to
your life and memory, I dedicate this book to you
with all my love.

I will love you forever.

Love has no other desire but to fulfil itself. To melt and be
like a running brook that sings its melody to the night. Life
without love is like a tree without blossoms or fruit.

Kahlil Gibran.

KOUSBAWI

Contents: Chapters 1- 51

Contents:

Contents:

KOUSBAWI

Chapter1: Encounter

Laura Quinn was tired, but feeling mildly elated as she
wearily made her way through the Prive club towards the
exit. The show had been well-received that night by an
enthusiastic Emirati audience, and everyone was still on a
high. The Prive, an exclusive night club and cabaret room,
was situated on the lower ground floor of the Holiday Inn
hotel in Abu Dhabi UAE. As Laura walked with her fellow
performers, she was blissfully unaware that before she
reached her hotel room that night, her destiny would be
rewritten. This was where it began for the young dancer, in
the early hours of January 2nd 1983. Laura was to embark
on a journey. No ordinary journey, but a journey of the
heart that would take her into the realms of fairy tales and
the abyss in equal measure. As Laura approached the exit
with the rest of the dancers and singers, the group were
intercepted. Alan, the clubs flamboyant entertainments
manager, called after them in an excited tone;

"Hey guys, before you leave there's a gentleman at the
bar who'd very much like to meet you," Alan informed.

People often asked to meet the act after a show; Laura
was used to it. Seemingly this would be no different from
the many introductions encountered during her performing
career. It was nearly three in the morning, and the fatigued
Laura had no desire to be chatted up by another stage door
Johnny at this late hour. But Alan was insistent, so along
with her co-band members, Laura reluctantly obliged and
followed him back to the Prive bar. With an exaggerated
rather camp flourish, Alan presented a tall, incredibly
handsome young man, who looked to be in his mid-
twenties.

"This is the young man who wishes to meet you," he
enthusiastically told them. "I'll leave you guys to it," Alan
said, then he discreetly walked away.

The young man smiled at Laura. She felt him slowly undress her with his eyes. His extremely attractive dark eyes openly conveyed he liked what he saw. He introduced himself;

"Hi, I'm Nicolas," he said in a in a deep masculine tone, appealingly wrapped in the most delectable foreign accent.

Laura met his alluring gaze and politely held out her hand to him. Nicolas took her hand but didn't shake it. Instead he lifted her hand to his lips and deliberately keeping his seductive dark eyes locked on hers, gently kissed it. As Nicolas's lips softly caressed her flesh, a pleasurable tingle ran through Laura's veins. There was a peculiar familiarity felt by both, as if they'd met before. It was quite unexpected, but something seemed to stir and awaken within them; like an electric pulse, igniting a long lost memory. For the longest time their eyes stayed locked together. Almost breathlessly Laura said at last,

"Lovely to meet you Nicolas, I'm Laura."

Nicolas was impeccably dressed. His appearance was not typically Arabian as he was wearing a light grey rather expensive-looking suit with a red silk tie, and not the traditional robes many of the men at the club wore. His look was more Mediterranean than Arab. With his name being Nicolas, Laura supposed he might possibly originate from Europe.

"Where are you from Nicolas? Are you European?" she asked.

This seemed to amuse him. Nicolas gave her a wide smile. He had beautiful chiselled features, and with perfect white teeth his smile was to die for. Laura had never experienced such charismatic vibes emanate from anyone she'd ever met before. The attraction between them was mutual and immediate. Unlike Nicolas, Laura was too shy to act upon it; modestly she maintained a cool, reserved persona.

"I am Lebanese, Christian Lebanese," he announced, proudly adding, "Phoenician, from the north."

He seemed keen to emphasize that he was Phoenician, and not of Arab descent. This emphasis was lost on Laura. She knew little of the Levant's history, or of Middle Eastern politics, so the significance of Nicolas's proud statement didn't really register. Laura was not acquainted with Lebanon either; she barely knew its position on the map. Her only knowledge of it came via the nightly news bulletins of its troubled war torn capital Beirut. But this strikingly handsome man was very proud, and fiercely patriotic of his beloved country. Laura was fascinated. They had barely been introduced, but already the obvious chemistry between them could have set the place on fire.

"Did you enjoy the show tonight?" she asked curiously.

"No, I didn't see, I just arrive from Beirut now," he told her. "Can I offer you and your friends some drink?"

Laura found his accent and imperfect English grammar endearing and rather sexy, but endeavoured to conceal her attraction. Somewhat less modestly, Nicolas had already marked Laura as his next conquest. In front of him she displayed cool indifference, quickly averting her eyes from his penetrating gaze. It was late, and hardly anyone was left in the Prive club. The bar staff were starting to close up. Laura looked around.

"The bar is already closing," she observably stated.

"They will open it for me." Nicolas said self-assuredly. He was demonstrating the kind of confidence exhibited by a man used to getting what he wants. Laura and the rest of the group were duly impressed, but all the same declined his offer. It was fast approaching 3.15am, and they were tired. Laura thought she sensed an air of disappointment in the handsome stranger. She gathered Nicolas was not often said no to, especially by women. With subtle diplomacy Laura quickly added,

"Why don't you come and see our show tomorrow night? We'd be delighted to join you after for a drink."

Nicolas had a temptingly attractive twinkle in his eye.

"Are you inviting me Laura?" he asked.

His overtly flirtatious manner threatened to make her

blush. Men flirted with the female performers all the time, but this sweet talking guy was on another level; Nicolas's irresistible charm was a perfected art. Laura was finding it difficult to refuse his enticing invitation to stay. But she held her composure telling him coolly,

"Yes I am inviting you, and look forward to seeing you tomorrow night."

Nicolas responded with;

"Okay…, then I will have the champagne waiting."

He gave a broad smile. Laura noticed how it lit up his whole face. The group bid him goodnight and left. Laura felt Nicolas's eyes follow her all the way to the exit.

Backstage the following evening while doing her warm up exercises, Laura wondered if Nicolas would be in the audience. She didn't know why, but she was excited at the prospect of seeing him again. It was inexplicable, considering they had been in each other's company for barely five minutes. All the same, Laura felt a weird connection to this charming, charismatic, Phoenician man.

As the group walked onto the cabaret floor to perform their first number, Laura spotted Nicolas. She could hardly have missed him sitting there at the very front table. He looked directly at Laura, lifting his whisky glass to her as a form of acknowledgement. She smiled back demurely. All through the performance Laura felt a quiver of excitement, conscious Nicolas was watching her every move.

Straight after the show, Alan flounced buoyantly into the dressing room congratulating the group on another successful performance.

"Oh and by the way," he told them, "Mr Nicolas is requesting your company at his table."

The group quickly changed out of their costumes, then proceeded to join Nicolas in the club. As they approached his table he stood to greet them. Nicolas then cordially introduced the other two people sitting with him. Mounir, also Lebanese, was a short little guy with greying hair who looked somewhat older than Nicolas. His other companion was Rajai, a tall handsome Jordanian.

After the introductions Nicolas signalled to the waiter. A perfectly chilled bottle of Don Perignon champagne was immediately brought to the table. Moments later a bottle of Johnnie Walker Black Label whisky followed. That night as the champagne flowed, Laura and Nicolas chatted and danced until the early hours. He thought her vivacious, feminine and sexy. With flowing auburn hair, green eyes, and a coquettish playful manner, Nicolas was extremely attracted; a fact he made no attempt to conceal. She found him intelligent, charming, and wittily mischievous.

Their lives and backgrounds couldn't have been more different. Laura had danced from the tender age of five, originally showing great promise in the art of ball-room dancing, before devoting her young life to the disciplined environment that was the world of classical ballet. Having travelled extensively with various companies and groups, she was an experienced performer, but a little deficient in worldly wisdom where men were concerned; especially men like Nicolas. Already he had quite turned her head, but Laura shyly continued to play it cool, politely resisting Nicolas's obvious advances. This only served to make him all the more determined to win her over. Her coyness enthralled him, especially as her eyes flirtatiously signalled a distinct and undeniable attraction. As Laura's tantalizing beauty continued to intrigue and fascinate him, Nicolas remained the perfect gentleman.

With a reputation to uphold in that he never failed to get any woman he set his sights on into his bed, Nicolas was determined to conquer this ice maiden. He didn't bank on it taking quite so long. Women normally fell at his feet. Within minutes of meeting this prince of charm, they would gladly succumb. Nicolas was persistent in his pursuit. Realising Laura was not going to fall for his charms as easily as he had hoped, he planned to change tactics. Falling in love was definitely not a part of that plan. But as they danced until dawn, this tiny little lady was captivating his heart, so Nicolas prepared to play the long game.

By 5 am the group of seven were the only people left in the Prive club. It had apparently stayed open just for them. Nicolas seemed to wield a lot of influence, which had not gone unnoticed by Laura, who was rather impressed by his obvious sway and confident charismatic charm. The group decided to go to the hotels coffee shop for breakfast. There were a few other early morning guests, and the coffee shops Filipino attendants were welcoming, as they happily served the group with breakfast.

At 7.am Mounir and Rajai left the hotel. Laura, Nicolas and the rest of the group, made their way to the lift to return to their rooms. Having recently given up his Abu Dhabi apartment, Nicolas now resided permanently at the Holiday Inn. His room was on the fourth floor and Laura's on the eighth. As the elevator doors opened at level four, Laura asked Nicolas what time he planned to wake up;

"Wake up?" He said with an amused air, "I'm not going to sleep; I will take my shower and go to my office."

Laura couldn't help feeling a little guilty. She would now go and sleep all day, while Nicolas would be working.

They arranged to meet later at the hotel's rooftop swimming pool for five o'clock tea. Earlier that evening Laura had kiddingly persuaded Nicolas it was an English tradition; a custom she and the others regularly adhered to. After wishing Laura a nice sleep, Nicolas got out on the fourth floor.

"See you at five for tea then," Laura called after him. Nicolas waved without looking back and disappeared along the corridor. It was a rare occasion that he returned to his room alone.

Laura slept easily until 3.45pm. At 4.30 she took the lift to the sixteenth floor, and then walked up the half dozen steps leading to the hotels rooftop pool. Some of the other performers were already there sunbathing. After saying hello to them, Laura took a seat at the poolside café. She anxiously waited to see if Nicolas would show.

Dead on the dot at five o' clock he arrived, looking

immaculate in his suit. This was the first time Laura saw Nicolas in daylight. She wasn't disappointed. As he came over to the table, her heart fluttered. Something appeared to be brewing within Laura's psyche; she felt goose bumps as he smiled at her. Nicolas was again accompanied by Rajai, his Jordanian companion from the night before. Rajai and Nicolas had become close friends, and were now virtually inseparable. Laura was amazed at how cool the pair of them looked in their suits, despite the intense Abu Dhabi heat.

"You slept well?" Nicolas politely asked as he took a seat.

"Yes thank you, but what about you?" Laura inquired. "You must be tired?"

"I slept for two hours this afternoon," Nicolas told her.

"Only two hours?" She exclaimed. "And you don't feel tired?"

"It's nothing," he said casually. "Many times I didn't sleep when I was fighting in the north."

Nicolas was referring to the Lebanese civil war which was still on-going.

"How about you Rajai, did you sleep?" Laura inquired of his Jordanian side-kick.

Before Rajai could utter an answer, Nicolas interrupted; "He didn't go to work; he slept all the day like you."

Rajai just shrugged. The two men said something to one another in Arabic and started laughing.

Three of the cabaret performers came over to say hello. Nicolas invited them for the traditional five o'clock tea. He and Rajai put two tables together to make enough room for everybody. Tea was ordered and when it arrived, they had a light-hearted discussion about the correct way to drink it. Nicolas and Rajai drank their tea black and found it amusing that Laura and the others added cold milk.

"It's the English way," Laura told them.

Nicolas ordered some sandwiches with more tea, and the six of them sat chatting in the late afternoon sun. At around 6.15pm, Nicolas announced he needed to go back

7

to his office. Everyone left together. Nicolas and Rajai said they would be at the Prive later to watch the show.

Every night for the next two weeks Nicolas was at the Prive club. He always sat at the same front table smiling at Laura throughout the show. Usually he was accompanied by Rajai or Mounir or both. Sometimes one or two others would be present in his little entourage. Nicolas couldn't take his eyes off Laura as she danced tantalisingly in front of him. After the show Laura and the other performers would join him at his table.

Some Prive club regulars protested that Nicolas always had the company of the cabaret artists exclusively at his table. Occasionally, the rivalry for the group's attention would develop into an argument between Nicolas and the other club guests, who jealously demanded the group accept invitations to join their tables. There was a bit of an altercation one night because Nicolas and his entourage constantly bagged the best front table. Laura and the rest of the performers, found the rivalry for their attention quite amusing.

On subsequent nights at the Prive Nicolas bought Laura the finest Dom Perignon champagne, while he drank his Black label whisky. Nicolas would always lay the whisky bottle flat on the table which amused Laura. She was never sure why he did this, and Nicolas never explained.

When they weren't dancing the night away, they talked endlessly; naturally Nicolas and Laura's connection grew progressively stronger. One little complication stood in the way of their developing relationship; Nicolas was married. When Laura inquired as to his relationship status, Nicolas was very upfront and never made any secret of the fact that he had a wife. Despite finding Nicolas incredibly attractive and enjoying his charming company, Laura was reluctant to take it further, believing that becoming romantically involved with a married man would most likely result in her getting hurt.

He had married the previous August, now barely four months into his marriage Nicolas confided to Laura he was unhappy. He openly confessed he had never been faithful to his wife, not even at the beginning. It was a brave and honest confession. Laura listened with a sympathetic ear, but wasn't prepared to be just another of Nicolas's many conquests. Laura would hold back from falling for a man who wasn't free, or with whom she wasn't completely enamoured. Nicolas wasn't free and at this point, although captivated by this sweet talking Phoenician charmer, Laura was not yet in love.

As for Nicolas, he was already quite smitten, but had not conveyed this fact to Laura. His initial plan had been merely to enjoy seducing her into his bed. So far that hadn't worked. The chase was all part of the game though, and Nicolas relished the challenge. There was something about Laura that was different, setting her apart from the many other women in his life. It was unknown territory for this Middle Eastern Casanova to have a woman hold back from him, the way Laura was doing. Nicolas always had a plan though, and if plan A didn't work, there was always plan B.

As is the custom with Middle Eastern men, Nicolas had a set of worry beads that he carried everywhere. While sitting with Laura after the show one night, Nicolas took the beads from his jacket pocket. So as to get Laura to notice them, he flamboyantly began twirling and playing with the beads in a very obvious fashion. Fascinated, Laura asked if she could have a look at them. Nicolas happily handed Laura the string of beads, telling her they had been a gift from his father. The following night Laura joined Nicolas as usual at his table. The broad smile he normally greeted her with, was tonight replaced by an intense rather solemn expression.

"Are you okay?" she asked. Nicolas's sudden change of mood concerned her.

"No, I'm not okay." The tone of his voice was serious as was the look on his face. "I need to ask you something."

"What is it?" Laura asked, wondering what could have upset him.

"You remember the beads I show you last night?" he continued.

"Yes, the ones your father gave to you. What about them?" Laura asked.

"I can't find them. Maybe you take them with you last night? I didn't see them since you hold them."

Laura looked at him in amazement. His English wasn't perfect, but it was clear what Nicolas was implying. Was he actually accusing her of stealing the beads? Laura looked him in the eye adamantly telling Nicolas;

"I don't have them, why would I?" Laura felt hurt that he would accuse her.

"Maybe you take them by mistake. Please, look in your bag." He insisted.

Annoyed and irritated by his accusation, Laura handed Nicolas her bag, telling him angrily;

"Here, you look if you think I have them. But I assure you they are not in there."

Nicolas tried to remain serious as Laura glared at him.

"I'm sorry I must find them, they are from my father."

Nicolas's sad, mournful expression made her feel sorry for getting angry. In a calmer tone, Laura asked him to recall his movements. They searched around the seats where they were sitting, and then Laura suggested he may have left the beads in his room.

"You will help me to look?" Nicolas asked innocently.

Laura agreed to accompany him to his room and help look for the missing beads, unaware this was exactly what Nicolas had hoped she would say. Together they entered room 110 on the fourth floor. Naïve to Nicolas's clever but deceptive tactics; Laura innocently started to search for the beads. Nicolas sat down on the sofa and somewhat over dramatically, he sighed heavily.

"My father gave them to me I must find them," he said mournfully.

His playacting managed to convince the gullible Laura who in a bid to comfort, immediately sat beside him. Determined to find the precious beads for him, Laura enthusiastically began searching behind the cushions. Putting her hand into the gap at the back of the sofa, she reached down to the floor where her fingers touched what felt to be a string of beads. Pulling the beads up off the floor she happily handed them to Nicolas. He gave her a convincing relieved smile, conveying heartfelt gratitude. Laura was blissfully unaware of Nicolas's sleight of hand in having planted the beads down the back of the sofa himself, while she busily searched the room. Again in a much exaggerated manner Nicolas expressed faked relief;

"Wow! You found them, thank you."

Having successfully pulled off his cunning ruse to get the unsuspecting Laura into his hotel room, Nicolas was feeling pretty pleased with himself, only to find his plan go completely awry a moment later. Drawing Laura towards him Nicolas kissed her lips. Looking into her green eyes he recognised a kindred spirit. Spontaneously he declared,

"I think I love you." The words left his mouth before he could stop them.

Surprised and shocked Laura just looked at him, unsure how to react to Nicolas's sudden unexpected outburst. Her silence and stunned expression clearly stated that she was not ready to reciprocate Nicolas's feelings towards her. The chemistry was there in bucket-loads and Laura was charmed and flattered. But love was something she took seriously; furthermore Nicolas was a married man. For this reason alone she'd held back; it would be so easy to fall for him. Nicolas was intelligent, strong, courageous and confident, with an enchanting sense of humour, not to mention gorgeous to look at. What was not to love?

"Its okay love, I know you don't feel the same," he told her in a more subdued tone.

"It's too soon," she insisted "I mean I hardly know you. Besides you are married" she said pointedly. But as she looked into his soulful dark eyes, they revealed the undeniable sincerity of his heart.

Nicolas gave out a long, regretful sigh;

"Oh love, I wish I had met you before."

Undeterred, Nicolas was more determined than ever to capture the heart of the resistant Laura. Once his mind was set on something, he would not give up easily. Failure was not an option to be contemplated;

"Let us go back down to the Prive," he suggested. "We will drink champagne and dance, and I will hold you in my arms. Maybe you will fall in love with me a little bit." He laughed.

"Maybe," she teased.

Over the next few weeks, Nicolas took Laura to dinner at the finest Abu Dhabi restaurants and to the best night clubs, where they often danced till the early hours.

One night after the show, Nicolas ordered six bottles of Dom Perignon champagne. Just for the hell of it, he and Rajai vigorously shook the champagne bottles before opening, then recklessly sprayed Laura and the rest of the band till they were completely soaked. Laura was utterly enchanted by Nicolas's impulsive, spontaneous, fun loving personality.

The cabaret acts residency at the Prive was coming to an end; very soon they would be moving on to their next venue. They were booked to perform at a hotel in Dubai for the following month. On their last night, Nicolas asked Tim the Prive's resident DJ, to play a song and dedicate it to Laura. The song Nicolas requested had been a hit for Ricci Valens back in 1960. It was appropriately called, 'Tell Laura I love her'. The DJ announced that he had a request from Nicolas to Laura and played the song.

Much to Laura's embarrassment, Nicolas insisted on loudly singing the chorus along with the record. When the song ended he persuaded Tim to play it again, not once but on a loop ten times over, to the point where people were threatening to leave the club if they heard that song played one more time. In the end Tim took the record off the turntable and gave it to Nicolas. Laura was touched by Nicolas's open declaration of love in front of everyone. The temptation to throw caution to the wind, follow her heart and just let herself fall in love was growing strong.

But Laura was unyielding; she would resist this oh-so-charming prince just a while longer. If Nicolas's intentions were really serious, then he would need to prove it. And to Laura's subsequent delight he did.

Travelling back to Beirut on business for a few days gave Nicolas some time away from Laura; time in which he was able to reflect on his situation and less-than-perfect marriage. There were now two women in his life, his wife and the woman he had unexpectedly fallen in love with.

While in Lebanon Nicolas found he was constantly thinking of Laura, to the point where he inadvertently called his wife by her name; which didn't go down too well, causing another argument. Via a friend, Nicolas sent Laura a telex telling her he loved and missed her, and that he hoped to be back soon to tell her in person. Laura was thrilled to receive the message, but with Dubai nearly two hours' drive from Abu Dhabi she wasn't expecting to see Nicolas quite as often as before.

One evening before the start of the show at the Dubai venue, Laura peeped round the stage curtain to see what the audience was like. She was overjoyed to spot Nicolas sitting at a table with Rajai. The show couldn't finish soon enough; Laura was excited and impatient to be with him.

Seated directly in front of Nicolas and Rajai were two women. When the show was over, a comment made by the women was overheard by Nicolas and Rajai. One woman said to the other,

"Isn't it nice to come and see a show without those two trouble makers from the Prive in Abu Dhabi?"

The other woman agreed with her friend,

"Yes, you mean that Nicolas and his Jordanian friend? I'm glad they're not here causing trouble."

Nicolas and Rajai looked at one another and started to laugh. Nicolas couldn't resist, he stood and tapped one of the women on the shoulder.

"Good evening ladies nice to see you both again."

The two women looked horrified and hurriedly left the venue. Nicolas and Rajai couldn't stop laughing, highly amused by the incident. Nicolas's reputation and notoriety in and around Abu Dhabi was something Laura was not yet fully acquainted with. When finally she joined him at his table he stood up, as always the perfect gentleman. Every time she left the table he would stand, and do it again on her return. Laura's colleagues were impressed by his old-fashioned manners, telling Laura she was lucky to have found a real Prince Charming. Deciding to put Nicolas's perfect etiquette to the test, Laura and a female friend mischievously played a game at his expense. Leaving the table a little more often than they really needed, they wanted to see if he would keep it up. Nicolas never faltered, but the knowing glint in his eye revealed he was on to them.

Nicolas remarked approvingly of the costumes Laura had worn on stage that night asking;

"Why you didn't wear those sexy dresses in Abu Dhabi?"

Laura explained that she'd considered them too risqué for Abu Dhabi audiences, but Dubai seemed more liberal. Nicolas laughed at this statement and said something to Rajai in Arabic.

There was no club or disco at this Dubai venue. They decided to go somewhere else where they could have a drink and dance. Laura invited one of the girls from the show to come along. While they waited for her downstairs in the hotel lobby, Laura instinctively took Nicolas's hand. As he put his arm around her, it felt familiar and safe; being with him felt so natural to her. They exchanged a look of deep affection. In that perfect moment, Laura realised something had changed. As the realisation hit her, she physically felt a distinct shift in her emotions and the inevitable happened. At precisely that moment, Laura knew she had fallen in love. Whispering softly to Nicolas she suggested,

"Let's go somewhere to be alone."

Nicolas understood immediately. Prepared to play the long game, Laura's sudden change of heart delighted him.

He couldn't hide the look of triumph on his face.

Nicolas drove the four of them to the Intercontinental hotel. They had a drink and a few dances in the hotels night club, before Rajai and Laura's friend decided to call it a night. After collecting a key from reception, Nicolas led Laura towards the elevator to go to a room he'd booked on their arrival.

Knowing they were about to become intimate for the first time, Laura was nervous as they stepped from the lift. She still had reservations that Nicolas was married, but felt she could no longer deny her heart. Laura always believed the heart must follow its own path; no one can judge what is right or wrong in love. With her emotions outweighing any feelings of guilt, Laura was ready to give everything to him. Nicolas was the man she'd waited her whole life for.

As they entered the room Laura nervously anticipated that first moment of intimacy. Nicolas took her by the hand leading her towards the bed. Seductively kissing and caressing, he moved his hands eagerly over her trembling body. His touch was passionate, warm and tender. Laura could feel his heart beating strong inside his chest. Nicolas began undressing Laura slowly, allowing his hungry eyes to drink in every inch of her petite svelte body. Nicolas may have played out this scenario many times, but for Laura it was more than just taking off her clothes to have sex; she would be opening her soul to explore and embrace this long awaited union with her true soul mate.

Unable to control his growing passion, Nicolas hastily removed his clothes. Without a hint of hesitation he lay naked on the bed in front of her. In contrast to Nicolas's bold confident manner, Laura shyly removed her remaining garments while he watched. Laura presented an air of modesty and coyness that intrigued. Nicolas found it quite alluring, feminine and sexy. Laura gazed at Nicolas's slim toned physique; the firm defined muscles of his chest and torso were those of an athlete. With his long legs he appeared taller than his height of six feet. Stretching out his hand he beckoned Laura closer to him. Nicolas softly encouraged,

"Come love."

The moment of their sexual intimacy was imminent. Laura briefly hesitated to engage in an act that would change her forever. Nicolas suddenly felt very protective. Her hesitation told him she was inexperienced. Daunted at the sight of his huge erection, Laura tried to cover up her apprehension with humour. She kidded nervously;

"Where am I going to put that," she giggled referring to his very impressive manhood.

Nicolas laughed, pulling the hesitant Laura down onto the bed. He drew her close. In a moment he would capture her innocence, and the treasure of her love would be his forever. Nicolas was in no doubt this was Laura's first full sexual encounter. The trepidation in her eyes was evident as he positioned himself over her trembling body.

"Don't worry hayati," he told her assuredly. "I know what I'm doing."

Nicolas was totally confident in his expertise, having played out the same scenario many times with numerous women. But this was different, in that he actually loved the woman he was about to have sex with. Laura's body automatically tensed. Sensing her unease, Nicolas resolved to take things more slowly. He began gently kissing and caressing her. Laura started to relax allowing his mouth and fingers to explore her intimately. The taste of his lips was sweet as Middle Eastern honey. As he continued to delight her senses, little by little, Laura let go of her inhibitions.

"I think you are ready," he whispered softly.

Pressing tautly against his shoulders, Laura made a vain attempt to push him away. Nicolas held her arms above her head whispering,

"Don't worry hayati; I'm going to make you happy. I will take you to paradise."

Grasping her hands he interlocked his fingers tightly with hers. Laura was overcome with emotion as he began to penetrate her. He kept murmuring the words;

"I love you hayati, eyouni."

Laura relaxed as the initial pain subsided, their bodies melting together to become one. No part of her was denied him as her body united with his, in rapturous surrender. Laura felt the whole universe open to her, as on that night they sealed their love amongst the stars. Nicolas guided Laura expertly through every step, transporting her into the realms of euphoric ecstasy. As the dawn rose, they lay exhausted in each other's arms. Laura dare not speak for fear of breaking the magic of that early morning bliss. Nicolas then uttered the words she hadn't dared dream of, or hope for;

"Laura, will you marry me?"

Laura's heart fluttered like the wings of a thousand butterflies. Nicolas gazed adoringly into her eyes. He looked at Laura as if she were everything he had been searching for his entire life. He waited expectantly for her reply. Laura couldn't speak; his words had literally taken her breath away. His dark eyes were like pools of unchartered water as they penetrated hers. Held within them were so many untold secrets. Laura felt she had momentarily glimpsed his soul. Nicolas kissed her with a passion that revealed the truth of his love. Suddenly Laura stopped him.

"Wait Nicolas, you are already married."

"I will divorce my wife." he promised as he continued to kiss her. He repeated his proposal;

"Laura, will you marry me?"

She searched his face; it was full of passion. There was no denying the sincerity portrayed in those dark eyes that were so hungry and impatient for her answer. At last she whispered;

"Yes I will. I would love to marry you."

As they embraced he murmured;

"Hayati you have made me so happy."

She felt all the emotion of his soul penetrate her heart as she lay in his arms. Laura wondered at the words he had whispered so passionately. She asked;

"What does hayati mean?"

"Hayati, it means you are all my life," he told her.

"And eyouni?"

"It means my eyes, but more. You cannot translate fully. These words you say to the one who is always in your heart."

Laura rested her head softly against his chest. She listened to the comforting rhythm of his heart beating inside; the heart that now belonged exclusively to her.

KOUSBAWI

Chapter 2: Man of Mysterious Ways

It was Friday, the Islamic holy day. The sound of the call to prayer rang out from the mosque echoing through the city. Her blissful slumber now disturbed, Laura half-opened her eyes. Noticing Nicolas was not in the bed beside her, the not yet fully awake Laura glanced around the room. Nicolas was standing near the window wrapped only in a towel, having just taken his shower. Laura stared admiringly at his toned body, glistening with droplets of water. Lighting a cigarette Nicolas turned to see Laura's sleepy face gazing at him. Smiling he said;

"Hey sleepy girl, you wanna eat?"

"What's the time?" she mumbled.

"One o'clock in the afternoon," he answered. "Go take your shower love."

Laura stumbled out of the bed and made her way to the bathroom, feeling slightly disorientated after seven and a half hours of sleep. Nicolas waited until she was in the shower before making a phone call. Refreshed and feeling more awake, Laura stepped from the shower; she could hear Nicolas talking on the phone in Arabic. As she emerged from the bathroom he ended the call.

"Who was that?" Laura asked.

Nicolas was sitting in the chair. Evasively he told her, "Someone."

"Someone?" she repeated.

Nicolas looked into her inquisitive eyes. He smiled, but his look revealed he didn't like to be questioned.

"Love, its business," he told her. Nicolas then changed the subject. "Hayati, how are you?" Stretching out his arm he beckoned her closer. Laura moved towards him.

"Come here hayati." Placing his arm around her waist, he pulled Laura to his lap. "Tiny little woman; you want me to order room service or you wanna go to the coffee shop?" Before Laura had time to answer he'd decided for her. "We will order room service, and have a dinner out tonight, okay hayati?"

Nicolas obviously liked to be in control and make all the decisions. It was something Laura would get used to. Even down to the way he carried himself and the way he talked, his whole demeanour ensured a powerful aura of confidence, leaving you in no doubt this was a man totally in charge. Women found it attractive and sexy. Laura had never met anyone like Nicolas before and was completely under his spell.

They ordered toasted cheese sandwiches from room service and snuggled up on the bed together, intending to watch a movie. Needless to say they were soon kissing and petting heavily. Nicolas caressed and explored every inch of Laura's body. The lovemaking was tender but intensely passionate; Nicolas was unselfish in his quest to satisfy. His prowess in the bedroom quite overwhelmed Laura. So absorbed were they in each other, the world could have disappeared and they wouldn't have noticed. Afterward they lay together without talking. Nicolas then lit two cigarettes, and passed one to Laura. After a time he asked;

"Hayati tell me, are you happy?"

"Very," Laura answered softly.

"Hayati, I know you want to ask me something; tell me love." He continued, "Its okay love, say it darling."

He had anticipated her question as though he were able to delve into her mind, and pick out her thoughts. Hesitantly she asked,

"Did you mean what you said last night about…?"

"About marrying you?" he interrupted before the words had a chance to escape from her mouth.

"Yes. Did you mean it?"

"Love I am Nicolas Chehade, Al Hajj, if I say I will do something I will do it." he reassured Laura.

"But what if she won't give you a divorce?"

"You cannot hold someone who does not want to stay," he told her. "It will take some time, but… she will make a mistake, and then I will divorce her."

Laura felt reassured, believing somehow he would make it happen. They dressed for dinner and while Laura was getting ready to go out, Nicolas spent most of the time on the phone. Not able to speak or understand Arabic, Laura had no idea what was being discussed. Judging by the authoritive tone in Nicolas's voice, she assumed it was most probably business related.

"Ready?" he suddenly announced.

"Yes, I'm hungry where are we eating?" Laura asked.

"We will meet with Rajai and maybe we will go to the Hyatt Regency hotel to eat before we drive back to Abu Dhabi."

"Oh, I thought we would be spending the evening in Dubai," she questioned.

"I have an early meeting in Abu Dhabi tomorrow." He informed as he picked up his room key and cigarettes.

Holding the door open for Laura, Nicolas impatiently ushered her through. They walked to the lift holding hands and once inside Nicolas protectively placed his arm around Laura holding her close. Rajai was waiting in the lobby. Nicolas spoke to the hotel receptionist and a moment later a driver brought his silver Mercedes to the front of the building. Laura sat in the front seat next to Nicolas, and he drove the three of them to the Hyatt Regency. As they drove through the busy city of Dubai they passed through several sets of lights. Stopping at the next red light Nicolas turned to Laura and said;

"You want to see something?"

He blew at the red light which immediately changed to green as if he had commanded it to do so. He proceeded to do this successfully at every red light all the way to the Hyatt Regency. He laughed saying to Laura;

"You see I am Al Hajj, even the lights obey me."

They ate dinner in the Hyatt's revolving restaurant. The night-time views of the gulf waters, Creek and city were spectacular. The sophisticated luxurious opulence of this desert state was quite impressive. Before driving back to

Abu Dhabi, Nicolas passed by Laura's hotel so she could pick up a change of clothing. During the nearly two hour drive, Nicolas and Rajai conversed in Arabic.

Unable to understand, Laura stared out the car window, not that there was much to see. It was dark, and the area was still being developed; nothing but flat dessert either side of the road. Laura slowly drifted off to sleep. She was awoken an hour and a half later by the sound of Nicolas's voice.

"Darling, wake up we are here."

Meeting them at the entrance of the Holiday Inn was a very tall, heavily moustached, well-built muscular guy, in his early twenties. He was dressed casually in blue jeans and white trainers. Nicolas spoke to him in Arabic and handed him the keys to his silver Mercedes. As they walked into the hotel lobby Laura asked;

"Who was that?"

"Milad, my body guard," Nicolas answered.

"Body guard?" she repeated with a surprised tone.

"Yes I have many. This one, he loves me too much," he told Laura smiling proudly as he said it.

"Why do you need a body guard?"

"Love I have many enemies," he said.

His tone was very matter-of-fact, as if having enemies and body guards was the most normal thing in the world.

As she walked with Nicolas towards the elevator Laura wondered who this man she had fallen for really was. He appeared powerful, and certainly seemed to carry a lot of influence in high places. Laura pondered what else would be revealed about him. Nicolas was an enigma, and his life a mysterious conundrum that Laura may one day unravel.

KOUSBAWI

Chapter 3: Flowers for the lady

Before leaving for his early morning meeting, Nicolas made a couple of calls. The sound of his talking on the phone in Arabic roused Laura from her slumber. She stretched and sat up slowly. Nicolas put down the phone and stood in front of the mirror adjusting his tie. Noticing Laura was awake he turned around, looking immaculate in his suit. He told Laura;

"Listen; be ready at noon, we will have lunch with my American business colleague Peter and his girlfriend."

Nicolas then made another call and Laura heard him say in English,

"And get some flowers for the lady."

Laura thought to herself, how considerate of him to arrange flowers for his colleague's girlfriend.

"Okay darling, I'll call you after my meeting. If you need anything hayati call room service; okay love."

Nicolas picked up his briefcase and left, leaving the still-sleepy Laura alone. She briefly considered getting up, but as usual her lazy side won over and she slept in. Laura finally rose from the bed two hours later, at 10.30am. As she took her shower and dressed, Laura's spirits were high. It seemed being in love totally agreed with her psyche. The light heady mood and floaty, dreamlike sensation, made concentrating on anything practically impossible. At last she understood the term 'walking on air', often associated with being in love. Falling for Nicolas had taken her by surprise. Unplanned and unexpected as it was, Laura had never felt so ecstatically happy. She couldn't wait for Nicolas's meeting to finish, being parted from him for even a short period, Laura felt strangely incomplete.

Dead on noon he called. He was downstairs in the bar with Peter and asked Laura to meet them there.

"I'm on my way," she told him.

Excitedly Laura grabbed her bag and the room key, and then hurried to the elevator almost skipping like a child. Pressing the button for the ground floor, Laura glanced at her reflection in the elevator mirror. Both her mood and appearance was glowing. Laura felt butterflies dance inside her. Her breathing quickened as the lift doors opened. She walked towards the bar where she saw Nicolas standing with two other people. He was clutching a huge bouquet. As Laura approached he smiled. Handing her the bouquet of pink roses, Nicolas said;

"Flowers for my lady."

"They're beautiful," she gasped. "Thank you."

"My pleasure hayati, I want you to meet my very good friend, Peter Garett and his girlfriend Lisa."

At six foot four Peter was a little taller than Nicolas. He had a thick mop of brown hair, brown eyes and a heavy moustache. Lisa was taller than Laura at around five feet four, with wavy blonde shoulder length hair. Lisa spoke with a lazy southern drawl. Laura smiled and shook hands with the American couple. The four of them made their way to the restaurant, which was adjacent to the bar. With his hand placed protectively at Laura's back, Nicolas guided her towards a reserved table. He remained standing until both women were seated, and then took the seat beside Laura with Peter and Lisa seated opposite. A waiter hurried over with a bottle of champagne on ice. During the lunch the atmosphere was relaxed and jovial. Lisa was hilariously outspoken and supremely scatty; the two women hit it off immediately. Laughing and giggling throughout the lunch, they engaged in light hearted conversation, teasing and mocking their male partners in a good humoured manner. The company was very relaxed and Nicolas was feeling particularly upbeat. He joked with Peter about how he could take on any man in a fight. Just then, a huge guy walked past their table. Peter said to Nicolas,

"Okay Nick, what about him?"

The two women giggled, the guy was built like a

gorilla. Nicolas answered confidently;

"Easy for me, nothing to do with size. I could put him down in two seconds," he boasted. "It's the technique."

The four continued to laugh and joke throughout the lunch. Nicolas suddenly grabbed hold of Laura and gave her a big kiss on the lips. Laura pulled back in horror, her lips burning.

"What the hell!" she exclaimed.

Mischievously, Nicolas had taken a large swig from the bottle of tabasco sauce on the table, which happened to be extra hot. Highly amused at his schoolboy antics, he sat grinning devilishly. As Laura's lips swelled he laughingly offered her an ice cube from the champagne bucket. Laura was not as amused. She desperately tried to cool her burning lips.

After lunch, Nicolas said that he wanted to sleep for an hour before going back to the office. He had arranged for a driver to take Laura back to Dubai at 6pm. Feeling tired after the champagne, Laura got into the bed next to him to take a nap. Lying on her side facing away from Nicolas Laura closed her eyes. Nicolas started to sensually kiss her neck. Tired but aroused, Laura just went with it, as Nicolas proceeded to make love to her. Both fell into a deep sleep until awoken an hour later by the ringing of the phone. Nicolas answered quickly and got up from the bed. He hurriedly started to dress, telling Laura;

"Love put your clothes; someone is coming to the room in ten minutes."

"Who?" she asked.

"It's business."

Nicolas wouldn't illuminate further. Laura dressed and exactly ten minutes later there was a knock at the door. Laura went to answer but was abruptly stopped.

"Never answer the door to anyone unless I say, and never when I am not here, okay?" he told her sternly.

Laura sat down on the bed leaving Nicolas to answer the door. A shady-looking Middle Eastern man entered the room. He was a lot shorter in stature than Nicolas, with a face that reminded Laura of a character from a gangster movie; he had the eyes of a killer. At Nicolas's request he sat down on the sofa. In a low gravelly tone he spoke in Arabic. Seated in the chair opposite Nicolas displayed a distinct air of authority. At no point did the man make eye contact with Laura, nor did Nicolas introduce him.

Laura couldn't understand what was being discussed, but gathered this peculiar little guy worked for Nicolas in some capacity. By his conduct and manner, he obviously revered Nicolas, but his presence gave Laura the creeps. Intuitively she felt there was something very underworld and sinister about him. It seemed strange that Nicolas would associate with such a character; the guy seemed out of place in Nicolas's soave extravagant world.

Seated facing Nicolas, who sat with his back to the mirror, the guy kept his eyes lowered when talking. His whole demeanour was one of submission in front of Nicolas. When Nicolas stood and walked to the other side of the room near to Laura to get a cigarette, the man's eyes didn't follow him, but stayed deliberately looking down to the floor. Eventually he got up to leave. As he walked towards the door, Laura noticed he again kept his eye line away from her. Laura found the behaviour odd, almost rude. She mentioned it to Nicolas after he'd gone and was told in no uncertain terms;

"Love if he looks at you even in the mirror, I will smash his face."

Laura realised that it was out of respect for Nicolas that the man had ignored her, not even daring to look at her reflection.

Nicolas was a law unto himself. People would run to him in times of trouble, knowing they could rely on his assistance. Whether legal or a business matter, or maybe something more personal, friends, family, and business colleagues alike, knew they could go to Al Hajj for help and receive it. When having dealings with others, honour and respect were high on Nicolas's list. It didn't matter whether or not you liked him, as long as you respected

him. Nicolas had a kind generous heart, which was alw
ready to help others. He was a champion for the und
dog. In return all he would ask was your loyalty; any kin
of betrayal was not tolerated. Betraying Nicolas was the
very worst you could do. As much as he opened his heart,
he would close it to anyone he felt had dishonoured or
betrayed him. It didn't matter who they were, or how
much he loved them, friends and family alike would be
wiped from his life in an instant. Nicolas would be totally
unmoved by their pleadings to be forgiven.

"They are dead to me." Is what he would say of anyone
who crossed that line.

Some found Nicolas's tough attitude over harsh and
inflexible; he could be rigidly stubborn. In time Laura
would witness his uncompromising inflexibility first hand.

Yet as Laura came to know Nicolas, she found that this
was only a part of the man he was. Underneath that tough
exterior, lay a passionate, sensitive being, with a heart of
pure gold. Nicolas felt things deeply and as much as he
was obstinately unyielding, he would be moved to tears
when something touched his heart.

Chapter 4:
,ace, a Lover and a Fighter

.th later Laura and her co-performers moved on to
,ther venue in Sharjah; it was the final destination of
.neir Emirates tour. The group were booked to perform at
'The Palm', a nightclub situated in the basement of the
Palm hotel. The group would be resident here for the next
three months. Sharjah was an hour away from Dubai, and
Laura was concerned the distance between her and Nicolas
was now even further. But distance would not be the only
obstacle encountered along the rocky road of true love.
Laura needn't have feared; as they say, where there's a
will there's a way, and Nicolas certainly had the will.

To her delight Nicolas drove to Sharjah as often as he
could. Rajai would often accompany him on the two and a
half hour journey. When he was unable to make the trip
himself, Nicolas would either send a driver or one of his
body guards. Laura would be collected after the show at
the Palm, and driven to Abu Dhabi so she and Nicolas
could spend the night together. Eager not to waste one
moment of their precious time, Laura would pack her
overnight bag and be ready to leave immediately the show
finished. Nicolas gave Laura his private office number so
she could talk to him anytime. He instructed the reception
staff at the Holiday Inn, to put her directly through to his
room whenever she called, day or night.

Since building his empire in and around the Emirates,
Nicolas had lived the ultimate hedonistic playboy lifestyle,
which continued despite his marriage. Nicolas's reputation
for successfully seducing the prettiest and most beautiful
woman in Abu Dhabi would often leave his friends and
colleagues astonished and frustrated; they'd comment that
perhaps he should leave a little something for the others.
When it came to women, Nicolas had his own unique

tried-and-tested method to woo them. If his old-fashioned etiquette, charm, and boyish good looks didn't succeed, then his sweet talk certainly would. It could even be said Nicolas had the ability to charm the bird's right out of the trees, if he chose to. He would boast,

"Give me a woman's ear for just ten minutes and she will be in my bed in five."

His friends liked to put his apparent unfailing technique to the test. They'd teasingly pick a woman they considered particularly challenging, and dare Nicolas to make his move. Nicolas revelled in such a challenge, and rarely if ever failed to meet it. During his short marriage he had indulged in many such dalliances with various different women; but that's all they were; dalliances. With Laura it was something else entirely. Just being with Laura felt warmly familiar; there was something about her that got right under Nicolas's skin. What started out as a challenge, ended up as something profoundly rare and unique. This unforeseen romance came at him like a bolt of lightning.

Whatever it was holding Nicolas to Laura, it struck a chord that resonated and echoed deep within his soul. It was the same for Laura; their two hearts had acknowledged their recognition of each other from the moment their eyes first met. This intriguing familiarity drew Nicolas in hook, line and sinker. Nicolas was in love, probably for the first time in his adult life. Undoubtedly this was going to be a problem as far as his marriage was concerned. In spite of the womanising and unfaithfulness, Nicolas was not mean or cold-hearted. He genuinely felt he had loved his wife; it was never his intention to hurt her. But his feelings for Laura could not be denied. Despite his being thrown completely off kilter, Nicolas had never been so happy. He admitted to Laura that he didn't remember a time in his life when he had ever felt this happy.

In light of his marriage proposal to Laura, sooner or later Nicolas would have to own up to the truth and deal with the complications it carried. Awakened to the fact that he was prepared to give to Laura what he'd never felt able to give any other woman, total commitment, was proof enough to convince Nicolas she was the one. Unable to continue living a lie, his marriage clearly would not long survive.

One night Nicolas sent his driver to collect Laura from Sharjah. On arrival at the Holiday Inn in Abu Dhabi, Laura was met at the entrance by Milad, Nicolas's number one body guard. He told her,

"Mr Nicolas has asked me to bring you directly to the Prive where he is waiting."

At six foot five, and built like a prize fighter, Milad towered above the tiny Laura as he protectively escorted her into the Prive. It was dark inside and very crowded. Laura couldn't see Nicolas amongst the crowd. Milad told her;

"Wait here, I will tell Mr Nicolas you have arrived."

Laura sat down at an empty table near the back of the club and waited. Moments later she saw Nicolas emerge out of the darkness; soon he was standing in front of her. He bent taking Laura's hand. Reminiscent of their very first meeting his eyes seductively locked with her eyes as he kissed her hand.

"Hayati," he said softly, "Come, I have champagne waiting for you."

Nicolas pulled Laura to her feet and offered her his arm. He then walked her to his table like a king with his queen. The men in his entourage stood respectfully as she took a seat. Whenever Laura needed to visit the ladies' room, one of Nicolas's entourage would dutifully escort her. They would wait outside until she came out, and then accompany her back to the table. Laura thought it very quaint, but enjoyed the attention. On this particular night Mounir escorted her. As Laura opened the cloakroom door to return to the Prive, she was surprised to find Mounir standing with outstretched arms blocking her exit.

"Go back, go back in Miss Laura," he said, ushering the bemused Laura back inside the ladies' cloakroom.

"What's going on?" she asked him.

"Please Miss Laura just five minutes, go back inside please," he insisted almost pushing Laura back through the doorway.

Bewildered Laura did as Mounir asked and went back inside the cloakroom. As she reapplied her lipstick and brushed her hair, she speculated as to what on earth was going on. Glancing at her watch she saw that five minutes had passed. Laura decided to look and see if Mounir was still blocking the exit. As she opened the door Mounir was standing right outside. Beckoning her out Mounir said,

"Okay now Miss Laura, come please out."

Laura followed Mounir back into the club. She asked him what had occurred.

"No nothing everything good Miss Laura," he assured in his broken English.

Anxiously Laura looked for Nicolas. She spotted him sitting at a different table looking relaxed and immaculate; he stood as she approached.

"Is everything alright?" she asked.

"Darling, everything is good because you are here," he answered handing her a fresh glass of champagne.

Laura noticed that not only their table was changed, but the champagne had been replaced with a new bottle. As she was the only one in the group drinking champagne, she inquired suspiciously;

"What happened to the other bottle? It was more than half-full; and why have we moved tables?"

"I thought you should have a fresh one," Nicolas said casually. At seventy pounds a bottle Laura thought this a little extravagant.

"And a fresh table too?" She added with humorous disbelief.

"Someone spill their drink on the seat," he lied.

Laura gave him a sceptical look, aware she wasn't getting the truth. Clearly something other than a spilt drink had occurred whilst she was in the ladies. Whatever it was, they had done a fine job of covering it up; either that or Mounir was completely losing his marbles. But Mounir's strange behaviour was not explained to Laura that night. It would be some time before she was eventually enlightened to the full story.

Shortly after Laura's arrival at the Prive that night, someone who was affiliated in some way to Nicolas's wife turned up. When they saw Nicolas all over Laura an altercation transpired, and the two men began arguing in Arabic. Disapproving comments were made regarding the way Nicolas was publicly flaunting his affair. Refusing to heed Nicolas's warning to mind his own business, the person in question unwisely continued to push Nicolas's buttons by persistently airing his judgmental views.

Unable to understand Arabic, Laura had been unaware that she was the subject of their heated conversation. The resulting consequence was inevitable. Highly vexed by the continuing criticism, Nicolas reacted. As soon as Laura was not there to witness it, he punched the guy. Subsequently during the ensuing fight the champagne got caught in the crossfire. Oblivious of the skirmish that had taken place, Laura enjoyed the rest of the night basking in the attention that Nicolas openly lavished upon her.

They retired to his room in the early hours of Friday, and slept until 10am. Friday was the Islamic holy day so there was no performance that night, which meant Laura could stay another night in Abu Dhabi. On Saturday Nicolas drove Laura back himself in his silver Mercedes. Rajai accompanied them to Sharjah. Nicolas and Rajai watched Laura's show at the Palm, and afterwards she joined them at their table. That night there was to be a performance by the clubs resident belly dancer, and Laura was looking forward to it.

Nadia, the Egyptian belly dancer was barely halfway through her performance when Nicolas removed his watch and bracelet handing them to a puzzled Laura. The look on Nadia's face was priceless as he suddenly jumped onto the stage. Performing an acrobatic handstand Nicolas started dancing across the floor on his hands in time to the music. Not only Nadia, but Laura too was surprised and amazed by Nicolas's impromptu acrobatic performance. Everyone in the room was impressed, admiring the strength, agility and stamina, required to perform such an acrobatic feat and keep going for as long as he did. It appeared it was not only in the bedroom Nicolas could perform so athletically. The audience went wild applauding and cheering him on; the place was in uproar. Being the centre of attention Nicolas was in his absolute element. The confused Nadia just stepped to the side. There was no point in even trying to continue her dance as no one was watching her; all eyes were on Nicolas. Eventually he stopped and nonchalantly returned to the table. Everyone in the whole place was on their feet cheering. Nicolas took his seat coolly replacing his watch and bracelet, feeling completely at home in the limelight. Laura was speechless eventually exclaiming,

"I didn't know you could do that."

Nicolas smiled and lit a cigarette, turning to Laura he told her,

"I am Al Hajj, I can do many things."

He was certainly full of surprises; Laura would surely never be bored in her life with him. She looked adoringly at him feeling proud he was her man. His dark eyes looked tenderly into hers as he asked,

"Are you happy love?"

"I'm very happy," Laura confirmed.

"And you love me, hayati?"

"Yes I love you totally."

Nadia continued with her belly dance trying her best to follow Nicolas's limelight stealing performance. But that night belonged to Nicolas, he was the star of the show gaining the admiration of all the men, and charming every woman in the room with his skilful display of masculine strength and virility.

KOUSBAWI

Chapter 5: Catch a Falling Star

The dreaded moment was fast approaching; Laura's tour of the Emirates, and her time with Nicolas was coming to an end. Saying goodbye was going to be a heart wrenching affair; after all they were engaged, albeit unofficially. Laura's last few weeks in the UAE seemed to fly past. Her cabaret act had been pre-booked for a follow up tour of Scandinavia, where they would perform predominantly at venues in Norway, with a few engagements in Sweden and Finland. Nicolas assured Laura their parting was just a temporary phase, and promised to call Laura every day. It was of little comfort; Laura would miss him terribly.

Getting a divorce was going to take time he explained. It would not be an easy process. Both Nicolas and Laura were mindful of the implications involved. For Nicolas continuing to live a lie was not an option, no matter how painful the alternative. Without doubt there would be difficulties. He was fully prepared to face some strong opposition; but no one told Hajj how to live his life. In his heart of hearts Nicolas knew if Laura had never entered into his life, he would not have remained faithful to his wife. The length, to which he was prepared to go to hold on to Laura, was proof enough that divorce was the only logical solution. If Laura left and Nicolas never saw her again, his marriage would still be lost; you cannot deny the heart its truth. In spite of the philandering and his overtly promiscuous behaviour, Nicolas actually preferred to be in a relationship. The unconditional love he had craved since childhood, he believed was found in Laura. His habitual womanising had been an unconscious searching for the elusive love his marriage had failed to deliver.

One night after the show, Laura was sat with Nicolas in the Palm night club watching another act perform. Laura loved to give support to the other artists. She knew their routines inside out, and was totally engrossed in the show. Nicolas looked at Laura's face; she was so into it as she watched the dance act perform. He could tell Laura was going through every step and movement with them in her mind. Nicolas could see the passion shine through Laura's eyes. He wondered at their future. Impulsively he grabbed Laura's hand and asked,

"Do they know they are going to lose one?" By 'they' Nicolas was referring to Laura's cabaret group.

"Lose one what?" she asked not quite understanding his meaning.

"Lose you from the group," he told her in a matter-of-fact rather determined manner.

Until now, Laura hadn't given a thought to such an idea. Seeing the surprised look on her face Nicolas added assertively,

"What I mean love, when you become my wife you will stay here with me." For Nicolas this was a given.

Dancing and performing had been Laura's life for as long as she could remember. This sudden out of the blue stipulation that she give it all up came as a shock to her. Laura was so in love with him, she hadn't fully considered the reality of what life with Nicolas would entail. She now pondered this actuality for the first time. Noticing Laura's look of reticence, Nicolas sat up and faced her directly asking,

"You love me Laura, right?"

Although Nicolas enjoyed being in a serious long term relationship, it needed to be on his terms.

"Yes, of course," she told him. "I love you more than anything."

"And I love you hayati. Laura I belong to you and you belong to me now. As my wife your place is here with me okay?" Nicolas's attitude was emphatic. He squeezed Laura's hand to reinforce his point.

"Of course it is. I know that," she answered sincerely.

Laura smiled, but her eyes couldn't hide just an inkling of reservation. Stopping her career was something she hadn't bargained for; not yet anyway. Nicolas was quick to observe Laura's misgivings. Smiling he announced;

"For you love I will buy a club here. You will dance with your group as much as you want. Okay hayati?"

The solution for Nicolas was as simple as that. Laura looked at him incredulously.

"You will buy a club?"

Nicolas smiled. His optimism and gritty determination prevailed, as he told her confidently;

"Hajj can do whatever he wants."

Encouraged by Nicolas's unwavering self-confidence, Laura tried not to dwell on the fact that she would soon be leaving, deliberately putting it out of her mind, in the blind hope that not thinking about it would delay the inevitable. Their last night together in the beautiful Arabian Gulf was emotional. Nicolas sent a driver to Sharjah who brought Laura to Abu Dhabi. Not wishing to share their precious last moments with anyone, they decided not to go down to the Prive club, but stay in Nicolas's hotel room. Unable to control her emotions as they made love, tears rolled down Laura's cheeks. They fell like the unstoppable flow of a river into the sea. As he kissed her face, Nicolas murmured softly;

"Hayati, eyouni, you are my life my love."

Looking into Laura's tearful eyes he gently told her,

"I know darling, I know what you're feeling."

Nicolas wanted to keep Laura by his side as much as she wanted to stay, but the circumstances wouldn't yet allow such an endeavour. Impassioned at the thought of being parted, the emotionally charged energy expelled was almost tangible. The intensity of their emotions and lovemaking made them hungry. Nicolas ordered room service.

Twenty minutes later a bottle of champagne and a large plate of toasted cheese sandwiches were brought to the room. Despite her hunger, Laura's feelings overwhelmed her. An emotional lump formed in her throat and she had difficulty eating. Nicolas watched as Laura picked at the food. There was a strong urge to hold her in his arms and never let her go. But Nicolas determined to demonstrate a show of emotional strength; stoically holding his emotions in check in front of Laura.

Lighting a cigarette, he walked out onto the balcony. It was a warm starry night with a light gentle breeze. It blew the smoke from his cigarette up into the heavens. Nicolas watched it swirl and drift into the inky night sky, finally dissipating into nothing. His heart was heavy and his head full of thoughts; Laura's leaving wasn't all that was plaguing his mind this night. The on-going civil war in Lebanon was never far from his thoughts, the indefinite outcome of which weighed heavy on Nicolas's mind. He would continue to play his part, whatever it took; fight to the death if necessary for his beliefs and the sovereignty of his beloved country.

But what of Laura, how could he expect her to live that way? Constant shelling and bombing, neighbours killing neighbours; the troubles had been raging now for over five years with no real end in sight. Families were being torn apart, and his country destroyed by a war that threatened to escalate for years to come. This would be a nightmare existence for Laura and Nicolas wished to protect her, and to never have her witness the much darker aspects of his life. Nicolas was a fighter. When he believed in something he would fight to the end; it was an uncompromising part of his character. If Laura were to witness this side of his life, he worried it may taint their relationship.

Nicolas was worrying unduly. Laura's love for him was unconditional. Despite his fears, Laura was pretty resilient. She would accept whichever side of himself he chose to show. Part of him already knew this, but he wanted his life with Laura to remain untainted and separate from certain things. Nothing must ever sully the purity of their love. By keeping his life with Laura untouched by the darker demons that haunted him, Nicolas would ensure he always had a place to retreat to. He called out from the balcony,

"Come love and look at the stars."

Laura moved to join him stopping at the balcony door. She was barefoot and reluctant to step out onto the dusty surface.

"I don't have my shoes," she told him.

Nicolas walked towards Laura,

"You don't need your shoes; you can use my feet."

He held out his hand to her. Laura took hold of it and Nicolas gripped her around the waist as she put her feet on top of his. Holding on tightly, Laura giggled as Nicolas slowly walked her out onto the balcony. They were both laughing as Laura tried not to slip off. They gazed up at the stars twinkling like diamonds above them. They were shining extra brightly tonight, and as a poignant reflection of the dreamy couples love, a shooting star suddenly flew across the Arabian night sky.

"Oh it's beautiful," Laura whispered in an exaggerated breathy tone.

Nicolas smiled boldly claiming,

"I put them there for us."

Together they stared up at the carpet of stars set against the black velvet night. A cool breeze blew making Laura shiver. Wrapping his arms around her Nicolas held her tighter.

"I will make you warm with my own central heating," he laughed. The warmth from his body enveloped Laura like a soft blanket. She wanted the moment to last for ever.

"Darling," he started, "When we are apart, look to the stars and think of me, I will be thinking of you, and you will feel all my love."

Soon Laura would be thousands of miles away, half way across the world. She would spend many nights looking at the sky thinking of Nicolas, imagining him somewhere in the desert; wondering if he too was looking up at those same stars and feeling the love her heart was sending.

The next day Laura was driven back to Sharjah by Nicolas's body guard Milad. It was the last show at The Palm marking the end of their tour in the UAE. Laura was disappointed Nicolas was unable to be there due to a prior engagement and some important meeting. Nicolas could easily have cancelled his meeting, but in truth he didn't wish to say goodbye to Laura. By avoiding going through the actual motion of seeing her leave, he could better deal with his feelings that were more fragile than he would wish to admit. He called her three times during the day, telling her not to worry his heart was always with her, even if he wasn't. She asked if he would be coming to the airport to say goodbye. Again Nicolas declined. Sensing Laura was upset he told her;

"Darling we are not saying goodbye. You are in my life now. Whatever happens all my roads lead to you. We will be together okay. Don't be sad hayati remember I love you."

In Nicolas's head, refraining from watching Laura leave the Emirates made the parting less real. Comforted by his words, Laura told Nicolas she loved him and was missing him too much already. He said he missed her too, and when she reached England he would call every day. Laura gave Nicolas her contact details, including an itinerary of the Norway tour.

As she left for the airport that morning Laura was sad, wondering how on earth she was going to survive the next two months away from Nicolas. It felt as though she were leaving a large piece of herself behind. Laura finally boarded the plane cheered by the thought that as Nicolas had assured, this parting was only temporary. Before too long she would be back to this exotic Arabian land, and returned to the warm arms of her Middle Eastern Prince Charming.

KOUSBAWI

Chapter 6: Song of Norway

Back in England Laura prepared for her trip to the frozen north. From the intense heat of the desert sun, she would now travel to the chilly Arctic Circle and the land of the midnight sun. Not a day passed when her head wasn't full of thoughts about Nicky, as she affectionately called him. True to his word, Nicky telephoned Laura every day, telling her how much he loved her, and promising to stay in contact during her Norway tour. Now they were living in different time zones, this was going to be problematic, especially as Laura and her band would be constantly on the move in Norway.

Contrary to the pain she felt at being parted from the love of her life, Laura was deliriously happy. There wasn't a doubt in her mind that she and Nicky would be together again soon. For now Laura would have to be content with their only contact being by phone or telex. Laura's heart raced with excitement whenever Nicky called her. Luckily the line was always so clear; Nicky could almost be in the next room. It was hard to believe he was actually 3,500 miles away. Before hanging up, he would ask Laura;

"Do you want anything; do you need anything, hayati?"

Laura's answer was always the same;

"Just you Nicky, I just want you."

"Soon darling, soon we shall be together always. Just give me time, everything will be okay," he assured. "I love you darling, hayati, my tiny girl. Take care of yourself, my love, and wait for me."

Reluctant to break the precious connection, they would both argue over who would put the receiver down first. Eventually they agreed to count to three and do it together. After Nicky's call, Laura would sit mesmerised by his tender words; completely lost in another world. His loving refrains would be ringing around her head, as she replayed their conversations over and over throughout the day.

Nicky's solemn promise that they would soon be back together, sustained Laura through the lonely nights and days. Giving up her career to stay with him permanently, now no longer seemed such a daunting prospect. Laura refused to give credence to people who felt her faith and trust in Nicky was misplaced. They may have meant well, but telling Laura a life with him was just an impossible dream, only served to make her all the more determined to prove them wrong. She agreed the situation was not ideal, what with his still being married, not to mention the huge geographical distance between them. Laura was starry-eyed in her belief that any obstacles would be overcome; they would find a solution somehow. As long as Nicky loved her, nothing else mattered.

The Norway tour was soon under way, with the group taking a ferry from Felixstowe to Gothenburg. On board they met up with Chris the DJ, who would be touring with them. Chris was an outgoing Yorkshire lad in his early twenties, and was to supply the disco that would follow on after the show at each venue. He had brought along his friend Bob to act as his roady. Bob was a reserved, thin lanky guy, with a pallid complexion and a rather dry, slightly caustic wit. Bob had been through a bit of a rough patch recently, and Chris suggested it would be a nice break for him, describing it as a sort of working holiday. Bob had not been keen on the idea, telling Chris he didn't feel up to it. Chris was insistent; saying to his friend the trip would be a nice relaxing break, and would do him the world of good. Against his better judgement, Bob reluctantly agreed to be Chris's roady on the tour. If only they had known what was in store; the Norway tour would reveal itself to be anything but a holiday.

The group were met at Gothenburg in Sweden by Eric their tour manager. Eric had apparently been Abba's tour manager at one time, so they assumed they would be in good hands. Eric was a native Norwegian, typically fair haired, tallish, and of stocky build. As with most Scandinavians, his English was good. Chris the DJ had brought his own van which carried all of the sound and lighting equipment. Laura and the rest of the group would travel in a separate minibus, along with Eric, and a Swedish driver called Henric.

They drove to Oslo and were checked into a hotel where the shows rehearsals would be held. The hotel was also to host their first public performance. A fashion show had been incorporated as part of the entertainment, and professional models had been booked. Laura's dance vocal act would perform three separate 15-20 minute spots. A week was spent rehearsing to gel everything together. The whole show would be rounded off with a two hour long disco. The rehearsals and first night's performance went off without a hitch, and the group were keen to get the tour under-way.

Stunningly beautiful, was the only way to describe the Norwegian scenery Laura thought. With its vast fiords, enchanting waterfalls, and picturesque Christmas card landscapes, this Nordic snowy wonderland was totally breath-taking. The downside of the tour was hours and hours spent in the minibus travelling between venues. By the time the first leg of the tour was over, everyone was tired. It was a gruelling schedule, far removed from the luxury lifestyle they had enjoyed in the Middle East.

Being a vegetarian in a country where the predominant population were meat and fish eaters had its drawbacks for Laura. She found it particularly difficult, surviving mainly on tiny side salads and chocolate. It was hardly substantial considering the extremely cold climate, combined with the work schedule and constant travelling. But most of the hotels and eating places did not have a vegetarian option. Laura's already tiny physique was shrinking. Despite this, the enthusiastic reception the shows received from the Scandinavian audiences and the breathtakingly beautiful scenery, sweetened the physically demanding experience.

When travelling long distances between venues, Laura

often wanted to sleep, but she was so entranced by the incredible beauty and spectacular views, she couldn't shut her eyes. As they crossed the Arctic Circle and visited the land of the midnight sun, Nicolas kept in touch by sending regular telexes on ahead to the hotels from the list Laura had given him. Often she would arrive at the next venue to find a telex waiting. Laura received two phone calls a week from Nicky, which was amazing considering their hectic programme.

Half way through the tour everyone began to feel the pressure and exhaustion. The band jokingly likened it to an SAS training course. They had covered the length and breadth of Norway, and Lapland. Poor Bob the DJ's roady was becoming paler and thinner by the day; so much for a nice relaxing break.

Bob and Chris normally travelled ahead of the rest of the group, to get the sound and lighting equipment set up at the next venue. One day having made good time, Chris and Bob stopped at a little Norwegian village to buy sandwiches. Further along the road they pulled over in a layby next to a field to eat their lunch. Still being ahead of time, they decided to stretch their legs in the adjacent field. Jumping the wire fence they took a ten minute stroll, breathing in the fresh mountain air which refreshed them for the next part of the journey. Bob was feeling more relaxed after some food and fresh air; he told Chris that with the nice scenery and fresh clean air, that maybe the trip wasn't so bad after all.

Walking back to the van Chris jumped over the fence closely followed by Bob. Suddenly Bob cried out; Chris turned around to see Bob wriggling around on the ground in the snow under the fence. Bob's jacket had somehow managed to attach itself to the wire fence which just happened to be electrified. Chris tried to help his friend get loose, but every time Chris touched Bob he also received an electric shock. The more Bob struggled the more entangled his jacket became with the electrified fence. While poor Bob wrestled with the fence, Chris was very unsympathetically doubled up laughing.

Eventually, after several electric shocks and a totally ripped jacket, Bob finally managed to wriggle free. Cold, wet, shocked and exhausted, he staggered back to the van where Chris was still clutching his stomach creased up laughing. Failing to see the humour of his plight, Bob and his soaked shredded jacket clambered into the van. In a distinctly unamused, annoyed caustic tone, he told Chris;

"The next time you want to invite me on a nice relaxing holiday, **DON'T!**"

A few days later they were crossing one of the many large fiords by ferry. Laura began to feel quite unwell. She had stomach cramps; she must be getting her period she thought. Laura had not had her period since she was in the Middle East. Unconcerned, she had attributed it to her low body weight. Sitting in the café she tried to relax but the cramps became increasingly painful. Laura made her way to the toilets where she discovered she was bleeding. Laura had in fact suffered a miscarriage. She had not paid attention to symptoms of dizziness and nausea, believing she couldn't be pregnant as she was on the pill. With the lifestyle she was leading in the Middle East, it wasn't unknown to miss a pill here and there. Thankfully within a few minutes, the excruciating pain subsided. Laura needed fresh air. Ashen-faced she joined the others up on deck. Seeing Laura's washed out appearance they remarked;

"You look awful, are you okay?"

Laura put on a brave face and told them she was fine. Her emotions were mixed; she felt some sadness for her loss, but thought it was nature's way of telling her the time was not right for a baby. Laura deliberated whether to tell Nicky, finally deciding to leave it until they were properly back together.

The rest of the tour went relatively smoothly, except for one day when all the fashion models decided to walk out over a pay dispute. There was no time to find replacement models, and as they say, 'the show must go on', so Laura and the rest of the cabaret group were recruited to stand in.

Being professional dancers they looked the part, and had no problem adapting to the last minute-changes in the programme. Unfortunately, there still weren't enough of them to replace all of the models. Someone then had the bright idea to enrol the DJ, the roady, the tour manager, and the minibus driver to make up the numbers. Frankly, these last minute recruitments made that part of the show look more like something from a 'Morecombe and Wise' or 'Two Ronnie's' comedy sketch. Most of the clothes didn't fit, Bobs were massively too big, and Eric's and Henrik's wouldn't do up over their rather large paunches. The guys did their best but they were hardly male models, with their pot bellies sticking out, terrible deportment, a complete lack of coordination, or anything even mildly resembling natural rhythm. The bemused audience didn't know whether it was serious, or an actual comedic routine. Either way it was entertaining, and the audience laughed and applauded just the same.

Throughout her stage career, Laura had experienced some rather amusing incidents. Countless times during live performances, things would go wrong that the audience was blissfully unaware of. This particular episode would go down in Laura's memoirs as being one of the most absurd, and definitely the funniest ever encountered.

KOUSBAWI

Chapter 7: Twist of Fate

On their return to the UK everyone was feeling exhausted. The group agreed to take a temporary break from touring. Laura was hoping to return to Abu Dhabi, but Nicolas had unfortunately been called away on business. His regular trips to Beirut worried Laura with the country in the midst of a bloody civil war. Beirut airport was often closed due to shelling, and Nicolas would be stranded sometimes for days. Frequently he would fly to Cyprus, and take the ferry to Lebanon, but again that depended on the roads being open and safe to travel on. Lebanon was now a very dangerous place to be, with fierce fighting, bombings and kidnappings a regular daily occurrence. Certain parts of Beirut were strictly off limits for Christians, namely the west. To venture into these parts during such troubled, turbulent times would be foolhardy. Laura would live on her nerves until she heard from Nicky that he was safe. But often phone lines would be down in Lebanon. Nicky called every chance he could, and when he couldn't, he sent messages via friends who would call Laura from outside Lebanon on his behalf.

After the Norway tour, due to mounting arguments and disagreements over their future, Laura's vocal dance group disbanded and everyone went their separate ways that summer. Deciding to return to the world of dance, Laura enrolled in regular dance classes. To audition for shows and to be 'seen', relocating to London was an absolute necessity. Laura loved living in the big city again, and the stimulating buzz from London's cosmopolitan atmosphere, enlivened her spirit. It was of course a temporary stop-gap, effectively filling the time until she could return to Abu Dhabi, and to Nicky.

With the continuing and escalating conflict between the warring factions occupying his beloved country, Nicolas's situation was complicated. Travelling between the Arab states to secure his business interests at this politically unstable time was crucial. Nicolas's trips to Lebanon were becoming more difficult and less frequent, with the constant bombing and shelling of Beirut. Lebanon was being crippled, as Syria and Israel raged their battles with one another on Lebanese soil. For the time being, Nicolas's wife Samra remained in Kousba in the north, a relatively safe distance from the war-torn capital Beirut. On his now infrequent trips back home, they would argue constantly. Samra was not so enamoured with his beloved Lebanon; not being Lebanese but of Syrian origin, she didn't share her husband's patriotism. She hated even more how Nicolas was constantly surrounded by his entourage. Frequently Samra would voice her opinions, making it clear she wanted Nicolas to change his ways. Samra wanted her husband to conform to her expectations, as if he was somehow flawed the way he was. For Nicolas, being accepted for who he was in any relationship was pivotal; Samra's insistence that he change not surprisingly had a ricochet effect.

They clashed and argued regularly, leading to volatile outbursts on both sides. There could only ever be one boss in the marriage, namely Nicolas; his wife was expected to bend to his will not the other way around. Samra was not completely blind to her husband's womanising and infidelity. Nicolas was unaware she knew as much as she did. However, he was acutely aware of her discontentment with his lack of conformity. Nicolas could only ever be the man he was; if people did not accept him that way, it was their problem, not his. Before they married, Samra agreed to accept Nicolas's ways, especially his need to be in control; her backtracking on this confused and upset him. Samra's insistence he change, pushed him further away.

Change would come in time, Nicolas wasn't incapable of it. But it wouldn't happen overnight, as Samra expected. Pushing him before he was ready was a pointless exercise. Nicolas refused to put on a show. He would not pretend to be something he was not, or ever could be. He hated how people would willingly sacrifice themselves just to follow the crowd. His confidence came from knowing his own mind, and never allowing himself or his beliefs to be compromised or influenced by the opinions of others. Nicolas celebrated his individuality. There was nothing remotely fake or contrived about him.

During their short marriage, Nicolas did his best to hide his extramarital affairs from Samra. He may have wished to spare his wife embarrassment, but she was only too aware he was regularly playing away from home. On one occasion Samra drove him to Beirut airport. Despite the shelling it had opened for a few hours, allowing Nicolas to take his flight back to Abu Dhabi. On his arrival in the capital of the Emirates, he immediately called Laura.

"How are you hayati, you still love me?"

"Of course, I love you more than anything." Laura was thrilled and relieved to hear his voice. "I've been so worried about you. I'm glad you're back from Beirut and safe in Abu Dhabi," she told him.

Sometime later Nicolas remembered he hadn't called Samra to check that she had arrived safely back to Kousba. In fact he hadn't given her a thought since leaving her at Beirut airport. No one could accuse him of being a selfish person; but Nicolas felt ashamed and selfish at his thoughtlessness. He may no longer be in love with her, but he cared for Samra. His behaviour was uncharacteristic and by no means intentional, although it drew to his notice the fact that when he wasn't with Samra, he rarely thought about her.

In complete contrast, he couldn't get Laura out of his head. She was 3,500 miles away, yet perpetually on his mind. This distinction confirmed that it was time and only fair, to allow Samra the freedom to live her life without him. Theirs was not a match made in heaven; it was more like a business arrangement than a love match. The sooner Nicolas rectified this, the better it would be for everyone. He resolved to tell his wife that he wanted a divorce on his next trip home.

Time passed and Laura accepted contracts for shows in and around London. Reluctant to be tied to anything that might delay her return to Nicky; she turned down any work that took her away for too long a period. In retrospect as things turned out, Laura need not have worried on that front. More than six months passed. At times Laura found the separation from Nicky intolerable. Although he called almost daily, she longed to be back in his arms.

Later that autumn, Nicky called Laura with devastating news. An emergency involving his wife Samra required his immediate return to Lebanon. While driving her husband's car, Samra had been shot. All of Nicolas's cars had windows with darkened glass. Aiming at the front seat and believing the driver to be Nicolas, the gunman fired two bullets. Samra's injuries were thankfully not fatal, but Nicky told Laura he needed to leave Abu Dhabi and go to her.

Hearing this news left Laura shocked and horrified; not only about Nicky's wife being shot, but that the assassin had actually intended the bullets for him. The realisation that Nicolas had real enemies, who wanted him dead, was difficult for Laura to digest. He had alluded to having enemies when she was with him in Abu Dhabi. At the time it had sounded fanciful, and Laura hadn't seriously taken it in. Now it suddenly made sense about all the body guards. Fearing for Nicky's safety, Laura dreaded even more every moment he spent in Lebanon. Nicolas was unperturbed, it was the life that destiny had decreed and he accepted its darker segments, as par for the course. What worried him was exposing Laura to such dangers. She would gladly follow wherever his road led. All the same, certain things Nicolas resolved to keep far away from Laura.

In light of this unexpected, devastating development, asking Samra for a divorce would have to be put on hold. Nicolas decided now was not the time to rock an already sinking boat. Samra needed him, and it was his duty as a husband to be by her side. Despite his failure to be faithful, Nicolas was an honourable man. He would put his feelings for Laura to one side, while helping his wife recover from her ordeal. After all, Samra was the innocent victim. He felt guilty that she had taken a bullet meant for him.

Laura totally understood his situation; fully confident in Nicky's love for her, she agreed the timing was not right to talk of divorce. If Nicolas had acted any other way, Laura would think him heartless. The unexpected turn of events meant Laura would have to wait a little longer. Desperate as she was for their reunion, Laura loved Nicky enough to let him go. She gracefully allowed him the time to do what he needed to. In Laura's perception, the delay would be a matter of months at most. While Nicky played the dutiful husband Laura waited, spurred on by his declarations of undying love for her.

Samra was under no illusions about her husband's numerous affairs. She hated that he was untrue, but she believed deep down he loved her. In spite of his many infidelities, Nicolas had at one time genuinely loved his wife. When things started to wane in their relationship, he was still prepared to continue with the marriage if only on paper. That was until the hand of fate brought Laura into his life.

Regardless of the disagreements and fights, Samra was confident she could influence Nicolas to settle. But nobody changed Nicolas except Nicolas. He too was under no illusions about his marriage. His wife did not love him unconditionally. Clearly they wanted different things from the union. Samra's endless attempts to get her husband to conform failed miserably. Nicolas rebelled fiercely against conformity whenever it was forced upon him.

Lately Samra was noticing something different in her wayward husband. It was more than the usual extramarital dalliance; Samra feared he was really slipping away from her. Positive she may be losing him, Samra determined to win her husband back. She would do it while Nicolas was conveniently at her side.

Back in London Laura was keeping busy with endless dance classes and rehearsals. The heavy schedule could be exhausting with nightly performances, plus two matinees a week. Dancers are always required to have huge amounts of stamina, along with a body that is not only aesthetically pleasing, but in tip top physical condition. Laura's salary had almost halved compared to what it was when working with the vocal group. If you danced you were expected to do it for the love of the art. With so much to occupy her, there was little time to dwell on the fact she was parted from the man she loved. Phone calls and telexes kept her going spiritually. Physically, Laura's body ached from the exhausting, strenuous performances, but it ached even more from missing the feel of Nicky's loving touch.

On a rare night off Laura would accompany a group of girls from the show for a night out on the town. There was never a shortage of men wanting to take Laura out. Guys tried to get close but Laura's eyes were blinded to all but Nicky's face, and her heart strictly off-limits to anybody who wasn't him. The other girls ceaselessly teased, calling Laura Mother Superior, referring to the fact that she was living like a nun, not allowing any other man near her.

"That Nicky must be really something," they would tell her, "You have the pick of any man in London, and you turn them away. Are you crazy?" Crazy in love is what Laura was, only Nicky held the key to her heart. As far as Laura was concerned no man could hold a candle to him.

In Lebanon Nicolas's wife made a complete recovery. Determined as Samra was to hold on to her man, it wasn't long before they were physically close. Like most men, Nicolas felt that love and sex were not necessarily related. With Laura away in London and Nicolas a normal, healthy red-blooded alpha male, the inevitable happened. With Samra well-recovered, Nicolas left Lebanon to return to Abu Dhabi. He called Laura most nights, and at the end of each call would tell her;

"I love you hayati, eyouni, see you in my dreams."

Laura would answer, "I'll be there my love."

Momentarily soothed by his sweet loving words, Laura kept hopeful that the long wait would soon be over. Like Cinderella waiting for her Prince to return her glass shoe, she patiently waited. But it was not a glass shoe Laura had left behind in Nicky's hands, but her heart. Nicky's constant assurances that he was working his way along the road leading back to her, was of little comfort when alone in bed at night. All Laura wanted was to feel the warmth of his body next to hers, and his strong arms around her again. Little did either of them realise that the road leading them back to one another's arms, would be littered with obstacles. Cruel twists of fate were about to test their long distance love affair to the absolute limit.

Leaving the troubled war-torn Lebanon behind, Samra left Kousba for America where her wealthy family owned property and businesses. It was from here that she called Nicolas with a bombshell to scupper his plans to leave her. Samra announced she was pregnant. Nicolas decided not to tell Laura, fearing she may pull away from him. In the face of this new development, things were to become a lot more complex. Resolute that Laura would be in his life one way or another, in spite of the changed circumstances, Nicolas determined to make it happen. Equally resolute, Laura would not forsake him. No matter how much people tried to dissuade her, Laura refused to believe she was wasting her life waiting for Nicky. In the eyes of the world she was blindly following a mere fantasy, a dream that would never materialise.

Laura wouldn't be moved; stubbornly refusing to listen to anyone who cast doubt on her firm conviction that she and Nicky were meant to be together. When feeling particularly down, she would purchase a bottle of Nicky's Chanel cologne and spray it around her room. As the sweet smell of her lover permeated the atmosphere, Laura would close her eyes imagining him beside her. With neither one prepared to give up on their quest to be reunited, against all the odds the bond between Laura and Nicky remained steadfastly unbroken.

Chapter 8:
Valentine's Star Crossed Lovers

The following January Laura made the decision to reform her vocal group and dance act. Laura needed a lead male vocalist to front the band. Straight away she began holding auditions. Many applied for the opportunity of a place in the group, and Laura was confident she would soon find someone with precisely the qualities she had in mind. For the role of lead male, the applicant needed to be strong on vocal talent but also able to dance a little as well. Laura wasn't looking for a trained dancer as such, but someone who would have no trouble picking up a few simple steps and routines. The successful candidate would require another asset too; to be easy on the eye. The new act must appeal to both male and female audiences.

After sifting through dozens of hopefuls, Laura began to wonder if she would ever find what she was looking for. Some applicants were rejected in Laura's mind from the moment they walked through the audition room door. But she gave everyone a fair chance, even though it meant sitting through some horrendous sights and sounds. Those who could actually sing were weeded out from the less-than-hopefuls. The successful applicants were invited to attend a second audition, aimed at establishing movability skills. Laura choreographed a couple of routines and put the guys to the test.

Again there was a disappointing result. They could all sing but when asked to dance, it was quite a different matter. Some were hopeless at picking up the simplest of steps. Laura never could understand why people, who obviously had musicality, could be so lacking in a sense of rhythm and awkward when it came to moving their bodies.

Those who did manage to pick up the routine seemed promising, but when Laura asked them to perform the moves and sing at the same time, it fell apart spectacularly. After many frustrating hours of endless auditions, the right guy was finally chosen and the position of the bands lead male vocalist was filled. For the next few weeks the group rehearsed like crazy. Professional publicity photos were taken, and costumes made. The act was booked to have its debut performance at a prestigious London venue on Valentine's night. This first engagement was an important showcase to publicly launch the band. It was an opportunity to show off the act to agents, who hopefully would book them to perform at other London venues. Laura was confident in successfully securing some good contracts and further residential work.

Organising the shows format and arranging all the choreography, Laura was in her element. Throwing herself into a new creative project kept her mind focussed, and deflected her attention from the absence of Nicky. It was Laura's way of coping while remaining apart from him.

Nicolas, meanwhile felt bad about keeping the news of his wife's pregnancy from Laura, but he didn't want to risk losing her. He was eager to bring Laura back into his life and with Samra away in America, Nicolas arranged for Laura to return to Abu Dhabi. He was happy about Laura's new venture for the time being, but he was unaware of the planned Valentine's night debut. Laura hadn't told him, superstitiously afraid that speaking about the big night might somehow jinx it. She was hoping to surprise him with good news of the bands success after the event.

Nicolas had very little interest in show business or what it entailed. The only reason he had ever gone to see a show was to eye up the female talent. And it was not their talent for singing or dancing that interested him either. Laura was under no illusions about Nicky's lack of enthusiasm for the profession that had been her life; this being so, she refrained from boring him with the details. Unfortunately this backfired; Laura's big night was already jinxed. With a conspicuous lack of details concerning Laura's schedule, Nicolas spontaneously went ahead and made arrangements without consulting her. A few days before the group's first public appearance he called;

"Love I've sent you a ticket to come to Abu Dhabi," he eagerly told her. "Your ticket is at Heathrow. They will send a driver to pick you up and take you to the airport. Okay hayati?"

Laura was over the moon; her heart was beating ten to the dozen as she relished the long awaited reunion. She excitedly asked Nicky when she would be flying out.

"Darling, your ticket is for after tomorrow, the 13th." Laura's heart sank.

"But that's the day before Valentine's," she said.

"I know darling, and I want the woman I love to be in my arms and in my bed on Valentines night. First we will have a nice dinner together, and then I am going to make love to you the whole night, okay hayati?" Still oblivious to Laura's prior engagement, Nicolas's confidence took him way ahead of himself.

"I can't," she exclaimed. "Not that day."

"You have to come that time," he insisted. "Darling, what's the problem?" he asked earnestly.

"Valentine's night is the debut performance for the new group," she told him. "I'll be able to come after, just not then."

Nicolas went quiet; he wasn't prepared for his act of spontaneity to receive such a negative response. It hadn't occurred to him Laura would possibly have other plans.

"Are you still there?" Laura asked after a painfully long silence.

"Yes love, I'm thinking," Nicky said, unable to hide the irritation in his voice. "You will stay with me for a short time, we will talk about everything, and then you can go back and make your show, okay hayati?" Nicolas didn't quite get that it really didn't work like that in the land of show business. "Love, I have to go away on business soon and I don't know when I will be free after that time."

If the circumstances were different, Laura would in a heartbeat happily drop everything and run to him. If only it could be that simple. But there were four other people in the equation to consider; otherwise nothing would get in the way of her longed for reunion. Everyone had worked so hard towards this one very important performance, not least of all Laura who was responsible for putting the band together. She tried to explain to Nicky; she wasn't a solo performer and could not let down her co-band members by walking out on the eve of their debut performance.

"How much are they paying you?" Nicky demanded. "I will double it."

Again Laura tried to explain it wasn't about the money. She had a moral obligation to the rest of the group, not to mention the club owner who would have difficulty booking another act for Valentines at such short notice. Besides the advertising had gone ahead, tickets were already sold out and important agents had been invited. Not only would it be disloyal to her colleagues, it would mean professional suicide for all of them to suddenly pull out. Laura couldn't understand what difference delaying her trip for a week or two would make; they had already been apart for months. She pleaded with him to change the arrangements and let her travel at a later date. But Nicolas was adamant.

"No it has to be now," he insisted.

Laura sensed the frustration in Nicky's voice. Unaware of the complex situations going on in his life, things he was as yet reluctant to reveal, Laura was perplexed by his attitude. Nicolas wasn't trying to deceive her; his feelings for Laura were never in question, but Samra's unplanned pregnancy was something he would rather explain face to face. Again the phone line went silent. Neither of them spoke for what seemed like an age. Within that silence the nervous tension between them was palpable.

Laura was miffed that Nicolas expected her to just drop everything; after all he was the one telling her it would take time for him to get out of his marriage. In his absence Laura had been forced to get on with her life; now it seemed to her Nicky couldn't wait even a few days for her to fulfil a commitment she was contracted to. As they told each other 'I love you,' their voices were tinged with annoyance and disappointment from both sides.

The atmosphere was decidedly cool as the conversation ended on a less joyous note than it had started; they said their goodbyes under a distinct cloud of anti-climax. Things would be different if Laura had been selfish and followed her heart instead of her conscience, but it wasn't to be. Rather than run to her lover's waiting arms Laura fulfilled her obligation to the band. Had she been blessed with the gift of foresight, might she have acted differently? Perhaps Nicolas should have been quicker to make a stand with Samra. At the time he wanted to have his cake and eat it too. His heart would pay for that mistake. Sometimes the smallest of decisions can result in a catalogue of events that can have an irreversible impact on one's whole future. Fate it seemed was against them, intervening in a less than positive way; a familiar scenario that would continue to plague their relationship. For the star-crossed lovers, their love affair was about to fall victim to a fate equal to that of any great, and tragic love story.

The show went ahead as planned on Valentines night, and was a huge success. The audience and the agents were impressed with the new act, resulting in the band securing more bookings. One impressed agent offered a contract to tour the continent of India performing at the Sheraton hotels. There Laura would again enjoy the luxury lifestyle reminiscent of her time in the Middle East.

Laura revelled in the new acts triumph, but its success was soured by the continued absence of Nicolas in her life. She felt more than an inkling of remorse at not going to Abu Dhabi. The ever-present regret stayed with her. While performing on stage Laura's secret sorrow was kept well hidden behind her smile.

Three weeks passed without further word from Nicky; they hadn't spoken since Laura turned down his invitation in favour of her commitment to the band. Laura felt sure he would appreciate and understand that she had been put in a tight spot. Clearly Nicolas had retreated into his cave to sulk. Laura believed he would come around once he had gotten over his huge male ego. Laura continued to write to him, expressing her deep disappointment at not being able to go to Abu Dhabi. It was important he understood she had not made the choice lightly. Laura would never have willingly passed up the opportunity to be with him.

Laura received no response, and the weeks quickly turned into months. It was a ridiculously long time to be sulking, even for a man Laura thought. She tried to remain positive, refusing to consider the possibility he had been stringing her along, as suggested by some. Laura was unwilling to believe Nicky would deceive her about his intention to divorce. Were his promises all an act? Had he been playing a game with her as friends insinuated? Laura didn't believe that was the case. She trusted her instincts. Despite how things looked, Laura refused to entertain the cynical views of others.

But time passed, and with that time Laura unwillingly came to terms with the cold fact that it was unlikely she would see Nicky again. Sadly, the love of her life appeared to have slipped through her fingers. Laura tried to forget him, and gave a good impression that she had. But secretly Laura ached for the man she believed it was her destiny to be with.

Contrary to how it appeared, Laura still believed Nicky loved her. Friends were quick to remind Laura that he was married, pointing out that very few men who say they will leave their wives ever actually do so. Over three months passed by with no word from him; Laura's affair with the elusive Nicky became the white elephant in the room she refused to discuss.

Eventually, although it was painful to do so, Laura was persuaded to move on with her life. There was nowhere else to go accept forward. Convinced Nicky was gone for ever, and with encouragement from her friends, Laura reluctantly started dating. The trouble was no-one made her feel the way Nicky had. But Laura would do what she did best; make the most of what she had. She had her career, she was young and there were no shortage of male admirers. Soon Laura started seeing a handsome young Italian. Three months down the line Alessandro presented her with an engagement ring. Laura accepted his proposal, and their wedding plans were promptly made.

Six months on, Laura was at her family home preparing for the big day; her parents had spared no expense to give their daughter a real fairy tale wedding which was to take place in two days'. Laura was in her bedroom getting ready to go out to dinner with her husband to be, when the phone rang. Laura answered and heard a familiar voice;

"Hello love, how are you hayati?"

Laura was momentarily stunned.

"Oh my God where are you?" she shrieked.

"I'm in Abu Dhabi," he answered.

Laura's heart was pounding; suddenly without warning all the feelings she had been suppressing for months, came flooding back. Her hands were shaking so much she almost dropped the phone;

"Where have you been why didn't you call or answer my letters?" she demanded.

"Love I have been through many, many problems. I was fighting in Lebanon, and there was big problem with my business and many things happen, I will tell you when I see you. But listen, I have my divorce, I am free now."

For a few glorious moments Laura's mind drifted right back. She was instantly transported to where she had been emotionally speaking, ten months previous; the last time she had spoken with him. For months Laura had clung to the hope Nicky would come back to her. Now, long after she had given up believing it would happen, he was at the end of the phone telling her he was free. Her wedding nuptials in two days' briefly escaped Laura's thoughts.

Suddenly the cruel irony of the situation came rushing towards her, along with the realisation that the hand of fate had again struck another fateful blow. Nicolas was free, and Laura was betrothed to another.

Laura's head spun as she struggled with her emotions. Frantically she searched for the words to tell him. Her heart started to break all over again. Laura slowly uttered what she could never in a million years have imagined saying to Nicky. Laura waited for his response to her news. For a while nobody said anything, but the silence spoke volumes. Nicky tentatively asked,

"Do you love him?"

Laura hesitated with her answer. Nicky asked again,

"Do you love him Laura?"

Laura took a deep breath then quickly replied,

"Yes, of course I do."

It wasn't a lie; she did love Alessandro in her way. But if Nicky had been in touch sooner it was unlikely Laura would be walking down the aisle with him in two days. Trying to make sense of such a surreal situation was impossible.

"It's too late Nicky. Everything is arranged for my marriage. I can't back out at the eleventh hour."

Again if Laura was braver, more selfish, or prepared to take a risk even; who knows? If Nicky were to arrive in person and fight for her, things would be different. But Nicolas was in a situation that prevented him from leaving Abu Dhabi. If he told Laura, she may be persuaded not to marry. Unwilling to cause a problem or to pressure her, Nicolas selflessly declined to tell Laura of his tenuous situation. Instead he put on a brave front, telling her,

"Love I'm not asking you to back out, if this is what you want I am happy for you."

"You are happy for me?" she questioned.

Nicolas was far from happy, but he did not wish Laura to feel guilty about her decision to marry. He was not in a good place financially like before. If Laura could be happy with someone else, Nicky would not interfere. Because he loved her, he was prepared to step aside and let her go.

"Maybe its better this way," he told her.

Nicolas struggled to stay upbeat and calm. He stoically hid his true feelings, as another part of his world tumbled down before him. Strong though he tried to be, Laura could tell he was hurting. Fate had made a travesty of their love, and another piece of Laura's heart broke as he asked,

"You love him more than you loved me?"

Laura didn't answer; she couldn't. Nicolas was not stupid he could read between the lines. Laura may appear to have got on with her life, but she was fragile in her emotions where Nicolas was concerned. Who was he to disrupt her life, and prevent her from having the security he was not able to offer in his present situation? He told Laura,

"You know I love you hayati, but I love you enough to let you go. Be happy darling and take care of yourself."

"Will you stay in touch; will I hear from you again?" Laura asked.

"I don't know love, but if you ever need anything I will be here. Go get married hayati be happy."

Nicolas put down the receiver and lit a cigarette. He poured himself a large whisky and sat alone in the dark with his thoughts. With a heavy heart he contemplated the irony of the fact that he had just let the love of his life go again. Perhaps he should have pushed harder, convinced Laura to leave and run to him. If his situation was different Nicolas would have pushed; he would have taken a flight, confronted Laura and challenged her decision to marry. Nicolas stubbed out his cigarette; he gave a long drawn out sigh.

"C'est la vie," he thought resignedly, "C'est la vie."

Laura went to dinner with Alessandro as planned. All thoughts of Nicky were relegated to the back of her mind. She dare not allow those feelings to emerge. She had chosen her path and would now focus her attention on her marriage to Alessandro. But her heart knew different. Hard as she tried, Laura was unable to completely silence the persistent voice that continued to throw doubt on her decision to deny and abandon her love for Nicolas. Even so, two days later Laura's wedding went ahead.

When they returned from honeymoon, Laura took up a pre-arranged five month contract to work in the Channel Islands performing in cabaret shows with her band. Laura and Alessandro had agreed Laura would continue working with the band while they saved for a house. Before long Laura discovered she was pregnant. She continued to work with the band late into the pregnancy; finally giving birth to a beautiful daughter they named Alyssa. Laura had planned to continue working in the entertainment industry, but as soon as her little daughter arrived, she knew she could not be parted from her to go off on tour. Her life as a dancer was now on hold indefinitely.

Laura devoted herself to married life and motherhood; unlike the unpredictability of show business, it felt stable and secure. For a while Laura was happy in her new role. She fully embraced being a wife and mother. It was the normality she thought she needed, and was determined to make it work.

But all too soon, despite her best efforts to make a success of the marriage, the cracks started to appear. Alyssa was barely a year old when Laura and Alessandro began to drift apart. Unable to delude herself any longer that she could make the marriage work, Laura gave in to the inevitable, and contacted a solicitor.

She and Alessandro separated and finally divorced. It was nobody's fault, they were just incompatible. Faced with the daunting prospect of bringing up her daughter alone, Laura was disillusioned by her failed attempt to have a normal life. But normal was not an adjective that would adequately describe anything about Laura's life; now or in the future.

It was time to face another truth. Nicolas was the love of her life. If Laura couldn't be with him, she wouldn't be with anyone. But where was Nicolas? Laura didn't know, and had no way to contact him. Reluctant to chase a dream that seemed to have long since fled, Laura resolved to focus her energy on her daughter.

KOUSBAWI

Chapter 9: The Power of Love

Laura adjusted to her single life as best she could. With Alyssa nearly two years old now, Laura was beginning to feel restless; she needed a change. Working in her father's business was one option available to her. Being a creative soul, Laura yearned to become involved with a project where she could embrace that skill. Involving herself in the world of dance again would satisfy her creative yearning. Laura had always loved choreography and been good at it. Teaching dance classes was an alternative she gave strong consideration to. Not surprisingly it had only been a matter of time before she suffered withdrawal symptoms from her previous incarnation as a dancer. One day while at home, Laura was sitting on the bed absorbed in play with her young daughter when the phone rang. Expecting a call from her mother, Laura leant over and picked up the receiver from the bedside table;

"Hi mum," she said casually, assuming her mother was at the end of the line. An extremely masculine voice with an unmistakably familiar accent responded;

"I'm not your mother."

Laura's heart skipped several beats.

"Laura, it's me love, how are you?"

This unforgettable voice caused Laura's heart to flutter furiously. With excited anticipation she asked,

"Nicky, is that really you?"

"Yes love, you remember me?"

Remember? How could she forget? His memory was imprinted indelibly in her heart?

"How you doin, love?" he asked in a rather laid-back, manner as if it were only yesterday since they had spoken. The masculine velvety tones of his eastern Mediterranean accent melted Laura's senses like ice cream on a sizzling hot summer's day. Just as Laura couldn't forget him,

Nicolas equally had never been able to forget her. They had been apart for a while, but still she pulled his soul like a river being pulled towards the sea. But much had befallen Nicolas since they last spoke. Laura struggled to compose herself as her heart continued to palpitate like a nervous seventeen year old on a first date.

"How did you get this number?" she asked finally.

During what was a very turbulent episode in his life, Nicolas had lost many of his personal possessions. Laura's contact details, along with many of her letters and most of his personal papers had gone missing. Exactly how this had come about was a long story to which Nicolas would enlighten Laura in time. Nicolas had re-acquired Laura's number again in a peculiar and most surreal way.

Having long since vacated his permanent residence at the Holiday Inn, Nicolas happened to be at the hotel one day for a business meeting. While standing in the hotel reception area, the manager passed by and straight away recognised Nicolas. They engaged in conversation and the manager asked after Laura. Nicolas told him that he had unfortunately lost contact with her. With that the manager said;

"Wait there Mr Nicolas, I have something that can help you."

The hotel manager disappeared into his office, leaving the bemused Nicolas wondering what he meant. He came back a short while later holding a piece of paper. Handing it to Nicolas he said;

"This is Laura's number."

Nicolas stared at him in amazement;

"How do you have this number?" Nicolas asked.

"Laura used to call her mother when she was staying here. I don't know why I kept the number all these years; but I'm glad I did. I never forgot you Mr Nicolas you seemed so in love with Laura."

Although he didn't expect for a moment that it would actually be the right number, Nicolas thanked the manager and decided to call it. With nothing to lose he dialled and waited to see who would answer. After a few rings a female voice came on the line. Nicolas didn't recognise the voice. Believing it must be the wrong number he apologised for disturbing the lady, explaining that he was trying to contact somebody called Laura.

"Laura is my daughter," the woman told him.

Nicolas couldn't believe it; it was the right number after all, what were the chances of that happening?

After a fairly brief exchange the woman gave Nicolas Laura's new number. He couldn't believe his luck. It was pure coincidence for Nicolas to be at the Holiday Inn that day; his meeting was originally scheduled to be held elsewhere. It was even more of a coincidence to bump into the manager who knew him and just happened to be on duty that time. More unbelievable was the fact that he had kept Laura's mother's number. Synchronicity working at its best you could say. Fate may have thrown many a spoke in the wheel, but in the end true love will always find a way to fulfil its destiny.

They talked for over an hour; it felt like they had never parted. Laura told Nicolas;

"I have a daughter."

"Let me hear her voice," he asked.

Laura put the phone to Alyssa's ear and told her to say hello. As Nicolas spoke to her, Alyssa made her usual baby talk sounds. He laughed and seemed genuinely happy to hear the little girl's voice.

"She's a lovely," he told Laura. His English was still delightfully imperfect. "Send me photo."

Laura promised she would, so Nicolas gave her his post office box number. He asked Laura;

"You still love me?"

Laura told him that she had never stopped loving him.

"What about you?" she asked. "Do you still love me?"

"Hayati eyouni, you are my heart. I will love you for ever," he professed sincerely.

Both of them were reluctant to end the call and like a couple of love struck teenagers, argued over who would put the receiver down first; just like old times. Everything felt natural between them. In their hearts time had stood still waiting for this moment to occur.

"When will I see you again?" Laura asked expectantly.

"Love, I'm in fucking situation now," he told her. "Remember I said you are on my road, every step I take, you taking with me. Love, I promise we will be together soon; just let me finish this fucking problem."

Nicolas didn't elaborate on his unfortunate situation or the problems he was facing. Laura didn't wish to spoil the moment by pushing him to talk of what she sensed had been a difficult and painful time. Nicolas was still Nicolas, but Laura could tell he'd taken some hard knocks in his life. She wished she could somehow jump down the phone line and hold him. Eventually they hung up the call. Laura sat on the bed feeling slightly stunned by the unexpected re-connection. Laura couldn't think straight. Her pulse was racing and her head spinning as though suddenly tossed into the centre of a whirlwind. Within a minute of Laura putting down the receiver the phone rang again.

"Well, it's about time," Laura's mother said in an irritated fashion. "I suppose you've been talking to that Nicky?" Her tone was a little sarcastic.

"Yes I have," Laura told her mother.

"Well I don't know what you can find to talk about all that time. I've been trying to get through for ages."

Laura's relationship with Nicky had never really been understood by her mother, who had displayed a cynical and negative attitude from day one. Today it didn't matter, because Laura was floating on air again, and nothing, least of all her mother's negative views, was going to burst her bubble. After putting Alyssa to bed, that evening Laura composed a letter to Nicky; she practically ran to the post box the following day to post it. She included some photos of herself and Alyssa.

Back in Abu Dhabi Nicolas took stock of his situation. Confident of his ability to reverse his spate of bad luck, he dared to consider a life with Laura. Nicolas had genuinely only ever wanted Laura to be happy, but while having told her he was sorry her marriage had failed, his heart secretly jumped for joy; it meant Laura was free to love him again.

There's no remedy for love as Nicolas was finding out. He and Laura both discovered that when true love seeks you out it will grip your soul, and take your breath away; it will drive you crazy like a furious dance, or leave you stunned like an insect caught in a web helplessly waiting to be consumed. Having tasted true loves sweet nectar, Nicolas could never settle for anything less and neither could Laura.

At last he dared to dream again; dream about a future, and of giving Laura the life he'd always intended for them. But the equation was changed; now there was a child to consider. Nicolas was aware this would ultimately take priority in Laura's life. An arduous journey lay ahead, but Nicolas was determined to climb back up to the top of the ladder and regain all he'd lost; his business, his money, and of course Laura.

Nicolas decided to write to Laura explaining everything that had happened. This required some help as he had never previously written anything in English before, and had never composed a love letter; until now he hadn't the inclination. As promised Laura sent pictures; Nicolas was overjoyed at receiving her letters and photos. The first letter he wrote back took a while to complete; but with perseverance and some help from a friend, soon he had written in excess of ten letters. Laura cherished his letters, keeping them in a red box tied with a red satin ribbon.

That first letter was the most precious. Laura would never forget the day it arrived through her letter box. As Nicolas hadn't revealed his intention to write, it came as a complete surprise. She was so excited at seeing the Abu Dhabi postmark, Laura shrieked with joy. It amused young Alyssa who laughed and giggled as her mother danced around the room waving the letter in the air, hugging it to her heart as if it were a precious treasure. Aware how hard Nicolas would need to work to write a letter in English,

Laura appreciated his effort all the more. Every time she heard the sound of the post being dropped through the letter box, her heart skipped in joyful anticipation as she eagerly sifted through the mail to see if there was anything with an Abu Dhabi postmark amongst the bills.

In those early days Laura struggled as a single mother financially. She taught dance class five days a week, and worked in her father's restaurant in-between. Later on when Alyssa was in school, Laura took a job working as a coordinator in women's fashion. To give Alyssa the best she could, sometimes meant working three jobs to make ends meet. Laura certainly didn't have money spare for a ticket to Abu Dhabi.

Whilst talking with Laura one day, Nicolas excitedly told her he had made some good money that week, enough to buy her a plane ticket. Laura desperately wanted to go but her mother refused point blank to take care of Alyssa, telling Laura she should give up this childish fantasy about Nicky, and start living in the real world. If Laura wanted to see Nicolas she would have to take Alyssa to Abu Dhabi with her. Nicolas didn't yet have the money to purchase another ticket, so Laura told him to put the money he had made into his business and she would come another time.

Nicolas would gladly have given his last penny to buy Laura a second ticket, but they agreed to wait until he was in a better situation. Life had been tough for them both. It felt at times their love was being put through the wringer. As Nicky said, too many spokes were being put in the wheel trying to bring them down. Whenever Laura spent her money on phone calls to him he would become angry telling her sternly;

"I get angry when you spend your money on the phone; I don't have as before to send you. Write to me love."

Laura did write every day, but sometimes the longing to hear Nicky's voice was overpowering. Unable to resist the urge to call him, Laura ended up with a few large phone bills. Nicolas called whenever he could and it was like a lifeline to her heart. Frustrated with his insufficient knowledge of English grammar when writing, and lack of finance to call Laura as often as he would like, Nicolas had the perfect solution. He would make a recording. Nicolas would record his voice and be able to say what he wanted to Laura without having to worry how to write it.

No matter what problems he was facing, and there were many, Nicolas remained positive. Laura would laugh at some of his more outrageous statements. For instance he would tell her that when he got his money, he would send his private plane to bring her to him. Laura took it all with a pinch of salt, but Nicky would convincingly insist;

"Don't laugh love, Hajj can do it."

Nicolas had big dreams and he wasn't giving up on any of them. He refused to be beaten. Any situation that reared itself threatening to destroy his hopes of success would be analysed and dissected. Like a snake in a tree, Nicolas would weave around any problem turning it inside out until he found an alternative route around it. Encouraged by Nicolas's unwavering confidence and optimism, Laura was convinced they would one day be together. Nicolas's hopeful outlook helped her deal with the cynicism she encountered. People were far from convinced that this long distance relationship would amount to anything. Laura's mother especially; citing on numerous occasions that she regretted passing on Laura's new number to Nicky. Laura resented her mother's flippantly insensitive remarks; it caused more than a little friction between them.

Laura could face peoples doubt and cynicism, because Nicky reliably kept her strong. Like an indestructible bridge, he carried Laura above the persistent negativity, pulling her from the waves of uncertainty flowing in the chaotic river known as life. Their love acted as a lifeline to each other's heart; in troubled times it would pull them through life's murky waters. Neither time passed, nor the distance between them, would prevent their written destiny from being fulfilled.

KOUSBAWI

Chapter 10: Al Hajj

Situated in the Khoura district of northern Lebanon south of Tripoli and east of Chekka is the village of Kousba.

One of the most populated towns in the region, Kousba (meaning hidden), takes its name from the old times because of the way it lies; snugly settled between the mountains. The young Nicolas was born and raised in Kousba. Sadly his mother passed away shortly after giving birth to Nicolas, who was her second son. Despite being cruelly deprived of his mother from birth, Nicolas had a relatively happy and care free childhood. He grew up never knowing her, but Nicolas worshipped his mother's memory. She had by all accounts, been a very strong woman, and Nicolas was blessed with having her indomitable strength of character. Losing his mother the way he did was to have a profound and lasting effect on his life.

Brought up by his mother's family, Nicolas was never permitted to celebrate his birthday. As a child he was told he could not celebrate the day that his mother died. Every year on his birthday Nicolas would be reminded that his mother had passed on that day, and it was clearly not a day for celebration.

Tragically, his family's insistence that they continually mourn the passing of his mother rather than celebrate Nicolas's birth, caused him to feel guilty; believing he was somehow responsible for the unfortunate circumstances of his mother's death. It was a heavy and cruel burden put on an impressionable young child, which needless to say emotionally scarred him.

In adulthood Nicolas continued to treat his birthday as a solemn occasion; reacting negatively if anyone attempted to bring him a cake or gifts. No matter how well-meaning their intentions Nicolas would become angry, adamantly refusing to acknowledge any kind of celebration.

Very few restrictions were placed on Nicolas or his behaviour while growing up, but crying about anything was frowned upon. Often he would walk in the village and overhear remarks referring to him as 'the boy whose mother died', it hurt and made him feel that life had disadvantaged him from day one. Feeling he was unable to cry, his strong emotions needed an outlet. His pain was redirected, often surfacing in volatile angry outbursts.

Nicolas was fervently encouraged to be a man and to stand against anyone who opposed him. There were few toys he loved more than his grandfather's rifle. At four or five years old he would proudly carry the rifle around and even insist on sleeping with it, as opposed to a teddy bear like other kids. His grandfather would wrap a cloth around it so that it would feel soft against the young boy's skin as he slept. Of course, the gun was never loaded when in the hands of young Nicolas.

In the old days family honour was everything. It was an accepted part of life especially in the north of Lebanon. A man, if he was a man, would be expected to seek revenge against anyone who dishonoured him or his family. Strongly influenced by his uncles and grandfather, Nicolas grew up with these notions of honour and revenge firmly set in his mind; it was a very Mafioso way of thinking. It was hardly surprising that in later years films such as 'The Godfather,' were Nicolas's favourite movies to watch.

Everyone loved the young Nicolas, especially the other kids in the village who would follow him around honoured to be part of his little entourage. From an early age it was noticeable that Nicolas was bright, and acutely intelligent. As he developed from a boy to a young teen, he would often be found courting the company of older men, happily conversing with them on subject's way beyond his years.

Despite his apparent intellect, Nicolas was seldom seen in school which he hated with a passion. Reluctant to accept any form of authority, he rebelled against anything or anyone that tried to tell him what to do, or restrict how he behaved. Every day was a fight to try and persuade the young Nicolas onto the school bus. He would vehemently refuse, and fought with anyone who endeavoured to force him. Putting Nicolas in a classroom environment was like trying to cage a tiger, or fit a square peg into a round hole. Nicolas clearly was never going to be just another brick in the wall. Exasperated, his family eventually gave up trying to force the issue and would allow Nicolas to stay home and do his own thing; much to the relief of the school teachers, who found their life a lot more peaceful when he wasn't there rebelling and being disruptive. Left to his own devices Nicolas was far happier.

This unwillingness to cooperate was frustrating to say the least, as Nicolas possessed a brilliant mind, if only he would apply himself. His out of control behaviour led to his being fundamentally denied the academic success he could easily have achieved. Consequently Nicolas barely made it through primary school; nobody was going to tell him what to do. Nonetheless he was very smart, and had a thirst for knowledge. Education was something Nicolas would acquire on his terms. His passion for books drove him to read voraciously anything he could lay his hands on. Books on history, politics or philosophy were his firm favourites. Strong-willed, rebellious and unashamedly outspoken, Nicolas was a born leader, and determined to be his own boss.

Contrary to his distinct lack of schooling and formal education, Nicolas was advanced in the University of Life. While the other kids were busy studying, Nicolas was busy making money. With a mind as sharp as a blade, by the time he reached his early teens Nicolas had already begun to put his entrepreneurial skills to use. Working in the local electric company and practically running the village cinema with his loyal band of mini mafia, he was well acquainted with how to turn a profit. With the gift of the gab as they say, he had a natural talent to coerce people into doing what he wanted. His tremendous self-belief instilled confidence in others.

Not surprisingly Nicolas was a true daredevil, and got a buzz from taking risks. With the other young boys in the village he would often play a dangerous game of jumping from the roof of a moving car. His lithe, supple body with its cat-like flexibility enabled him to jump, twist and turn without ever sustaining any serious form of injury from his thrill inducing escapades.

Being so naturally athletic Nicolas was keen on sports. He became an accomplished junior gymnast and was a talented young boxer. Because he was so quick and light on his feet they nicknamed him the dancer in the boxing ring. Nicolas literally danced circles around any opponent, having developed a technique that would floor any guy no matter how big they were. Nicolas was highly competitive and he enjoyed playing Ping-Pong (table tennis) and beach volleyball with his peers; naturally he excelled at that too.

Possessing such talents could have led to a great future in the sports arena. His gymnastics coach wanted to enter the young Nicolas into the junior Olympics. Unfortunately Nicolas lacked the discipline and dedication required to follow such a vocation or career. Instead he preferred to follow his nose for business and making money.

In Lebanon the nickname for anyone called Nicolas is Hajj, and this was the name he was commonly known by around the village. Early on in his life Nicolas displayed a passionate and volatile temperament. Even as a teenager he had little patience to tolerate any kind of disloyalty or disrespect. Often he would fly into a rage if things didn't pan out the way he wanted. Those who crossed him did so at their peril. With his hot temper, Nicolas's reputation for fighting and disruptive behaviour went before him. On occasion this would invariably lead to him being blamed for things he didn't actually do. If something occurred in the village, the word would go around that Hajj was up to his tricks again. Often Nicolas would be innocently sitting at home having his dinner, or not even be in the village at all. This was the price of such notoriety.

Notwithstanding being so rebellious, Nicolas was a

very loyal friend; he had integrity which people genuinely loved and respected him for. The local police had occasion to incarcerate young Hajj from time to time, usually for fighting or causing a disturbance in the village. But they too couldn't help but be charmed by the charismatic personality and likable nature of the incorrigible young man. Many times the police officers would sit and play cards with the teenage trouble maker, even leaving his cell door open allowing Nicolas to come and go as he pleased.

His arrest was only ever a mere formality as the police had rules to adhere to, even if Nicolas didn't. Nicolas's uncle was very influential in the village, and whenever informed of his nephew's arrest would make a phone call or have a persuasive word in somebody's ear. Nicolas was always immediately released without any charges ever being brought against him. Despite being regarded as a trouble maker Nicolas was well liked, but he didn't see eye-to-eye with everyone.

There was one boy in the village who regularly stirred up the furies in him. Pierre was born in Lebanon but of French descent and the same age as Nicolas. For some reason they disliked one another on sight, and whenever they came face to face it was like waving a red rag in front of a bull. It was almost a daily occurrence for Nicolas to start a fight with Pierre whenever he saw him until friends intervened and pulled them apart. One day Nicolas's cousin Veni tried to encourage a truce. Veni was friends with Pierre, but he also loved and respected his cousin.

After some persuasion from Veni, the three of them walked together in the village. The atmosphere was at first strained, but it wasn't long before young Hajj and Pierre realised they had a lot more in common than they thought.

From that day, instead of fighting they became like brothers, quickly developing a firm and lasting friendship. Nicolas's loyalty to his friends was such that he would go to the end for them, recklessly putting his own life at risk to protect those he cared about.

Later people would refer to him as Al Hajj, a mark of

great respect. Al Hajj was fearless and would stand against the world, alone if he had to. This kind of bravado gained Nicolas kudos and almost heroic status. You could say Al Hajj became a bit of a legend with people talking about and remembering his escapades for many years after the event.

Wishing to leave the ghost of civil war behind, those who fled the northern Lebanese village to other safer countries, would gather together in later years and often reminisce about the old days in Kousba. Whenever the village's expats congregated, Nicolas's name would crop up many times with people saying,

"Remember when Hajj did this; do you remember when Hajj did that?" Once you had encountered Al Hajj you didn't easily forget.

Following the path of all true heroes meant Nicolas had enemies, mainly because he had the balls to stand for his convictions. Rarely would he back down from anything, even if his views were not shared or accepted. Nicolas never required anyone's permission to act. For him there was no joy to be found in people pleasing. With such strong self-belief he was never envious of others. The only person Nicolas would ever compare himself to, was the person he was yesterday. Of course his reputation aroused jealousy, and some would like nothing better than to bring Al Hajj down. But as they say, a man with no enemies never did anything really great in his life. To others it may have looked as though he were sowing the seeds of his own destruction, and that one day 'Al Hajj' would surely fall victim to a fate equal to that of any tragic hero.

Al Hajj's word was his bond. He would never backtrack on a vow or promise once made. To do so would mean losing face in front of the people; an option never undertaken by Al Hajj. Going back on your word in Nicolas's eyes was not only dishonourable, but cowardly.

"Nobody can put Hajj nose-down," he would say, and nobody ever succeeded in doing so.

During the years of the Lebanese civil war, Nicolas

played his part in defending his country and its Christian territories. Lebanon was everything to Nicolas; he would willingly fight to protect its sovereignty and freedom.

"Lebanon is a paradise on earth," he would say; one that he would die for.

In spite of his staunch patriotism and unquestionable loyalty, Nicolas was told that he was not a good soldier. He was way too fearless, and believe it or not, didn't easily follow rules; especially if he believed there was a better way. Hajj preferred to act on his own initiative.

One time whilst fighting in conjunction with one of the Militia's in the northern territories, a dangerous situation arose where Nicolas was alone and heavily outnumbered by the enemy. While enthusiastically defending his territory he strayed from the rest of his Militia group. Determined to stand his ground and see off the enemy, Nicolas soon ran out of ammunition. Hajj had forgotten one very important rule; to save a bullet for himself. Being captured by the enemy would be a fate worse than death.

The adrenalin was pumping as he listened to the coded sounds and calls of the enemy who now surrounded him. Resigned to his fate Nicolas calmly lit a cigarette and waited for the inevitable. It was pitch black and Hajj knew that the light from his cigarette would alert his enemies to his exact position; typically he was showing reckless defiance. The enemy were so close he could smell their breath. Suddenly he felt a firm hand on his right shoulder. Hajj didn't jump; nothing ever made him flinch or jump. He slowly and calmly turned to face his would be captor. As they made eye contact the man raised a finger to his lips indicating for Nicolas to remain silent. Hajj recognised a fellow Christian Militia fighter. The enemy had drawn close expecting Nicolas to be alone, but now they were the ones surrounded. Fortunately for Al Hajj, his co-militia fighters alerted to his predicament came to his rescue in the nick of time. That day Nicolas stared death in the face with the same bold rebellion with which he faced life.

During a training exercise one day, Hajj and the other

fighters were ordered to eat grubs and insects to prepare for the time when normal food may not be available during conflict. Hajj flatly refused. Reprimanded by his superior, he argued that while normal food was available to him he would not resort to eating rodents or insects. Rebelliously, he told his militia leader that he didn't need to play-act to prove he could survive. Again Nicolas was told he needed to prepare for such an event. Moving towards the man Hajj looked him directly in the eye, then calmly stated;

"If I'm faced with such a situation, believe me I will survive." Continuing to hold direct eye contact Nicolas moved closer still. He then boldly declared, "I will even eat you if I have to."

The Militia leader never brought up the subject again.

Such rebellious behaviour was sure to ruffle a few feathers here and there. Various complaints had been made about Nicolas's antics in and around the village. In the north different factions of militia groups, who should have been on the same side, started to fight amongst each other disagreeing politically about how to proceed in the war. It was an extremely volatile and dangerous time. It had come to the attention of certain authorities in Kousba that Al Hajj was causing yet another disturbance. Having set up a road block he was not allowing anyone access in or out of the village.

Concerned for Nicolas's safety, his friend Pierre tried to convince him to leave Kousba. Nicolas refused and stood his ground, and in typical Al Hajj defiance, declared he was not going anywhere. Certain influential people frustrated at being unable to control or rein Al Hajj in, eventually asked one of the warring factions to intervene. In other words get rid of Hajj; he was becoming a problem and was considered by some to be a 'loose cannon'. After being persuaded by his friend Pierre that his life may be in danger if he stayed, Nicolas reluctantly agreed to leave Lebanon until things cooled.

Still only twenty years of age, Nicolas went to work in his father's construction company in Abu Dhabi. Aware of

Nicolas's astuteness for business, his father gave him a free hand in running the company. Wheeling and dealing came naturally, and Nicolas soon proved himself; making his first million by the time he was twenty-one. With a keen eye and sharp mind he knew how to expand the company and make it profitable. His prestige abounded in Abu Dhabi, and Al Hajj was soon known as the guy to do business with. People unfamiliar with Nicolas's reputation and status would soon be put wise if they disrespected or attempted to belittle him. You simply don't mess with Hajj, not unless you want him to mess with you.

Within a few short years the millions grew, along with his reputation in and around the Emirates. At twenty-six years of age Nicolas was at the top of his game. Amongst his peers he was well-liked and respected for his fairness, loyalty and integrity in the business world. Nicolas now had real status, money and power.

Hajj was a man's man who loved women, and he took full advantage of the playboy lifestyle that his wealth, charm, and boyish good looks afforded him. It was well known in certain circles that the female cabin crew of a particularly popular airline would flock to the Holiday Inn in Abu Dhabi, where Nicolas had taken up residence.

Every night at the 'Prive' club they would seek out the occupant of room 110. No woman ever left that room disappointed. His legendary performance in the bedroom was no myth; Nicolas more than lived up to his reputation.

During the years when he was suffering a distinct lack of resources, Hajj never quit. Rather than agonise over setbacks he would focus his energy on finding a solution. A force to be reckoned with Al Hajj could be a loyal friend or your worst enemy. Those privileged to know him as a friend saw him as a generous hearted individual; a real prince amongst men. This is the legend of '**Al Hajj.**'

KOUSBAWI

Chapter11: Trials, Tribulation, Expectation and Betrayal

Little by little Nicolas gradually revealed to Laura the full extent of his misfortune, and the subsequent events that led to his catastrophic financial collapse. Prior to his divorce from Samra, his company was drastically at risk of falling into bankruptcy. Not because Nicolas wasn't taking care of things, but because he was treacherously betrayed. One Lebanese named Joseph, whom Nicolas considered a friend, worked for a company he had previously done business with. The company owed Nicolas a vast amount of money, but were disputing the issue and refusing to pay him. Nicolas promptly took them to court. Joseph was a key witness in Nicolas's case against them. On the day of the hearing bribed and persuaded by Nicolas's opponents, Joseph deceitfully lied on oath in the court. As Nicolas listened to the evidence in a case that was guaranteed to rule in his favour, he became furious and dismayed at the lies pouring out of Joseph's mouth. He knew someone had got to Joseph and paid him to lie; still Nicolas couldn't believe Joseph's cowardly betrayal. In the past Nicolas had been instrumental in giving Joseph a helping hand up the ladder of success. Now thanks to his deceit, the judge ruled against Nicolas in favour of the other company. The irony was it was Nicolas who had introduced and secured Joseph a very good job with this company. Angered, and utterly confounded by the court ruling, Nicolas appealed the judge's decision and a second hearing was arranged.

Outside of the court Nicolas couldn't control his fury. He grabbed Joseph by the arm and angrily demanded to know why he had lied and betrayed him. Understandably Nicolas's temper exploded. Friends had to restrain him from physically attacking the spineless liar. Apologising profusely, Joseph blamed pressure from his company but promised to tell the truth at the next hearing.

While all this was happening, Nicolas's wife was in the late stages of her pregnancy. After receiving a call telling him that she was about to go into labour, Nicolas flew to America to be with Samra for the birth. His daughter was barely five days old when he received the devastating news from his colleagues in Abu Dhabi. In his absence the second hearing had been held. Aware Nicolas was outside of the Emirates; Joseph accepted his company's bribe and blatantly lied on oath giving false evidence to the court. Consequently without Nicolas there to defend himself, the judge ruled in favour of the other company. Consumed with rage Nicolas vowed revenge and took the next flight back to Abu Dhabi, determined to confront Joseph who had dared to betray him a second time.

Fearing the consequences of his betrayal, Joseph was reluctant to face Al Hajj. He took a flight straight after the court hearing. By the time Nicolas arrived, the treacherous coward had already fled the country. Back in Abu Dhabi Nicolas searched high and low for Joseph, but to no avail. Then with help from 'his people', Nicolas discovered the traitor had escaped to Canada.

With millions at stake, Nicolas bore the huge cost of Joseph's wicked lies. Joseph's betrayal was the catalyst that sent Nicolas on a downward spiral financially; one that would take years to recover from. Nicolas swore to one day seek Joseph out and take his revenge.

In the UAE writing a bad cheque can easily land you in jail; fortunately Nicolas was able to pay back every penny demanded by the court. For a while he managed to sustain his business assets, but with the escalating Iraq / Iran war, the already fragile political state of the Middle East was on a knife edge. Few were willing to invest their money in the construction industry at this politically critical time until things stabilised.

Due to the industries instability, Nicolas's big Bahrain project fell through as funds from would be investors were suddenly withdrawn losing him millions more. The crisis in Lebanon caused the Lebanese pound to drop drastically against the American dollar, making it impossible for Nicolas to sell his property and land there. With one catastrophe after another, it finally bankrupted him. Soon practically nothing remained of Nicolas's vast fortune. The courts confiscated his passport to ensure he didn't flee the country without paying his debts.

As Nicolas's world collapsed around him, his wife sent him divorce papers which he signed without even reading. Angry that Nicolas didn't fight for their marriage, Samra challenged him. He said he had merely given her what she asked for. If sending him divorce papers was meant as a ploy by Samra to make Nicolas run after her, then it didn't work. People don't play games with Al Hajj. Samra had made the mistake Nicolas was waiting for. Nobody could hold Hajj if Hajj did not want to be held; it would be as futile as trying to keep a wave upon the sand.

Samra tried to pull him back by offering to finance his building a new company in the states. She suggested he could live in the same house for the sake of their daughter. When Nicolas refused, Samra said he would be free to live his own life. Nicolas tested her motive by asking;

"So you agree I can bring my girlfriend there?"

Samra's response was predictable;

"What are you crazy, no way?"

After this Nicolas would never lay eyes on his daughter again. Bitter he would leave her so easily; Samra refused Nicolas further contact with the child, not even allowing him a photograph. Knowing he couldn't leave Abu Dhabi Samra vengefully told Nicolas,

"If you want to see your daughter, come to the USA."

With his daughter's name deliberately changed, it was difficult for Nicolas to trace her. At first Samra's cold hearted actions hurt him badly, but as the years rolled by Nicolas accepted the situation, saying maybe it was for the best. But the blows kept coming. It was shortly after this dramatic episode that Nicolas discovered Laura was betrothed to another.

Marooned in Abu Dhabi without his passport, no company, and no money, Nicolas would have to start from scratch to rebuild his life. Faced with such adversity, many would give up. But the intrepid Nicolas held his head high. Now miraculously reconnected with Laura, there was at last light at the end of a very long, dark tunnel. During this unsettled time, Laura's letters helped keep Nicolas's spirits up. Having something to hold on to, had a profoundly positive effect on his psyche. Nicolas passionately held Laura's love in his heart; her love was to him the life-force that flowed through his veins.

As the years passed, things were far from easy. Laura struggled at times to stay positive. She frequently doubted whether her dream of being reunited with Nicolas would ever materialise. It was a dream that was still unsupported by friends and family who couldn't understand why Laura continued to put her life on hold, waiting for this fairy-tale ending; it was a fantasy they believed had no hope of ever coming to fruition.

Sometimes the negativity got to her, and Laura's faith wobbled significantly. While shopping in the supermarket one day, feeling extremely downhearted, she began to wonder if perhaps everyone might be right after all. Maybe she should give up on this fairy tale, as her mother still liked to call it? As this negative notion entered Laura's thoughts, something rather bizarre happened.

A song suddenly blared out from the super-markets in-store radio station. Laura hadn't been aware of the stores radio till now. Stopped in her tracks, Laura dropped her shopping basket to the floor as she heard the unmistakable intro to Richie Valens song, 'Tell Laura I love her' play. Standing in the supermarket aisle amongst the pasta and tins of beans Laura was mesmerised, as the song echoed loudly around the store.

She felt herself slip back in time to that unforgettable night at the Prive club. The night Nicolas coerced the DJ into playing the song on loop. As she clung to the precious memory, Laura could feel Nicolas's love wrap around her, instantly hugging away any doubt. As the song ended, she was abruptly jolted back to the present by a fellow shopper who concernedly asked,

"Are you all right love?"

Tears had automatically fallen onto her cheek. Quickly wiping them away Laura told him;

"Yes, I'm fine thank you; it was just that song made me feel sad."

The man gave her a quizzical look and asked;

"What song?"

"Oh it doesn't matter, I'm just being silly."

Feeling more than a little embarrassed, Laura picked up her shopping basket and hurriedly walked away. Naturally Laura being Laura, she took it as a sign. Similar incidents occurred whenever she was on the verge of doubt. Not just in supermarkets, but in clothes shops, restaurants, and many times on the radio, Laura would hear their song play. Considering the song was no longer popular, it was uncanny. Whenever Laura heard it, any negative emotion would be overturned, and her faith firmly re-established. Outside forces were perhaps conspiring; convincing Laura to stay strong and wait for Nicky.

Albeit from a distance, with the passing years Nicolas witnessed Alyssa grow from a baby, to a toddler, to starting school, now she was almost a teenager. He enjoyed seeing the many changes via Laura's regular updates, sent to him by way of photographs. In his heart Alyssa became as his own daughter. Every year on her Birthday, Nicolas would send a gift or cheque so that Laura could buy something she wanted or needed. Nicolas talked and interacted with Alyssa often, firstly by phone and later over the internet. They would type messages to one another and in later years, thanks to the marvels of the developing technology; they would converse through calls on Skype.

But it wasn't enough for Laura. The time had come to stop putting her life on hold and take matters into her own hands. Desperate to see Nicolas again, Laura resolved to bring the long years of separation to an end. She concluded it was now make or break for their long distance romance.

Before there was time to over think it, Laura went immediately to the travel agent to find out about flights to the United Arab Emirates. She would pay for her ticket by credit card. That night, Laura excitedly told Nicky of her plans to travel to Abu Dhabi. He was overjoyed at her decision, but predictably argued about paying for her ticket, insisting he would send the money. Laura refused, telling Nicky he could reimburse her when he was rich again. Nicolas was an incredibly proud man and wanted to be in a position to offer Laura a decent life. Laura didn't care whether or not Nicolas had money; she was in love with the man not his bank balance; she would gladly live in a tent in the desert just to be with him.

Laura booked her flight without revealing her plans to anyone else. Having made up her mind, she didn't want to be bombarded with any negative response trying to throw doubt on her decision. Laura left it to the last minute to tell her mother, whom she felt certain would do everything in her power to dissuade her. Eventually Laura confided in a friend who said she would gladly take care of Alyssa if Laura's mother refused.

A few days before her flight, Laura finally told her mother of her plans. As expected Laura's mother was not particularly impressed by the news. Predictably, she asked what Laura intended doing with Alyssa while she went gallivanting in the Middle East, as she put it. Laura said she had arranged for a friend to take care of Alyssa. Seeing Laura would not be dissuaded, her mother relented, agreeing to look after Alyssa rather than leave her with 'a stranger'.

The preparations were quickly made, and Laura was ready for her assignation with what she believed was her destiny. Laura felt a sense of relief. Whatever the outcome of this long awaited reunion, she couldn't delay it any longer. On the eve of her flight, it felt good to be saying to Nicky, 'see you tomorrow'. In a few hours' Laura would again set eyes on the man who had held her heart in limbo.

At this point in time, they didn't yet have video calls on Skype. Over the years Laura had kept Nicky updated with photos, but despite her numerous requests, he had failed to send her a picture. When Laura asked if he was afraid to show how much he had changed, Nicolas would insist he looked exactly the same as when she had last seen him, confidently claiming;

"I'm still the same lovely boy."

Laura laughed, amused by his claim. Unless Nicolas possessed a Dorian Gray-type painting, he must have changed a bit. Soon enough she would discover the truth. On the way to the airport her emotions were a jumbled mix of elation, excitement and nerves.

After an eight hour flight, Laura arrived at Abu Dhabi international airport. Her heart was pounding furiously as she waited to retrieve her suitcase. Laura was nervous about coming face to face with Nicolas after fourteen long years apart. What if she didn't recognise him? What if the chemistry and physical attraction wasn't there? What if she was still attracted but he wasn't, or vice versa?

What if? What if? What if? It was time to dispense with what ifs and discover exactly what is!

As a porter wheeled her trolley past the customs into the arrivals terminal, Laura was greeted by a sea of faces. She felt anxious as she failed to see Nicolas amongst the crowds. There was no sign of him, where was he? Just as the anxiety was beginning to build, Laura heard a familiar voice to her left say;

"Laura, I'm here. What you didn't recognise me?"

Laura turned around. There he was, tall, slim, and still handsome, although a little paler than she remembered; he looked tired. Overcome with emotion, Laura couldn't at first speak. Nicolas kissed her on the cheek to welcome her. With the same mischievous humour she remembered, he remarked cheekily,

"You look older girl."

Laura smiled; she was thinking the same about him and

retorted back;

"Yes, fourteen years older to be precise."

The atmosphere between them was a little strained and awkward. They had waited so long for this moment, and now finally it had arrived. Overwhelmed and nervous they struggled to know what to say to each other. Taking her luggage from the porter, Nicolas led Laura outside to a waiting car.

KOUSBAWI

Chapter 12: Reunited

It was the end of July, not exactly the best time of year weather-wise to visit Abu Dhabi. As Laura stepped from the cool, air-conditioned airport terminal, the immense heat and humidity took her breath away. It felt as though a hair dryer on the hottest setting was pointed directly at her face. The last time Laura was in the Emirates, she left at the end of March before the summer began, so she had never actually experienced the extreme searing heat of the summer months in the UAE. Nicolas opened the car door. Laura hurriedly got into the back of the air conditioned vehicle. Nicolas sat in the front and introduced his friend Marcel who was driving. Marcel had a friendly disposition and playful tongue-in-cheek sense of humour, with which he mercilessly enjoyed teasing Nicolas. He turned to face Laura and smiled.

"Welcome to Abu Dhabi Laura." With an impish expression and cheeky laugh Marcel quickly added,

"Hajj has been waiting for this moment for a very long time."

Nicolas smiled broadly and asked,

"How was your journey love?"

"It was good but I'm tired," she told him.

As they pulled away from the airport terminal and headed to the main highway, it was already dark. They made polite chit chat, but for most of the journey Marcel and Nicolas spoke on and off to one another in Arabic. They were headed to Mussafah; a place Laura had never heard of. Situated on the outskirts of Abu Dhabi, Mussafah was an industrial estate. Pulling off the main road into a badly lit area, Marcel stopped the car.

"Are we here?" Laura asked;

"No love, I have to collect something, just five minutes, wait here."

Nicolas got out of the car and disappeared into the dark. There was hardly any lighting in the area, but from what Laura could see, the place looked kind of desolate and run-down. She chatted politely with Marcel who asked her about the UK. Five minutes later Nicolas reappeared. He went to the back of the car and put some bags in the boot alongside Laura's. Holding a strange-looking box under his arm, Nicky got into the back seat next to Laura. As he held the box protectively on his lap, some weird sounds were coming from inside. Nicky opened the top, and out popped a furry face;

"This is Bingo," he said smiling.

Laura had heard a lot about Nicky's cat Bingo. As they drove back towards Abu Dhabi, Nicky talked in a soothing affectionate tone to his pet. Laura noticed how tender and gentle he was with the animal. This was a soft nurturing mellow side Laura hadn't witnessed before. She was quite touched by his sincere affection; he clearly adored Bingo.

Driving through the centre of Abu Dhabi, Laura was amazed at how much the place had developed and changed since the eighties. Suddenly it had become so built up and modern. There wasn't a wandering camel in sight. With all the bright lights it was reminiscent of London, but with its modern skyscraper buildings Abu Dhabi was more on a par with New York.

Bustling with people, it was in complete contrast to the place they had just left in Mussafah. They didn't say much to each other as they drove through the brightly lit streets of the Emirates capital. Laura had a catalogue of emotions swirling about her head. It was hard to grasp that she was actually back in Abu Dhabi with Nicky beside her. Nicolas had been equally as nervous anticipating their reunion.

Tired, jet-lagged and emotional, Laura was noticeably reserved and tense. Sensing the awkwardness, Nicky tried to deflect it by focussing his attention on Bingo. Their first meeting after years of separation had so far not played out the way either had envisioned.

This long-awaited reunion had been rehearsed over and

over, many times in Laura's imagination. Now the reality was somewhat disillusioning. Nicolas had greeted Laura by gently kissing her on the cheek. Acting very polite and courteous, with no hint of the passion he had expressed in his phone calls and letters. There had been no proper kiss, or romantic embrace; not exactly the fairy tale scenario Laura had been imagining.

Nicolas was dressed casually in a simple pale blue shirt and jeans. The sleeves of his shirt were neatly rolled back to just below his elbow, and he was wearing casual loafers without socks. As always he looked immaculate. Laura liked his more casual apparel; it suited him. She had only ever seen Nicolas dressed in formal attire. It was probably the reason Laura hadn't instantly recognised him at the airport; in her mind she had pictured him as she remembered, dressed more formally. Now they had actually met again in the flesh, Laura feared Nicolas might not feel the same, or maybe he didn't find her attractive. Everything felt a bit strained, and a little too polite.

If Laura had looked closely, she may have glimpsed the fiery passion burning in Nicolas's eyes. Far from not being attracted, he couldn't wait to hold Laura in his arms and make love to her. Laura was older now but more beautiful he thought; a woman not the naive girl he had encountered fourteen years earlier. Nicolas picked up on the strained vibes; he too was concerned that Laura was disappointed with what she saw. But Nicolas was always so completely self-confident and instantly brushed away his doubts. Laura's distant, slightly cool manner reminded him of how she was the first time they'd met at the Prive club. All the same, her reticence nagged just a little at his ego.

Laura wasn't purposely being distant, and with the heat was feeling far from cool. It was merely nervous inhibition causing her cagy reserve. Nicky hadn't a clue Laura was expecting a big show of romantic affection. Caught up in her imagined fairy tale reunion, it briefly escaped Laura's mind that she was now in an Islamic country. Displays of affection between couples in a public area, was deemed inappropriate, and frowned upon. It was not unheard of for people to be jailed for just holding hands. Nicolas had behaved cautiously, exactly as he should; this was after all Abu Dhabi, not Paris.

Twenty minutes later they were pulling up outside of an apartment building. Nicolas carefully closed Bingo's carry box, and got out of the car. After helping Laura from the vehicle, he led her towards the buildings entrance. Holding the door open he quickly ushered Laura inside directing her towards the elevator. Nicolas put Bingo's box inside telling Laura to hold the elevator doors open, while he and Marcel brought the luggage from the car. Laura waited in the lift with Bingo who was making the strangest noises from inside his box. Amusingly he didn't meow like a normal cat, but appeared to have his own unique language. Laura smiled, perhaps Bingo was speaking cat Arabic.

Within a couple of minutes Marcel and Nicolas were back with the bags. Using his key, Nicolas pressed the elevator button. As they stepped from the lift on the fifth floor, Nicky adamantly refused to allow Laura to carry anything other than her hand luggage. He may have lost many things over the years, but none of his etiquette and gentlemanly good manners. After unlocking the apartment door Nicolas stood back, allowing Laura to enter in front of him. Marcel wished them goodnight and diplomatically left them alone.

Once inside the apartment Laura started to feel more relaxed. Nicolas put her case in the bedroom and left her alone to unpack a few essential items. He went into the kitchen to fetch something from the fridge. Curiously Bingo followed Laura to the bedroom. Exhibiting typically inquisitive feline behaviour the white tabby began jumping in and out of her suitcase. Laura expressed that she wished to freshen up after the journey. Nicolas called to her from the lounge,

"Don't be long love."

Laura stared at her reflection in the bathroom mirror, a mixture of excitement and apprehension gripped her. It felt unreal, almost dreamlike to be back again in Abu Dhabi with Nicky. Since her marriage ended, Laura had not been sexually intimate with another man. In his letters Nicolas repeatedly asked Laura to wait for him. Willingly she stayed true, vowing to wait for their eventual reunion. For years Laura kept her promise dreaming of this day. Now that the longed for moment was imminent, why was she delaying? Nicolas was growing impatient.

"Love, what are you doing? Come!"

Nicolas didn't want to rush her; he could tell Laura was nervous. But typically he was eager to re-establish their intimate relations, besides Laura hadn't come all this way to hide in the bathroom. Eventually, after taking some deep breaths to regain her composure, Laura emerged. She walked to the lounge where Nicky was patiently waiting. Laura hesitated, stopping momentarily in the doorway. Exhausted from the journey and pent-up desire, she needed to acclimatise emotionally to this long awaited moment. Nicky was seated on the sofa wearing shorts and a T-shirt. Laura stared at him; she felt relief that he wasn't stark naked and ready to pounce on her.

She stepped into the room and moved towards him. Nicky turned to see Laura standing there. The sight of her was like a vision; a waking dream of desire. His heart pounded strong and fast inside his chest. It took all the control he could muster not to tear the clothes from her, and ravish her like a hungry wolf. Playing the gentleman he controlled his fevered desire, but beneath the surface, that raging wolf was salivating ready to devour. Laura gave a shy nervous smile as she sat down beside him. Their eyes met and the chemistry automatically reignited; it burned like petrol poured onto a naked flame. A rush of adrenalin caused Laura's heart to race. Nicky handed her a glass of perfectly chilled Chablis, her favourite wine. The low table in front of the sofa was laden with strawberries and other exotic fruits and nuts.

The apartment belonged to Nicolas's cousin John who was away in Lebanon. Nicolas had loaned it from him specifically to romance Laura. He planned everything with the utmost care down to the last detail, filling the fridge with Laura's favourite vegetarian foods and wine.

With dilated pupils, Nicolas's dark eyes revealed his long awaited passion; he intended to seduce his lady all over again. Chinking his glass to hers, he murmured softly;

"I love you hayati. Cheers girl."

Smiling back at him Laura affirmed,

"I love you too."

Being too wound up with stomach tightening nerves and excitement, Laura hadn't eaten during the flight. Now she could feel the ice cold wine trickle all the way down to her empty stomach. The light-headed rush it gave her felt good, immediately relaxing her mood. Nicolas seductively fed Laura with strawberries and tantalisingly whispered erotically into her ear. Laura quickly became intoxicated; not from the wine but from Nicolas's well-rehearsed sensual persuasion.

Removing the wine glass from Laura's hand he placed it down on the table. Building on Laura's growing passion Nicolas tenderly kissed her mouth and neck. Still the master of the game he knew exactly how to gently lead Laura where he wanted. Slowly he undid her top. As it slipped provocatively from Laura's shoulders he caressed and kissed her small but perfect breasts.

For so long he had dreamt of touching the soft pale flesh of the woman he loved. Behind his dark eyes, Laura saw the want and hunger as it fully awakened within his heart. Nicolas's passion grew; he no longer felt able to control his yearning. Laura's body was willing but it trembled with anticipation. Pure primal instinct took hold as Nicolas impatiently pulled away Laura's clothes, revealing the unfettered beauty of the woman he had fantasized about so many times over the years.

His passion at its height was almost savage. Laura felt herself submit completely. Sweeping her up into his arms Nicolas carried her to the bedroom. After laying her down on the bed, he hastily removed his shorts and T-shirt.

Nicolas was still built like an athlete; strong and lean, like a prize stallion. Laura was filled with lustful admiration as she focussed her eyes on his toned torso and felt the firm flesh of his slim thighs push against her. Nicolas had the sexiest thighs, and between them his impressive manhood swelled to its maximum potential, the sight of which fuelled Laura's desire further; a desire that had lain dormant far too long. Nicolas held Laura tightly, repelling any resistance to his claim on her flesh. Laura was not resisting; after years of waiting her prince had returned to awaken her. All her sensualities came alive and Laura melted into blissful submission. With each penetrative move, she held more tightly to Nicolas's lithe, strong masculine body.

Every fervid pulsating movement was felt intensely, as was every beat of his impassioned heart as it vibrated within her. Leading with the expertise and skill Laura remembered, Nicolas's intense raw passion devoured her. As she climbed to the height of ecstasy, it felt they were making love for the first time all over again. Like a drum, Nicolas's heart beat heavy to the rhythm of Laura's erotic sighs; Nicolas felt ready to explode into the stratosphere as Laura's breathless moans increased. Her heart quickened, and the blood pulsed through her veins like a speeding runaway train. Laura arched her back sighing breathlessly as her muscles tightened and contracted in a frenzied rhythm, as she performed the sensual dance of love.

Blissfully entangled, their fevered bodies locked in joyous reunion and their souls merged. The moment was perfectly timed when finally a prolonged orgasmic climax was reached. As they lay silent and glowing, their hearts rejoiced.

That night Laura slept soundly, safely back in the arms of the man she was born to love forever.

Chapter 13: Fire in His Blood

Laura awakened from a deep dreamless sleep to the sound of Nicolas rattling around in the kitchen. As she stretched her tired jet lagged limbs, she embraced a sense of joy. Hearing Nicky in the room next door lifted her mood to a vibration of contented bliss, which immediately overcame the feelings of fatigue. In this heavenly state of serenity Laura practically floated out of the bed. Grabbing her robe from the top of the open suitcase, she walked dream like towards the happy sounds coming from the kitchen. A conversation was taking place between Nicky and Bingo. Standing silently near the door, Laura observed unnoticed. Nicolas talked to his feline companion as if conversing with a young child. He spoke Arabic so Laura didn't understand the words, but his tone was one of utter affection. Devotedly following his owner's every move, Bingo responded to Nicky's words with his unique form of vocalisation. Laura was completely mesmerised by the engaging scene. Nicolas pottered around the kitchen totally at ease tidying away the glasses and dishes from the night before. Laura knew she was seeing a side to him that few if any, had ever witnessed. She smiled as the little scenario played out in front of her. The mutual love displayed between the two companions warmed her heart. Nicolas was still unaware of Laura's observation, making it all the more charming to witness. Laura felt privileged to have glimpsed yet another facet of this extraordinary man. He was full of surprises, and every time Laura discovered another piece of him, she fell more deeply in love. Nicolas turned to see Laura watching him.

"Hi love, you wake up."

Laura smiled and walked over to him. Nicolas reached out pulling her close. His eyes reflected a look you might expect to see in a man who had just won the lottery.

"Come love, what can I get you?" he asked holding her tightly around the waist from behind, resting his chin on her shoulder.

Laura turned to face him. She hung her arms around his neck. Gazing into his smiling eyes she answered;

"I have all I need right here."

"What do you think if I make eggs?" he asked full of excited enthusiasm.

Laura smiled, amused by his eagerness. He was like a little boy on Christmas morning about to open his presents.

"Sounds good, just let me take a shower then I'll help," she told him.

Nicolas kissed Laura on the lips telling her,

"Go take your shower love, but be quick."

Laura showered and hurried back to the kitchen to help Nicky prepare the breakfast.

"Go sit in the lounge and relax," he ordered.

"You don't want help?"

"No," he said in a confident manner. Nicolas as usual had everything under control.

In the lounge Laura made herself comfy on some large oblong shaped cushions, which were positioned around a low table next to a Shisha in the corner. A little while later Nicky appeared carrying a large tray of food.

"We will sit on the cushions and eat Arabic style," he said placing the tray down on the low table.

It was so exotically Middle Eastern. Laura could easily imagine herself as an eastern princess and Nicolas her handsome Arabian prince, reminiscent of a certain TV advertisement for a Turkish inspired chocolate bar.

Nicolas presented a delicious array of food consisting of scrambled eggs with tomato accompanied by something he called Labneh with houmous, olives, baby cucumber, traditional Lebanese bread, and tea with honey. On the tray Nicolas had lovingly placed a glass holding a single white flower. Nicolas sat on the cushion next to Laura.

"For my special lady," he said handing her the flower. His romantic gesture was far more delightful than a bar of

'Turkish Delight'.

"I forgot milk for your tea," he suddenly announced.

"I'll drink it black, Arabic style," Laura assured him.

As always before eating Nicolas crossed himself. Laura was famished; she ate everything. Nicolas laughed at her. It amused him how someone as petite as Laura was able to demolish so much food. Food always tastes better when prepared with such love. After they'd eaten Nicky picked up the tray.

"I'll do that," Laura said.

"No, stay there love," he insisted.

"You don't want me to do anything?" she asked.

"No love, you are my guest and I am at your service," he told Laura with a smile.

Laura sat back down; she wasn't used to being spoilt this way and was rather enjoying it. Nicky returned from the kitchen and handed Laura a glass of wine.

"Wine, at this time?" she exclaimed taking the glass from his hand.

"Today no time, just relaxing, drinking, talking, making love; time not existing, okay hayati?"

Laura had slept till well gone noon; it was almost 3 pm so although they had just eaten breakfast, it wasn't early. Nicky went back to the kitchen returning with a bottle of Johnnie Walker black label. He poured a large whisky into an ice filled glass, and placed the bottle on the floor beside him. Chinking his glass to Laura's he said;

"Cheers love, here's to us."

Nicolas relaxed back onto the large cushions. They talked together effortlessly and time slipped by unnoticed into early evening. The rapport was strong; the years apart now felt quite irrelevant. Picking up from where they had left off fourteen years ago, seemed as natural as breathing.

"I feel very comfortable with you. You feel so familiar to me," Nicky confided.

Laura understood totally; she felt equally at ease in his company; like she had come home. Each found in the other a mutual recognition, like a past memory from an unfinished story that was being replayed and reflected back. Both let down their guard, allowing the other access to their innermost thoughts and reflections.

During the days that followed Nicolas entertained with his many amusing tales. Laura listened as he filled in the blanks of his rather chequered life. Laura attended to every word as he talked of his family, and expressed his thoughts on his doomed marriage. Nicolas's politics, his philosophy and religion were openly discussed. In-between they ate delicious Lebanese food, and made love. An unknowable amount of time passed when the rest of the world ceased to exist. As Nicolas had rightly proclaimed, for now they were outside the dimension of time.

After several days of not leaving the apartment, Laura asked if they could go out for a change of scenery. Abu Dhabi had changed enormously in fourteen years. Laura was keen to see it at least once in the daylight before leaving. Nicolas gave her an incredulous look.

"What?" she asked innocently. "I like the heat."

Taking Laura by the arm Nicolas marched her over to the window. Opening it he slid back the fly screen then deliberately held her arm on the outside.

"You feel that?" he said.

The immense heat was burning. Laura tried to pull her arm back inside but Nicky held it firmly.

"People die in this heat and you want to go out there?" he exclaimed, raising his voice to her as if she were a child who'd asked for sweets before dinner. "Are you crazy?"

As the heat seared into her skin Laura felt foolish for making the request and pleaded for her arm back;

"Okay! I get the point," she said. "Sitting in here with air conditioning on I'd forgotten how hot it was outside."

Nicolas let go of Laura's arm quickly shutting the window. He tutted, shaking his head at her;

"Crazy woman!" he scorned.

Feeling a little guilty for reacting negatively to Laura's innocent request, Nicolas immediately relented. In a much softer tone of voice he told her,

"I will take you to lunch tomorrow; Rene will come and drive us somewhere. Okay love?"

As promised, the following day Nicolas arranged for Rene to pick them up at noon. He drove them to a pizza restaurant in the centre of the city. Laura hadn't met Rene before today. She knew of him though. Over the years her letters were sent via Rene's PO Box; for whatever reason Nicolas didn't have one. Rene was a lot shorter in height than Nicolas, and a little portly. In contrast to Nicolas's confident forthright excitable nature, Rene was less candid with a quieter, more placid disposition. Although he and Nicolas were of a similar age, with his hair being almost completely white, Rene did look older. Nicolas couldn't resist teasing him. Jokingly he said to Laura,

"Have you met my father?"

In the restaurant Rene sat alongside Nicolas with Laura seated opposite. When the waiter came to take their order, Nicolas ordered everything vegetarian. Laura didn't have a problem with people eating meat around her, but Nicolas was insistent. He ordered garlic bread with melted cheese, followed by three thin crust Gardinière pizzas and three side salads. Later while waiting for their coffees to arrive, Nicolas became agitated. He was talking in Arabic with Rene, so Laura didn't have any understanding of what was said. Something clearly was upsetting him, but Laura had no clue as to what. He looked directly at Laura telling her,

"Move your chair."

Laura didn't understand.

"Why?" She asked.

Seated behind her were four men. They were wearing western clothing and were probably of Lebanese or Syrian origin. Glaring at Laura Nicolas repeated,

"Laura, move your chair."

His eyes blazed furiously. Confused, Laura did as he asked and edged her chair closer to the table, oblivious of the problem. Noticing Laura had moved her seat, the man sitting directly behind her apologised.

"Oh I'm sorry," he said.

All four men then got up to leave. As they passed by the table Nicolas said something to them. The men stopped in their tracks. Nicolas stood to face them; his face like thunder. Rene tried to placate him. Nicolas's altercation appeared to be with one guy in particular, the one who had been seated behind Laura.

The restaurant went quiet. Everyone sat with bated breath waiting to see what would unfold. Laura was suddenly nervous, she had no idea what had caused Nicky's anger, but intuitively sensed it somehow involved her. One minute they were enjoying a peaceful lunch, now it looked as though there was going to be a brawl. The men appeared to not want any trouble and genuinely seemed a little perplexed, as was Laura.

During their lunch, one guy from the group had repeatedly turned his head to stare at Laura. Not only was he openly ogling her in front of Nicolas, but he had consistently placed his arm near to her. From Nicolas's view it looked like he was making a deliberate attempt to touch Laura. With her back to him, Laura was unaware of his inappropriate behaviour. The situation calmed as the men apologised to Nicolas, it was a misunderstanding they said and they meant no disrespect to him. They apologised to Laura and quickly left. Nicolas's eyes followed them all the way to the door. When he finally sat down, the tense atmosphere relaxed and the restaurant returned to normal. Within seconds the coffees arrived.

"We're leaving," Nicky said. He asked the waiter for the bill.

"What about the coffee?" Laura asked.

"Leave it," he told her brusquely.

The restaurant manager hurried over to the table and told Nicolas that the meal was on the house, by way of an apology for the incident. Nicolas thanked him but insisted on paying for everything in full, and they left.

Back at the car Laura asked what had occurred to make him so angry. Nicky explained telling her,

"That bloody guy was leaning back in his seat looking

at you, and I saw his hand move trying to touch you."

"Really?" she said in a surprised tone. "I didn't notice."

"I was going to smash him, the motherfucker."

Having calmed significantly Nicolas was now laughing adding,

"Maybe he touches you by accident, but believe me I was going to smash his face."

Rene started to laugh;

"I thought there was going to be a fight; I was worried I'm too old for fighting," he joked.

Now everyone was laughing and Laura was most relieved their outing hadn't ended with a brawl. Nicolas had a volatile side, and his fiery temper could explode quickly. But as long as he wasn't goaded he would calm down just as quick. As they drove away Rene remarked;

"Hajj has fire in his blood,"

The incident reminded Laura just how wound up Nicky would become if he thought he was being disrespected. A guy trying to make a move on his woman right in front of him was definitely a step too far.

Over the next few days Nicky shared with Laura his hopes and dreams for the future. As he talked and opened his soul to her, he insisted Laura keep eye contact. Vulnerability was not something Nicolas was comfortable with. If Laura looked away, he would turn her face back towards him. He was very adept at reading people; there was no point in being anything other than honest, Nicolas wouldn't long be fooled.

During her stay with him, Nicolas treated Laura like a queen. Towards the end of her short visit, he took her out to buy gifts for Alyssa. He was so generous and insisted on paying for everything. Whenever Laura took out her money he would tell her,

"Put your money away love." Nicolas was extremely proud.

In recent years he had gone through many hardships; there were occasions when he couldn't afford to buy bread to eat. Now he had a little money again, Nicolas wanted to spoil Laura. He proudly stated;

"Love I have, better than before. I am making again."

The last day of their reunion arrived. Laura's flight was booked for two o' clock in the morning, which meant they still had a whole day to spend together. Laura packed her things and helped Nicolas clean the apartment. Bingo had become very comfortable inside Laura's suitcase. She joked with Nicky that she may have to take Bingo back to the UK with her. Around three o' clock in the afternoon, Marcel arrived and drove them to Mussafah. Laura had no idea where Nicky had been living, but she was about to find out.

As they drove through the centre of Abu Dhabi, Laura was amazed as she stared out of the car window. Densely packed concrete buildings were punctuated with modern skyscrapers, which shone and gleamed in the hot Arabian sunshine. The city had its own particular charm, with its stark contrasts between the old world and the new. Men in traditional dress drove modern expensive cars along wide well-built roads. Driving past contemporary hotels and magnificently opulent shopping malls, Laura was surprised to see many green areas and tree lined roads and parks. As they drove along the beautiful cornice the turquoise sea of the Arabian Gulf sparkled in the sun, as though sprinkled with thousands of glistening diamonds.

The landscape abruptly changed as they approached the road leading to Mussafah. Now the road either side was bordered by great expanses of rolling desert. On reaching Mussafah the scenery became much more industrialised. Marcel pulled into an enclosed area with no built up road. He stopped the car outside of a concrete building situated amongst the industrial businesses. Nicky got out of the car; Laura followed. He took her hand and helped her up the half a dozen steep concrete steps leading to a residential complex. Laura stared at the rows of shoes that were lined up outside of the apartment doors. Nicky unlocked one of the doors and told Laura to go inside. She stepped into a sparsely furnished room.

The first thing to catch Laura's eye was a huge red and white wooden cross hanging on the wall. It was unusual in that it had a diagonal cut at the base. Nicky explained that it was the Lebanese force's cross. The Lebanese forces were part of the main Christian resistance during the civil war, and the political party to which Nicolas held strong allegiance. Their own special cross had been officially launched at the church of St. Charbel (a Maronite monk and priest) in Lebanon in 1984. It held deep significance in exemplifying the Lebanese Christians suffering throughout history. The diagonal cut at the bottom of the cross Nicky explained, represented their determined will to keep the cross of Jesus firmly planted in that region of the world.

Nicolas put down Bingos carry box and told Laura not to open it until he had brought the rest of the luggage in; he didn't want Bingo to run outside. He went back to the car and Laura looked around. There were Christian crosses everywhere along with pictures of the Virgin Mary and a small carving of Jesus on the wall. The apartment didn't look particularly inviting; there was a distinct lack of home comforts. Laura knew times had been difficult for Nicky, but it shocked her to see with her own eyes how he'd been living. As she scanned the room Laura's eye was drawn to a glass vase filled with dark coloured earth. One wall was covered with cards and photos. Laura moved to take a closer look. Nicky had made a collage of everything Laura had ever sent, including Christmas, Valentines and Easter cards. All of the photographs of her and of Alyssa were proudly displayed.

Laura felt sad as she surveyed the rather drab meagre apartment. A single dusty rug barely covered the concrete floor in the lounge area. There was a beaten up old brown leather sofa, a TV and video recorder that had definitely seen better days. She could see into the bedroom. It had a small sized double bed with a cross painted in red on the wall above it. To the left were the toilet and shower room. There was a very basic kitchen area with a sink, fridge, one cupboard and a small cooker with just two gas rings, similar to the portable type you might use on a camping trip; everything a person needed to survive was there, but nothing more.

One thing stood out in these basic living quarters, and that was the books; absolutely hundreds of them, and they were everywhere. Nicolas was an avid reader; he once told Laura he had read at least three thousand books. Seeing just how much Nicolas had lost, brought tears to Laura's eyes. Nicolas's demise began when he was betrayed in court by the cowardly lying Joseph; his unprecedented downward spiral into bankruptcy was triggered by that one fateful event. Laura understood why he sought revenge.

Moments later Nicolas was back. Noticing Laura's sad expression he said;

"Don't be sad love. I am Al Hajj; I will be back on top soon, I swear."

Fiercely proud and resilient, Nicolas would overcome any situation life chose to throw at him. His determined tenacious spirit, plus a zealous enthusiasm to succeed were qualities to be envied and admired. Laura asked about the vase with the earth.

"That love, is a piece of heaven; soil from Lebanon, from my village Kousba, I can touch it whenever I want."

Nicolas's eyes glazed when speaking of his beloved homeland. Despite the misfortunes he'd been forced to endure, Nicolas remained stoically undefeated; a real man in every sense. It made Laura feel proud. Nicolas would never waste time feeling sorry for his losses, nor would he accept help or entertain pity from anyone. If the truth be known, most people were in awe, wishing they could possess a little bit of what Nicolas was made of.

"You will stay with me here?" Nicky asked.

"I'll stay with you anywhere," Laura told him. "Being with you is all that matters to me."

Nicolas held Laura close, happy in the knowledge she loved him for himself. Rich or poor Nicolas was still the same man, and Laura loved him unreservedly.

Rene's business was situated nearby. He called to wish

Laura a safe journey. Nicolas invited Rene round and an entertaining afternoon was spent watching some old videos from Nicolas's past, recorded at the time when he still had his vast fortune. Later on Nicolas ordered some pizza's for dinner. When the pizza's arrived they were as usual vegetarian. Nicolas's unselfish consideration was typical; he would always put Laura's needs above his own.

Soon it was time for Laura's departure. With a heavy heart she gathered up her bags. Rene wished her a safe trip saying he hoped to see her back in Abu Dhabi before too long.

"She will be back," Nicky told him assuredly.

Laura liked Rene, but she was quietly pleased when he diplomatically made his exit before Marcel arrived to drive them to the airport. Although she'd spent nearly the whole vacation alone with Nicky, Laura jealously guarded every precious moment of time they had left. She was filled with sorrow at having to leave again, uncertain of when they would next be together. Nicky held her close whispering;

"Its okay, soon you will be with me for ever."

Naturally Nicolas was upset at Laura's leaving, but remained strong in front of her. Trying to make light of things, he used humour to deflect from his true feelings. Even before she was gone Nicolas felt an uncomfortable emptiness. He was desperate to turn around his misfortune. Spurred on by Laura's love, he would taste the sweet life of success once again. Nicolas believed that he had never reached his peak in life; he was sure the best was yet to come. It would be bigger and better than before. In the past Nicolas had taken his wealth for granted. Now he revelled at how fragile success can be; how easily one's life and fortune can be ripped away in the blink of an eye.

Nicolas's phone rang; it was Marcel waiting for them outside. Laura gave a deep sigh as she picked up her hand luggage. Nicky took her suitcase. The tears welled as she said goodbye to Bingo, and had a last glance around the shabby apartment.

"Okay hayati, you have everything?" Nicky asked.

Laura nodded and they went outside to the waiting car. Walking down the stone steps Nicky took hold of Laura's hand to ensure she didn't fall in the dark. As Laura got into the car Marcel asked if she had enjoyed her stay.

"Yes very much, I don't want to leave," she told him mournfully.

"Hajj doesn't want you to leave either, you must come back to him soon or he will go crazy." Marcel laughed.

As they set off for the airport, nobody spoke too much. Marcel switched on the car radio in a bid to disguise the silence and sombre atmosphere. The first song that played was 'My heart will go on', by Celine Dion, the love theme from the movie Titanic. Simultaneously Nicky and Laura reached for the other's hand.

It would be the last opportunity to be physically close. Once they reached their destination they would be obliged to abide by the strict Islamic laws of no public displays of affection. They held on tightly to each other all the way to the airport.

Despite the huge differences in culture, Laura knew she would miss this sunny desert land. She would miss hearing the sound of the ancient call to prayer every day, swirling around the buildings as it's carried on the breeze echoing through the dusty streets at sunset and dawn. She'd miss the scorching heat and delicious eastern cuisine. But most of all Laura would miss going to bed and waking up beside Nicolas each day. The talks, the cuddles, and the laughter they had shared, and of course she would miss feeling the closeness of his body when they made love.

Much too soon Marcel pulled up in front of the airport terminal. Laura stepped from the car and straight away a porter came running over with a trolley ready to take her luggage. As the porter took the suitcase and bags from the boot, Nicky gave Laura a quick peck on the cheek aware that eyes were watching.

"Soon love, soon," he told her.

Laura fought desperately to keep the tears at bay.

"I will call you tomorrow, okay love? Take care hayati,

remember I love you."

Laura's throat tightened with emotion as she tearfully blurted;

"I love you too."

Reluctantly she let go of his hand. Nicolas turned away, and with a heavy heart he walked back to the car. Laura watched him. He wound down the car window; Nicolas waved and blew her a kiss. Laura blew one back, and as Marcel's car drove away from the airport she stayed rooted to the spot watching, unable to take her eyes away until the car was out of her vision.

"Okay madam?" The porter asked.

Laura nodded and forced a smile. She was too choked up to respond verbally. After checking in her luggage and clearing passport control, Laura had two hours to wait for her flight. She wandered aimlessly around duty free. The Abu Dhabi duty free lounge was amazing; a real shopper's paradise. Laura looked but didn't buy; she already had plenty of gifts that Nicky had bought. After meandering for a while longer, she decided to pass the rest of the time in the departure lounge coffee shop. Laura sat quietly sipping tea while her thoughts reflected on the past two weeks. Her mobile suddenly rang; it was Nicky.

"How are you love, everything okay?" he asked.

It was just over an hour since he'd left her, but he was missing her like crazy. Laura hadn't expected to hear from him until she reached the UK, and was thrilled to hear his voice.

"Hi, yes I'm okay. I thought you would be asleep by now. I'm so glad you called, I miss you," she told him.

"I couldn't sleep," he said.

Hanging on to the conversation as long as possible, they chatted for half an hour until Laura's flight was called at I.30am. Making her way to the boarding gate Laura felt the same empty feeling she had felt fourteen years earlier. Once again she was leaving a big chunk of herself behind. Nicky's words echoed inside her head; Laura wanted the sound of his voice to remain locked in her memory. Once on board and settled in her seat, Laura pulled her blanket over her and tried to get some sleep.

She was abruptly woken a few hours later by the cabin crew wheeling the breakfast trolley down the aisle asking people if they wanted tea or coffee. Laura was starving so decided to take breakfast, eagerly tucking into scrambled eggs and French croissant with jam. After an eight-hour flight, the plane landed at London Heathrow at 6.55am. Laura altered her watch to London time. There was a time difference of three hours, with Abu Dhabi being ahead.

Laura checked her passport at the UK border control; then grabbing a trolley, headed towards the baggage claim. There were no porters on hand like in Abu Dhabi, and Laura struggled to retrieve her luggage from the revolving carousel. Laura gripped tightly to the handle of her case as the carousel threatened to drag her around with it. Luckily a kindly gentleman saw he predicament and came to her aid. After rescuing Laura and her luggage, he obligingly placed the case onto her trolley. Laura thanked him and walked towards the exit. After passing through customs, she fervently looked for her taxi driver who would be carrying a card with her name and destination on. At last she spotted him, Quinn Southampton the card read.

Outside of the terminal Laura was greeted by the dreary grey skies of the typical British summer. Surprisingly it wasn't raining, but the distinct early morning chill was a shock after the extreme heat of Abu Dhabi. It was strange to suddenly be over three thousand miles away from Nicky. Yesterday she was in his arms; now Laura wasn't sure when she would see him again. Inside the taxi Laura switched on her mobile phone. Already there were three missed calls from Nicky. She tried to call him back but failed to get a signal.

Meanwhile in Abu Dhabi Nicolas was sitting in the office of his friend drinking coffee. It was just after eleven in the morning, and Nicolas was becoming frustrated at not being able to contact Laura. His friends teased saying she had run away and left him.

"Oh look how Hajj is in love," they kidded with him.

They continued to tease as he persisted in trying to get hold of Laura on the phone, not realising Laura was unable to receive a signal from inside the taxi. He went back to the apartment at lunchtime and made a sandwich although he didn't feel hungry. Nicolas ate without really tasting, his mind was on Laura. Bingo jumped onto his lap as if to comfort him. Glad of the company Nicolas gently stroked his cat. Over the years Nicolas had felt incredibly lonely at times. Having Bingo meant he didn't come back to an empty apartment each day.

Nicolas decided to take his customary afternoon nap. Bingo followed him to the bedroom. Jumping up onto the bed he snuggled close to Nicolas. After half an hour of tossing and turning, Nicolas was unable to fall asleep. Frustrated at not sleeping he got up. Nicolas made a coffee and sat on the sofa. After lighting a cigarette he tried once again to call Laura. Still she was not answering. After several more attempts Nicolas became irritated. Stubbing out his cigarette he immediately lit another.

Due to the heavy traffic caused by road works, Laura's journey took longer than expected. Finally she reached her house after a two and a half hour drive. She had barely got in the door and put down her luggage, when her mobile rang. Frantically Laura rummaged through her handbag to find her phone before it stopped ringing. At last she retrieved it and answered. It was Nicky;

"Love I called many times, I was worried." His voice sounded anxious. Laura sensed his irritation.

"I've just this minute arrived at my house; I tried to call you, but couldn't get a signal from the car," she explained.

"Okay love, no problem," he said.

The annoyance and frustration quickly evaporated from him now he knew Laura had arrived safely.

"I'm missing you so much," Laura told him. "Are you missing me?"

Nicolas was missing Laura like crazy but didn't want to admit to it. Being soppy and romantic wasn't his style. At least that's what he told himself. Instead he typically covered his true feelings with a cheeky response;

"Yes love, I miss your ass and your tits."

Reluctant as he was to admit in actual words he missed Laura, she knew he did, and he knew she knew. All the same Nicky continued with his subterfuge, which amused Laura who could see through it.

"Love you girl," he said "Go now, I will call in a few days."

Laura told him she loved him and they reluctantly said their goodbyes. No sooner had she closed her phone when it rang again instantly. Hoping to hear Nicky's voice again Laura eagerly answered.

"Where have you been?" It was Laura's mother. "I've been ringing for hours."

"I couldn't get a signal in the cab then Nicky called me, we've been talking." Laura explained.

"You've had two weeks talking to him," her mother said. There was annoyance in her mother's tone as she asked rather impatiently, "When are you planning to come and collect Alyssa?"

Laura felt the hackles rise; her mother could have asked about her trip first. But it was no real surprise that she'd deliberately not mentioned it. Laura asked if Alyssa could stay one more night. She was really tired from the journey and would appreciate it if she could leave collecting Alyssa until the next day. Reluctantly her mother agreed. Laura asked to speak to her daughter. Alyssa came on the phone,

"Mum when are you going to come?"

"Hi darling, how are you love, have you had a nice time with Nanny? I missed you."

"No, I haven't, and I want to come home now," Alyssa answered petulantly.

"Tomorrow darling, I'm really tired now, and I need to sleep." Laura told her.

"But mum I want to come home now," Alyssa pleaded.

"Darling stay one more night and I will be there in the

morning. I have gifts for you from Nicky."

Laura's mother took the phone again;

"Alyssa is perfectly fine here."

"Are you sure she's okay?" Laura asked.

"Positive," her mother answered. "Well, tell me how it was then?" She inquired at last referring to Laura's trip.

"I'm too tired now; I will talk to you tomorrow," Laura answered, deliberately holding back any details of her visit with Nicky.

Laura was annoyed by her mother's curt attitude and initial lack of interest. Nothing would alter her mother's opinion. Laura made up her mind that she would keep the details of her relationship with Nicky to herself. No one was ever going to fully understand their love, or the extent of the circumstances that had kept, and was still keeping them apart. Why bother explaining it? Laura had tried in the past, only to have her explanations met with negative comments and looks of scepticism. Laura could tell by people's faces that maybe they thought she was delusional in her quest to be with the mysterious Nicky, the man from the Middle East who none of her friends or family had ever met in person. To them he was just a voice on the end of a phone, or a face in a now very old photograph. Maybe their love affair was the stuff of fairy tales, or of dreams, but a life without dreams is not a life.

Chapter 14: Another Twist of Fate another Spoke in the Wheel

It is said that the path of true love never runs smooth. The truth of that saying was to become all too apparent for Nicolas and Laura. Their path had already been full of twists and littered with obstacles, but it wasn't about to get any easier. Presented with such an unfortunate path many would have given up, or fallen at the first hurdle. But defying all logic, their love affair had overcome numerous adversities; conquering even the huge distance between them. Nicky and Laura continued to follow the road set out by their hearts. With the bricks that life threw, they built that road stronger. Nicky would tell Laura;

"I am always by your side hayati, even when I am far away."

But the misfortunes fate had metered out were far from over. A few more trick cards waited in the wings ready to play their role in this theatre of travesty. Backstage an unpredictable turn of events was unfolding. Again Nicky and Laura's quest to be together would be unavoidably thwarted. As the musician John Lennon once famously declared; 'Life is what happens when you're busy making other plans', a statement that would ring all too true for the ill-fated lovers.

Alyssa was hovering on the brink of a devastating and potentially fatal illness. The signs were at first subtle, resulting in her symptoms being misdiagnosed. Alyssa was becoming increasingly fussy with food. Initially Laura put it down to teenage behaviour. She herself had acquired some strange eating habits during her early teenage years. The world of ballet demanded that dancers be a certain shape and size, and although Laura, like Alyssa was naturally slender, as a young ballet student it was easy to fall into the trap of obsession where food was concerned.

Alyssa was behaving as many young teenage girls, and as Laura had. With assurance from others that it was just a phase, Laura believed there was nothing to be concerned about. But as time went on, things didn't improve. Increasingly concerned by her young daughter's erratic eating habits, Laura was not satisfied with the diagnoses that it was a teenage phase; Laura sensed something a little more sinister may be at play.

Slim and petite with lustrous waist length hair and strikingly beautiful dark eyes, that were as clear as sparkling polished glass, Alyssa didn't look ill. Her energy levels were high, so on the outside there didn't appear to be anything wrong. It seemed Alyssa's fussy eating was purely a desire to be healthy. But behind the scenes Alyssa was obsessed with counting the calories of everything she ate. In private she was constantly weighing herself. Alyssa had not stopped eating completely, but she ate very little; barely enough to survive. Keeping up the deception, Alyssa cleverly hid her diminishing body size under layers of clothing and baggy tops. At the time all teenagers were dressing this way so it didn't seem odd. As yet no doctor had actually bothered to weigh her; if they had done so they would have realized much sooner that Alyssa was drastically underweight, and was in fact suffering from anorexia nervosa.

The characteristics typically associated with girls who become anorexic were apparent in Alyssa. She was bright, intelligent and ahead of her peers academically. Creative, talented and sensitive, Alyssa was also a perfectionist; traits often associated with anorexia. One day, weakened from lack of food, Alyssa collapsed and the doctors finally paid attention. When given a proper examination, the shocking truth was revealed and it was discovered how tiny and frail Alyssa was underneath the layers of clothing. The doctor was horrified to discover Alyssa's weight had dropped dangerously low. Weighing barely four stone (25.4 kilos), Alyssa was instantly rushed to hospital and admitted into intensive care.

Laura was frantic. She sat outside the children's ward waiting for news of Alyssa's condition when her mobile rang. It was Nicky who somehow, sensing something was wrong had felt an immediate compulsion to call. From the urgency in Laura's voice he could tell she was worried and extremely upset. As she confided what had happened, Nicolas's heart went out to her. Laura needed his calming support. He would provide that support as best he could from a distance.

"Don't worry; love everything going to be okay. We are together with this. If I had my passport I would be at your side. Remember love I am right there with you, and I will pray for your daughter," he told Laura.

As Nicolas put down the phone he became upset. The distress he heard in Laura's voice alarmed him. He was angered by his situation. Nicolas wanted to run to Laura, hold her in his arms and comfort her at this time when she needed him most. Trapped by his circumstances, Nicolas was on the edge of his nerves. Frustrated, he lit a cigarette. Nicolas stared at the collage of pictures on the wall in front of him. They showed Alyssa's development, from a cute baby to a beautiful young girl. He had enjoyed seeing the changes as she grew up; something that was denied him with his daughter from his marriage to Samra. Over the years he had formed a strong attachment to Alyssa, often telling Laura he felt she was his daughter. Stubbing out his cigarette Nicolas sighed heavily. He decided to do the only thing he could and pray for Alyssa's recovery.

It was late, but Nicolas didn't feel like sleeping. Instead he filled a glass with five ice cubes and poured himself a large whisky. Sitting down in the chair his mind became overwhelmed with thoughts of Laura and little Alyssa. Unable to settle, he stood and lit another cigarette. The anger rose in him as he paced the room. In a fit of temper he kicked at the chair knocking it over. He began cursing in Arabic. After releasing his pent up frustration, he gradually calmed. Nicolas turned to see Bingo looking up at him. He bent down and picked up his cat.

"I'm in fucking situation Bingo."

The white tabby meowed as if to agree, his huge green eyes communicating a knowing expression. Nicolas kissed the top of Bingo's head then put him down. After picking up the chair he'd knocked over, he lit yet another cigarette. It was an unconscious action Nicolas indulged in when troubled.

He sat quietly contemplating the catalogue of injustices that had befallen his and Laura's life over the years. Bingo jumped onto his lap and started purring. The sound of his cat's purrs helped him relax as he gently stroked the animal. Nicolas's anger was fuelled by the exasperating situation he was in. Being unable to leave Abu Dhabi and fly to Laura's side had provoked his volatile tendencies. Sitting alone in the semi darkness those feelings of anger slowly subsided. But as he let go of his vexed emotions, they were replaced by uncharacteristic despondency at his lost liberty.

Back in the UK Laura anxiously waited at the hospital. After what seemed an eternity, a nurse eventually came over and told Laura the consultant wished to speak with her. Moments later the consultant appeared in front of her. He introduced himself and then directed Laura into a private room. Laura listened intently as the consultant informed her that Alyssa's condition was extremely grave. Her vital organs he said had begun shutting down. There was a strong possibility that her heart may give out, having been weakened by the anorexia. Alyssa was in very real danger of suffering cardiac arrest. The consultant gently explained to Laura how the heart would be the last organ to give out, but with Alyssa's other organs already closing down, there was too much strain on it. Laura was told Alyssa may not survive the next twenty-four hours; she was in fact dying. Laura felt her heart sink to her feet at the devastating prognosis.

Trying to comprehend the dreadful news Laura's mind was in turmoil. Alyssa could actually die. It was just too awful to imagine and she couldn't at first take it in. Laura called Alessandro, telling him to come immediately.

Three and a half thousand miles away and unable to sleep, Nicolas called Laura again. It shocked him to hear the heart breaking news. Laura was highly distraught and he did his best to calm her. Reassuringly he told her,

"Remain strong love, I am with you."

Despite being unable to be close physically, Laura was much comforted by Nicolas's supportive calming words. He urged Laura to keep thinking positive, but after talking with her, Nicolas was himself despairing. He had to stay strong for Laura, but the seriousness of Alyssa's condition broke his heart. He took Alyssa's picture from the wall and held it. A happy, healthy, pretty young girl was smiling back at him. Alone in the apartment Nicolas reflected on the upsetting turn of events, and he wept.

When finally permitted to see Alyssa, her parents felt totally helpless as they sat at their daughter's bedside. It was distressing to see her so tiny and frail, connected to all sorts of tubes, drips and monitors. Weak and extremely fragile, Alyssa was barely able to talk or move. Right before their eyes their little girl was slowly slipping away. Laura and Alessandro stayed at Alyssa's bedside all night. As their daughter's life hung in the balance, they silently pondered on why and how this could have happened right under their noses.

Laura questioned why everyone had missed the signs. How could they have not seen that Alyssa was suffering from anorexia? There was no point in playing the blame game, Alessandro told her. All that mattered now was that Alyssa would somehow pull through. It was a very long and stressful night; the outcome of which nobody could guarantee.

To her parent's great relief Alyssa managed to survive the crucial twenty four hours. Their relief was short lived, as the consultant warned them Alyssa was far from out of danger. It was now safe to insert a feeding tube to nourish Alyssa's fragile weak body, and hopefully reverse some of the damage. Alyssa was dangerously anaemic; Laura and

Alessandro had blood samples taken in case a transfusion was required. Laura called Nicolas to give him an update on Alyssa's condition. He was greatly relieved to hear she had made it through the night.

"Thanks my God, thanks my God," he rejoiced in his imperfect English.

Emotionally sharing in Laura's pain and fears Nicolas had stayed awake the whole night.

"I didn't sleep all the night; I was right there with you love, believe me I was living it with you."

Laura said Alyssa was not out of the woods yet, but she was sure his prayers were helping.

The hospital nursing staff made up a bed for Laura next to Alyssa. Physically and mentally exhausted Laura would now be able to stay with her daughter, and get some much-needed rest. The nurses checked Alyssa's condition every half an hour, she was still critical and the danger of having a relapse or possible heart failure was very real.

Forty-eight hours after her admission to intensive care, Alyssa's condition gradually stabilised. Laura had another meeting with the consultant, who informed that recovery would be a long slow process. Alyssa would be required to remain in hospital for the foreseeable future. As with most severe cases of anorexia the consultant explained, recovery is seldom guaranteed to be permanent. For Alyssa it would become a lifelong battle; one she would have to control, and hopefully overcome. Several weeks down the line Alyssa was out of immediate danger. Monitored hourly, there were numerous tests and scans to check her progress. Fortunately, much to everyone's relief, Alyssa's vital organs and bones hadn't suffered permanent damage. Alyssa was able to occasionally get out of bed and into a wheelchair. She wasn't permitted to walk on her own or go anywhere unaided as she was still too weak.

After many anxious days and long sleepless nights, at last Laura felt she could begin to relax a little. Plans for her return visit to Abu Dhabi were postponed indefinitely; Laura would need to stay with Alyssa while she recovered.

Nicolas had been a tremendous source of positivity and strength, supporting Laura every step of the way through what was a most traumatic experience.

"We have time love, be with your daughter now, and as soon as I get my papers I will come to you," he told Laura.

Encouraged by Nicolas's optimism, Laura believed he would soon obtain his passport and official papers from the court; then he would be by her side.

Eight weeks later, shortly before Christmas, Alyssa was transferred to another section of the children's ward. She had made satisfactory progress, and no longer required such intensive monitoring. But it would be at least another month until she was finally allowed home.

Meanwhile, Nicolas was having several meetings with influential people who had promised to help resolve his ongoing case to reclaim his passport. There was no way to get the required paper work or passport returned without going through the official court system. But every time they got their hopes up that his situation would be resolved quickly, something would go wrong.

First the elderly sheik, who had formerly agreed to speak in the court on Nicolas's behalf, was suddenly taken ill. Then on the day of the hearing the judge dealing with his case was called away at the last minute, and the case had to be adjourned. Nicolas's court hearing was hindered yet again when an important document was lost in the system, resulting in another postponement and long delay. Before his case could be heard, the lost document would need to be reapplied for. There was a constant stream of one hindrance after another.

Murphy's Law says 'anything that can go wrong will go wrong'. This old adage it appeared, was working at its best. It felt at times that the whole world was against them. It was putting a tremendous strain on Nicolas who just wanted his life back. The still unresolved situation was an aggravation that caused him to have violent outbursts. Unexpectedly he would lose his temper, often resulting in his shouting at Laura if she pushed or asked too many questions about why everything was still taking so long to sort out. Laura did her best to remain calm when Nicky became volatile. But she too was increasingly frustrated with it all. Laura understood his anger was not directed at her, but rather a reaction to the tenuous position he was in. Even so it was causing unnecessary friction, when all they wanted was to be together.

Apart from the occasional volatile outburst, Nicolas was for the most part, tremendously hopeful. Regrettably, despite his optimism, the problem he was facing would be endured for a while yet. Laura busied herself with work while they remained apart. She tried not to dwell on what, after so many years of waiting, was still missing from her life. Alyssa was making steady progress and would soon be allowed home. Thankfully no permanent damage to her health had been suffered, but if Alyssa were to become that ill again, she may not be so lucky.

In Abu Dhabi things gradually started to pick up for Nicolas. Although he was still without papers or passport, his business initiatives were going well and he was making a pretty decent living. With his days tied to his business undertakings, Nicolas had little time to write to Laura. It would frustratingly take him forever to write one page in English. But as always Nicolas had a solution, an idea that he had considered before. That night he told Laura;

"You know what I am going to do. I will make a tape recording, then you will hear my lovely voice whenever you want, okay hayati," he laughed. "I will do it tonight," he promised.

118

KOUSBAWI

Chapter 15: Recorded, and Delivered.

True to his word, the following night Nicolas prepared to make a tape for Laura as promised. It was well after 11.30 pm by the time he finally got started with it. Bingo was sleeping; only the monotonous hum of the air conditioning interrupted the silence of the otherwise peacefully quiet room. Nicolas turned the AC off; now all that could be heard was the ticking of the clock and the faint sound of Bingo's soft purr. With a glass of whisky and his cigarettes close to hand Nicolas felt relaxed as he leant back in the chair, resting one foot on the coffee table in front of him. Taking a large sip from his whisky, he considered how to begin. Trying to imagine that Laura was in front of him; Nicolas decided to say whatever came to his mind and pressed the record button.

The quiet dimly lit room created a subdued atmosphere. One small lamp cast shadows across the wall. Nicolas lit a cigarette inhaling deeply. He exhaled releasing the smoke from his lungs. A swirling misty haze wafted in front of him, slowly dissipating into invisibility. Feeling at first a little awkward and still grappling with what to say, Nicolas began hesitantly,

"I, I er… don't know how to start," he faltered slightly. "Because you know this is the first time that I record by my voice."

Nicolas took a sip of whisky and forcibly cleared his throat.

"What I wanna tell you?" He continued, "You know love I have told you many things of my life, but if I wanna tell you the whole story it will take hours and hours, years even."

Retreating deeper into his imagination, Nicolas tried to focus, envisioning he was talking to Laura rather than into a machine. His senses heightened and he began visualising

Laura's presence. Gradually, despite the unfamiliar setup the words started to flow. As Nicolas began speaking with ease, a diverse sequence of events from his rather dubious youth unravelled. Many of these stories Laura would have heard before, but Nicolas loved to tell his stories over and over. He spoke from his heart and with a natural humour. Subjects he'd been unable to convey adequately in a letter were unfolding. He related stories of life in Lebanon and his mountain village. Openly and unashamedly disclosing incidents from his somewhat chequered past, Nicolas delivered his thoughts with total abandonment. He shared some rather cheeky facts and eyebrow raising revelations. As he expressed his desire to one day return to his beloved country, there was palpable emotion in his voice as he told Laura;

"Lebanon is not from the earth, like our singer Fairuz say, Lebanon is a piece of heaven that fell from the sky." Nicolas paused dragging heavily on his cigarette before continuing;

"Lebanon is all my life, is in my blood. You know love, you have to come with me one day; I want to take you to Lebanon, to my village. Lebanon is the best place on earth. I'm not saying because I am Lebanese, all the peoples they say it."

His sentiment filled tone, reflected the passion he held for his beloved homeland. He became wistful. But the playful cheeky spontaneity and slightly irreverent manner, soon returned. Reminiscing in his grammatically imperfect English and delightful style of speech, he continued to wax lyrical about Lebanon.

"But love, we have crazy people there, the best people, crazy and lovely."

Nicolas began laughing, as light- heartedly he mocked a tradition in the north.

"When we have any wedding there the men will take out their gun and shoot up at the sky because they are happy. Sometime one of the bullets by accident will go in someone and they fall, and then they have, how you say, funeral? Then in the funeral the men take their gun again, and shoot in the sky because they get angry someone die. Someone will catch a bullet and fall from a balcony and then will be another funeral."

Nicolas started to laugh at the irony of the scenario. With his sometimes incorrect use of grammar, he related his stories with satirical irreverent charm. Typically, Nicolas made light of the situations that had been forced upon him. He talked of the millions lost, and how these misfortunes had led to his downward spiral and present circumstances. Without a trace of self-pity he referred to his spate of bad luck with a resigned,

"What can I do love? C'est la vie."

Speaking with startling candour, Nicolas shared his hopes, his dreams, and his fundamental plans for a better future. The bold manner and unique delivery, was both amusing and brutally honest. When relating his rather unconventional background, Nicolas admitted that he had enjoyed his promiscuous playboy lifestyle. Laura wouldn't be fazed by his frank exposes; she had never been under any false illusions concerning Nicolas's wandering eye, and fondness for women and sex. From day one Laura knew Nicolas had been quite a player where women were involved.

Talking frankly now of his past indiscretions, Nicolas was careful to reassure Laura, insisting the many women were no more than bodies he had taken momentary pleasure in.

"Love, don't worry about the women from my past.

You get angry?" he asked. "Love, don't be jealous," he said telling Laura, "those girls I was with before, all those women, they were only body to me, and I don't have any feelings. But you Laura, you are different. I can talk to you. I can hold you and feel something about you."

Nicolas paused lighting another cigarette. His love for Laura was as intense as his dynamic, fiery, hot blooded personality, and it came across clearly in the recording.

"Don't be jealous, I gave my cock to everyone but my love I give to you; my heart only to you. Okay love, you are waiting for me?" He dragged on his cigarette. "Okay hayati? Hayati, eyouni, I love you. Wait for me darling. If any man touches you, I will kill him!"

Nicolas gave a wicked laugh, then coughed as he exhaled the smoke, and cleared his throat.

Talking of sex and his love life so openly was making him incredibly horny. Predictably his dialogue became more intimate, and sexually orientated. But even with the occasional profanity, it didn't deter from his unique charm. Nicolas's desire to have Laura in his arms and feel her body close to him was now overwhelming; he didn't wish to continue on this line of thought.

Quickly changing the subject, he turned to his other passion. Nicolas went on to describe his invention; it was a new system for building that he had secretly been working on for years. Excitedly referring to this new system as 'his baby', Nicolas felt he was on the threshold of great success, believing he had developed something that would revolutionise the building industry. His eyes came alive; alight with passionate pride, and his voice was filled with excited enthusiasm as he talked of this ingenious creation. Emphasizing its limitless possibilities and potential, Nicolas claimed 'his baby' would one day totally change the world of construction. Nicolas's unique creativeness and imagination was beyond the vision of most mere mortals, and definitely bordered on genius. The down side to his ingenious mind were the fluctuating emotions. Nicolas could be incredibly moody, and temper flare ups were common. Continuing with the recording, he spoke determinedly of his plans to recoup all the money he had lost, revealing his unrelenting desire to exact revenge on those who had betrayed him.

"I have to kill that bloody bastard Joseph," he vowed. "But the others," he slowly dragged on his cigarette. "They are like, how you say in English?" With another wicked laugh he stated; "They are my five o' clock tea."

Nicolas compared his intention to deal with his enemies and betrayers, as being no more than a trivial pastime which he would partake of at his leisure.

"They are still young; they are not going to die yet. I have time to take my revenge." He laughed again at his own dark humour.

The casual manner in his voice, disguised the reality of his deadly intention. When alone, usually when drinking his morning coffee, Nicolas frequently hypothesized how he would achieve his justice. While conveying his love for Laura and for Lebanon, his voice carried genuine warmth, which was in contrast to talk of revenge, expressed earlier in the recording.

Nicolas was full of complexities. As much as he was positive and upbeat, he equally had periods when he would become morose. On such occasions' of his moroseness, Nicolas retreated from the world, only reappearing when he had sorted whatever was bothering him. Seldom would he share his problems, refusing to talk of them until he had reached a solution. Those closest learnt to leave him be, trusting he would soon bounce back with everything resolved. Never wishing to show weakness stemmed from Nicolas's upbringing, where it had been instilled in him to always be the man. Unfortunately it meant Nicolas would suffer alone rather than share his burdens. Refusing to admit to a problem or accept help, he would stubbornly soldier on. The weaknesses Nicolas never allowed himself to show, contradicted the generosity of spirit he would grant others. He understood and accepted their weakness, but not in himself. Nicolas was like a man of steel with the heart of an innocent baby.

It was late into the night, and Nicolas had easily filled both sides of the cassette. From initially not knowing how to start, incredibly he had made a recording lasting ninety minutes. If the tape had not run out when it did, no doubt he would have carried on talking. Now in the early hours Nicolas was wide awake. As he sat alone in the semi darkness, the memories resurrected whilst recording were called again to his mind. Pictures from his past continued to dance through his imagination, in a kaleidoscope of changing patterns and colours. A wry smile crept across his face as he pondered the incredulous events he had just revealed.

Nicolas lived without regret or apology. Some thought him reckless and impulsive. His life may well have been easier with fewer adversities, had he been willing to accept other ways of dealing with things. But then he wouldn't be Nicolas; Al Hajj, who nobody could ever put in a box and label. His convictions governed his actions. There was only one objective, to do it Hajj's way or not do it at all.

Nicolas sat blowing smoke rings into the air, his mind buzzing with new ideas. Making the recording had given him an adrenalin rush. Nicolas's over-stimulated brain made sleep impossible. The silence of the early morn was abruptly broken by the call to prayer ringing out from the local mosque. As the sound echoed around his humble dwelling, a shaft of sunlight invaded the dark eeriness of the room. Outside people were scurrying along the dusty streets of Mussafah, faithfully answering the call to prayer. As the approaching dawn proclaimed the advent of a new day Mussafah gradually awakened, and this predominately industrial area sprang to life, as did Bingo. Roused from his peaceful sleep, the cat stood and arched its back then slowly stretched out his front paws. Jumping off the sofa Bingo walked over to the chair where Nicolas was sitting. Sat expectantly at Nicolas's feet, Bingo gazed patiently up at his owner. For a while longer Nicolas sat puffing on his cigarette deep in thought, enjoying the solitude. The peace and silence rapidly gave way to the sounds of industry. Bingo paced the room and meowed constantly, he wanted to play, but his owners mind was elsewhere. Nicolas appeared to be oblivious of the noise from outside or his cats incessant meowing.

The sun was now fully up. Nicolas rose from his chair stretching and yawning to relieve the stiffness in his body. The need for caffeine kicked in, and he walked slowly to the kitchen. Bingo immediately followed. His expressive green eyes curiously watched as Nicolas made his coffee and opened another packet of cigarettes. Inquisitively, Bingo tagged behind Nicolas as he carried his coffee to the lounge. Picking up the TV remote he switched to his favourite Lebanese news channel. Nicolas took a cigarette from the newly-opened packet, and reached for his lighter. He paused for a moment listening to the early morning news headlines before lighting up. The impatient Bingo jumped up onto his lap. At last acknowledging his pet, Nicolas stroked and talked to the cat who purred loudly; happy to finally have his owner's attention.

Several cups of coffee, and equally as many cigarettes later, it was time to shave and take a shower, whereupon Bingo dutifully followed him to the bathroom. Nicolas encouraged his pet, playfully engaging with him in a child-like conversation in Arabic. Bingo responded vocally to Nicolas's every word. Both clearly enjoyed the interaction.

After showering and dressing, Nicolas removed the cassette from the tape recorder, carefully placing it inside a large envelope. His mobile rang; it was his friend Philipe calling to say that he would be outside in ten minutes. Nicolas had arranged for Philipe to take him to a meeting in Abu Dhabi. He dutifully refreshed Bingo's water bowl and topped up his food dish with the cats favourite dried biscuits. Nicolas patted his shirt pocket checking that he had his wallet and the little blue bible which he never left the house without. Before leaving the apartment he spent a few moments in prayer, and then gathered together his keys, worry beads, cigarettes and lighter. Nicolas picked up his briefcase, not forgetting the all-important envelope containing the recording. Before leaving he turned off the air conditioning. Walking past the rows of shoes, he made his way along the passage and down the stone steps.

Stepping into the bright sunlight made him squint. Nicolas lit a cigarette as he waited for his friend; his pale olive complexion was warmed by the morning sun. It was still early, but the heat was building; today he believed was going to be hot and humid. Moments later Philipe arrived pulling up just in front of the apartment block. Nicolas got in the car and they drove out of Mussafah towards the city.

Within thirty minutes they reached their destination, managing to park close to the office where the meeting was to be held. It was lucky; the centre of Abu Dhabi is renowned for being difficult to find parking. Pumped full of adrenalin, Nicolas was raring to go. He had a confident feeling about this meeting. He loved business meetings, all the wheeling and dealing was right up his street; Nicolas thrived on the buzz it gave him. In business he knew how to play the game; he could seal a deal better than anyone. His knowledge and authoritive confident delivery when speaking was impressive. When it came to negotiating, Nicolas was the master. Today his intuition had not failed him, and as hoped the meeting turned out to be productive. Nicolas was more than happy with the outcome.

After the meeting, their host invited them to partake of refreshment. While Nicolas and Philipe sat drinking their coffee, an unexpected familiar face arrived at the office; one Nicolas hadn't seen in some time. Dennis was English and had been working in the Emirates dealing in insurance for a number of years. Dennis and his Polish wife were well acquainted with Nicolas. Spending most of his time as he did in Mussafah, Nicolas hadn't seen Dennis for a while. During their short conversation Dennis mentioned to Nicolas that he was taking a trip back to the UK the following day. Seizing the opportunity, Nicolas took the envelope containing the tape from his briefcase. Passing it to Dennis he asked if he would post it to Laura when he reached England. Dennis said he was very happy to oblige. Nicolas wrote down Laura's address urging Dennis to post it as soon as he reached the UK. Dennis told Nicolas not to worry; assuring Laura would receive it promptly. Nicolas thanked him and they said their goodbyes. Now Laura would have the recording so much sooner than if Nicolas posted it from the UAE.

Three days later it arrived via recorded delivery. Laura

knew immediately what it was, and couldn't wait to listen. Excitedly she opened the package. There was a little note from Dennis with the tape, telling Laura that he had met with Nicolas unexpectedly at the office of a mutual friend. Dennis said Nicolas had given him strict instructions to deliver the tape immediately he arrived in the UK. Dennis had written his address and phone number, and asked Laura to contact him to confirm she had received the tape.

The post had arrived just as Laura was about to leave for work. She quickly ran upstairs and retrieved her old Sony Walkman from the top of the wardrobe. It was a bit archaic; a relic from the eighties Laura had bought in Abu Dhabi the year she met Nicolas, but it was the only tape recorder she possessed that was portable with headphones. Hurrying back down the stairs Laura put the tape and the Sony Walkman inside her bag. Grabbing her keys from the table Laura hurriedly left to catch the bus.

She raced to the bus stop with seconds to spare before the bus arrived. Laura took a seat and excitedly retrieved the tape recorder from her bag. Carefully placing the cassette inside, Laura put the headphones over her ears. Pressing play she waited eagerly for the recording to start. Nicky sounded so natural. If Laura closed her eyes she could believe he was there beside her. She listened to the deep masculine tones of his voice, and his adorable accent. When Nicolas spoke English, the occasional misuse of a word or incorrect pronunciation was utterly appealing.

During the bus journey Laura was lost in the recording, but all too soon she reached her destination. Tucking the tape safely back inside her bag, she got off the bus. Laura would have to wait until her lunch break to continue listening. Luckily it was a busy day at work, which meant the time passed quickly. When her break arrived Laura chose not to waste the time eating. She was eager to hear the rest of the tape. Ordering just a coffee she took the old Walkman from her bag. For the next hour Laura immersed herself. The humour and outspoken directness with which Nicky expressed his thoughts, made her smile.

Laura's break came to an end. Reluctantly she switched off the tape. Her colleagues were curious as to what she had been listening to that kept her so amused for the past hour. Laura told them it was a recording from Nicky. They responded by asking if they could hear his voice. Laura denied their request, insisting the tape was far too personal and private.

Shyness was not something Nicolas suffered from; he certainly wasn't reticent when expressing intimacies. Parts of the recording were clearly meant to be heard only by Laura. The recording was not the only thing Laura would be required to keep private. Over the years Nicolas sent numerous cards and letters; few of which Laura could openly display or allow others to see or read. Nicolas couldn't resist writing intimate messages inside her birthday cards and the letters he sent. Once he sent Laura a birthday card with a beautiful heartfelt message, telling her how much he missed and loved her. Laura proudly displayed the card until her young daughter Alyssa who was four or five years old at the time, picked it up and asked her mother;

"Mummy, why has Nicky drawn this picture on the back of your Birthday card?"

Laura quickly grabbed the card and looked at the back. She was to discover Nicky had made a drawing which she hadn't noticed. Cheekily he had drawn a bed with the word 'SOON' written across it. The young Alyssa wanted to know what it meant. Taken by surprise and a little shocked at the rather naughty discovery, Laura explained to her daughter that Nicky wanted to tell her he was going to buy a new bed; to which Alyssa replied;

"Why didn't he just write it?"

Awkwardly Laura told Alyssa that Nicky liked to draw things. Her young daughter looked at her quizzically for a moment and then said,

"I like to draw too. I will draw a picture for Nicky."

Straight away young Alyssa started to draw a picture that Laura sent with her next letter to Nicky. Nicolas was thrilled to receive Alyssa's drawing; but he did laugh when Laura told him over the phone what had happened with the birthday card. Cheekily Nicolas asked Laura if she had ever shown his cards or any of his letters to her Mother.

"No way, are you kidding?" she shrieked.

Nicolas laughed at Laura's bashful response to the idea of disclosing anything he'd written to her mother; nothing ever embarrassed him, he was totally incorrigible.

The recording was proof to all the doubters that Nicolas was serious about his intentions, even if Laura couldn't let anyone hear it. By now Laura was long past caring what others thought. If they wished to invalidate her relationship with Nicolas, so be it. Laura knew the truth and that's all that mattered.

KOUSBAWI

Chapter 16:
Home is Where Your Heart is.

Not yet ready to commit to a residence in a more upmarket location, Nicolas resourcefully made the best of what was available to him and began renovating his apartment. When most of the work was complete, Nicolas called Laura to tell her he was in the process of putting the final touches to the paintwork and décor, keeping secret exactly what he had done with the place; he wanted to surprise Laura. He worked tirelessly to make the apartment ready for her eventual return. This part of Mussafah may not be the smartest place to live, but for the time being it suited Nicolas's purposes. Despite the cosmetically-unattractive industrialised neighbourhood, it had some advantages.
Nicolas moved here during a time when he wished to go underground and keep a low profile for a while; it offered the necessary privacy and seclusion he sought. Secondly this area of Mussafah was ideal in being close to where Nicolas conducted most of his daily business.

The transformation Nicolas achieved was incredible; by the time he had finished with the place, it didn't look like the same apartment. Gone were the ugly grey concrete floors and battered dusty old rugs, replaced by white marble tiles which were laid throughout. By altering the position of the kitchen Nicolas expanded it, turning it into an open plan complex. Purposely emphasized in the new décor, was the old Lebanese style which Nicolas loved. This he accentuated by adding shutters on all the windows and wooden beams on the ceiling. New furnishings gave the place a warmer ambiance, while strategically placed mirrors added to the illusion of space. The completed renovation captured the old style ambiance Nicolas had wished to imitate; recapturing his childhood memories of his family house in Kousba.

Apart from the plumbing, Nicolas did most of the refurbishment himself. The apartment now resembled a home, although Nicolas would never refer to it as such. In Nicolas's heart one place and one place only, was home. Satisfied with his enterprising achievement he proudly surveyed the finished effect. He couldn't wait for Laura to see the result of his creativity.

Alyssa was recovered enough for Laura to consider making plans, and fulfil her desire to return to Abu Dhabi. Nicolas was overjoyed to hear Alyssa had made a full recovery. When Laura communicated she was ready to return to him, Nicolas was over the moon.

With Alessandro, doting grandparents and Laura's sister, enough people were around to ensure Alyssa was well cared for. Laura didn't hesitate to book her ticket, and a couple of weeks later she took the night flight from Heathrow, arriving at Abu Dhabi international airport at 7.30am.

Nicolas was waiting anxiously in the arrivals terminal. He was talking on his mobile when he spotted Laura in the distance. Quickly ending the call he smiled broadly as she approached. He had been anticipating her arrival all week, and felt an excited surge of adrenalin as Laura smiled back at him. Nicolas handed some money to the porter who had helped with Laura's baggage.

"How are you love, everything okay." Nicolas asked as he gave Laura an affectionate welcoming kiss on the lips.

"Is that allowed?" Laura inquired.

Nicolas exhibited his usual defiance.

"If anybody says one word I will smash him."

Laura smiled; amused by Nicolas's rebellious attitude, although she was acutely aware it wouldn't take much to trigger his hot temper in a flare up of confrontational anger if he were challenged. Changing the subject he asked;

"How was your flight?"

"It was fine, but I'm so tired," she told him smiling. "I didn't get much sleep."

"You can sleep when we get to the house if you want,"

he suggested.

In spite of the exhaustion Laura felt ecstatic to be back with Nicky; the moment she laid eyes on him she felt at home. Placing his arm protectively at her back, he guided Laura towards the terminal exit. They walked outside into the already hot morning sun. As the brightness hit, Laura quickly pulled her sunglasses over her eyes and removed her cumbersome jacket. Swathed in the gentle caressing warmth, her pale English skin felt soothed. Standing there beside Nicolas in the sunlight, all the problems and stress of Laura's life melted away. His engaging smile had a wonderfully calming effect on her, it was almost hypnotic. As they stood in the Arabian sun, Nicolas made a call to somebody. When he had finished talking on his mobile Laura asked,

"Who's picking us up?"

"Nobody, we will walk," he said smiling as if to make fun of her. "Or you will sit in the luggage trolley and I will push you," he continued teasing. Lighting a cigarette he turned to Laura; "Or, I will bring my camel," he laughed.

Laura rolled her eyes and shook her head, pretending to be un-amused by his teasing. Within moments a car pulled up in front of them. Nicolas opened the door for Laura and she got into the back.

"Hi Laura, how are you?" said a voice that she vaguely recognised.

It was Rene; Nicky's close friend whom Laura had met on her previous visit.

"Welcome back to Abu Dhabi," he told her.

"Thank you. It's nice to see you again Rene."

"Nicolas is excited you are back," Rene revealed.

"That's good I'm happy to be back," she answered.

"Oh Hajj talks about you all the time," he confided.

Laura smiled at Rene's revelation, she knew Nicolas would never admit this to her. Luckily he was out of earshot putting Laura's bags in the boot. He walked to the side of the car taking one last drag on his cigarette before dropping it then stubbing it out his with his foot. Nicolas got into the front seat next to Rene. Turning round to face Laura he affectionately patted her leg. With a mischievous glint in his eyes he asked;

"Hi love how you doin girl? This is Rene; do you know Rene have you met before?" Nicolas teased.

Nicolas's teasing playful humour made Laura smile. He continued mocking her and pretended to introduce Laura to Rene, as if they had never previously met. Rene laughed and made a comment in Arabic. Nicolas responded with laughter; Laura could tell he was in good spirits. She loved to see him in such a relaxed happy mood.

Nicolas was charmingly young at heart. People found it attractive and appealing, leading them to believe him years younger than his actual age. When he was a very young entrepreneur running his own construction company, his associates and business partners were always much older. It was not uncommon when representing his company at a business meeting, for Nicolas to initially be ignored. When a deal was being discussed, people would mistakenly tend to converse with his older associate, who was in fact Nicolas's employee. Amused by their faux pas, Nicolas would purposely keep quiet until it came to signing the deal. It was only then; much to everyone's embarrassment that he would reveal himself to be the boss. No one could believe someone so young was running such a successful business.

As Rene pulled away from the airport terminal, Nicolas turned around to face Laura. They made direct eye contact. As they engaged in this longed for soul reconnection, for a fleeting moment time froze as if somebody had pressed the pause button. Simultaneously energy from some unknown source miraculously released Laura's fatigue; suddenly she felt wide awake.

They drove towards Mussafah. All the way Rene and Nicolas conversed in Arabic. Laura relaxed back in her seat and looked out of the car window. Abu Dhabi dazzled in the bright sun, with its palm-lined roads, fountains, and perfectly designed parks, adding colour and sophisticated beauty throughout the island city. Laura was entranced by the stunning distinctly Middle Eastern ambiance. It was May and the temperature would reach to around 30 – 35 degrees as the day progressed. The pleasantly warm early morning, was in stark contrast to the rather uncomfortable blazing July heat encountered on her last visit.

Driving out of the city they entered Mussafah situated on the outskirts. Although still relatively under developed compared to the large metropolis of the Emirates capital, Laura noticed quite a few changes; Mussafah was fast becoming a lot more urbanised, with many parts being progressively developed. Residential complexes, along with huge shopping malls and businesses, were constantly being built; where once there was nothing, construction sites were springing up everywhere. There were still many open spaces, but now with proper roads and uniform street lighting, stretching across what was formerly just desert. Mussafah was so expansive. It would still take a few years before it was fully developed, and on a par with Abu Dhabi. Finally they reached the industrial area, and soon were pulling up in front of the tiny apartment complex where Nicolas resided. Laura thanked Rene and said she hoped to see him soon.

"You are very welcome," he told her. "Enjoy your stay with Hajj, he is happy now."

Nicolas made a comment in Arabic, to which Rene laughed retorting with something amusing. Laura wished she could understand Arabic and appreciate the good-humoured banter. Nicolas took Laura's bags from the boot and opened the car door for her. Laura got out and so did Rene who insisted on helping. He and Nicolas tussled over Laura's suitcase, with Nicolas stubbornly refusing help but Rene would not give up.

Nicolas quickly ushered Laura up the stone steps, and along the passage where the familiar rows of shoes were lined up outside the other apartments. Taking the key from his pocket, Nicolas unlocked and opened the apartment door. He stood back allowing Laura to enter in front of him. Rene put Laura's suitcase down just inside. Nicolas invited him to stay for coffee, but Rene declined with the excuse that he had work to do. Laura knew Rene was being politely diplomatic, not wishing to intrude on their reunion.

"Wow! It's amazing," Laura exclaimed, as her eyes surveyed the newly refurbished residence.

"It looks completely different."

"You like it?" Nicky asked expectantly.

"It's beautiful," she told him.

Nicolas smiled happily; delighted at Laura's positive response. Taking her by the hand he excitedly proceeded to show off the rest of the apartment. As he led her room by room proudly displaying his clever handy work, Laura was speechless. The place was unrecognisable from the shabby abode Laura encountered before. It broke her heart when she was here last to see the bleak drab surroundings Nicolas had been living in. Now his environment was much more pleasant. The joyous look on Laura's face confirmed his innovative venture had not been in vain. She marvelled at the kitchen with the marble topped breakfast bar, and the new bathroom again finished in marble. There was a brand new TV and a computer complete with desk in the lounge; Laura loved it. She found the old style features utterly charming. Clearly Nicolas had done it all as a testament to his love for her.

"Who did all this?" Laura asked.

"I made it all myself," he proudly admitted.

Of course Nicolas left the best till last.

"Come see the bedroom."

Laura followed as Nicky led her by the hand to see his prize purchase; a huge king-sized bed. Either side of the bed the walls were mirrored. The wall directly facing the bed was adorned with nine black and white poster size framed pictures of scantily clothed, almost naked women, in various provocative poses.

"You like it?" Nicolas asked eagerly awaiting her response.

Laura wasn't sure what to say, she loved the new bed, and the furnishings, the mirrored walls were a bit daunting, but she would soon get used to that. The slightly risqué pictures Laura wasn't so keen on, but was reluctant to say.

"You don't like it," Nicky said answering for her.

"No, its beautiful. I love it." Laura reassured him, "it's just...er...well." She started hesitantly; "It's just I'm not sure about those." Laura pointed at the erotic pictures.

"Love I needed to put something on the wall," he said unconvincingly.

"And that was all you could find?"

Nicky smiled cheekily.

"Yep," he answered adamantly.

Laura had to admit the pictures didn't seem so bad the more she looked. She liked the black and white theme, and how each picture depicted a different era, from the 1920's through to the 1980's. In an erotic sort of way they were moderately respectable. But Laura was never going to tell Nicky that.

"Are you hungry or you wanna sleep?" Nicky asked.

"Both." Laura laughed.

"Okay we will sleep some and then eat," he decided.

Laura went to the bathroom to freshen up.

"Don't shower!" Nicky shouted from the bedroom. "And don't put makeup or perfume! I don't want to fuck Estee Lauder."

Laura smiled amused by Nicky's outspoken demands. Nicolas liked Laura to be as natural as possible, and didn't believe in gilding the lily. He preferred the natural scent of her body. After lightly freshening up, Laura put on a small silk robe which she tied loosely in a bow. She walked back to the bedroom. Nicky was waiting, lying stark naked on top of the bed displaying a huge erection. He beckoned her towards him.

"Come love I'm horny."

"I can see that," she said untying her robe purposely letting it slide seductively off her body to the floor.

"Yeah, yeah love, I've missed you," Nicolas murmured

approvingly, excited at the sight of Laura's alluring nakedness.

Laura smiled temptingly at him; deliberately holding his gaze she climbed seductively across the large bed towards her eager lover. Highly aroused Nicolas kissed her passionately, moving his mouth from her lips to her breasts. Laura came alive at his touch, and the exhaustion from her journey soon abandoned her.

Fully awakened and aroused, Laura began to pleasure him. Kissing, and caressing, she sensually encouraged his stimulated manhood. Laura continued to gratify his senses, turned on by his satisfied erotic sighs and murmurings. He began to penetrate her slow at first then as the intensity of his passion grew stronger, he asked her to turn so he could penetrate her from behind. Laura caught sight of their reflections in the mirror. Her excitement intensified as she watched the refection of her lover's uninhibited moves. His eyes suddenly met the reflection of hers in the mirror. Nicolas's dilated pupils made his sultry dark eyes appear darker. Reflected in those dark pools Laura saw everything she would ever need. The look of unbridled pleasure on his face as he made love was matched by Laura's own ecstatic expression.

"Oh Laura I've missed you so much," he uttered. "You are mine you belong to me."

"I'm totally yours," Laura breathlessly whispered.

The pent-up desires both had been forced to hold on to for so long was now completely unrestrained, releasing itself like a dam bursting of its waters. Lost in the moment, their rapid breathless sighs increased, until simultaneously they reached a fevered climax of euphoric revelry. In the blissful afterglow their bodies yielded to exhaustion, with neither able to resist any longer the call of much needed sleep.

"We will sleep some, one hour," Nicky said setting the alarm clock.

Laura drifted into a contented slumber, happy in the knowledge they would live in each other's hearts forever.

Nicolas looked adoringly at Laura sleeping beside him; the unrivalled Queen of his heart. Kissing her softly on the lips he silently watched as she slept. He lay down beside her and the gentle rhythm of her breathing fell in time with his as he too succumbed to his fatigue.

Repeatedly battered and bruised along the way, the journey leading them back to each other, had been fraught and burdened with misfortune. At times it had felt like a very long climb up an imposing mountain. But if asked, both would do it all over again in a heartbeat.

KOUSBAWI

Chapter 17: Loving the Devil you know

The obtrusive sound of the alarm going off abruptly roused Nicolas from his much-needed sleep. Reaching across to the bedside cabinet he quickly turned off the insistent shrill before it woke Laura. Momentarily pausing to gather his senses, Nicky lay back on the pillow blinking deliberately in an effort to force his tired eyes awake. Glancing to the left he looked at Laura; she appeared dead to the world but for the gentle rhythmic sound of her breathing. She looked so peaceful with her long auburn hair trailing across the pillow, and the sensual curve of her soft lips. He resisted the urge to kiss them afraid she would wake.

Hesitantly Nicolas raised himself up off the pillow, the large iron framed bed creaked. Laura stirred, disturbed by the sudden movement. Half opening her eyes, she sleepily watched as Nicky slowly walked out of the door towards the bathroom. The masculine gait of his naked body with its exquisitely defined muscles, and firm slim thighs was ample provocation for Laura to become aroused. But the extreme fatigue and lack of energy, was equally enough to suppress any inclination to do so.

Hearing Nicky return from the bathroom Laura again pretended to be sleeping, anxious not to let him think he had woken her. He moved gingerly around the bedroom very carefully taking a pair of shorts and a T-shirt from the wardrobe. Quietly he slipped them on. Laura's arm hung over her face conveniently shielding her secretly half open eyes. It warmed her to observe the way Nicky selflessly crept about, careful not to disturb her sleep. Blissfully unaware of Laura's already awakened state, he silently closed the bedroom door behind him.

He entered the lounge leading to the open plan kitchen. The air felt very humid. Nicolas switched on the AC, then opening the fridge he took from it a mini sized bottle of

Perrier water. Nicolas unscrewed the top and took a large swig, then replaced the bottle back inside the fridge door. The cool water refreshed him instantly.

Laura slowly sat up stretching her arms above her head; with a weary yawn she flopped limply back down onto the pillow. The initial motivation to get up, quickly subsided as Laura succumbed to her body's yearning for more sleep. Curling into a ball she snuggled into the bedclothes, reluctant to leave the cozy environment. Try as she might to regain access to the world of dreams, Laura's mind became so energized by the sheer thrill of being back in Abu Dhabi, it refused to switch off. The impulse to pander to her exhausted body's request for sleep was instantly over-ruled. Infused with sudden euphoria, Laura felt like a small child on a trip to Disney, full of excited anticipation. Laura's heartbeat quickened. Saturated with adrenalin that was now pumping through it, her body had no choice but to awaken. Sleep could wait she thought, as she joyfully celebrated the realization of being back with Nicky.

The sound of him making coffee in the kitchen invoked Laura's craving for caffeine. Slowly coaxing her unwilling limbs out of the bed, she bent to pick up her robe that was draped across the floor. Laura felt a mild head rush as she stood up; it was some hours since she had eaten. Slipping on the pink silk robe, Laura pulled the tie around her waist fashioning it into a neat bow. Shuffling to the bathroom her reluctant body ached from the eight hour flight. Laura washed her face, the cool water refreshed and stimulated her skin helping to relieve the physical signs of fatigue.

Laura strolled from the bathroom to the lounge. As she pushed open the door, her eyes were partially blinded by a shaft of bright sunlight that streamed through the small window filling the room with light. Bingo was lying on the window sill basking in the warmth. Sitting in front of the TV with the volume turned down, Nicolas was sipping his coffee. He turned as Laura entered the room; Bingo lazily lifted his head out of curiosity;

"Hey sleepy girl, how are you?" Nicky smiled at Laura.

I'm good, but I definitely need coffee," she groaned. "Why is the sound down on the TV?"

"I didn't want to wake you love, make your coffee and come sit with me," he told her.

Laura poured her coffee into the red mug that Nicky had put ready for her. A wave of contented bliss wrapped around her like an invisible cloak. After stirring a rather generous spoonful of honey into her coffee, she joined him in the lounge. Taking a seat next to Nicky, Laura tucked her bare legs underneath her and snuggled into the chair like a bird huddled tightly in its nest. The oversized arm chair was reminiscent of one her grandmother once owned. She almost disappeared into its large cushions making her feel very small, like Alice in wonderland down the rabbit hole. The air conditioning blew a cold breeze through the sunlit room. Laura held her mug of coffee close to her face, cupping both hands around it. The steamy heat rose up from the mug warming her a little against the chill from the AC. As she gently sipped the hot liquid caffeine, the honey soothed the dryness in her throat which had been aggravated by the AC. Outside the temperature was close to 33 degrees, yet Laura was practically shivering inside the apartment.

"What, you cold?" Nicky asked noticing the way she was huddled into the chair.

Laura nodded; "A little bit," she answered meekly rather understating the fact; she was actually freezing.

Immediately Nicky got up from his seat and turned off the air conditioning. He disappeared into the bedroom, returning a moment later with a blanket which he lovingly wrapped around the shivering Laura.

"Thank you, that's much better," she told him, greatly appreciating his considerate gesture.

Once the AC was off the room warmed quickly, Laura decided to take a quick shower, and dress. Nicky would not leave the AC switched off for long. The humidity he said would ruin his book collection. He never really felt the cold, whereas Laura was always freezing. Growing up in the mountains with the snowy winters of Kousba had made him quite resilient. Nicky would joke telling Laura that he had his own in built central heating, due to the hot Lebanese blood pulsating through his veins.

Revitalized after showering Laura dressed hurriedly and went back to the lounge where Nicky was watching the news now with the TV at full volume.

"Are you hungry?" he asked.

"Yes I'm ravenous," Laura answered.

"What's ravenous?" he inquired not understanding the word.

Laura giggled. "It means very hungry."

Nicky tried to repeat the word;

"Ravious, what rani raneous?"

Laura wickedly laughed at his attempt.

"No, ravenous," she repeated correcting him.

Nicolas endeavored to repeat the word several times, eventually with more success.

"Bloody English, what a fucking language you have!" Nicolas remarked disparagingly, poking fun at the English vocabulary. Laura couldn't help but love it when he mixed up his words or mispronounced them. She secretly hoped he would never speak English too perfectly.

The next few days were bliss; Nicky was in exuberant mood and treated Laura like a princess. He insisted it was her time to relax, not allowing her even to wash the dishes. He was totally at her service, just as he had been when she stayed with him at his cousin's apartment in Abu Dhabi. He self mockingly joked telling her,

"If anyone see me washing dishes they won't believe it." Presumably Laura was much honored in having such special treatment bestowed upon her.

Nicolas enthusiastically cooked their meals, adamantly refusing any assistance from Laura. He was keen for her to become familiar with the Lebanese cuisine though, and encouraged her to watch as he proudly displayed his culinary skills. Laura had not expected to witness such competence, and was impressed with the delicious results.

He seemed to be in his element showing off his newly-acquired proficiency in the kitchen. While creating his mouthwatering recipes, Nicolas would get Laura to repeat the Arabic name of each dish, correcting her pronunciation until she said it right. Laura couldn't help thinking this was payback for all the times she had laughed at, and corrected his English.

Nicolas was at his most comfortable being in charge, he thrived on it. His life was defined by the control he could wield; never a follower always a leader he would say. This was demonstrated by the way others saw him, as he was always the first port of call for anyone who needed advice. If Hajj couldn't solve the problem no one could.

Like a hand in a snug-fitting glove, for the most part Nicky and Laura worked together perfectly. Being as this was the longest period they had spent living together, it was natural to discover aspects of one another's character not previously encountered. This being so, sooner or later they were going to clash. Nicolas's pet hate was to feel he was not being listened to. He would become impatient and irritated with Laura if he thought she was being frivolous or not paying attention.

One day Nicolas was starting to prepare a meal, Laura said she would help by preparing the salad. Lovely as it was to be spoilt she wanted to contribute. Reluctantly he agreed. Passing Laura a large sharp knife Nicolas watched closely as she began slicing the tomatoes. It made her feel uncomfortable that he was looking over her shoulder so intently.

"No! Not like that!" he snapped swiftly removing the knife from Laura's hand. Nicolas tutted impatiently; "You have to do it this way."

He then demonstrated the correct way to slice a tomato. Somewhat bemused, Laura watched him patiently saying nothing. Passing Laura another tomato he handed her back the knife.

"Now do it the way I show you." he commanded.

Laura felt the hackles go up; but restrained herself from

143

commenting. Placidly humoring Nicolas Laura sliced the tomato exactly as he had shown her, or so she thought. Laura could feel the tension rise as Nicolas tutted again, taking back the knife telling her in a much irritated tone;

"You have to hold the knife this way."

Laura was determined to keep her cool, but felt he was being a touch pedantic. She could have prepared the whole salad in the time taken over one tomato. As Nicolas continued to instruct her on the correct way to hold the knife, Laura couldn't control herself any longer. Suddenly seeing the funny side of the scenario she spontaneously had a fit of the giggles. Nicolas failed to see the humor. Infuriated at Laura's flippancy he snapped angrily;

"I'm trying to teach you something! You want to learn or you don't?"

Failing to comprehend why Nicolas was making such an issue out of it she retaliated;

"For goodness sake Nicolas it's a flaming tomato!"

With that Nicolas grabbed the T-towel that was slung over his shoulder professional chef style, angrily throwing it down on the marble worktop. He glowered at Laura before storming to the lounge cursing in Arabic as he went. Laura speculated whether he had seen an episode of 'Hell's Kitchen'; he appeared to be emulating an angry TV chef. Nicolas sat down in the armchair and lit a cigarette. Laura at first amused was now stunned. Nicolas's volatile reaction to her light-hearted comment was mystifying. Following him to the lounge she sat in the chair opposite and tried to make eye contact. Nicolas's body language reflected his annoyance, as he stubbornly refused to look at Laura.

Again Laura refrained from responding to his moody outburst. She was bewildered by how quickly and easily he would flare up over what she regarded as nothing more than a triviality. From Nicolas's point of view there was nothing trivial about his pride, which had been dented by Laura's glib attitude towards his well-meaning critique. Sitting in silence for a minute or two Laura puzzled as to

144

why Nicolas was so upset with her. He puffed hard on his cigarette in a deliberate manner. Giving an exasperated and over-exaggerated sigh he stubbed it out in the ashtray. Indignantly he turned his head to face Laura who tactfully remained silent. With a steely disapproving look which a father gives to a disobedient child, he glared at her. Laura felt herself recoil inwardly. She wanted to protest but thought it wiser to use diplomacy and try to pacify him. Apologizing she explained;

"I'm sorry you thought I wasn't taking you seriously, but I was upset by your constant criticism."

Laura's apology and submissive tone had the desired effect. It forced Nicolas to reconsider his behavior. After a few moments mulling it over, he considered that he may have been a little hasty in his angry response to Laura's off the cuff remark. Justifying his actions he told her;

"It wasn't criticism, it was an observation. If you hold the knife that way you are going to cut yourself," he argued defensively.

"Oh, I see," Laura compliantly agreed, although she was still irritated. "You were aiming to protect me?"

There was more than a hint of sarcasm in her voice that Nicolas thankfully didn't pick up on. Once he had explained that his critique was out of concern for her wellbeing, Laura began to understand his motive; admittedly she had never been good around sharp objects. In an amenable gesture Laura held out her hand to him.

"Why don't you show me again?" she gently coaxed.

Taking Laura's hand Nicolas stood pulling her tightly to him.

"Bloody woman, come let me show you," he said leading her back to the kitchen.

Assertively Nicolas continued with the lesson of the day as Laura patiently watched. He fascinated her with his knowledge of herbs and spices, explaining the health benefits of each. Nicolas used the Lebanese name for some ingredients which meant Laura would have to troll through the dictionary to find the English equivalent for the ones

145

she didn't recognize. Laura wrote down all the recipes, in the hope that once back in England she could practice; away from Nicolas's watchful gaze.

Unfortunately she was never able to find the exact same ingredients, so consequently never had the opportunity.

Life was a lot easier when Laura just let Nicky do his thing. She quickly learnt not to take things too seriously. Nicky was naturally hot blooded and volatile, this was his way. Laura soon learnt to live with and accept it. Provided he wasn't provoked Nicolas's volatility was always short lived. Laura's placid nature went a long way in helping him keep a lid on his explosive temperament. She was no walkover though. Nicolas could be patronizing but never deliberately, and always held Laura in the highest esteem. Laura's willingness to accept him unconditionally meant he was comfortably free to be himself. It would take time to get used to each other's eccentricities, but it was all part of the fascinating journey. Becoming familiar with one another's strengths and weaknesses strengthened their bond; the resulting effect was to draw the best out of both personalities.

Over the coming weeks they had long talks. That is to say, Nicolas would talk, and Laura would listen. Anyone who knew her would find it hard to believe that Laura would sit quietly, and let someone else talk without having an input. Nicolas could converse on any subject. Laura did not blindly agree with him on everything, and there were numerous occasions when she just had to have her say.

Interrupting Nicolas though was not tolerated, and if Laura dared to do so he would give her one of his looks, signaling it was time to shut up. It wasn't that he didn't allow Laura an opinion; he just always thought his view of things was the right one. Annoyingly, Laura found that nine times out of ten Nicolas did know best.

It wasn't all roses around the door; far from it. Nicolas could be controlling, moody, and difficult. But Laura was more than capable of handling Nicolas's acutely stubborn impetuous ways. Laura's strong personality was a match for Nicolas any day, which was just as well, because the controlling aspect of his character would play out at every given opportunity. Compromises were made on both sides, albeit on a 40-60 ratio, which would fluctuate to 30-70 at times with Nicolas having the majority percentage in his favor of course. They learnt from each other, and in time Nicolas mellowed. He no longer felt he had to play the tough guy 24/7. Under Laura's influence his warm, compassionate, softer side flourished.

Disagreements were rare but not entirely absent from their relationship. Nicolas liked to be in charge, but deep down he knew they were equals. As with any relationship worth its salt, both were willing to accept and enjoy their differences. Nicolas adored Laura and she worshipped the ground he walked on. Neither was perfect, but together they came pretty close. Two sides of the same coin, twin flames, soul mates whichever narrative best described their unique beautiful coupling.

Chapter 18: David.

During her extended stay, Nicky told Laura many more stories from his life. His revelations were always peppered with humour and elaborate detail. Laura could listen for hours and never tire of his incredulous often amusing tales. He had a way of talking that gripped a person's attention.

One day they were chatting, and Nicky recalled a time when he had flown to America on a visit to the home of his business associate and close friend Peter Garrett. Laura remembered having met Peter back in the eighties at the Holiday Inn hotel. On arrival at Peter's house in Florida, Nicolas, somewhat jet-lagged from the long eighteen hour journey was greeted by a flurry of people scurrying around talking about the arrival of someone called David. This David person appeared to be held in very high regard, as everyone dashed about saying;

"David is coming. We must get ready David is on his way."

Nicolas planned to have a short nap to recover from his jetlag, but thought instead that he would take a shower and dress ready for the arrival of David. Taking his suit from the suitcase he carefully laid it out on the bed. Nicolas went to the en-suite bathroom to freshen up. He showered quickly as he had been told that David could arrive at any time. Always ready to wheel and deal Nicolas was keen to meet this David, maybe they could do business together he thought. Refreshed from his shower, Nicolas dressed in his smart light bluish grey suit and silk neck tie. It was a hot day but he wanted to make a good impression. Checking his appearance in the mirror, he tidied his hair and sprayed on his favourite Chanel cologne.

"Hmm....not bad," he thought, satisfied that he was suitably well-groomed and immaculate for the impending arrival of David.

Nicolas eagerly made his way downstairs to join the other people who had gathered at the house, obviously for the important encounter. He casually sauntered down the staircase into the large reception area, where it soon became apparent that the other guests had not made quite so much of an effort. Noticing Nicolas's conspicuous entrance, everyone stopped rushing about and stared at him. A little perturbed by the puzzled looks on their faces, not to mention their informal apparel, Nicolas innocently inquired;

"What? I'm too early?"

"Too early for what?" Peter asked in a rather bemused tone.

"David, he's coming soon right?" Nicolas questioned.

"Yes Nick, David is expected at any time."

"Well, you said to be ready."

The other people, who were dressed casually in shorts and T-shirts, looked at one another perplexed. Peter asked; "Nick, why are you all dressed up?"

Peter was baffled at Nicolas's impeccable but over-the-top attire. Mystified as to what was wrong Nicolas asked;

"This David guy, he's important yeah? Everyone was saying to be ready so I thought I should make an effort," Nicolas explained. "What's the problem?"

Nicolas now started to feel a little embarrassed. Clearly he had misunderstood something about the dress code, as everyone else was dressed so informally. People began to giggle and laugh as it dawned on them that Nicolas had miss-interpreted their apprehensive behaviour concerning the imminent arrival of 'David'. Peter put his hand on Nicolas's shoulder in a jovial manner telling him;

"Go and get changed my friend, it's much too hot for this formal dress." Still laughing he added; "Oh and by the way, you're right Nick; David is expected to arrive soon." Chuckling Peter continued; "But my dear friend, 'David' is a hurricane, not a person."

Needless to say, Nicolas's faux-pas highly amused everyone for quite some time after.

Laura was in stitches on hearing this story. She could just imagine poor jet-lagged Nicky dressed to the nines for the arrival of a hurricane.

Nicolas's stories were always entertaining. Laura was impressed by his incredible memory and the attention to detail he displayed when recalling each event. Nicolas told Laura he had inherited his excellent memory from his aunty. Apparently Nicolas's aunty had amazing recall, and would recount details of events that had occurred twenty or thirty years back in the past. Unbelievably she was even able to remember exactly what she had been cooking at the time.

Nicolas was a great talker and story teller. He had the knack of holding people spellbound, it was a gift. Always at his best in front of an audience, he would easily draw people's attention, mesmerising them with his charismatic interpretation. No matter what subject was discussed, his expertise was impressive. Nicolas modestly attributed his boundless knowledge to having read so many books. Laura felt it was more profound than that; he was blessed with a rare gift that no book could impart. No university could teach the skills Nicolas possessed naturally.

He enriched Laura's life in many ways. As for him, this maverick of a man found in Laura true love, acceptance and understanding. Many arms had held him, but none had ever captured Nicolas's heart so completely.

In spite of being hideously tested time after time, Nicky and Laura's relationship had triumphantly beaten the odds. The difficulties faced paled against what was gained. Their unique union was powerfully transforming for both.

Chapter 19: The Proposal.

Whilst Nicolas was working, Laura found there were too many empty hours to fill. He would leave early at around 8.30am, go to the office or a meeting, and come back for lunch at around1.30. Laura would usually sleep until late morning. Apart from reading or watching television, there wasn't much to occupy her; obviously she couldn't go outside, Nicolas wouldn't allow it. Laura preferred to leave any housework or laundry until the afternoon when it was cooler; it gave her something to do, effectively filling the time while Nicolas was out again, often until 8pm.

Nicolas was a creature of habit. When arriving back at the house he always performed the same ritual before he did anything else. First he would remove his outdoor shoes placing them neatly on the exact same spot, alternating them for what he called his slippers, which were more akin to slip-on beach sandals as opposed to the English version. Laura regularly had to re-position his shoes or slippers, after repeatedly tripping over them while sleepily walking from the bedroom to the bathroom after waking. Nicolas always insisted on placing them most inconveniently right at the entrance to the bedroom.

After the shoe changing ritual, he would go straight to the bathroom and spend time thoroughly cleansing his hands. Any tiny interference with his daily routine did not go down well. Nicolas would become irritated at not finding his slippers exactly where he had left them. Equally frustrated at constantly tripping over, Laura would persistently move them. The scenario of Laura moving his shoes or slippers to a different location, and Nicolas placing them directly back in the middle of the bedroom doorway, went on for a while. Finally Laura convinced him to relocate them just a little to the side if she were to avoid breaking her neck every time she got up to go to the bathroom. Nicolas's customary way of doing things was fine while he was living alone, but now Laura was permanently in the picture, he would need to adapt a little. Nicolas was not incapable of change; he just wasn't very fond of it.

When returning from work, Nicolas was often keen to discuss with Laura what was happening on the business front; enthusiastically detailing projects he was currently working on, or considering becoming involved with. Laura looked forward to and enjoyed this interaction. She loved hearing about his day; it meant things were going well. It was when Nicolas was silent or not in the mood to talk that she would be concerned his day had not gone to plan.

Characteristically, Nicolas would only communicate the positive aspects; problems if any, were never divulged until he had found a solution. Exasperated at always being left out of the loop until after the event, Laura asked Nicky why he felt unable tell her his problems. His reply would be;

"Because love, I didn't want you to worry."

Stubbornly Nicolas would never admit to being worried for the outcome of his business ventures; or anything else for that matter. But despite his dogged 'I can handle anything' tough exterior; Laura only had to look into his eyes. Like mirrors to his soul, those dark eyes reflected all the emotion held inside him. Excitement, disappointment, frustration, and hurt; all could be read at a glance. When Nicky was particularly quiet and reflective, Laura worried. If she asked if he was okay, he would consistently give the same stubborn answer,

"Love, I have many things in my head."

Experience had taught Laura that until he was ready, Nicky would not illuminate further on what was troubling him. If she pushed, he would just fob her off with a vague un-enlightening response. Nicolas was characteristically mindful in keeping his troubles or concerns to himself. Laura tried not to pester him with questions to which she would rarely receive a straight forward answer. All the same, she wished he wouldn't insist on carrying all his burdens alone. Laura knew he wanted to protect her, but she wasn't made of glass.

Nicolas was very old-school in his ways, believing it was the man's job to always protect the woman in his life. Any problem was firmly left at the door when he arrived back to the house. Laura was never informed of any glitch or setback, unless it directly involved her in some way; and only then if her involvement was absolutely necessary. His strategy worked on a need to know basis, and if Laura didn't need to know, then she didn't.

His private time with Laura was like an oasis, a refuge, where he could relax and enjoy moments of peace, untainted from the troubles and hassles in his life. Any wolves banging at his door, were kept firmly muzzled and at bay, until he was ready to deal with them.

There were never any trust issues; rarely did Laura feel the need to question Nicolas's activities. She knew he guarded his privacy, and trust was an important element in their relationship. At times Nicolas appeared secretive, but only because he didn't wish to fill Laura's head with things he believed were not her concern or worry.

Interfering in his business unless invited to do so, was not appreciated. It took a little while for Laura to become accustomed to Nicolas's very individual ways, but she adapted. When away from the house it wasn't uncommon for him to call her two or three times, just to check she was okay, or to ask if she needed anything. Nicky was taking good care of her, and for the time being Laura was content with the status quo.

Nicolas wasn't exactly what you would call obsessive compulsive, but there was a definite trace. He was fussy, and liked things to be done in a particular fashion; a trait probably inherited from his uncle. Like Nicolas his uncle was a handsome man but shorter in stature, with blond hair and striking blue eyes. He was extremely fastidious to the degree that he would practically soak himself in Arak due to its antiseptic qualities; cleaning his hands with it and wiping it over his face and body. Nicky always kept a few bottles in the house. A favourite Lebanese tipple especially in the north, Arak, Nicky told Laura, was a refined version of the anise spirit family. Often locally made in Lebanon from fresh aniseed, it is famous for its potency. Nicknamed the milk of lions, it turns milky white in colour when mixed with water or ice. Nicolas had shown Laura how to prepare it for him with just the right amount of water, but with an alcohol content of 40-65% or more, she was reluctant to partake of it herself. Nicky teased saying;

"When I take you to Lebanon and to my village, you will drink one Arak okay? Or they will not allow you in Kousba."

Nicolas had never been entirely comfortable living with a woman for a prolonged period. Even when married to Samra, he had never spent so much time alone with her as he was now doing with Laura. At the beginning there were a few hiccups, nothing major, just the usual getting to know the others individual needs and nuances. One day whilst cleaning, Laura noticed Nicky's desk was dusty and dishevelled.

Carefully removing his things, Laura enthusiastically polished the desk to perfection. She then set about putting everything back in a more ordered state. Unable to read Arabic, Laura inadvertently repositioned what looked like nothing more than random scraps of paper. Laura placed them into neat piles. Nicolas had the habit of writing himself little notes, reminders of important things he needed to do. Returning from work that day, he was horrified at not being able to find his notes. In her defence, Laura pointed out that his desk was untidy and full of dust, telling him she didn't see how it was possible to find anything amongst such chaos. Nicky insisted that before her intervention he knew exactly where everything was. He strongly specified that in future, Laura was not to move anything. From now on he would clean his own desk. Nicolas was aware Laura's intention was to be helpful. He blamed himself for not explaining to her how he hated his things to be moved. Other than empty his ever overflowing ashtray, Laura was mindful thereafter not to interfere with anything on the desk.

Nicolas was even more fastidious about his books. Just like him, Laura was an avid reader. Nicolas was more than happy for Laura to take whatever she chose from his vast library. He encouraged her by suggesting books he elected she should read. There was one rule; to treat his precious books with the utmost respect. Laura was instructed not to remove any markers he had placed inside, or bend or fold the pages. Nicolas had hundreds of books and many were in near pristine condition. He would be infuriated if Laura failed to put a book back exactly where it belonged. Laura couldn't always remember which shelf she had taken a book from randomly placing it where she thought was close enough to its original position. This was not good enough for Nicolas. He would constantly berate her for haphazardly disrupting his very precise library.

After accurately memorising the exact placement of each book, Nicolas didn't appreciate them being moved. Amazingly he could at any given moment, put his hand on a particular book, open it at the exact page required, and go directly to the passage or sentence he wished to read. Laura was impressed by his incredible knowledge and astonishing memory skills. Realising Nicolas's need to be able to refer to a certain book instantly, Laura understood his irritation if unable to locate it. Duly respecting his wishes, if in future she failed to recall where a book belonged, Laura gave it to Nicolas to replace himself, rather than incur his wrath by upsetting his meticulously planned library. Over time Laura grew accustomed to his eccentricities.

His business meetings were rarely set in stone and would often be rescheduled. Today was one such occasion. Nicolas arrived back to the house earlier than normal to find Laura was still sleeping. He took off his outdoor shoes and put on his slippers.

"Hey, sleepy girl," he said gently shaking Laura. "It's

time to wake up."

Bingo was curled up asleep on the bed beside Laura. "Oh, what's the time?" Laura groaned sleepily, surprised by Nicky's unexpected presence.

Nicky smiled, amused at the synchronicity with which Laura and Bingo stretched and yawned. Raising herself slowly to a sitting position Laura inquired;

"How come you finished early?"

Bingo quickly jumped off the bed meowing as if to ask the same question.

"My meeting was cancelled, the bloody guy couldn't make it," Nicky explained while walking to the bathroom to wash his hands.

Laura scrambled out of the bed and slipped on her robe. While Nicky changed out of his formal work clothes into something more comfortable, Laura fetched him a cold beer from the fridge, placing it on the coffee table with a small bowl of nuts. This was another daily ritual to which Laura lovingly adhered. Taking off his perfectly pressed shirt Nicolas hung it on the wardrobe door. He then put on the clean white T-shirt Laura had laid out for him. He stayed in his jeans which he often wore to work as much of his time was spent outside in the heat, visiting construction areas not conducive to wearing a suit. Nicolas sauntered to the lounge and sat in his favourite chair with his beer in front of him. Picking up the TV remote, he switched the television on flicking straight to the Lebanese news channel. Nicolas took a sip from the refreshing cool beer then lit his cigarette. After routinely checking the news uninterrupted of course, he eventually asked;

"How are you Loulou?"

Loulou was the name Nicolas now affectionately called Laura by. He said she had reminded him of the French girl in the1980s commercial for a fragrance of the same name. When he called her Loulou, Laura would playfully imitate the commercial by responding with, 'Oui c'est moi.'

Their closeness meant that both were sensitive to any small change in the other's mood. Today Laura sensed in

Nicky an air of serious contemplation. After eating a light lunch he wanted to sleep for an hour. His afternoon siesta was another regular habit. Laura got into the bed next to him and snuggled up close.

"Love, I need to sleep," he told her.

"That's okay; I just want to lie here beside you," she answered innocently, knowing that no matter how hard he tried to sleep, Nicky would quickly become aroused.

After they'd made love, Nicky set the alarm to wake them an hour later. It never ceased to amaze him how Laura, who had already slept for probably ten hours, could manage to sleep for another hour with ease. Laura blamed the humidity, saying it made her tired.

On hearing the alarm go off, Laura wrapped her robe quickly around her and went to make the coffee. Nicolas followed close behind. Lighting a cigarette he sat quietly in his chair. Laura felt the urge to chatter on about this and that, but Nicolas was deep in thought oblivious of Laura's ramblings. Frustrated by his prolonged lack of response to her chattering she complained,

"You're not listening to me." Nicolas was clearly in another world and probably didn't even hear her.

"Love I'm thinking," he eventually answered. Five minutes or so later Nicolas suddenly asked;

"Yes love you were saying?"

By now Laura had forgotten what she'd been rambling on about. Nicky asked teasingly; "Now what was it you wanted to talk about Loulou?" He knew full well she had already forgotten.

Nicolas liked to enjoy his first coffee upon waking in complete silence, while he gathered his thoughts, after which he would happily converse as much as Laura wished. Once Laura became familiarised, Nicky's habits and behaviours were relatively easy to contend with. After a time they effectively flowed together like a tranquil sea, instead of two opposing currents.

Secretly Nicolas was thankful Laura slept late, it meant he had the early mornings peacefully to himself. If Laura woke early which was extremely rare, apart from saying good morning to him she knew to leave Nicky alone until he was ready to chat.

"Loulou fix two coffees and come, I want to talk to you," Nicolas suddenly announced. His tone of voice was playfully authoritative.

Laura did as he asked. Taking the coffees to the lounge she sat down in the chair next to him and waited. Nicolas picked up his coffee and took a sip. Stubbing out his cigarette he immediately lit another. Laura gave a look of disapproval, which he stubbornly ignored. Staring into space he silently rehearsed his words. For a moment or so longer he stayed deep in thought. Then after another exaggeratingly long drag on his cigarette Nicolas reached for Laura's hand;

"What I wanna tell you?"

Mentally planning his dialogue, Nicolas took another lingering puff. Keeping hold of Laura's hand he leant back in his seat. Nicolas turned his head to look directly at her, scrutinising Laura's face for a moment without speaking. His delaying made Laura a little apprehensive. While she expectantly waited for his pronouncement, he annoyingly began blowing smoke rings in the air. He was purposely keeping Laura in suspense, mischievously prolonging the subject of his declaration. Stubbing out the cigarette, he suddenly sat up straight. Facing Laura and toying with her like a cat with a mouse, he deliberately repeated;

"What I wanna tell you?"

The twinkle in his eye revealed he was about to say something exciting. Laura was inclined to say 'Get on with it' but resisted the impulse to do so.

"You love me?" he asked at last.

"You know I do," she replied. "What a question."

"And do you think you can live with me, and stay here in Mussafah?" he continued, firmly fixing his eyes on hers.

Laura gave him a quizzical look.

"You will live with me here in Mussafah?" He pushed her to answer.

158

"Yes of course", Laura confirmed. "Isn't that what I'm doing already? Why are you asking?"

"Good! Then Loulou you will marry me. We will go to the Islamic court," he announced confidently.

With both of them being divorced their marriage could not take place in a church; not in Abu Dhabi anyway, and Nicolas was as yet unable to travel outside of the country.

Surprised by his brazen declaration Laura smiled. This was a proposal? It was not as if he hadn't asked her before, but this time he seemed to be telling Laura rather than asking. She felt his unabashed confident manner was a little less romantic than the first time he had proposed to her back in 1983, when perhaps he had not been so sure of her answer.

Laura didn't answer him straight away. She became unusually quiet. Nicolas stared at her; anxiously trying to read her expression. His eyes scanned her face. Without saying a word, Laura stood up and turned away from him. She slowly walked towards the kitchen. This was not the reaction Nicolas had expected. He was quite taken aback, thrown by Laura's weirdly silent response.

"What you don't want to marry me?" he exclaimed in a disbelieving tone.

Now was Laura's turn to play with him. She purposely kept her back turned so Nicolas couldn't see her smile.

"Loulou, you will marry me?" he asked again. This time his manner was much less assured. For all his confident bravado, Nicolas would be stunned if Laura refused his proposal.

Laura felt fit to burst. Teasingly she prolonged the agony before giving an answer. Gathering her composure Laura embraced a serious look and turned around. Keeping her tone low-key she asked;

"You are asking me to marry you? And you want me to live with you, here in Mussafah?"

"Yeah what's the problem?" Nicolas asked indignantly. "Just as we doing now, but you will be legally my wife."

Nicolas stood and lit a cigarette, unsure how to respond

159

to Laura's rather muted reaction. There was nothing Laura wanted more than to be his wife, and she was struggling to remain serious. Unable to control herself any longer Laura ran to his arms;

"Of course I will marry you; I can't wait to be your wife." She told him excitedly.

"Bloody you, you making me wait for an answer? You like to play game with me huh? Bloody you Loulou, you think you make me worry? Me Al Hajj, worry? No way!" Never in a million years would Nicolas ever admit to being worried at her answer. But her delayed response caught him off guard and as he hugged her, Laura could feel the relief in him at her acceptance. Laura knew she had successfully played him at his own teasing game. It was a rare triumph.

"When will we marry?" she asked.

"When you come back the next time to Abu Dhabi," he told her.

"Why not this time?" she asked.

"Because you have to get papers, I have to get papers, there is much to arrange. It's not Las Vegas you know it's Mussafah; they are very strict with the rules everything has to be in order."

"What papers do I need?"

Nicky took Laura's hand and led her to sit down. He kept hold of her hand as he sat down opposite her.

"You will need your birth certificate, divorce papers and a letter of consent from a close family member. Your father is dead and you don't have a brother, so your mother will need to give her consent by letter."

Laura smiled at the thought. Her mother had never been fully convinced of Laura's relationship with Nicky, asking her to write a letter consenting to their marriage would be tricky.

"Loulou, we will have to get our blood tested for the licence," Nicky continued. He squeezed Laura's hand tightly, "Okay hayati, you happy?"

"I couldn't be happier," Laura answered, returning an

160

affectionate squeeze of his hand as she told him,

"I can't wait to be your wife."

"Good! But listen." Nicolas took on a serious tone. "I have to be the boss."

Laura smiled. "You want to be the boss?" She said light-heartedly adding, "No change there then."

Nicky on the other hand retained his sombre aura.

"I'm serious now; I don't want you to lie to yourself or to me, like her."

By 'her' Nicky was referring to his ex-wife. Samra had been unwilling to change anything in her life, yet expected Nicolas to change overnight. That marriage was a mistake he wasn't prepared to repeat. Being the boss was not about being a control freak; for Nicolas it was a matter of honour and responsibility; unlike Samra, as his wife Laura must respect his role as the dominant partner in the marriage. He reiterated his non-negotiable requirement;

"You accept I'm the boss Loulou?" his eyes reflected his need to be obeyed.

Laura responded honestly;

"Yes, but within reason."

"What you mean by within reason?" He challenged not quite getting her drift.

"I mean I will still want to have a say," she explained.

Nicolas narrowed his eyes. Leaning towards Laura he intently held her gaze as he told her;

"Love, nothing going to change we will be as now. I'm not going to do anything bad because you are my wife. I'm not that kind of weak man. Of course you will have a say Loulou. But I have to be the boss, I have to," he accentuated. Nicolas held Laura's hand more tightly to stress his point. "You got me Loulou! You got me?" Nicolas continued; "You know love, I am not saying we will never discuss, we have to discuss. What I'm saying is if we disagree on something and cannot solve it together, we solve by my way. Okay Loulou?"

"You mean you will always have the last word?" Laura mockingly surmised.

To which Nicolas confidently affirmed;

"Yep, that's right."

Laura raised her eyebrows at him.

"Listen love I don't need to show myself be something in front of the people. I don't want to make myself a man he has to show he's boss. No love, because you know why? I'm real man! And a boss! In front of the people or behind the people, I'm the same. I am Al Hajj, leader not follower."

Laura smiled at his entertainingly incorrect grammar.

"What, you laughing at my English now?"

"Of course not," Laura unconvincingly assured.

"Bloody you Loulou! You want to make fun of me?" he exclaimed half laughing at himself. He knew Laura was amused by his grammatical mistakes. "What I wanna say, I'm the boss okay! You accept. Loulou you accept me?"

"Yes I accept," Laura answered.

"Good for you," he said, with triumphant satisfaction.

Lighting yet another cigarette Nicolas took a very long drag on it then slowly exhaled. Becoming serious again he told Laura, "Nothing going to change love. First of all, you are already my wife. I don't need fucking piece of paper to prove I love you. In my heart you always been my wife. Second of all, you love me and I am the boss. That's it nothing more, okay Loulou?"

The delightful imperfections of his English, irresistible accent, and irredeemably confident manner, melted Laura like soft butter on hot toast. Nicolas gave a mischievous laugh, then just to be certain he reiterated his terms;

"You accept me as I am; you agree I'm the boss."

Laura smiled; knowing she would be in good and safe hands she was happy to confirm her acceptance of his terms. Nicolas again scanned Laura's face for the slightest hint of doubt. He radiated with joy at not finding a trace. He could feel it in his bones; Laura was the woman he would grow old with. She was his lady, and Nicolas was unequivocally Laura's man.

KOUSBAWI

Chapter 20: The Gift.

That evening Nicolas was full of joie de vivre, confident that Laura was prepared for what she would be taking on by marrying him. He had waited a long time. After the struggles to get to here, their future could now blossom. With a relaxed, cheerful swagger he walked to the kitchen.

"Let's have a drink to celebrate," he said.

Opening the fridge he took out a bottle chilled Moet Chandon. Returning with the bottle in one hand, and two champagne flutes in the other, he placed them down on to the low table in front of Laura. She watched Nicolas skilfully remove the cork. There was a loud pop and a smoky essence escaped from the bottle; he didn't spill a drop. Nicky poured the champagne and handed a glass to Laura who exhibited an amused expression.

"What?" he asked, while still holding her glass.

"No, nothing," Laura answered unable to stop herself from releasing a giggle.

"Why you laughing?"

"I was just thinking."

"Tell me Loulou," Nicky jokingly ordered. "Or I am going to take the champagne away." He teasingly moved the glass out of Laura's reach.

"I was remembering how cavalier you were when we first met, how flamboyantly you would open champagne."

"What it mean cavalier?" Nicky asked.

"It means careless, carefree." Laura smiled, amused at Nicky's lack of comprehension.

"Aah…!" Nicky exclaimed.

The bemused expression was quickly replaced by one of triumphant understanding as he grasped the meaning.

"And the other word, how you say flambiant what?" he said, endeavouring to pronounce this baffling new word.

"Flamboyant," Laura repeated, she was trying hard not

163

to laugh again at his determined struggle to get to grips with the English vocabulary. "It means showing off," she clarified.

"Oh yeah, you meaning when I use to shake the bottle and shower the champagne over you?" He laughed at the fond reminiscence. "That was when I had my money. That time I could fill a bath with champagne if I want."

There was a moment of pensive wonderment; smiling wistfully Nicolas's eyes twinkled as he recalled the warm memory. Briefly taken back in time he became immersed in fond recollection of those happy go lucky days. He then self-mockingly stated;

"Yeah, yeah love, now I'm poor guy, and don't want to waste my money."

A fleeting tinge of melancholy was present in his tone, but no real regret reflected in his eyes; Nicky was happy. The past was gone and this was a new beginning. He passed Laura her champagne. Nicky raised his glass.

"Cheers to you girl. To us Loulou." He leant forward to kiss Laura, softly whispering, "Love you girl."

"I love you too, and I can't wait to be your wife," Laura whispered back as their lips tenderly touched.

Nicolas picked up the packet of Marlborough from the table. He removed a cigarette telling Laura assuredly;

"Don't worry girl, we going to have a good life."

Laura smiled; encouraged by his single-mindedness. "You believe me Loulou?" His penetrating dark eyes searched hers. He needed to be reassured of Laura's faith in him. Soulfully Nicolas's eyes looked for any hint of uncertainty. But all he saw reflected was love; her eyes, like his hid nothing. Laura had total and complete faith in Nicolas. If he were to tell her that tomorrow he would rule the world, not a bone in her body would question it.

It wasn't blind faith or delusional gullibility; it was the certainty that Nicolas would never say or promise anything he wasn't a hundred percent convinced he could deliver. He then confidently proclaimed;

"Going to be good year Loulou, I can feel it."

He topped up their glasses, and again chinked his glass to Laura's insisting;

"Drink Loulou, today we are celebrating."

The champagne tingled on her lips. In this sweet moment, Laura felt her life begin again. All the worry and uncertainty seemed light years away now as she gazed at the champagne bubbles racing joyously to the top of her glass. Laura's mood echoed them; she was floating high on top of the world, euphoric with the bliss of the moment.

Laura's dreamy, pensive, faraway expression and odd preoccupation with her glass of champagne caught Nicky's attention.

"What you thinking?" he asked.

"I'm watching the bubbles floating to the top of the glass, so light and free, rushing towards the unknown with total abandonment," she answered dreamily. "That's how I feel right now."

"Crazy woman, my lovely crazy woman in love," he said removing the glass from Laura's hand and placing it on the table.

Nicolas stood up. Grasping Laura's hand he pulled her to her feet. Then taking her in hold as if to commence with an old-fashioned waltz he asked,

"You wanna dance Loulou?"

They slow danced without music, but a whole orchestra played in their hearts as they held one another's adoring gaze. Like Cinderella with her Prince Charming, the fairy tale was finally coming true for Laura. As Nicky held her close, she felt the rapid beating of his heart; the strong rhythmic sound was reassuring. For the first time in years Laura felt a weight of uncertainty lift. With her head against his chest, feeling the warmth from his body as it radiated heat into hers, Laura remembered the night they had stood on the balcony at the Holiday Inn looking up at the stars. Just as she had on that night all those years ago, Laura again silently wished for the moment to never end.

"Come," he said softly taking her by the hand." Let me show you a different kind of dance." Nicky said as he gently guided Laura towards the bedroom.

That night their spontaneous lovemaking was intense. As their bodies synchronized, the vibrancy of their passion overflowed with burning desire; cascading over them like an electrical charge from a solar wind. Laura felt his love channel through her soul filling every atom with ecstatic pleasure. Nicky's strong warm hands gripped her flesh; Laura's undulating hips, pressed ever more tightly to his.

For a moment they were held in an altered state, as the alchemy of love and physical ecstasy transcended the physical realm. The pure erotic orgasmic delight was like the language of angels, transcending and lifting their souls to a higher plain of consciousness. The ever intensifying sequence of lovemaking was reaching its climax. Laura gripped the wrought iron bedframe behind her head. Nicky's life-force entered into her like a warm golden rain. Laura moaned, breathlessly vocalising her ecstasy. As her muscles spontaneously contracted, she felt the powerful essence of his love within her.

For a timeless moment that intangible wave of love was visible to their united souls. Laura quivered with ecstatic pleasure as Nicky released his life giving glory. Wishing to prolong the ethereal climatic rapture before it vanished into the ether, they held tightly to one another's throbbing damp flesh. In blissful exhaustion, both lay motionless and silent. Nicky sighed as he slowly regained his breath.

"WOW!" he exclaimed breaking the silence. "Was good Loulou?"

Laura silently acknowledged agreement. Words were inadequate to define the intense feeling of her jubilant satisfaction. Nicky rose from the bed and slowly made his way to the bathroom. As Laura stood to follow him she felt her head swoon. Her legs turned to jelly as her body struggled to co-ordinate. Quivering like an arrow hitting its target, Laura slowly recovered her body's equilibrium. The physical weakness was in contrast to the energised emotional high she was feeling.

Nicky turned to see Laura hovering in the doorway

looking as high as a kite. Her legs felt more like Disney's Bambi on the ice than her own. Concerned Nicky asked;

"You okay love?"

"I can't stop shaking." Laura laughed; the euphoria was still holding her.

Nicky smiled telling her;

"You used all your energy. We will eat something."

Laura prepared the table while Nicky rustled up a tasty snack. They ate with the unrestrained enthusiasm of two people who had been starved for weeks.

For days Laura stayed floating in a continuous bubble of blissfulness. It was difficult to remember a time when she had been so happy. She couldn't wait to call her family and tell everyone her happy news.

The following day Nicolas arranged to take Laura to the supermarket; they needed to stock up on food. This would be the first time Nicolas had taken Laura with him. She was looking forward to the experience of doing normal everyday stuff together. Laura was impressed by how organised Nicky was, he even had a list. But even in the supermarket Nicolas had the need to be in control. It amused Laura how he insisted on pushing the trolley. She was more than happy to let him take over; she never could get those trolleys to steer straight. With Nicky in command of the shopping trolley Laura was free to wander.

She relished every moment of the experience, although every time she was out sight for more than two minutes, Nicolas was calling her mobile insisting she stay close. Laura was intoxicated by the alluring smell of the fresh baked Arabic bread and cakes at the bakery section. After choosing his Lebanese bread, Nicky said something to his Sudanese friend Mohamed who had driven them to the mall. Turning to Laura Nicky told her;

"Loulou, stay with Mohamed and put whatever you need in the trolley."

"Why? Where are you going?" Laura asked.

"I need to look at something, don't wander off, I'm coming after ten minutes. Okay love? Loulou stay with

Mohamed."

Nicky walked away, and quickly disappeared out of sight amongst the hordes of shoppers and their trolleys.

Being as it was the first time that she had ever been to an Abu Dhabi supermarket, Laura was awestruck to see all the different products on sale. Of course there were many familiar brands filling the shelves, but there was so much variety and choice. The fresh food section displayed many different vegetables and fruits; some of which Laura couldn't recognise let alone name. It was all very exotic, especially the spice section. The intoxicating aromas and vibrant colours filled her senses, and were a distinct reminder that Laura was in the Middle East.

Twenty minutes or so later Nicky reappeared.

"Okay love; let's move to the pay area. You have all you need?"

Laura nodded but was a little disappointed to be leaving so soon; there was still so much she would have loved to look at. But Nicolas was insistent. Laura didn't argue, he seemed preoccupied and in a hurry. As they moved to the front of the checkout queue, they put their items onto the conveyor belt to be scanned. Laura moved past Nicolas to start packing the purchases into plastic bags.

"What are you doing?" he asked, steering Laura away from the counter.

"I was going to pack," she answered, confused by his question.

"Leave it, the boy will do it."

Nicolas ushered Laura to the side, and they both stood and watched as their shopping was neatly packed and put into the trolley by a young Filipino boy. Laura would soon get used to the different lifestyle. It was nice not having to do everything herself, as was the case in the UK. Nicolas paid for the shopping and passed the trolley to Mohamed. Nicolas insisted on paying for Mohammed's purchases as a thank-you for driving them. They exchanged a few words in Arabic, and Mohamed left pushing the trolley in the direction of the car park.

"Come Loulou, I want to show you something," Nicky said leading Laura towards a jewellery shop.

They went inside and Nicolas spoke in Arabic to the Lebanese assistant who seemed to be acquainted with him. The male assistant answered him in English saying;

"Yes Sir the one you chose, I have kept it for you."

Laura looked at Nicolas her eyes full of curiosity as to what was going on. Nicolas ignored her unspoken request for an answer, and again said something in Arabic to the assistant. The young man disappeared into the back of the store. He reappeared moments later with a tray of gold bracelets which he set down on the glass counter in front of them.

"Which one you like?" Nicolas asked, turning to Laura who was taken aback by the impromptu rendezvous.

Coyly she viewed the tray of glittering gold bracelets. They were all very beautiful, but one bracelet in particular stood out. It was unusual, like two bracelets in one, joined at the centre in a love knot. You couldn't tell where one band of the bracelet ended and the other began.

"That one." Laura pointed at her choice.

The assistant laughed;

"The one you chose Sir. It's good your wife likes your taste."

Laura smiled, thrilled to hear someone refer to her as Nicky's wife. Nicky picked up the bracelet and fastened it around Laura's left wrist. Nicolas had previously chosen that particular bracelet, but wanted to be sure Laura would like it before he purchased it. He had asked the assistant to place it on the tray with the others in case she preferred another. It was one of the few occasions when Nicolas doubted his own decision; it was important for him to get it right.

"It suits you," he said with a smile, happy that Laura's choice had matched his.

Laura admired the bracelet delicately draped around her wrist.

"Oh I love it, it's so beautiful," she gushed. "Thank you

darling, I love it so much."

"You are most welcome my lady."

Nicolas playfully simulated a little bow. Laura smiled, and was about to hug him when she quickly remembered where she was; no public displays of affection allowed. Nicolas paid the assistant, who asked Laura,

"You want me to put it in a box for you madam?"

"No thank you, I want to keep it on," Laura answered admiring her beautiful unexpected gift.

"Very well madam I will give you a beautiful box to keep it in."

Laura thanked him and took the box. She would never keep the bracelet in it though. Once Nicky had placed it on her wrist, Laura had no intention of ever removing it. Laura felt the unusual design was very symbolic of their love.

On first seeing the bracelet, Nicolas thought the unique design of the conjoined bands of gold encapsulated the way he felt. He and Laura would be always together, forever connected like two golden threads. Bound tightly by their love, they would be eternally entwined.

Chapter 21: Prenuptial Bliss.

A couple of weeks later Laura travelled back to the UK to collect the necessary documents required by the Abu Dhabi court. Serenely happy, she excitedly told friends and family of her impending nuptials. It felt satisfyingly good to prove wrong those who had consistently cast doubt on her long distance love affair, telling her it would never amount to anything. Laura couldn't resist showing off her beautiful gold bracelet to envious eyes. Her precious pre-wedding gift never left her wrist, even whilst bathing and sleeping. Some found it inconceivable that Nicolas was still powerless to leave Abu Dhabi. Laura had no intention of arming the sceptics with more ammunition to fire at her; going into long explanations of the whys and wherefores would only be met by blank disbelieving looks. In their cynical eyes, a future with the mysterious man from the Middle East was at best dubious.

Definitively, whatever Laura's future, her faith hinged on the unshakable belief she and Nicky were meant to be together. Over the years, the distance separating them only served to strengthen that faith. It humoured Laura to hear of couples who failed to make their relationship work because they lived a few miles apart. When love is strong, neither time nor distance can intervene. If what lay ahead for them was perhaps dubious, it was a risk worth taking.

After obtaining her father's death certificate along with a copy of her birth certificate from the local registrar, and the decree Nisi from her lawyer, there was just one more thing left to do. Although pretty sure of what the answer would be, Laura endeavoured to ask her mother to write a letter approving of the marriage. Predictably Laura's request was declined.

Her mother stubbornly defended her reluctance, saying she couldn't be expected to agree to the marriage when she had never met Nicolas. Laura challenged her mother's logic by reminding her that despite the whole family having met Alessandro, the marriage still failed. Laura's mother adamantly refused to budge on the subject, reasoning that if Nicolas was so keen to marry Laura, then he should come to England and meet her family.

Exasperated, Laura gave up; tired of continually trying to justify Nicky's motives to pessimistic minds. Elaborating on the details would not halt their incessant questions. Besides, it didn't matter that others perceived the situation as incredulous; Laura understood the circumstances and as much as she wished it were different, Nicky was unable to just jump on a flight and that was that. Adamant nothing would cast a shadow over her prenuptial joy, Laura ignored the negative remarks.

Later that evening Nicolas called. Laura explained her mother's unwillingness to write the letter of consent. Nicolas was not at all perturbed by the news; it seemed he had been expecting it. Nicky's laid-back approach lifted Laura's spirits, alleviating her gloom at her mother's less than compliant attitude.

His marriage to Samra had its many difficulties, often exacerbated by constant interference from his ex-wife's mother. Countless times Nicolas had confided to Laura about his ex-mother-in-laws unwanted meddling, which caused many problems in their already fragile marriage. Nicolas felt his ex-wife's mother never approved of him. He told Laura calmly;

"Don't worry love, I will find a way."

He gave Laura a fax number, instructing her to send the documents via fax immediately. The following evening he called confirming their arrival, telling Laura he had passed the documents directly to the court in Abu Dhabi that day.

"You will come back here in ten days'," he informed. "September 7th, okay love? When first you arrive we will have the blood tests and make everything ready. Okay Loulou?"

Excitedly Laura expressed she couldn't wait.

Ten days flew by, and before long Laura was again on her way back to Abu Dhabi. As the plane took off from Heathrow, Laura's mind was overflowing with a multitude of thoughts; all dancing chaotically inside her head. She had to practically pinch herself, as she revelled in the realisation that the next trip back to London would be as Nicolas's wife. Laura had waited a long time for Nicolas to fulfil his promise to her. She wished she could bypass the seven and a half hours flying time, and be instantly transported to the arms of her husband-to-be.

Equally as excited to have her back, Nicolas eagerly anticipated Laura's return. He was anxious if she would like the surprise he had waiting. Standing inside the arrivals terminal Nicolas was on his nerves. Laura's flight was already over twenty minutes late. It was just after eight o' clock Abu Dhabi time, when it finally landed. The airport was busy that morning. Crowds always caused Nicolas to become slightly agitated; he went outside to smoke. Once away from the busy terminal, he called Laura's mobile. It went straight to voice mail.

Tired from the seven-and-a-half hour flight, Laura was relieved to pass through the security control swiftly. She hastily made her way to the baggage re-claim. As usual a porter was on hand to help retrieve her suitcase. A lot of people were huddling around the luggage carousel, but Laura spotted her suitcase immediately. It stood out, thanks to the brightly coloured ribbons she had attached to the handles for easy recognition. After reclaiming her luggage, Laura passed straight through customs without a hitch into the arrivals area.

Her tired eyes scanned the terminal for Nicolas. When she didn't see him amongst the waiting crowds, she took her mobile from her bag to call him. Laura realised she had forgotten to reset her phone from airplane mode.

Already there were three missed calls from Nicky. Whoops! Laura knew he would be irritated that she hadn't answered. Possibly the fatigue had caused her to suffer a mild amnesia. Hurriedly rectifying her absent mindedness,

Laura anxiously called him back.

Nicolas was standing in the shade just outside of the airport terminal, when finally he received her call. Not hearing from Laura had put him on edge; concerned if everything was okay. Flicking his cigarette away, Nicolas answered his mobile. A wave of relief swept over him on hearing Laura's voice. He was unable to hide his irritation though. His response was rather brusque due to his built up tensions.

"Why you didn't switch your phone on sooner?" He questioned harshly.

"I'm sorry, I forgot," Laura admitted apologising for her remiss.

"Okay love no problem, I'm waiting outside."

Lighting another cigarette he exhaled deeply, releasing the stress that had built. More relaxed now, Nicolas waited patiently in the sunshine. Laura walked towards the exit accompanied by a porter pushing the trolley laden with her luggage. Laura could see Nicolas talking on his phone. He smiled as Laura approached cutting the call. He handed the porter a tip and dismissed him.

"How are you love, how was your flight?" he asked, his tone of voice was markedly calmer now.

Nicolas welcomed Laura with an affectionate kiss on the lips. His impulsive action made her a little uneasy. Tentatively she looked to see if anyone had seen. Sensitive to Laura's nervousness, Nicolas exclaimed in a tone loud enough for others in the vicinity to hear;

"What, I can't kiss my wife?"

Amused at Nicolas's outspoken defiance, Laura gave a nervous laugh. Nicolas disliked bureaucracy, and hated anything that contradicted his beliefs.

The sun was getting rapidly hotter as it moved higher in the clear blue Middle Eastern sky. The stark brightness of the morning was too much for Laura's tired eyes. Taking her sunglasses from her bag she put them on, giving her eyes a much needed respite from the harsh glare.

A moment later a car pulled up in front of them driven

by Nicky's friend Asma. As they drove towards Musaffah, Nicolas conversed on and off in Arabic with him. Laura felt relaxed as the sights and sounds brought a wave of pleasing familiarity to her tired eyes, and mind. The palm lined roads and parks with exotic vibrant flowers, clear blue sky and warm sunshine, all made Laura feel instantly re-energised. As the familiar ambiance seduced and lifted her spirits, Laura felt totally at ease with the prospect of living in the UAE permanently. For a moment it seemed quite surreal that she and Nicolas would soon be husband and wife. She was again inclined to pinch herself; afraid she would wake up and find it was all a dream.

As they entered the district of Musaffah, Asma drove towards an industrial estate. Turning into an area that was unfamiliar to Laura, he stopped the car outside of a large building.

"Where are we?" Laura asked Nicolas, as Asma began taking her bags from the car.

"This is the new house," Nicolas answered.

"What new house?"

All Laura could see was a warehouse type building next to an auto repair shop. There was a joinery close by and several other industrial businesses. Nothing in the vicinity even vaguely resembled a house. Nicolas smiled as he helped the bewildered Laura from the car. They stood in front of the warehouse's huge heavily padlocked entrance door. Nicolas unlocked the solid metal door sliding it open. He reached for Laura's hand;

"Come I will show you."

Grabbing her hand Nicolas led the confused Laura into what could only described as a cross between Aladdin's cave and a storage warehouse. Surely he was joking; this wasn't a house? As Nicolas led her through the dimly lit building, Laura was amazed at what she saw. There were a variety of items within this expansive storage unit.

As they walked through the two story warehouse, they passed a variety of construction materials. In one area Laura saw pieces of furniture sealed in dust proof plastic

175

coverings, along with ornate chandeliers and mirrors. There were various other ornamental accessories, typically Middle Eastern in style. As Nicky continued to guide Laura along a passage-way, she was silently awe-struck. They reached the end of the passage and were suddenly facing a door. Nicolas unlocked it. The familiar sound of Bingo's unique meow greeted them as they stepped into a dark space. Nicolas switched the light on, revealing the new residence in all its splendour.

"Stay here while I fetch the bags," Nicky told Laura.

He left the mystified Laura and Bingo alone while he collected her bags. Laura surveyed the new surroundings. Bingo stayed close to the door vocalising loudly awaiting Nicolas's return. Laura looked around the large room; on one side was an open plan kitchen with a marble-topped breakfast bar that was an exact replica of the one from the old house. Everything was painted in the familiar green and yellow, with a low beamed ceiling and marble tiled floors. Large sections of the walls were mirrored. Shelves around the room were adorned with Nicolas's impressive library. He was soon back with her suitcase and called to Laura from the other side of the door;

"Laura be careful of Bingo when I open the door."

Laura quickly ushered the impetuously curious feline away from the door as Nicky brought in her luggage.

"You don't like the new house?" he asked putting down her case.

"Yes, but I've only been gone a few weeks. When did you do all this?"

"I was making it when you were here the last time but I didn't tell you," Nicky confessed. "It's more private and I am close to everything for the business."

"Where's the bathroom?" Laura inquired eager to freshen up after her long journey.

"It's through here." Nicky directed.

Laura followed him through an enormous doorway that was typically Middle Eastern, with an intricately carved solid wood door. It led to a bedroom with a walk-in wardrobe at the far end, and an en-suite bathroom at the other. The same wrought iron extra-large king-sized bed, dominated the room. Three of the walls were mirrored from floor to ceiling. Again the wall facing the bed was decorated with the infamous pictures of the semi-naked women. Laura smiled when she saw them.

"You had to bring those?" she teased.

"Loulou I need something sexy to look when you're not here." Nicolas diplomatically answered grinning cheekily, as he justified their place in the bedroom.

Laura thought the bedroom rather lacking in natural light. At the end of the room adjacent to the bathroom was a small window with shutters. Unfortunately it admitted hardly any light into the room. By contrast the en-suite was quite bright decorated in traditional white marble.

As Laura freshened up, she was gripped by a wave of fatigue. Lack of sleep and jet lag began to take hold. Fighting the impulse to collapse onto the bed and sleep, Laura put some eye-drops into her tired eyes, refreshing them instantly. After brushing her teeth and hair she joined Nicolas who was waiting for her in the lounge.

"Come and see the garden," he said excitedly.

"There's a garden?"

Laura's mood lifted immediately; she anticipated with delight being able to sit outside in the sun. Nicky opened the glass patio doors and beckoned to Laura;

"Come Loulou, see the garden."

Laura stepped out into a small courtyard. A high white stone wall completely enclosed the area. To the right side in the far corner was a fountain, and to the left various plants were growing out of huge terracotta pots. Softly scented, pink and crimson flowers depicted a colourful display. Nicolas had put lanterns along the wall so that there would be lighting at night. Under each lantern he had ingeniously placed a large mirror, to which he'd fixed wooden frames with shutters either side. This ingenious idea gave the impression of windows, adding reflected light and the illusion of space. Beside the fountain, a garden table, chairs and a bench were painted in green and yellow, with yellow seat cushions in keeping with the colour scheme and rustic style of the house.

Nicky was like an excited boy enthusiastically showing Laura everything. Switching on the wall lights he proudly displayed his handiwork.

"You like it?" he asked.

"It's amazing, I can't believe you kept this a secret," Laura gushed.

Delighted by Laura's positive response Nicolas smiled contentedly. Despite his cavalier attitude to the opinions of others, Laura's endorsement was important. Confidence and unabashed self-belief aside, Nicolas still keenly sought Laura's approval and reassurance that he had delivered. Nicolas had more than delivered; Laura was ecstatic with the result. Making this secret hideaway into a homely cosy abode was a commendable achievement. Granted it wasn't in the best of locations, miles from anywhere and right in the middle of an industrial estate, but Nicolas had resourcefully made a safe and secure little haven.

"We will take tea out in the garden later," he suggested. "But first we will go to the bed."

Nicky winked saucily, beckoning Laura back inside the house. His forthright command made her smile. Whenever he looked at her in a certain way Laura's pulse would race. She followed him to the bedroom. Undressing quickly they lay down on the huge iron framed bed. It creaked noisily as they reached for one another; their eyes became momentarily locked in a tender gaze.

"I missed you girl," Nicky whispered moving his hands eagerly over Laura's body.

He began caressing every contour, his tongue exploring intimately as Laura lay open to him like a flower being seduced by the nectar searching honeybee. Nicky's hands gripped tightly at Laura's flesh as his mouth moved sensually over her body, hungrily kissing and sucking at her neck and shoulders. With his passion swelled to its maximum capacity, he moved his lips to her mouth, kissing Laura passionately as he penetrated her. Engaging in a pulsating feverish dance, her hips moved rhythmically beneath him.

Laura's sighs increased as he satisfied his voracious sexual appetite. Rapidly she was delivered to the height of orgasmic bliss. In a tight passionate embrace, their bodies pressed against one another as they reached a fevered climatic crescendo. Nicky's heart pounded with a strong rhythmic timbre. As he held tightly to Laura, she felt its resonance and rhythm, as if it were the echo of her own pulsing heartbeat. Her fingers pressed tight into his warm firm flesh, sighing as he thrust his hips against her. The sensation heightened her senses to almost tear inducing emotion, as he spontaneously released his life force into her. Lying silent in Nicky's arms, Laura soon gave way to a deep much needed sleep.

It was around midday when Nicolas decided to wake Laura from her slumber. He had devotedly prepared lunch. He stood motionless in the doorway hesitating to disturb his sleeping princess. Moving close to the bed, he watched as Laura slept; standing over her like a guardian angel. He debated whether he should just leave her be, but he was keen for Laura to eat something, as he knew she would not have eaten during the flight. If he were honest, Nicolas selfishly craved Laura's company. In spite of his joking and kidding with her as to how peaceful his life was when she wasn't there, in truth he desperately missed her.

The incessant chattering, and inquisitive questions, her talking and interrupting when he was listening to the news, not to mention leaving her stuff all over his desk, and tidying away his things so he couldn't find them; annoying as he found all of this, life just wasn't the same without Laura around. Nicolas couldn't imagine his life without her. So he would indulge himself and be a little selfish. He gently nudged Laura;

"Hey sleepy, you want something to eat?"

Laura opened her eyes to see Nicky standing by the bed looking down at her.

179

"Five more minutes," Laura answered sleepily.

"Okay Loulou."

Laura rolled over and immediately went back to sleep. Nicolas wandered to the lounge, the midday news was on. He sat in his chair and lit a cigarette and watched the Lebanese news channel while Laura slept soundly in the other room. Half an hour later he went back;

"Hey, it's 12.30pm come and eat."

"Okay," Laura answered but didn't move.

Nicolas pulled the covers from her;

"Now!" he ordered, "I've made lunch."

Stretching slowly, Laura reluctantly rose from her dream-filled sleep. She sauntered wearily to the bathroom. After splashing her face with water she felt pleasantly and unexpectedly revived. Quickly pulling on a pair of jeans and a comfy baggy T shirt, she joined Nicky in the lounge. He smiled on seeing her;

"Hey Loulou, come love, eat some lunch."

The dining table was laden with freshly prepared salad, a plate of sliced tomatoes, spring onions, houmus, olives and traditional Arabic bread. In the centre of the table was a bowl filled with something hot Nicky called Lebanese Foul.

"Oooh what is this?" Laura asked.

"It's called foul, try it you will like it."

Nicolas served a large portion of the fragrant hot dish onto her plate.

"Eat love," he insisted.

Strangely Laura wasn't particularly hungry, but Nicky had prepared a beautiful selection of Lebanese Mezze, she couldn't refuse. As she breathed the intoxicating aromas and tasted the delicious flavours, Laura's taste buds sprang to life.

"Oh, this is really so delicious." Laura told Nicky, and enthusiastically began tucking into everything.

With her appetite fully regained, Laura continued to devour everything on her plate and the table. Nicky stared at her in astonishment. He was quite full and had finished eating. Noticing his incredulous gaze, Laura stopped stuffing food into her mouth;

"What?" she asked innocently. "I'm hungry."

"Bloody you Loulou, you ate everything. Where are you putting it?" Nicky laughed.

He looked under the table, jokingly insinuating she had perhaps hidden the food somewhere.

"What do I have here, a vampire?" he said, amazed at how much food Laura had managed to consume.

Laura laughed, then light-heartedly retorted;

"I think it's you Nicky who is the vampire!"

Slipping her T shirt off her left shoulder Laura revealed a bite mark.

"Oh yeah........ I did that?" Nicky smiled impishly as Laura pointed to the mark. "Loulou you know you like it," he teased. "Do you know in Lebanon we eat raw meat? When you come there Loulou, maybe we will eat you." He laughed again, adding wittily; "But I cannot eat you, you are too tiny. You will be my hors'd'oeurve."

Their good-humoured banter continued as they cleared the plates away together. Laura began washing the dishes. "Leave it love we will do it later. Come and sit, there is a nice film."

Nicolas made a beckoning gesture indicating for Laura to come and sit by him.

"I prefer to do the dishes now," Laura insisted.

"Okay love, as you wish. You are the lady of the house," Nicky acknowledged.

Laura swelled with pride at being referred to as, 'The lady of the house'.

Lighting a cigarette Nicky sat in front of the television. Once the dishes were washed, Laura sat alongside him. Nicolas reached for her hand interlocking his fingers with hers.

"Love you girl," he declared, lovingly squeezing her hand.

"I love you too," she murmured.

They settled down to watch the movie together.

During a commercial break Laura left the room to go to the bathroom. During Laura's absence Nicky changed the channel. On her return Laura found him randomly flicking from one channel to the other. Channel hopping was one of Nicky's foibles that Laura had not paid any attention to before.

"What are you doing?" she asked, unable to hide the annoyance in her voice.

"Hey!" he snapped, giving her a stern look. "What's the problem?"

"I thought we were watching the film?" Laura snapped back defensively.

"We are; I'm just looking to see if there is anything."

Nicky scowled, unaccustomed to having his actions challenged. He abruptly switched back to the movie. Laura was most irritated to find he had forced them to miss the beginning of the second half of the film, thanks to his indiscriminate channel-hopping. This was only one of Nicky's little eccentricities. Laura quickly learnt that to argue with him would merely result in receiving a defiant look, firmly establishing his undisputed control over the TV remote. It was not uncommon for Laura to leave the room to fetch a drink or snack from the kitchen and come back to a completely different film or programme from the one they had started watching. Over time she got wise. Without Nicky noticing, Laura would secretly take the remote with her, or hide it down the back of the chair.

Around dusk the following day, Nicolas took Laura to a private hospital where they were to have their blood tested; this was the final step required to apply for the marriage licence. Inside the hospital they were led to a small room where they sat on a white couch opposite one another. A doctor came into the room and spoke to Nicolas in Arabic.

"What's happening?" Laura asked as the doctor left the room.

"He will take our blood now and test it."

Nicky smiled at the apprehensive look on Laura's face.

"If you have any disease I won't marry you," he said,

pretending to be serious.

Laura stared at him.

"Don't worry love," he reassured her. "We don't have any disease."

The doctor came back with a syringe in his hand. Laura felt a wave of nausea. Nicolas looked at Laura intuitively picking up on her apprehension. Laura had a needle phobia but didn't want to show she was afraid. She braced herself as Nicolas instructed the doctor to take her blood sample first. As the doctor took her arm and looked for a good vein to insert the needle, Laura became light headed with apprehension.

"Okay love?" Nicolas asked, trying to draw Laura's attention away from the needle.

"Yes, I'm fine," she lied.

Fixing his eyes firmly on hers, Nicolas willed Laura to stay looking at him, averting her focus as the needle went into her vein. His bid to calm Laura without letting on he knew she was scared worked, as she concentrated on his reassuring expression. Even so, she still felt quite nauseous as the syringe drew the blood from her. It was soon over and Laura relaxed, as the doctor changed needles ready to take Nicolas's blood. Laura felt pleased she had managed to hide her fear, unaware she hadn't fooled Nicolas at all.

"My turn," he announced confidently.

He then pretended to be scared adding mockingly;

"Oooh I'm afraid."

Laura smiled, she envied Nicolas's fearless approach to everything as she witnessed him calmly watch without blinking, as the needle entered his vein. Having been shot three times in Lebanon, it was unlikely Nicky would be fazed at the sight of a needle. They left the hospital and got into Nicolas's Syrian friend and business associates car. Salman had driven them to the hospital and waited outside for them.

"Loulou we will stop at the supermarket before we go back to the house," Nicolas informed.

Laura was happy not to be going back to Mussafah yet.

Her attention was drawn to how Nicolas always used the expression 'going back to the house'; she had never heard him refer to it as going home. She asked why he never said going home. Nicolas was resolute in his answer;

"Home is Lebanon."

Laura didn't suffer from such stoic patriotism. For her, home would be wherever she and Nicky resided. Nicolas was under no illusion that he would automatically return to Lebanon. He desperately wished to revisit his homeland, but doing so would bring its own personal difficulties. Retiring to Kousba, his village in the north of Lebanon, was a dream Nicolas hoped to one day fulfil. Before this dream would ever be realised, there were old scores to settle. Even if he were to never go back, in Nicolas's heart Lebanon and only Lebanon, would ever be called home.

Chapter 22: Chaos in the Court.

Within a couple of days the blood test results arrived along with the certificates. Nicolas had paid privately to get the results quickly, ensuring there would be no delay in going forward with his marriage to Laura. The results confirmed both were in good health and it was discovered they shared the same blood group, O positive. Nicky joked that they would be able to be donors for one another if ever the need arose.

"Loulou if I give you my blood then you will become Lebanese," he teased.

The next day he took the certificates with him intending to drop them at the court on his way to the office. This was the final paperwork needed for the completion of the marriage licence. At ten to four in the afternoon he left the house for the court. Laura made herself a coffee and took it into the little garden. It was still very warm so she sat in the shade near the fountain. The trees behind the stone wall cast dappled patterns of light over the small garden enclosure. The men at work in the joinery next door had stopped working for a prayer break. The sudden respite from the monotonous noise of their machinery brought about an almost ethereal ambiance, to the now peaceful surroundings.

As she drank in the atmosphere enjoying the pleasant warmth of the late afternoon sun, Laura was entertained by Bingo's antics. She watched amused as Bingo climbed up the trellis fence like a little monkey onto the balcony that Nicky had lovingly constructed for him. Today Laura felt exceptionally peaceful and at one with the universe, embracing a feeling of total contentment as she sipped her coffee. Even the sound of the workmen starting up again with all their banging and electric sawing, failed to disturb her relaxed tranquil mood. Behind the white stone wall, the tops of the trees were visible from where Laura was seated. An occasional bird would fly past, setting Bingo off in a manic frenzy as they flew from tree to tree above his head. Temptingly close but out of Bingo's reach, they would happily chirp away a joyful song or two.

From the vantage point of his balcony at the far end of the garden, unlike Laura, Bingo was able to survey the world on the other side of the stone wall. Nicolas had constructed a pergola style wooden frame that covered the whole garden. He had erected a rainproof canopy over the seating area in front of the patio doors. A wire netting had been attached to the roof of the Pergola, strong enough to keep Bingo in and fine enough to keep insects and flies out. It covered the entire area, allowing plenty of light and air to enter the enclosure. The little garden gave Bingo a safe haven where he was able to run and enjoy the outdoors within a secure protective environment.

Typical of the Middle East, a large number of stray cats roamed the area. From time to time they would walk across the top of the wooden beams, often stopping to gaze curiously at Bingo inside the enclosure. A very spoilt, pampered Bingo, was until recently blissfully ignorant of the fact that he was a cat. Nicky and Laura would laugh at the way Bingo would sit in a chair, resting his front paw up on the arm, which looked amusingly human like. Bingo never meowed properly, but instead had his own unique language. Hilariously, when Bingo vocalised he sounded as though he were mimicking actual words. Only when Nicolas moved him to this new residence, did Bingo encounter at close quarters another of his species.

Fascinated with all things new, Bingo was initially happy to be in close proximity of the curious strays. But the other cats took liberties sitting on the top of the netting, cat-whaling and tauntingly looking down on Bingo stuck inside. Frustrated by their constant presence, Bingo would respond by making the most blood curdling screeches in a bid to intimidate the unwelcome guest. Eventually, the audacious outsider would reluctantly remove itself from his property, and saunter nonchalantly away, only to return again the following day. Bingo was feeling intimidated by the impertinence of local alley cats.

After witnessing Bingo's altercation with the strays, when Nicky arrived back at the house that evening Laura suggested to him that Bingo needed something to raise him up higher than the other cats. A higher position Laura explained, would make Bingo feel more secure and less threatened. Nicky set to work immediately. Within a few days he had constructed a three-foot-high wooden lookout tower that Bingo could access from his balcony. Nicky even fixed a ladder for Bingo to climb up to his balcony, eliminating the need for him to monkey climb the trellis fence. This would now be put to better use for the plants to climb instead.

Laura was captivated by the caring attitude expressed by Nicky for his beloved cat. Found as a kitten wandering alone and hungry outside his door eight years ago, Nicky had taken pity on the tiny ball of fluff. Before Laura came to live with him, Bingo had been Nicolas's only constant companion. The cat was a source of tremendous comfort to Nicolas during some stressful and lonely times. The way the two had bonded was utterly enchanting. In Nicolas's opinion Bingo was special. Adamantly he proclaimed his pet had qualities that made him distinctly superior to other mere moggies.

"Bingo is not a cat," he insisted. "He's different, he's the best!"

Laura laughed at Nicky's proclamation. She purposely teased telling him,

"All cats do funny things, Bingo is no different."

Having owned several cats Laura was well acquainted with the delightful diversities of their characters. Nicolas was adamant his cat was different, the best-looking and the most intelligent. Laura just agreed because Nicky would never accept otherwise.

With his newly erected tower Bingo was much happier. Now that his head was the highest he was the one looking down on the cheeky neighbourhood strays. Being well fed and cared for, Bingo was more than twice their size and solidly built. Every day he would sit closely guarding his territory, permitting only the cats of his choosing to sit or walk along his garden roof. With a shady tower protecting him from the hot Arabian sun, Bingo confidently took his position as the supreme alpha male, just like his owner.

Every day she spent with Nicolas, was an opportunity for Laura to discover something new. Marriage to this man was clearly never going to be uneventful. Laura felt she was really getting inside his head, which was not an easy task. The predictabilities of his character were mirrored by just as many complexities and contradictions. But she soon became acquainted with what made him tick; whichever side of himself Nicolas chose to reveal, Laura never once doubted she had made the right decision. Even the slightly negative aspects of his temperament strangely held their own kind of charm.

During the coming days, some lucrative business opportunities were brought Nicolas's way, and he had important meetings to attend. It meant his arriving back at the house late in the evening; some of these meetings would go on much longer than anticipated. Nicolas was concerned about leaving Laura alone in the house at night. Once all the nearby businesses were closed for the day, the area was pretty isolated. In the past he had managed to work his business schedule around Laura's visits; coming home early and even conducting a lot of his business over the phone to ensure Laura was not alone for hours on end. Now she was here on a permanent basis, he could not afford to do this indefinitely. Nicolas had lived alone too long needing only to think of himself. Having brought Laura to the UAE to become his wife, he endeavoured to be a good husband and take care of her. In order to get his business moving in the right direction it was imperative he attend these sometimes late meetings. Securing a few good deals and contracts would elevate him back up the ladder; back at the top where he rightly belonged. Nicolas found a temporary solution. He would send Laura to Abu Dhabi. She would stay with Lebanese friends for a few days.

Laura had met Hani and his wife Jana a couple of times before. She was excited and looking forward to spending time in the Emirates plush capital. Laura packed a small suitcase, and Nicky's friend Salman drove them to Hani's apartment which was situated very close to the opulent Abu Dhabi Mall. Nicky stayed with them for dinner then left by taxi at 11 pm.

"I will come and collect you when the papers are ready. Okay hayati? We will go straight to the court from here to marry." He then kissed Laura adding, "Take care love I'll call you in the morning."

Laura thoroughly enjoyed her impromptu stay in Abu Dhabi. It was a change from Mussafah where she hardly ever ventured outside of the house. Being able to visit the nearby mall, which was within walking distance of Hani and Jana's apartment, felt so liberating. Laura never got to walk anywhere in Mussafah. Nicky would not permit her to go out without him, telling her it was too dangerous. At times Laura felt his attitude a little over protective, but she respected his decision, and never argued about it.

Nicolas, of course had his personal reasons for his over vigilant behaviour. His fiercely possessive nature and jealousy was not, as you might suspect, the only reason for his domineering conduct. It was not unknown for weeks to pass without Laura ever leaving the house. Nicolas knew his behaviour might be seen as somewhat controlling, but jealousy aside, there was another motive behind his wanting to keep Laura close and away from prying eyes. Whether she was aware of it or not, Laura was in fact Nicolas's Achilles heel.

Secretly Laura had nicknamed their new residence 'The Cave', in reference to its hidden location and severe lack of natural light. If it wasn't for the little garden, Laura would never see the light of day. But her activities here too were soon to be curtailed by the over protective Nicolas.

Being in Abu Dhabi for a few days gave her a welcome

respite from the 'Cave'. She felt like a kid in a candy shop. Having the freedom to walk outside alone, and go to and from the Mall as she pleased, made Laura realise just how restricted her life was in the 'Cave'.

Laura relished feeling the warmth of the Abu Dhabi sun on her pale English skin. Nicky called her two or three times every day. On the fifth day of Laura's little vacation, he informed her that the court had everything ready for their marriage. Nicolas arranged to pick Laura up at 9.30 am. That night as she laid out her clothes ready for the morning, Laura tingled with nervous excitement. She retired early but lay awake envisioning what the following day at the court would entail. Too excited to sleep, Laura wondered what was going through Nicolas's mind on the eve of their marriage.

Back at the 'Cave', Nicolas fixed a glass of Arak, and relaxed in front of the television. Of course he had no nerves. Nicolas was completely at ease about the following day's proceedings. All the same he was looking forward to getting the formality of it all over and done with.

In total contrast to Nicolas's laidback manner, Laura was full of nerves. Regretfully she would not get to wear the dress bought especially for the occasion, but a simpler outfit. Laura was disappointed at not being permitted to dress as she had planned. Nicolas had been emphatic, insisting Laura be suitably covered. Even her head would need to be veiled in front of the judge at the Islamic court. Nicolas was happy for Laura to wear whatever she liked around the house, in fact the less she wore the more he liked it; provided of course there were no visitors. His possessive nature would ensure Laura obeyed his own strict rules. His reaction to the dress she originally planned to wear was a little over the top Laura thought. Initially she was upset but adhered to his demands and chose another outfit. Laura's dress was not by any means over-revealing by European standards, but Nicolas considered it too alluring for an Islamic court.

Finally Laura fell asleep and was awoken seven hours

later by her alarm ringing on her mobile. She hurriedly showered, and after dressing packed her things ready to leave. In spite of having to cover up Laura was determined to look her best for the big day. She styled her hair and applied her makeup with the utmost care; though her hands trembled with nerves. Hani and Jana offered her breakfast, but Laura was too nervous to eat.

Dead on 9.30 am Nicky called her mobile to say he was waiting in the car downstairs. Laura thanked Hani and Jana for their hospitality before making her way to the elevator. Hani and Jana decided to accompany Laura down to meet her bridegroom.

"You look beautiful," Jana told her as they walked to the elevator.

As the lift doors opened, Nicolas stepped out. He had decided to come up and get Laura. Smiling affectionately at her, he gave an approving nod of the head regarding her appearance.

"Okay hayati, are you ready?"

"As ready as I'll ever be." Laura smiled nervously.

Hani and Jana congratulated them on their imminent nuptials, and Nicolas escorted Laura down to the waiting car. As they stepped outside Nicky told her;

"Don't be nervous love, you look beautiful." He held open the car door for Laura and asked; "You have the thing for your head?"

"Yes, do you want me to put it on now?" she asked.

"No not now love, when we get to the court."

Laura was anxious as they drove to the court; she took out her mirror to check her appearance for the umpteenth time. Nicolas sat in the front; he turned to look at Laura. Grasping her hand to reassure her, he smilingly told her;

"It's okay girl, nothing to worry. Relax Loulou you going to be my wife soon."

Aiming to calm her nerves he gently squeezed Laura's hand. Laura tried to quell her anxiety and relax, but as they pulled up outside of the court her heart started pounding again. She had never entered a court before, let alone an

Islamic one; it looked intimidating.

Nicolas's cousins Antony and Elias were waiting for them outside the court; they were to be witnesses to the marriage. Taking the Hijab from her bag Laura carefully placed it over her head. Nicky told her to wait in the car while he talked with his cousins. Again Laura anxiously checked her reflection in the mirror. As her hands trembled and her heart raced, she silently told herself;

"Pull yourself together; you've waited a long time for this moment."

Laura glanced over at Nicky standing a few feet away talking to his cousins. He looked so masculine and so in control.

"This is where I finally marry my Prince Charming." Laura thought, and like fairy tale magic a sense of serenity descended melting her tension away. Nicky walked back to the car and opened the door.

"Ready Loulou? Let's go love."

The group of four walked towards the courts entrance and went inside. Immediately a man hurried over and started speaking with Nicolas. Munir was a friend who worked at the court; they exchanged a few brief words in Arabic. Laura didn't understand what was being said, but Munir seemed flustered. He invited Nicolas and Laura to take a seat, and quickly disappeared down a corridor.

They sat together in silence. Nicolas gave his bride a reassuring glance, but Laura picked up on some tense vibes. Nicolas wasn't nervous in the same sense that Laura was, but being in the court brought back unwanted memories of his previous encounters with the legal system. Thankfully this time wasn't going to be a battle for justice. As much as Nicolas hated the formalities, by the end of the day Laura would be his legal wife.

After waiting for what seemed an absolute age, Munir reappeared with some papers. Nicky and Laura followed him to another section of the court. Munir asked them to take a seat again and disappeared into another room. The way Munir was scurrying around in and out of different rooms and corridors, reminded Laura of the white rabbit from the story of 'Alice in Wonderland'; who constantly run about disappearing down different rabbit holes.

"What's happening?" Laura asked Nicky as they took a seat in the corridor opposite a row of doors.

"We are waiting for the judge," Nicky replied calmly.

Munir appeared again from one of the rooms and spoke with Nicolas, and then disappeared yet again. Five minutes later he was back with Antony and Elias in tow. The four of them engaged in conversation while Laura sat patiently listening but she was only able to understand an occasional word or two. Suddenly one of the office doors opened in front of them. A serious looking court official beckoned the group inside. Laura looked anxiously at Nicolas as they entered the judge's room. The judge welcomed them inside and shook hands with the men. He invited everyone to take a seat. The judge smiled and briefly acknowledged Laura, then continued to speak in Arabic with Nicolas and Munir.

Repeatedly the judge picked up the papers in front of him and shrugged; Laura quickly gathered something was amiss. She wanted to ask what was going on, but instead sat quietly observing. The ensuing conversation seemed to be causing Nicolas some irritation.

Suddenly they all stood and without speaking, Nicolas indicated for Laura to follow him outside. Once they were back in the corridor Laura tentatively asked if there was a problem. Nicolas was still speaking to Munir and didn't answer. Noticing her anxious look Antony turned to Laura and informed her of the situation;

"There are some papers missing," Antony told her.

"What papers?" Laura asked.

"Your divorce papers," Antony answered.

Laura gave him a look of dismay;

"But we gave them to the court weeks ago," she said.

"They lost them." Nicky suddenly exclaimed.

There was irritation in his voice, and his manner was becoming tense as he cursed in Arabic.

"So what happens now?" Laura asked.

"They are looking; we will go for a coffee and come back later," he explained.

Outside the court Nicolas lit a cigarette; his nerves were frayed with the inaptitude of the court in mislaying vital documents. Antony opened the car for Laura to get inside out of the heat. Laura got into the back while Antony sat in the driver's seat. They waited patiently inside the car while Nicolas finished his cigarette.

"Don't worry these things happen." Antony reassured a confused Laura.

The party left to go to the nearby Maziad mall. They went for some much-needed refreshment in 'Apple Bees' one of the Malls coffee shops. Just under an hour later, Nicolas received a call from Munir and they all promptly returned to the court.

They were led to another department where a different judge welcomed them into his chambers. This judge would conduct the marriage as long as Laura signed a statement saying she was legally free to marry. The missing papers would have to be reapplied for and sent to the court in due course. The judge sent them outside while he prepared the documents. Again the party sat and waited. Nicky looked at Laura who was feeling disappointed that things had not gone to plan. By now they should have been celebrating.

"Don't worry love we will marry, if not today Loulou then tomorrow." His mood was a little more relaxed. "The court has messed up not our fault love."

A few moments later the judge sent for them. Another court official with a far more pleasant demeanour escorted them into the judge's office. The judge then spoke directly to Nicolas. By his expression Laura could tell it was not good news. Again the judge kept waving papers around in an apologetic fashion, conveying his regret at the courts mislaying of the crucial paperwork. It was then he dropped the bombshell. He was not after all, at liberty on this occasion to commence with the proceedings. Once again everyone stood and went back out into the corridor.

"So what was all that about?" Laura asked, bemused by the whole chaotic affair.

"We will go home," Nicky announced.

"So we aren't getting married."

"Not today love."

Laura was understandably disappointed. They walked to the car in subdued silence. Both were feeling downcast with the calamitous outcome of what should have been their wedding day.

Chapter 23: Hajj Loses his Cool

A few days later Laura rose at 9.30 am, which was early for her. Nicolas had left the house for the office an hour earlier. Having so enjoyed the feel of the sun on her skin when staying in Abu Dhabi, Laura decided to spend a little time in the garden relaxing with a book. She opened the patio doors and stepped outside into the hot morning sun. Laura positioned a chair in the middle of the garden and went back inside to change into something more suitable for sun bathing. After dutifully applying sun protection to her fair skin, Laura hurried back out with her coffee and the book she was currently reading from Nicolas's library. Keen to get some colour, Laura planned to sit out for a couple of hours before it became too unbearably hot.

As she relaxed and became engrossed in her book the noise from the carpentry next door was hardly noticeable. Just before 11.30 am Laura was still reading; she didn't hear the patio doors open. Having arrived early from work, Nicolas was surprised to find Laura sitting outside in her bikini.

"What are you doing?" he asked.

Laura jumped; startled at the unexpected sound of his voice.

"Oh you made me jump; I didn't hear you come in," she said catching her breath from the shock. "What time is it?"

"It's 11.30 am," he told her. "I came early because there is no meeting." Nicky explained. He was not happy to see Laura was so exposed. "Why you don't sit closer to the house?" he suggested.

"It's too shady there; I wanted to get some sun." Laura argued.

Nicolas tried to cover his jealousy but couldn't handle Laura sitting outside dressed, or rather undressed as she

196

was, while he was away from the house. It wasn't just his jealous streak fuelling his unease; Nicolas worried Laura may be at risk if anyone knew she was alone in this predominantly male isolated area of Mussafah.

"Put something on," he demanded.

"Why?" Laura questioned, baffled by his objection to her perfectly normal beach attire.

"Someone might see," he declared.

Bemused Laura looked around the completely enclosed private garden. Apart from the stray cats or an occasional bird flying overhead, no one could observe her. Laura could see no legitimate reason for Nicky's concern.

"But there is no way anyone could possibly see me," Laura protested.

Nicky was adamant insisting;

"They will look over."

Laura smiled at the thought. Someone would need to be at least twelve feet tall to look over the garden wall.

"Who will?" she demanded, baffled at the absurdity of Nicky's logic.

Nicolas pointed to the adjacent carpentry business. The building had a level higher than the garden wall. Laura had heard plenty of noise coming from the men at work inside, but had never seen a soul. In fact to view Laura in the garden below, they would need to scale the buildings wall to reach the carpentry's high windows, then lean right over and stand precariously on the narrow window ledge. But Nicolas was unrelenting, arguing that if they knew she was there, they would look.

"How will they even know I am here?" Laura persisted against his absurd reasoning.

"Maybe they will hear you talking to Bingo." Nicky claimed, obstinately adding; "Better you stay inside when I'm not here, or I will have to kill someone if they look at you."

Nicolas had said it light-heartedly and with a smile, but she sensed he wasn't joking, but deadly serious. All the same Laura was speechless at his resolute demand she stay out of sight. Reluctantly she went inside to get a robe.

"Bring me a beer and come and sit." Nicky called after her.

Laura took a cold beer from the fridge and a small bowl of nuts out to him. He was sitting in the shade under the canopy. Laura sat beside him. The men had stopped work at midday, and it was suddenly peacefully quiet again with just the sound of the birds. Nicky sipped his beer looking admiringly at Laura. Her silk robe was loosely tied resting gently against the contours of her body. Nicky found it most alluring. Wickedly he pulled her robe open, revealing the soft curve of her breast. The pink silk fell sensuously against her lightly sun kissed skin. Nicky fondled Laura's thigh seductively squeezing at her flesh. His hand slid to the top of her leg as he continued to fondle the toned warm flesh of her thigh. His eyes stayed lustfully focussed on her breasts.

"Yeah love, you make me horny now."

Laura smiled, consciously aware of the effect she was having on his over active libido.

"But you know I have to sleep."

"Okay you sleep." she teasingly replied.

"You bloody, you know I'm not going to sleep now." he confessed. "How I can?" Nicky stood revealing his very obvious arousal. They went inside and made love, sleeping until 3pm.

The next day Nicky came back to the house with news that they would be going back to the court. Alessandro had obligingly faxed replacement copies of the divorce papers that were lost by the court. A week had passed since their unsuccessful attempt to marry. Nicolas told Laura to be ready at 4pm; his cousin Antony would be picking them up. Again Laura prepared herself, and at four o'clock on the dot Antony arrived to drive them to the court for their appointment with the judge at five pm. They arrived at the court in plenty of time. Laura checked her hijab was in place before stepping from the car. She was still a little apprehensive but much calmer now she knew what to expect. Elias had been unable to make it, so in his place Nicky's friend Salman met them outside the court. Inside people cordially acknowledged Nicolas; he seemed to have connections everywhere.

Laura stayed close to his side. She naturally had the inclination to take his hand, but was mindful not to in the court. It would not be appropriate despite the fact they were about to marry. Once again they were led along a corridor and asked to take a seat. Nicolas engaged in casual conversation with Antony and Salman while they waited. After ten minutes they were invited into one of the offices. At the judges request they all took a seat. Laura listened, but was unable to understand the conversation that followed between the four men.

Moments later Laura became aware of a distinct change in the atmosphere. Clearly agitated Nicolas started to raise his voice. Laura felt the nervous tension rise rapidly, and observed Nicky's anger increasingly manifest in his tone and manner. She watched him tentatively. Suddenly Nicolas stood to leave signalling that Laura follow him. Dutifully Laura stood up and made her way towards the exit behind Nicolas. On reaching the doorway Nicolas stopped. He turned quickly around to look at Laura. Like hot burning coals his dark eyes smouldered furiously as he looked. Without warning in front of the judge, Nicolas forcefully ripped the hijab from Laura's head defiantly exclaiming;

"And you can take that stupid thing from your head."

If Laura wasn't nervous before, then she certainly was now. She couldn't wait to get out of the court for fear of what Nicky might do next, he was clearly not happy. Once they were outside and safely in the car park, Laura felt able to breathe. Nicolas's tendency to blow up was unpredictable. When he exhibited such volatility it was scary; a good analogy would be to imagine a freight train coming straight at you at full speed. In those few seconds Nicolas was capable of anything. Provided he was not antagonised, he would quickly calm.

By the time they reached the car he had already cooled down and was joking with Antony; Laura felt it was safe to ask him what had occurred. Nicky enlightened Laura as to the cause of his fury;

"They lost your father's death certificate this time, and the fucking judge wanted to know why no one from your family gives permission for you to marry me."

His volatile mood may have eased, but Nicolas's words were tinged with obvious anger. Laura looked at him with an expression of incredulous shock.

"I don't believe it! So now we have to get another death certificate?"

"No love, they will find it; or I swear I'm going to kill somebody!"

Nicolas laughed through his anger but Laura sensed more than a grain of vengeful intent. A man didn't get the reputation Nicolas carried by not following through with a threat once that intention was set.

A fortnight later Nicolas informed Laura that the court had found the lost certificate and they would go back to the court to complete the marriage. Salman drove them from the house and Antony was to meet them there. Not surprisingly Laura was apprehensive as they entered the court; as it turned out with good reason. They sat in silence in the waiting area. Nicky was swinging his worry beads in an attempt to remain cool, but Laura could tell he was on the edge of his nerves. Laura felt uncomfortably ill at ease whenever Nicky was agitated this way. It was four weeks and counting since their first visit. Laura was becoming quite familiar with the place. She worried how Nicolas may react if there was another court mess-up or delay.

An official beckoned them into yet a different judge's office. How many judges were there in this place Laura thought? By now they must have gone through all of them.

This time Salman accompanied them into the judge's office while Antony stayed outside in the waiting area. Again Laura understood nothing as the proceedings were conducted in Arabic. Nicolas was seated beside her with

Salman opposite. The judge made a couple of phone calls, as he and Nicolas continued to converse in Arabic. Unbelievably there was another mix up over the official paperwork. Laura looked on incredulously as the judge kept picking up the papers in front of him and shrugging his shoulders.

"Here we go again," Laura thought to herself.

Nicolas conversed in a calm controlled manner. But as Laura would discover, the fact that Nicolas was not raising his voice was not necessarily a good indication that he was not about to lose it. The judge made a third phone call to another department. As he put down the receiver, he again nonchalantly waved the papers in the air. Nicolas said something with which the judge stood up shrugging his shoulders in a dismissive fashion. Laura had no idea what was happening. Whatever the judge said next was like a red rag to a bull. One minute Nicolas was seated calmly beside her, and in a flash he was across the room with the judge pinned to the wall. It happened so fast neither Laura nor Salman saw it coming.

Salman desperately tried to calm Nicolas who had the judge by the throat and pinned to the wall. Nicolas was refusing to loosen his grip as the fire inside of him erupted like a volcano. Hearing the commotion Antony entered the room followed by a court official. Eventually the situation calmed and Nicolas relinquished his iron grip from the terrified judge's neck.

The whole thing was just too surreal. Laura felt like a spectator to a movie scene. She feared they would all be arrested instantly. In a complete turnaround, as quickly as it had arisen everything suddenly calmed. Though visibly shaken, the judge profusely apologised to Nicolas. Laura gathered he must have disrespected Nicolas in some way. The menace she'd seen in Nicolas's eyes was unrelenting. No one, no matter who they were, would ever be permitted to talk down to Al Hajj without facing consequences.

The group walked from the court unhindered; nobody said a word to any of them. Nicolas walked calmly out of the court back to the car as if nothing had happened. He sat in the front seat next to Salman who was driving them; Nicky's cousin Antony left in his own car. As they drove away from the court Salman and Nicolas were laughing and talking in Arabic. Suddenly remembering Laura was there, Nicky turned around to look at her;

"Are you okay love?"

Laura was still reeling from the scary ordeal.

"Yes, just about. What the hell happened back there?"

"You know love, what can I say? This is me!"

His tone was typically unapologetic.

"You love me?" Nicky asked in a more dubious tone, as if to check his little display at the court had not changed Laura's mind about marrying him. Giving him a reassuring smile Laura replied;

"Of course I do,"

"Good for you," he said almost triumphantly.

By now Laura was wholly aware of what she would be taking on by marrying Nicolas. Nothing he did detracted from her unconditional love. On the contrary, Laura was proud. Being with a man so demonstratively unafraid to stand up and be counted was liberating. His unwillingness to be compromised in his convictions made him real. Nicolas's imperfections, if you could call them such, were what made him the man he was. In Laura's eyes he was the perfect man. Laura wouldn't change a hair on his fiery hot head.

A week passed and Laura was beginning to wonder if their marriage would ever take place. Then unexpectedly Nicky announced that the court had contacted him with the news that all of the paperwork was at last complete and ready. Two days later they were at the court again. This time it was Antony and his brother Elias who accompanied them. Salman for some reason was suddenly unavailable; Laura suspected he may not have recovered from the last visit, and was afraid of a repeat performance. Nicolas told Laura to wait in the car while he and Antony went inside.

"Why? I'm not coming with you?" she asked.

"I don't want to take you in there just to be told there is another delay. I want to be sure everything is ready before you have to put that stupid thing on your head."

Nicolas never hid the fact he absolutely hated the idea of Laura wearing the Hijab. She waited in the car with Elias while Nicky and Antony went inside. Half an hour passed; Laura was becoming increasingly concerned. She fretted that perhaps Nicky had lost his temper again. Elias made light conversation with her, but Laura could tell he too feared the worst. Knowing Nicolas's hot blooded temper could explode spectacularly if the wrong buttons were pushed had them both on tenterhooks. How many times can you threaten a judge in his own chambers before being thrown in jail; even if you are Al Hajj? Moments later to Laura's relief, Nicolas and Antony reappeared looking relatively unscathed. They were all chatting in Arabic as Antony drove away from the court.

"What's happening?" Laura asked, puzzled.

"None of your business," Nicky deliberately teased. Then straight away added excitedly, "Love, we are going to be married on Saturday evening at the judge's house."

"What?" Laura thought he must be joking.

"They don't want Hajj in the court again he's a trouble maker," Antony laughed.

They all started laughing and Nicky seemed a whole lot more relaxed.

"Your husband has fire in his blood, no one can handle him," Elias added.

"Hey Loulou, what do you think about we order pizza tonight?" Nicky suggested. He was suddenly like an excited little boy.

"Sure, why not?" Laura agreed.

She was happy and relieved Nicolas was in such a good mood. Needless to say Laura was also hugely thankful that they wouldn't be required to make another nerve-wracking visit to the court.

Chapter 24: At Last.

Saturday arrived and Laura was full of excitement at the prospect of finally becoming Nicolas's wife. Nicolas told her that to be married by the top judge outside of the court was highly unusual, and was to be regarded as quite an honour. Nicolas's connections and reputation had certainly enabled him to pull a few more strings. This particular judge rarely performed such ceremonies except on special occasions. Laura sat nervously waiting for Elias; he was to drive them to the house in Abu Dhabi. Today her nerves were more of anticipation than fear induced apprehension.

Nicolas of course was as cool as a cucumber. Although the ceremony would take place in a private dwelling all the witnesses, both Muslim and Christian, would be male. Nicky was emphatic Laura cover up again. She decided to dress as she had for the court.

Dead on the dot at five, Elias arrived to take them to Abu Dhabi. Laura picked up her handbag and the hijab for her head.

"You don't need that," Nicolas said, roughly grabbing the hijab from Laura's hand and throwing it down in an aggressive fashion. "It's a private house, not the court. You don't have to wear that stupid thing."

Nicky's antagonism towards an innocent headdress amused Laura; all the same she was relieved to dispense with wearing it. Nicky's hostility subsided and in a more jubilant tone he announced,

"Come Loulou, let's get married."

Laura smiled; Nicky's eagerness made her feel special. But one thing worried her. Laura remembered how Nicolas had once described his feelings on the day of his marriage to Samra. Revealing to Laura he felt trapped and overcome by feelings of confinement. He told Laura that when it came to the signing of the register, he looked at Samra, and in that moment had an inexplicable feeling of hatred towards his new bride. This shocking confession stuck in the back of Laura's mind. She feared he may suddenly feel the same way towards her, and would again regret his decision to marry. But Laura need not have worried; this time around Nicolas was one hundred percent sure. With all the hassles encountered just to get to this day, if Nicolas had any reservations, there had been plenty of opportunities in which to back out. The numerous delays and mix-ups at the court had tested his resolve to the limit. There were probably moments when Nicolas would gladly have said to hell with it all. But he didn't; Nicolas wanted Laura to have the respectful place she deserved as his legal wife.

Taking Laura's hand Nicolas led her along the dimly lit passage towards the entrance of the warehouse. Once they reached the secure metal door he unlocked and slid it open. He told Laura to wait inside a moment while he scanned the area. Satisfied there were no prying eyes, Nicolas ushered Laura into the back of Elias's four wheel drive BMW. Whenever they left the house or entered it, he always behaved in this odd manner. Laura thought his behaviour a little peculiar, but Nicolas never explained his rationales for such extreme caution.

On the way they stopped to pick up Nicolas's employee and friend Mubarak who was from Yemen and to be one of the Muslim witnesses. Salman, who was making his own way, was another witness, along with Asma, Antony and Elias. On arrival at the house they were greeted by the owner's wife; apart from Laura she was the only other female present. The judge was waiting for them inside. Nicky whispered to Laura;

"This is the top judge in the whole of Abu Dhabi."

A few moments were spent while everyone introduced themselves before being shown into the large reception room. Dressed in his official robes the judge greeted them. His demeanour was relaxed and smiling. The judge then spent a few minutes checking the paperwork until he was satisfied that everything was in order. He displayed a kindly pleasant disposition as he asked if they were ready to begin and invited everyone to take a seat. Laura and Nicky were directed to sit next to each other. Smiling the judge turned to Laura and asked,

"Do you love this man?"

"Yes I do," Laura replied.

"You are willing and ready to marry of your own free will?" the judge asked.

"Yes I am," Laura confirmed.

Nicolas and Laura were required to sign a document for the license. After which the judge declared;

"Good let's begin."

From then on the marriage service was conducted in Arabic. Taking Nicolas's hand the judge recited verses and read out passages from a religious book. In the appropriate places Nicolas repeated phrases and said vows. Laura watched Nicolas's face closely as he repeated and recited the verses; he spoke confidently and with conviction. To Laura's relief there was no hint of hesitation. The service itself was very formal. Numerous prayers and religious songs were performed by the judge. The witnesses were required to join in some prayers. All the vows were spoken by Nicolas. Laura was required to speak only twice. In English she was again asked if she loved Nicolas, and to confirm that she was free to marry and was doing so of her own free will. Towards the final part of the ceremony, the judge placed Laura's hand together with Nicolas's and more prayers and blessings were said.

The whole proceeding took forty five minutes, ending with the judge singing a very long prayer. Laura didn't understand what he was singing, but secretly found this part rather amusing as it did go on for quite a while. At the end of the service, the judge took Nicolas and Laura's hands and placed them together. He performed a blessing adding in English that he hoped they would be very happy in their life together. Everyone congratulated Nicolas and Laura on their marriage.

Immediately the lady of the house brought in some refreshment. Trays of traditional Arabic snacks were laid out on a table, with fresh juices and mint tea. No alcohol of course. Thirty minutes later Nicolas and Laura thanked their hosts before leaving to return to Mussafah as husband and wife.

As they walked slowly back to the car hand in hand, the judge came hurrying over. He expressed his apologies to Nicolas for all the delays and problems encountered at the court. Nicolas thanked him for conducting the ceremony. In English the judge wished them a long happy marriage. The newlyweds set off for Mussafah, dropping Mubarak off on the way. Before today Laura had only ever seen Mubarak dressed casually in jeans, but today he had worn his finest white robes. Mubarak told Nicolas he would call the following day to discuss a job, and again congratulated the couple on their marriage. Nicolas thanked him for being a witness.

Back at the house, (the Cave), Nicky and Laura changed into more comfortable attire, and settled down to a relaxing evening; their first as husband and wife. Nicky opened a bottle of Moet Chandon and poured out two glasses declaring;

"Cheers Mrs Chehade." He gave Laura a kiss on the lips. "Love you girl," he told her affectionately.

"I love you too," Laura said gazing adoringly into her husband's smiling eyes.

After six extraordinary calamity filled weeks, Nicky and Laura were finally married. Both felt sure it was worth every calamitous step.

Some years back Nicolas had been forced to let Laura go. But she had come back to him and stayed through all the many unprecedented ups and downs. As he sat with his new wife, Nicolas recalled a quote he had once read by a famous Lebanese writer and poet;

'If you love someone let them go, if they return to you then they were always yours.'

Chapter 25: Married to Kousbawi.

With the formalities over and Laura now at last his legal wife, Nicolas felt more relaxed. Against all the odds he had succeeded in achieving what he set out to do a long time ago. Now no one would question the validity of their relationship. Laura was safe and protected under the law. The first few weeks of their marriage were blissful; a continuous honeymoon. While Nicolas was working Laura busied herself with the usual things that need doing around the house. Once the obligatory mundane jobs were done, she would fill the time by reading or watching television.

Initially perfectly content, Laura hardly noticed that weeks passed by without her ever stepping out of the 'Cave'.

Not surprisingly, after a little while Laura began to feel claustrophobic in her unchanging surroundings. Venturing into the tiny garden to hang out laundry was the furthest she ever got to being outside. After spending time one day looking on the internet, Laura discovered there were all sorts of wonderful things to see and do in this fascinating Middle Eastern country that was now her home. She wanted to explore and get to know Abu Dhabi, and all it had to offer. Laura decided to broach the subject with her husband, perhaps he would agree to her visiting the places she had seen advertised. Unfortunately her husband was not of the same mind-set; on the contrary Nicolas had no intention of loosening the reigns or advocating Laura go out and about alone.

Nicolas arrived back from work that day in a happy relaxed mood. Laura grasped her opportunity. As usual he presented Laura with a small posy of white flowers that he had picked and wrapped carefully in a paper cone. This incredibly sweet romantic act Nicolas performed whenever returning to the house from outside. It was the sweetest gesture and beautifully demonstrated Nicolas's sensitive side. Laura put the flowers in a glass of water and placed then in the centre of the table.

After changing from his outdoor shoes into his slippers, Nicolas went to the bathroom to perform his hand washing ritual. Laura followed him excitedly chattering on about the interesting places in Abu Dhabi she had discovered on the internet. He made no response as he dried his hands and walked to the bedroom to change out of his formal work clothes. Laura sat on the bed babbling on about all the wonderful sites she hadn't yet visited.

"Are you listening to me?" she asked, frustrated by her husbands continued lack of response.

"What's that love?" he asked with a vacant expression. Nicolas was pretending not to have taken in any of what Laura was saying.

"Sometimes I get bored here alone when you're out working. I'd like to take a taxi one day, and visit some of the places I haven't been to," Laura repeated.

An uncomfortable edginess began to infiltrate Nicolas's formerly relaxed mood. He wasn't sure how to respond to Laura's unexpected request, so he said nothing. He walked to the fridge and took out a cold beer. Grabbing a handful of almonds from the jar on the breakfast bar, he made no comment as Laura persisted with her innocent appeal.

Nicolas was playing for time. Caught off guard, he now struggled to find an excuse that sounded vaguely feasible. Laura repeated her wish to explore the exciting capital of the Emirates.

"Wha..at?" he said, in an exaggeratingly dismissive fashion. Beer in hand, Nicolas nonchalantly walked to the lounge and sat down in his favourite chair. He picked up the remote and switched on the TV hoping to find something of importance on the news, so as to avoid answering Laura. There was nothing particularly attention grabbing and annoyingly Laura wasn't giving up.

Exasperated by her husband's unresponsive attitude, Laura followed him into the lounge. Sitting down opposite him, she gave her husband a questioning look. Nicolas faked a disapproving glare in a bid to dissuade her from continuing to bother him. Quite undeterred she questioned his expression;

"What does that look mean; are you actually saying I can't go out?"

Nicolas responded with an affirming nod of his head.

"Why?" she argued, "Why can't I go out?"

Nicolas's stubbornness prevailed telling Laura in a firm authoritive tone;

"Because I said so!"

Was that really the best he could manage? As he said it, Nicolas knew it was an unfair and inadequate explanation. Taking Laura's hand he attempted to change the subject.

"Loulou, what shall we make for dinner tonight?"

Laura refused to be fobbed off by such a feeble excuse; it was clear he was avoiding the issue. Dissatisfied with her husband's unreasonable response, Laura challenged him, defiantly saying,

"What if I were to do it anyway?"

"Do what?" he asked vaguely, pretending not to know what she was talking about.

"Walk to the main road and take a taxi to Abu Dhabi."

Irritated with Laura's persistence on the subject, which to Nicolas was non-negotiable, his stubborn controlling tendencies automatically came into play and his response was unyielding;

"Try it, and see what happens!"

He smiled as he said it, but Laura got the message loud and clear, and didn't ask again.

Laura was thankful that Nicolas possessed such a large library; she read voraciously and found she slept a lot to fill the lonely hours when her husband was at work. Laura was glad of Bingo's company. Nicolas would always call her before arriving for lunch or dinner to check if Laura needed anything from outside. He would arrive back to the house bringing whatever was needed in the way of household items or food, and of course never forgetting Laura's little posy of flowers.

Nicolas was faultlessly generous and a loving husband; whatever Laura needed he would go out of his way to bring her. The only need he didn't cater for was Laura's desire for more freedom to go out. In this he remained rigidly inflexible.

On his days off Nicolas helped Laura with anything that required doing in the house, and would spoil her by cooking dinner. He treated Laura like a princess; albeit a princess locked away from the outside world. Occasionally they ventured out together, but mostly people came to visit them. Friends would be invited over at the weekends, and they would have barbeques in the little garden. Laura loved these occasions, but wished they could do more things away from the house. She couldn't wait for Nicolas to return in the evenings. Like a child she would be excited if he mentioned they were going anywhere at all. Laura never believed she would find such delight in a trip to the supermarket. She began to cherish any event that took her out of the 'Cave'.

Laura was willing to accept her husband's stubborn ways because she loved him; believing it must be a culture thing that he didn't let her go out. But her eyes were soon opened to the fact that this was not entirely the case. When friends visited they would sometimes offer to take Laura out somewhere, or invite her to their home. They would tell Nicolas to call and make the arrangements. He would half-heartedly agree at the time, but when Laura asked him to follow up on the invitations he would make an excuse, or flatly refuse to acknowledge the invite. Some of his Lebanese friends were bemused by his attitude. Jokingly telling Laura;

"Hajj is afraid someone will take you away from him." They would laugh and make light of it, and Laura could tell this possessive behaviour was a characteristic of Nicolas rather than a cultural thing. Despite his obstinate streak, Nicolas was the ultimate prince of charm. Laura accepted his obsessive behaviour as a small price to pay for the total commitment and love he bestowed upon her.

On trips back to the UK Laura could come and go as she pleased. Uncannily Nicolas didn't object, maybe because he knew it was out of his control. Laura was obliged to leave the UAE on a regular basis to renew her visitor's visa. Sometimes Nicolas would have Laura's passport stamped by the court. He would happily pay the fee to extend her visa, rather than have her leave the country. It cost about the same as a ticket back to the UK anyway. When Laura was visiting Alyssa, he would call her frequently, sometimes two or three times a day and when apart they would spend hours on Skype video to one another. When he recovered his passport and had all his residency papers in order, Nicolas planned to add Laura to his visa; relinquishing altogether the need for her to travel out of Abu Dhabi. Many more doors would open for Nicolas once he had these long awaited legal documents in his hand. Without them he was unable to put anything in his name. Once this was resolved restarting his company was a priority.

Laura enjoyed her time spent with friends during visits back to the UK. Naturally they would ask about Abu Dhabi. There wasn't a great deal Laura could tell them, as she never went anywhere. Laura's friends were shocked to discover she rarely ventured out. They told her Nicolas was too controlling, and she should put her foot down and demand to go out. Such suggestions made Laura smile; she couldn't imagine anyone putting their foot down with Nicolas or demanding anything from him. Regardless of the shocked disbelief by friends at her revelation, Laura was never in the least bit doubtful of her marriage. Nicolas had many positive attributes, which far outweighed the negatives. Deep down Laura suspected something more than he was admitting to, lay behind his over stringent protectiveness. She didn't dig, as she knew a logical explanation wouldn't be forthcoming. Nicolas's seemingly irrational obsessions were the product of something he would rather not share with Laura; it was an underlying, and decidedly more dangerous side to his life.

Chapter 26: Plan B

The next few years of their marriage were for the most part blissful. Nicky and Laura had become so familiar neither could ever imagine their life without the other. It appeared their destiny was so firmly cemented whatever happened, nothing would separate them again.

Nicky worked hard, and every spare minute was spent perfecting his invention. Laura would quietly read while he worked meticulously on his drawings. She would keep him supplied with endless cups of coffee, and empty the overflowing ashtray while he sat silently at his desk fully engrossed with his 'Baby', as he called it. Occasionally Laura would look up from her book, and be fascinated by the inspired dedicated commitment Nicolas poured into his project. It filled her with awe to witness this genius mind at work. Reluctant to disturb Nicky's concentration, Laura refrained from doing anything noisy like vacuuming or playing music. If she put the TV on, the volume was so low it was barely legible. Intermittently Nicolas would pause from his work, leaning back in his chair he would give a satisfied sigh, indicating his pride in what he had achieved.

It was Thursday afternoon the start of the weekend in the Arab world. As usual Nicolas was working at his desk on his 'Baby'. Suddenly he joyfully announced;

"I don't believe what I have done. Loulou, no one will believe what I have made."

"Is it finished yet?" Laura asked enthusiastically.

"It was finished long time, but you know love there are many ways to use it, many things to build from it. That is what I am figuring, and it's unbelievable."

Laura had no idea how this invention would work as it was designed in such a way that only Nicolas held the key; only he would be able to fathom its secrets. To Laura or anyone else who looked, all they would see was a jumble of drawings. Without Nicolas's brain, no one would be able to decipher the meaning. It was the way he wanted it; ensuring no one would ever be able to steal his idea, even if they had all the drawings in their hands. Laura's belief in Nicolas was as strong as his belief in himself; she would devotedly support whatever he decided to undertake.

That night after dinner, he decided to go into one of the chatrooms on the internet. Nicolas got immense enjoyment from debating and discussing politics or philosophy with other Arabic speaking people around the world. It enabled him to gage people's thoughts on the political state of the Middle Eastern region. He never gave out his true identity, always going under the guise of his pseudo name Kousbawi. Frequently he would be asked questions, or to advise and give his views on precarious political topics. Many times while debating, Nicolas would refer to his vast library.

As she now witnessed for herself, Laura understood his need to be so meticulous about his library. Being able to instantly put his hand on the book he required, and read passages or comment on certain texts, was crucial during these politically orientated, sometimes heated discussions. Nicolas was much in demand as a speaker, and it was obvious to Laura he was in his element when passing on his much sought after expertise and wisdom. He had people hanging on his every word. Often these talks would go on for hours, sometimes late into the night. Tonight was one such occasion. Laura lay in bed with the bedroom door open, listening to the hypnotic tone of his voice which eventually lulled her to sleep.

Surprisingly, Nicolas never lost his cool or raised his voice in anger during these debates; fully confident he had the upper hand when it came to being knowledgeable on a subject. Invariably he would talk till four in the morning, having taken total control of the chatroom. People were so keen to hear him speak; they were reluctant to let him go. Nicolas was gifted in being able to enthral an audience.

People were spellbound by his unique flair with words and natural charisma. Not speaking Arabic, Laura couldn't appreciate these brilliant discussions and speeches by her husband. But even without understanding the language, the way Nicolas delivered his words was mesmerising.

Later that week he arrived back to the house with something on his mind. Straight away Laura picked up on the vibes. Concerned she asked;

"What's wrong?"

"Nothing love, I'm just tired, and it's very hot outside."

Laura wasn't fooled by her husband's flippant answer; he was clearly ill at ease. Nicky was deep in thought as he ritualistically washed his hands before changing into more comfortable attire. Laura fetched him a clean white T-shirt and his cotton sarong. When it was just the two of them in the house, he preferred to dress in this comfortable relaxed fashion. It was nearing the end of August and unbearably humid. The temperature would reach a suffocating 45 to 50 degrees. The house was relatively cool, but Nicolas insisted on having the air conditioning on full blast; he feared the humidity would ruin his books. Being a chilly mortal, Laura hated the AC, and would often switch it off for a short while when Nicolas wasn't at home.

While sipping his cold beer Nicky checked the news for any development on the political front. They made a light lunch, and once he was more relaxed, Laura again asked if everything was okay. Nicky began to explain;

"You know love I was planning to demolish this house, and rebuild it again on two levels?" It was an idea they had briefly discussed some months back.

"Yes I remember. Are you planning to start?" Laura inquired.

The rebuilding of their house was not the thought plaguing his mind. Nicolas took another mouthful of his sandwich, keeping Laura waiting for an answer. He did so repeatedly. This was Nicolas's usual way of stalling while he figured what he was going to say.

"Fetch me another beer and I will explain," he said,

stalling again. Laura fetched the beer and handed him a glass. Nicky refused the glass;

"No I will drink from the can, you cleaned it yes?"

Laura always scrubbed the beer and Pepsi cans before putting them in the fridge to ensure they were clean as Nicky had a thing about germs. He would insist telling her;

"You never know who has handled them."

Laura sat at the table opposite her husband, and waited for him to continue with what he was saying;

"As I said," he started, "I have plans to rebuild the house." Nicky took another sip from his beer; "But first I have to renew the lease."

"When does it run out?" Laura asked.

"In two months'." Nicky replied casually lighting a cigarette.

Laura gave him a quizzical look;

"Only two months? Is there likely to be a problem with the renewal?"

"No problem," Nicky said, calmly dragging on his cigarette. "But the guy who owns it, you know the local who owns all the land here, he wants to demolish the area, and build something else."

"Oh I see. Then we will have to move?"

Laura felt a tinge of relief at the prospect of moving out of the isolated 'Cave'. Nicolas on the other hand loved the house, but then he did get to go outside of it twice a day. She never complained, but Laura hated the isolation and loneliness. When Nicky was at work, at times it was too much. Laura equated the claustrophobic sensations she sometimes felt, as being like a frog trapped in a dry well.

Nicky got up from the dining table and strolled to the lounge. Laura followed, and they sat down together. Nicky took hold of Laura's hand;

"No love, we will go to the court and get an extension on the lease, me and the other leaseholders."

"Can you be sure they will agree to renew the lease?" Laura asked sceptically.

Nicky lit another cigarette.

216

"They will. They did last time." His words carried the usual unshakably confident air.

Laura gave a surprised look;

"Last time?" she exclaimed. "What do you mean last time? Last time when?"

Nicky dragged hard on his cigarette;

"Six months ago," he reluctantly admitted.

Laura was taken aback; astonished by his confession.

"You mean six months ago you knew this?"

"Yep!" he told her with a wry smile.

"And you didn't think to mention it?"

"Yeah so? None of your business." It was what Nicky always said when faced with a question or situation he preferred not to explain.

"None of my business?" she repeated with dismay. "I live here too don't I?"

Laura stared incredulously at her husband; aggrieved he had taken the decision not to share something that clearly affected them both. Not telling Laura was Nicolas's way of protecting her. In his defence, he had hoped to resolve everything without the need to unduly worry his wife. But now the situation had become critical he couldn't keep it secret from her any longer. Nicky could see Laura was annoyed at being kept in the dark. He smiled reassuringly; with rugged determination he told her;

"Nothing to worry Loulou, I'm fixing everything love," adding with cool assertion, "Don't worry, Hajj will fix it."

"And what if you can't?" Laura was never quite as confident.

"Then we have plan B," he assured boldly.

"What's plan B?" Laura probed.

Nicky stood up from his seat;

"Plan B is plan B," he answered coolly stubbing out his cigarette in the silver ashtray on the sideboard.

Clearly he was not going to elaborate further. Laura had the distinct impression there was no plan B in place; not yet anyway.

"You should have told me about this when you applied

for the extension six months ago," she criticized.

Nicolas gave Laura a stern look; he hated having to explain his motives.

"Love, why do I have to tell you? To make you worry when I am fixing it?" He glared annoyed by her criticism. "There is not a problem," he affirmed.

"And if there was, would you tell me?" she questioned back at him.

"No!" Nicolas's answer was firm but honest.

As a husband Nicolas did not fall short; whatever the problem, whether big or small, he would never shy from his responsibility. Laura understood his wish to protect her, but she disagreed with Nicolas's obstinate insistence to carry the weight of every problem alone. She adamantly maintained;

"You should have told me."

With the heat, and the tenuous situation of the house, and now Laura's criticizing his decisions, Nicolas was becoming irritated. The smile slipped from his face. He gave Laura one of his looks, the one he gave to anyone daring to question his actions. Although annoyed with him, Laura felt herself recoil from his penetrating gaze.

"So if I told you what would you do?" he scowled.

"Well I don't know," she said meekly. "But at least I could share it with you."

"Why! So that two people have to worry. What exactly does that achieve?" his tone was scathing, he scowled again at her.

Reluctant to antagonise him further, Laura stayed silent. He would never say it, but Nicolas was seriously concerned at the prospect of losing the lease on the land. The isolation of the house meant no one could easily find him unless he wanted them to. Faced with the possibility of having to move from this secluded hideaway, was unsettling for him, a fact he refused to disclose to his wife. Nicky took a cigarette from the packet of Marlborough on the table. After lighting it he turned to face Laura;

"So now you want me to tell you all my problems?" he

shook his head disapprovingly. "You can't solve this!"

Nicolas used anger to deflect Laura from his growing uneasiness with the unfolding situation of the lease. With exaggerated rage his eyes bore into her.

"I am the man, I will solve it, got it?"

His hostile reaction had the desired effect. Nicolas effectively concealed his apprehension. Laura now felt bad for mistrusting her husband's ability to take care of things.

"GOT IT?" he repeated louder, demanding she answer him.

"Yes okay, I get it," she answered him submissively, wishing she had not pushed the issue.

Laura was no fool; she knew her husband well enough to realise he often used anger as a way to disguise what was really bothering him. Content that he had managed to curtail Laura's questioning, Nicolas sat down again and switched on the TV. Laura cleared the table and washed the dishes from lunch. She resolved not to speak on the subject again unless her husband initiated it.

Nicolas sat flicking through the TV channels; his mood had lightened. Laura went to the lounge and took a seat beside him. Turning to face her, Nicolas deliberately faked a scowling expression pretending to still be angry. Laura could at times make his blood boil, but he never stayed angry with her for long; though he would pretend to be. Laura smiled coyly. Unable to keep up the pretence, and in a mocking but undeniably affectionate tone he declared;

"Bloody woman! Always pushing, always wanting to know everything!" Nicky switched off the TV and took Laura's hand. "Plan A," he started. "I need to sleep for one hour."

"Okay I will wake you in an hour with your coffee," Laura said cheerily.

Nicolas stood up flamboyantly discarding his sarong to reveal his obvious arousal in all its glory.

"Plan B, Loulou I wanna fuck you." He then boldly proclaimed;

"Loulou, I think we will go straight to plan B."

KOUSBAWI

Chapter 27: A Little Piece of Heaven

Laura's UAE visitor's visa was due for renewal. Nicolas's papers still hadn't arrived, so he wasn't at liberty to add Laura to his residence visa just yet. Laura's mother had been taken ill with what was thought to be Parkinson's disease, rather than get the court to stamp her visa, it was decided Laura would take a trip back to the UK for a few weeks. Laura was keen to spend time with her sick mother, as well as check all was okay with Alyssa and the house. Nicolas arranged Laura's ticket; she would fly back the following weekend. Constantly sat at the back of Laura's mind, was the worry that the lease on the land where the house (Cave) was situated, may not be renewed.

It was no secret Laura was not enamoured with the place. Locally named as Mussafah Sanaya, this predominately male occupied industrial area was she believed, the reason Nicolas refused to allow her to go out alone. Laura was confident she would have more freedom once they moved to a more residential area. Despite her desire to leave the 'Cave', she knew Nicky was reluctant to vacate the area that afforded him the privacy and seclusion he enjoyed. Plus, if the lease was refused, it would be a headache for him to find storage for everything in the vast warehouse.

On the surface Nicolas remained upbeat and positive; but underneath that façade of certainty, Laura was only too aware that her husband would be desperately trying to find a solution. The look he portrayed to others was that he was gliding effortlessly through any setback, but like a swan that appears to glide serenely along, beneath the surface Nicolas too was paddling like mad to keep himself afloat.

Until now, their married life had been relatively trouble free. Laura said nothing of her fears about the lease to Nicolas, mindful not to let him see she was worried. But it was like a dark cloud descending on an otherwise beautiful sunny day. Truly convinced they would be granted a reprieve of two to six months, Nicolas was confident he would have enough time to look for a suitable residence.

Before leaving for the UK, Laura packed up all of her belongings into boxes, bags and suitcases. Convinced there was still plenty of time, Nicky said it wasn't necessary; he would arrange everything himself. Laura was a little more sceptical of the outcome. If things didn't go to plan, she knew Nicky would have enough on his plate, without the added hassle of packing up all her stuff. It was Laura's way of trying to make life a little easier in case anything happened while she was away.

On the day she left for the airport, Laura had a funny feeling in the pit of her stomach; she would not be going back to the 'Cave' on her return. She kept this thought to herself. Less than a week later, her intuition proved correct. While talking with Nicolas via Skype video, he broke the news to her that they had lost the appeal.

"How long do we have?" Laura asked.

"Two weeks," Nicky revealed.

Uncharacteristically, he didn't even attempt to hide the fact he was gutted at not being granted more time. Laura felt hugely disappointed for him. As much as she was keen to move from the 'Cave', Laura was acutely aware Nicky had banked on a different outcome to the court's decision. He tried to be his usual positive self, but it was the first time Laura had ever seen a chink in his armour; her husband looked and sounded so defeated.

Nicolas hated to lose at anything. If ever things went belly-up, he always had several back up plans. Clearly he had not expected such a short term of notice to vacate the premises, and there was no such plan in place. To her utter dismay Laura discovered this was the third occasion in which Nicolas and the other lease holders had applied for an extension on their land leases. They had all been informed by the land owner that he wished to demolish the area, over a year ago. Twice before the court had granted a reprieve; it wasn't likely to happen a third time.

Typically Nicolas had been a little too optimistic that he could turn things around at the eleventh hour. Not so this time; as the saying goes, the fat lady had well and truly sung, done her encore, and left the building. Nicolas tried to make light of the situation, but two weeks was not very long in which to find new accommodation.

He had hoped for enough time to sort his residence papers and look for a villa. A villa would be a long term commitment and he wanted to take his time in finding one that properly suited their needs. With so little time Nicolas would look for somewhere temporary, until they were ready to commit to a more permanent dwelling. Besides, while the issue of his passport and papers etc. remained unresolved, a villa was not viable. One more year was all Nicolas required, one year and everything would be in his hand; if only he were granted more time. Once again the uninvited fickle hand of fate was knocking a little too loudly at his door.

As they talked on skype Laura sensed the tension in his voice. He denied it, but Laura could see he was worried. He may fool others, but Laura knew Nicolas too well. He smiled and joked playfully with her, but Laura saw another story reflected in his dark eyes. What his smile concealed his eyes couldn't help revealing.

"Do you want me to come back now?" Laura asked.

"What for?" As usual Nicky stubbornly insisted he could manage.

"To help you pack everything up." Laura was ready to take the next flight; he only had to say the word.

"No love, I have people to do that. Better you stay there till I find somewhere to live," he insisted.

Laura desperately wanted to support her husband at this uncertain time, but Nicolas was right; there was nothing Laura could help with that he couldn't arrange by himself. She would only be in the way, and a distraction. Better she stay put until he found somewhere. If push came to shove, he would put everything in storage and bunk down at a friend's. With Laura in tow, it would be more complicated.

Within a week Nicolas had removed everything from the house as well as the warehouse. He put everything into a shipping container he had previously acquired and had been keeping on a friend's property. For a while Nicolas had been storing things there; collecting items he wished to eventually ship to Lebanon; things intended for their eventual villa there. Once all the legalities were in order, this was Nicolas's long term plan. He had discussed with Laura many times his plans of retiring to Lebanon. Nicolas told her of the land in Kousba at the top of the mountain. He had shown her pictures on the internet of where he would one day build their home. It was Nicolas's dream that he and Laura would grow old together in his mountain village.

Nicolas's dream quickly became Laura's. Many times they would laugh, imagining themselves in their twilight years. They imagined sitting on the balcony of their villa overlooking Kousba; very old but still very much in love.

Laura couldn't wait to see this land that held such a dominant place in her husband's heart. Nicolas told Laura his former girlfriend's and even his ex-wife Samra had been jealous of his love for Kousba and Lebanon.

"What about you love?" he once asked Laura. "Are you jealous of my love for the most beautiful place on earth?"

Laura's answer pleased Nicolas;

"How could I be jealous?" she told him. "Lebanon is part of you. I love you so I will love Lebanon."

Her sincere heartfelt statement warmed him immensely. Nicolas held Laura close.

"You know love, it's not just talk," he told her. "One day I will take you. Loulou you will see all of Lebanon's beauty for yourself."

There was no place on earth like Lebanon for Nicolas. He would talk of his country incessantly and with great pride, repeatedly boasting to Laura;

"We have there the best food, the best fashion, the best people the best everything. When God made the earth, he put a little piece of heaven and he call it Lebanon."

Aside from Laura, Nicolas's greatest love was clearly Lebanon. Their cultures may have been different, but Laura had nothing but admiration for her husband's patriotic love for his homeland; it made Nicolas the man he was, and Laura whole heartedly embraced it. When you truly love a person you must embrace everything about them.

Over the years Laura learnt much from Nicolas. He taught her many things, not least to be true to her heart. Patience though, was a virtue they both had to embrace. After waiting for years just to be together, they were still waiting to be free from the bureaucracy preventing Nicolas from enjoying the normalities of life others took for granted. At times Laura became frustrated with their less than ideal situation. At such times Nicolas would tell her;

"Everything happens for a reason Loulou, and in the right time."

Inspired by Nicolas's innate ability to see the positive in life, as his wise steadfast philosophy encouraged, Laura like him, began to trust and believe. Undoubtedly Nicolas was Laura's earth angel. It was therefore fitting he should hail from a heavenly place.

Laura couldn't wait to be shown this little piece of heaven on earth called Lebanon; the only place Nicolas would feel truly at home. But before realising this long awaited dream, Nicolas had a sworn vow to uphold. In his heart he craved freedom from this self-imposed burden, but in his mind Nicolas determined to maintain his honour and control his destiny. Both these objectives would come at a price for Kousbawi.

Chapter 28:
Out of the Cave into the Light

While in the UK Laura spent a good deal of time visiting her sick mother. She had become noticeably frailer since Laura's last trip back. Almost every day Laura took the fifteen minute walk to her mother's house. She would often stop at the local shop to buy a cake, or a packet of her mother's favourite biscuits. They would chat over a cup of tea, and if the weather was nice enough, Laura encouraged her mother to sit outside. Normally her mother would have initiated the idea of sitting in the garden, but since the onset of her illness, she had developed an unusual aversion, refusing even to open windows or doors. She had acquired a weird phobia of insects entering the house. Laura tried to persuade her mother that these fears were irrational.

Diagnosing her with Parkinson's disease, the doctor prescribed what was considered appropriate medication. Laura's mother obsessively read every piece of literature on her supposed illness, typically picking up on all the negative aspects. This resulted in her becoming terrified at the prospect of living with an, as yet incurable disease. Despite being told she was in the very early stages of the illness, Laura's mother feared its progression, failing to see anything positive in her future. Consequently she fell into depression; repeatedly proclaiming she had no desire to face what she considered a hopeless bleak future. Laura was not entirely convinced Parkinson's was the correct diagnoses. Apart from a slight shake in her left hand, Laura's mother displayed few other symptoms, but she was increasingly delusional. Laura suspected her mother's delusions and odd behaviour, was more in line with a form of dementia.

Laura and her sister, tried to persuade their mother to

seek a second medical opinion. This was to no avail, as their mother refused point blank to entertain the idea of seeing a different doctor. Frustrated by her stubbornness, Laura attempted to arrange a home visit by another doctor. Unfortunately without her consent, which her mother naturally refused to give, this couldn't be accomplished.

Beset by an increasingly depressed mind-set, Laura's mother had become resigned to feelings of hopelessness, insisting there was no point in seeking another opinion as nothing could be done for her. Laura felt she was banging her head against a brick wall; her mother flatly refused to listen to reason. After a visit, Laura would invariably leave feeling drained and somewhat depressed herself.

On subsequent visits, Laura suggested to her mother that perhaps she should refrain from reading too much about the illness. Indicative of her mother's nature, she tended to focus on all the negativities. Laura's mother had always been inclined to emphasize what could go wrong rather than focus on the positive. Her mother's rapid decline and obstinate refusal to seek help had a knock on effect. Before long Laura began to feel some of those negative emotions creep into her own psyche.

Laura took refuge in her conversations with Nicolas. He was a Godsend, knowing exactly the right thing to say. His way of looking at life was in contrast to her mother's. Even the sound of his voice had an immediate uplifting effect on Laura's mood. With everything he was himself facing, Nicolas continued to be a pillar of strength; a solid rock Laura could always lean on. Never once did he say he was too busy to listen to her, or that he had problems of his own.

On the contrary, regardless of what he was dealing with, Nicolas was there for Laura. Difficulties that might otherwise overwhelm, he helped her cope with. Like a beacon of light, Nicolas provided a place of emotional safety where Laura could seek sanctuary from life's storms. After a dose of Nicolas's positivity, Laura felt balanced and recharged; ready to face whatever life threw.

Equally supportive, Laura provided Nicolas with the unconditional love he had sought since childhood; she saw him as he wished to be seen. He knew Laura loved and accepted him, even at times when he wasn't particularly lovable, or behaving in an acceptable manner. With Laura he could just be himself without fear of rejection. Her non-judgmental approach encouraged his volatile temperament to calm. Laura's open hearted vulnerability brought out his protective side; a role he felt happy and comfortable with.

People had unfairly judged Nicolas in the past, likening him to a walking time bomb. As a young man growing up in Kousba some people had written him off, proclaiming he was nothing but a trouble maker. With no formal schooling or education and with such an explosive hot temper, they predicted he would most likely spend half his life in jail. Unable to see beyond Nicolas's seemingly self-destructive image, they wrongly prophesized he had no future. His unwillingness to conform never worried Laura.

What others saw as non-conformity she saw as strength of character. Nicolas's impulsiveness and risk taking, was in Laura's eyes courageous. Nicolas had a fun daring side to his personality that Laura admired. As for his lack of education, nothing could have been further from the truth. Nicolas was living proof that there's much more to gaining an education than robotically memorising information to pass exams just to acquire a certificate, a piece of paper that tells everyone you are educated. Although it clearly wasn't for him, in some ways Nicolas admired people with the mind-set to buckle down and conform. Deep down though, Nicolas also believed conformity meant willingly bowing to the pressure of society's tight control. Definitely not for him!

The deadline to vacate the house in Mussafah was fast approaching. Laura did her best not to allow the worry of the situation to consume her. Instead she trusted Nicolas would find a place in time. As it turned out she didn't have to wait too long for that trust to be rewarded. That evening when he called, Laura could tell by the upbeat tone in his voice Nicolas had good news. A Lebanese friend had for some time been renting an apartment in Mussafah that he rarely used. Tony's work took him away, sometimes for weeks at a time, to the desert and other parts of the Emirates. Hearing about Nicolas's desperate situation, he offered to accommodate them at his apartment where he had a spare double bedroom. Tony told Nicolas;

"You and your wife are welcome to use the apartment for as long as you need."

"What's it like?" Laura asked excitedly.

"Beautiful," Nicky told her. "It's not exactly what I'm looking for long term, but its okay until we find a villa. Loulou it will give us some time."

With being homeless now no longer an issue, there was breathing space and the pressure was off. A lifeline thrown at the eleventh hour meant Nicolas could relax and look for a villa at his leisure. Nicolas worked tirelessly over the next few days moving everything into the new residence. He insisted on paying the full rent to his friend in advance. It was agreed that Tony would retain his room there for use between jobs, and his frequent travels to and from Lebanon. Nicky insisted Laura stay in the UK for another week or two, just while he properly settled in. The apartment had nothing in the way of furniture, and no internet connection. They would temporarily have to forgo their nightly chats on Skype until Nicolas had things up and running.

Exactly two weeks later Laura was on her way back to Abu Dhabi. She couldn't wait to see the new apartment. It was dark when her plane landed just before 9pm. She was met as usual by Nicolas whose friend Asma had driven him to the airport. Laura had met Asma several times, being as he worked for Nicolas and had been a witness to their marriage. Asma spoke little or no English, barely enough to ask Laura how she was, and to say, 'welcome back to Abu Dhabi'.

Fifteen minutes or so later, they were pulling up in front of a five storey residential block. Being only twenty minutes' drive, the new residence was closer to the airport than the 'Cave' had been. Asma helped Nicolas take Laura's bags from the car, and obligingly carried them inside. Even though it was dark, Laura could tell this part of Mussafah was very different from the location of the 'Cave'. As they entered into the buildings reception, a watchman greeted Nicolas. Asma insisted he carry the suitcase to the elevator. Nicolas thanked him and said goodnight, then quickly ushered Laura into the lift. Stepping into the mirrored elevator Laura asked;

"What floor is it?"

Nicky gave her the usual teasing reply,

"None of your business."

Reluctant to touch anything used by the general public with his bare hand, Nicolas used his door key to press the elevator button. Because of his germ phobia, when out and about in public, Nicolas would make sure he held his worry beads in his right hand, wrapping them around his fingers ready to use as a legitimate obstruction against any unwanted possibly germ contaminating, full on handshake.

The lift doors opened and they got out at the third level. Nicky made a left turn and Laura followed him along the marble tiled corridor. At the end of the passage next to the fire escape, Nicolas put down Laura's suitcase in front of a large wooden door. He then unlocked it telling Laura;

"This is it, Loulou."

He turned on the light switch and hurriedly steered Laura through the large door, gently pushing her quickly inside the hallway. Laura put down her bags and looked around. Directly to the right of the hall was a moderate sized kitchen, and to the left of it, a cloakroom. Past the kitchen a long passage led to the two double bedrooms, one being Tony's, with the main bathroom at the far end. Opposite, at the other end of the passage and to the left of the hall, a large doorway led into a huge reception room. To the back of the kitchen via a glass door, was a balcony. Laura became excited at the prospect of having a balcony. Disappointingly, on closer inspection it revealed itself to be rather small with not much room for anything other than a washing line. The balcony looked over an alleyway that ran between the residential buildings. There was no view other than the adjacent apartment block. To Laura's consequent delight though, the apartment had big windows ensuring plenty of natural light during daytime hours.

There was nothing at all in the apartment when Nicolas arrived. He had fitted it out with all the appliances and his own furniture, including two large fridge freezers brought from the 'Cave'. He had fitted a new washing machine, a new gas cooker and microwave oven. All the furniture in the lounge was new, including an impressive flat large screen TV. A long sofa in a pretty shade of eggshell blue was placed along the wall underneath the widow, with a matching arm chair positioned so it directly faced the TV. Naturally this would be Nicolas's chair. A very large square coffee table, a dining table and four chairs were all new editions. All of the new furniture Laura recognised; it had been in storage in the warehouse behind the 'Cave'. Nicolas's desk with his laptop was in the corner of the room, plus a brand new printer and scanner. Standing on top of a cabinet beside the television, was the all-important glass vase containing the precious earth from Nicolas's village in Lebanon.

A few favourite books along with some framed family photos, adorned the shelves above his desk. The majority of his book collection was still unpacked, stored in boxes distributed in various locations around the room. Nicolas had brought the huge wrought iron bed with the beautiful ivory coloured bedroom furniture from the 'Cave'. He had now added the matching wardrobes that were previously in storage. Unlike the 'Cave' with its low wood beamed ceilings, the new apartment had very high ceilings giving a light airy open feel to the place. White Marble flooring ran throughout. Nicky was keen to get Laura's approval;

"What do you think Loulou, its okay for now?"

"It's great!" Laura assured. "Thank God you found somewhere."

Although there were many unpacked boxes the place was very liveable.

"We will have a drink then sleep, okay Loulou?"

Nicky changed out of his shirt and jeans into his preferred attire for relaxing in; a white vest top and his comfy white cotton sarong, wrapped loosely around his naked lower half. He poured a large whisky and a glass of wine for Laura. It was a relief to relax. A very uncertain period was thankfully over; the stress had mentally exhausted them both.

The tension and fatigue visibly lifted from Nicky's face, as he further relaxed, enjoying his reunion with Laura in their new abode. The edginess in his mood that surfaced when things were more dubious was gone. Nicolas was back in the driver's seat; back in control, which was always his favourite place to be. Now able to exhibit a calmer disposition, his sense of humour was uninhibited and back in full throttle. Mischievously he inquired;

"Did you see the bedroom Loulou?"

"Yes, briefly." She answered.

"Let's go and take another look," he said winking as he directed her to follow him. "You have to see it properly," he smiled cheekily. Continuing in a playful tone he then asked Laura;

"Did you see the new wardrobe Loulou, its beautiful right?" Nicolas pointed like a child.

Not entirely sure where his absurd conversation was leading, Laura humoured him.

"No, you had it in storage, remember?"

"And the dressing table you saw it before I think; right Loulou?" He continued with the nonsensical banter.

Patiently Laura played along with her husband's bizarre dialogue.

"Yes, we had it at the old house."

Displaying an irreverently naughty expression, Nicky untied his sarong proudly showing off a very conspicuous erection.

"And what about this Loulou, did you see it before?"

"Oh wow! Yes I think I may have seen that before," Laura laughed.

"Come and have a closer look to be sure," Nicolas insisted, impatiently pulling Laura to the bed, where he proceeded to celebrate the new dwelling in the appropriate manner.

The following day Laura could survey the apartment in daylight. As she opened the drapes she was blinded by the enormous amount of light that came streaming in. It was so different from the dark 'Cave'; they had literally gone from one extreme to the other. Laura smiled at the irony of having to keep the drapes closed at certain times of the day, because too much light flooded in. Also the apartment was warmer, even with the air conditioning on, unlike the 'Cave', which sometimes felt like the North Pole when Nicky insisted having the AC on full blast.

Laura had a good feeling that things were on the up. Once settled in their new surroundings, she had renewed hope for the future. She decided to give the apartment a thorough clean. Although Nicky had cleaned everything when he moved in, the place was very dusty due the area. Abu Dhabi could be rather dusty, but Mussafah was so much worse. With its hidden location, 'The Cave' had been more protected from the environment. After she had finished cleaning the kitchen and bathroom, Laura stopped to make coffee.

Nicky was sat at his desk working on his project. Laura wanted to wash the floor but needed to vacuum it first. She was concerned the noise would disturb his concentration.

"It's okay", Nicky told her. "I'm going to stop with this now. But love you don't have to do everything in one day, take it easy. You want me to help you Loulou?"

Laura smiled at her husband's generosity, but declined his offer. It didn't take too long to clean. When she'd finished Laura happily informed Nicky;

"This place is so much easier to clean than the 'Cave',"

"The Cave?" Nicky repeated in a surprised tone.

Nicolas gave an incredulous look; shocked at Laura's

unflattering reference to their old house.

"I loved that house and you calling it the Cave," he retorted.

Laura giggled as she realised Nicky had not been aware of her nickname for their old residence. Aiming to justify her less-than-complimentary description Laura explained;

"Well, it was hidden away in the middle of nowhere, and it was so dark, it felt like living in a cave."

Nicolas pretended to scowl. He may have loved the old house, but Laura never felt comfortable, especially when alone. While Nicolas was out at work, Laura was always restless until he came home. The obscurity and isolation may have suited him, but Laura was never at ease with it. She never even knew the address of the old house; Nicolas told her she didn't need to know its whereabouts. Instead of telling her the address, he gave Laura a list of people she could call in an emergency if unable to contact him. Sometimes Laura wondered if her not knowing the address was perhaps Nicolas's way of insuring she didn't take a taxi alone anywhere.

A few years back, Laura was in the 'Cave' making her morning coffee. Nicky was out at a meeting somewhere. Suddenly there was a very loud knock at the door. At first Laura thought it was Nicky who had perhaps forgotten his keys. She was about to call out to him, but stopped herself. She reasoned if it was Nicky, he would have called her mobile to say it was him.

Whenever anyone visited the 'Cave', they would call Nicolas's mobile to say they were outside. He would go out through the warehouse to let them in. In order for anyone to knock the door of the hidden house, someone would first have to breach the securely locked metal door then walk the length of the warehouse, before reaching the entrance of the concealed dwelling. Repeatedly Nicky had told Laura she was never to answer the door to anyone, even if he was there with her. He was adamant she adhere to this rule. Frozen with fear Laura called Nicky's mobile to inform him someone was banging on the house door.

Nicolas told Laura to remain quiet, and lock herself in the bedroom.

"I'm on my way," he told her.

Laura went quickly to the bedroom as her husband instructed, and locked herself in. Eventually the banging stopped. Whoever was there appeared to have given up and left. Highly unnerved, Laura stayed put until Nicky arrived. Less than ten minutes later he was there. Laura was shaken by the episode; even though Nicolas reassured her everything was okay.

Despite his reassurances to Laura, Nicolas was greatly disturbed that someone had infiltrated his private domain while his wife was alone inside. Without disclosing his fears to Laura he reinforced the locks, and thought to set up a security camera. Although he had put his wife's mind at rest, it didn't escape Laura's notice that soon after the incident Nicky placed a large machete on a shelf above the door.

Nicolas may have loved his secret hideaway, but Laura was much happier being out of the dark lonely isolation of the 'Cave'.

KOUSBAWI

Chapter 29:
Fairy Lights and Champagne

With Christmas just around the corner, Nicolas suggested they put the tree up. Laura was in the kitchen washing the fruit Nicolas had bought at the market earlier that day. There was so much; Nicky never purchased anything in small quantities. Laura decided to make a fruit salad snack. Nicolas loved fruit and constantly tried to persuade Laura to eat more. She wasn't a big fruit eater like him, but Nicky always brought home such a delicious variety.

It was Thursday afternoon the start of the weekend in the Emirates. From time to time there would be the occasional meeting to attend, but mainly from Thursday lunchtime till Saturday morning Nicolas would be free. He fetched down the box containing the Christmas tree from the top of the wardrobe. While Laura was preparing the fruit, he began assembling the tree. Laura took two bowls containing fresh kiwi, strawberries, sliced apple, banana, red grapes and peach slices to the lounge. Nicolas had finished erecting the tree and was busy testing the lights. Thankfully they were in good working order. Nicky placed the tree on a low table by the window. He then proceeded to distribute the lights onto it which took him all of five seconds. Satisfied with his arrangement of the lights Nicolas stood back. Taking a bowl of fruit from Laura's hand he told her;

"We will decorate it this evening with the champagne."

Decorating the tree together was an intimate little ritual they both enjoyed. It had become a Christmas tradition that every year they would celebrate the act with a bottle of Moet Chandon. Whilst visiting Alyssa before Christmas one year, Laura had failed to get booked onto her planned flight back to Abu Dhabi. Being as it was the busiest time of year, Laura didn't manage to secure a seat on a flight until the night before Christmas Eve. Nicolas wouldn't decorate the tree without Laura. So that year although Nicky put it up, the tree didn't get decorated until the last moment on Christmas Eve.

They sat down to eat their fruit snack. Laura looked at the tree. She smiled at the way Nicky had positioned the lights onto it. It was the same every year, too many lights bunched together in one place and great big gaps where there were none at all. There wasn't much Nicky couldn't turn his hand to, but he just didn't have the same artistic flare as Laura when it came to decorating the Christmas tree. This year he had placed all of the lights at the front, leaving the sides completely bare. Of course Nicky saw nothing wrong with his effort, but Laura was determined to rearrange the lights when he wasn't looking.

This little scenario played out every year. Laura didn't know if her husband was aware she changed his lighting arrangement; if Nicky did notice he never said anything. Sometimes he would place the lights so haphazardly Laura wasn't sure if he had done it on purpose.

For the rest of that afternoon Nicky was glued to his laptop checking out antique websites. Over the years he had developed quite an interest in antiques, and become fairly knowledgeable on the subject. Keen to know what was holding her husband's attention so devotedly, Laura leant over his shoulder to look. Affectionately placing her arm around him she asked;

"So is there anything of interest there?"

"Yeah love, many things," Nicky told her. He then unexpectedly announced, "I'm thinking to start a business with antiques."

Laura knew her husband had a fondness for antiques, but the idea of starting a business, came right out of the blue. This was the first time he had revealed any such inclination to her. But as per usual, Nicolas only ever enlightened Laura to ideas when he was sure it was viable.

"Really?" she said, surprised by his declaration. "When did you decide this?"

The idea had been mulling around his head for a while, but it was only now Nicky felt he could successfully pull it off.

"I've been thinking some time now to start something different. I think antiques will be a good business here, we will do it together. What do you think Loulou?"

Laura was momentarily taken aback. Nicolas talked of doing many things, but antiques weren't something she envisioned he would start a business with.

"But I don't know about antiques," Laura confessed.

"I'll teach you," he proclaimed confidently.

Laura gave her husband a sceptical look. He leant back nonchalantly rocking and swivelling in the black leather desk chair. Then sitting quickly up again, he put his arm around Laura's waist. Grinning at her like a Cheshire cat he cheekily stated;

"You know plenty about antiques." He winked at her. "You know why Loulou?"

"No Nicky, why don't you tell me," Laura said wearily, waiting for his rather predictable witty comeback.

"Because Loulou, you are one." He laughed at his own lame humour declaring; "I'm such a lovely boy."

"Oh ha ha, you're very funny Nicky!" Laura retorted pretending to be offended. "But just remember you are older than me." Then countering with caustic humour she told him; "You're right though, I probably do know a lot about antiques; after all I've been living with one for years."

"Ah you think yourself funny? Shut up your face and make me coffee," Nicky retorted light-heartedly.

Laura gave a satisfied smile knowing she had outwitted him. Sharing as they did a similar sense of humour both enjoyed playing with it, and took immense pleasure in teasing the other. Carefree banter was a common daily factor in their relationship which they mutually delighted in. Laura went to make Nicky's coffee.

"Just a small one!" he shouted after her.

"What shall I make for dinner tonight?" Laura asked as

she placed his coffee in front of him.

Engrossed with looking at antiques he didn't answer.

This is typical Laura thought to herself; whenever Nicky was fixated on something new, she may as well be invisible.

"If I could have your attention for just a moment," she uttered with more than a tinge of sarcasm.

Preoccupied, Nicky wasn't concentrating on Laura's words and totally ignored her in favour of his antiques. She repeated the question of what to make for dinner. Conscious Laura had spoken, but without looking away from his computer screen he muttered;

"Whaa…h?"

"Dinner!" Laura exclaimed with obvious annoyance. "Well, what shall I make?"

Again there was no reply to her question. Nicky was far too absorbed with his new project. Laura picked up the TV remote and sat down in Nicolas's favourite chair. Just as in the 'Cave', Nicolas had one particular chair he favoured, and was reluctant to sit anywhere else. His special chair was like his Throne; it dominated the best position for watching TV and was always the most comfortable. When Nicky wasn't using it Laura would steal it for herself.

Laura huffed loudly, and randomly flicked through the TV channels. She had no real interest to watch anything, but continued to flick through the channels in a determined huffy manner in a bid to demonstrate her growing irritation at being ignored. It worked; Nicky leant back in his chair and looked over. Laura pretended not to notice him and carried on staring blankly at the television. With an air of candid innocence he asked;

"Yeah love, what did you say?"

Laura turned her head to face him. Even when he was being his most irritating she couldn't resist his ingenuous boyish charm and smile.

"Dinner!" Laura repeated. "What shall I make?"

His reply was less than helpful;

"Loulou, make whatever you want." Then with irony

he stated;

"Loulou you're the boss."

"Oh yeah, really? As if," Laura said dryly, as she got up from her seat to go to the kitchen.

As she passed by him, Nicky grabbed Laura's hand pulling her to his lap.

"You know Loulou I believe antiques will be good business for us." His enthusiasm sparkled right out of his eyes; "Yeah Loulou, I believe we're gonna make good money with this."

Whenever Nicky had a notion to do something new, he was like an excited little boy discovering a new toy. The childlike positivity he exuded was infectious; you could almost touch the ideas working inside his head. The difference between Nicolas and other mere mortals was his gifted vision to see potential where others couldn't; above all he had the courage to take a risk.

As much as Laura would love to stay in his arms and wax lyrical, dinner wasn't going to cook itself. Dragging herself up, Laura reluctantly continued to the kitchen. She opened the cupboards and pondered what to make. Staring at the ingredients Laura waited for a flash of inspiration. Nicky was suddenly behind her. His unexpected presence made Laura jump. Placing his hand on her shoulder he gently squeezed it saying;

"You know what I fancy Loulou?"

"Yeah I can guess," Laura teased. "But I have to make dinner."

A mischievous smile crept across Nicky's face.

"Yeah, but you know what else I fancy? M'dardarah, Loulou make M'dardarah."

One of Nicky's favourite Lebanese dishes, M'dardarah was made with rice and lentils. Laura agreed;

"Okay, that's what we shall have then."

"Loulou, do you need anything from outside?" Nicky asked.

"No, I have everything," Laura confirmed gathering the ingredients together.

It was one of the things Laura enjoyed about living in a residential area, if they ran out of anything Nicky would call the local supermarket and a boy would bring it to the door within minutes. It was a normal part of Emirati life.

Because of their traditional pre-Christmas celebration of decorating the tree, they would eat earlier this evening around 8.30pm; usually it was nine or even ten o'clock before they sat down to eat. Laura had just finished cooking when there was a knock at the door. Nicky still wouldn't allow her to answer it, except on very rare occasions. For instance, if they were expecting company and only then if the person expected called to say they were already outside. Nobody just arrived without calling first. It was an unwritten law everyone adhered to. While Nicolas answered the door, Laura took her opportunity to adjust the Christmas tree lights. Nicky opened the door to a boy from the store delivering his packs of Marlborough cigarettes. He would usually purchase 600 at a time. Laura continued fussing with the tree lights while Nicky paid the boy, and put his stash of cigarettes away in the kitchen. After distributing the lights more evenly, Laura stood back to check. Satisfied with the result Laura went back to the kitchen to prepare to serve their evening meal.

Both being as sneaky as each other, while Laura was out of the kitchen Nicolas had decided to inspect Laura's cooking. He wasn't disappointed; to his delight, as usual Laura had cooked the M'dardarah exactly as he liked it. Nicolas was amazed how quickly Laura had become so accomplished at cooking his favourite Lebanese dishes. Laura walked into the kitchen and caught him having a sly taste;

"Leave it! I'm just about to dish up," she ordered.

"Umm, smells good let's eat girl." Nicky loved home cooked food. "You want me to help with anything?" he asked.

"No, go and sit I will bring it through."

Laura enjoyed their evening dinners; Nicky was always appreciative of her efforts to please him. After she had set the table, Laura served his favourite dish accompanied by a large salad of shredded white cabbage tossed in a lemon and garlic dressing, and traditional Lebanese bread. Before eating, Nicky always crossed himself.

"Umm, it's good Loulou," he said enthusiastically tucking into his dinner. "You know Loulou, when I get the villa I'm going to employ you to be my cook," he joked.

Laura smiled; she knew his teasing was a compliment to her culinary skills.

"You know, I'm happy you love antiques so much." Laura suddenly announced. Nicky gave a quizzical look;

"Oh yeah, why's that?" he asked.

Laura smiled at him across the table,

"Because the older I get, the more you are going to appreciate me," she laughingly told him.

Nicky smiled at Laura's subtle wit;

"Is that right?" he responded mockingly.

Straight after eating, Nicky lit a cigarette and asked Laura to fetch the champagne. She put the chilled bottle on the table with two champagne flutes. Nicky opened the champagne and poured out two glasses. Passing a glass to Laura he said;

"Love you girl," he leant over and kissed her. "Merry Christmas love, here's to us, going to be good time ahead. Believe me Loulou things are gonna be good from now," he promised as he chinked his glass to hers in the usual way; "Okay Loulou, you love me?"

As if he needed confirmation on that score; yet still he would ask. Laura looked into his eyes. There was no doubting she utterly adored him.

"You know I do. I love you more than anything."

"And tell me Loulou, I'm a good husband. Yes or no?"

He genuinely didn't seem sure if he was or not.

"The best," Laura affirmed.

Satisfied with her answer Nicolas smiled. He knew he could sometimes be difficult, and perhaps at times a little demanding, and maybe just a teeny weeny bit controlling; but whichever way he behaved it warmed him to know he could always count on Laura's love.

Together they decorated the tree finally placing a gold star at the top. Nicky took a small Lebanese flag from the bookshelf. He stuck it in the tree just under the star. He did this every year. When decorating their first Christmas tree together several years back, they never had a star for it, so the small Lebanese flag took pride of place at the top. It was now a permanent addition.

They stood back to admire their artistry. With its twinkling lights and sparkling baubles, the tree looked really pretty.

Happily sipping their champagne, Nicky and Laura felt confident their future held great promise. Both believed they were due a break. Holding hands, they made their Christmas wishes. Nicolas silently wished for a prosperous future and to one day be able to return with Laura to his homeland. Staring dreamily at the tree Laura also made a wish. She wished to have her beloved Nicolas forever by her side and to grow old with him.

But as they both silently wished their wishes, storm clouds were already gathering along the horizon of their almost perfect little world.

KOUSBAWI

Chapter 30: A Step too far

The day started pretty much as normal, Nicolas had risen at 6.30 am and was enjoying his early morning quiet time with his coffee and thoughts. He practiced the same ritual every morning. Sitting in silence while he drank his coffee, Nicolas mentally rehearsed his strategy; going over his plan to keep the vow he made long ago. During their years together Nicolas had tentatively touched on the subject with Laura; many times he spoke of executing his desire for revenge. He wasn't sure how much Laura understood, or believed. Maybe she thought he was kidding. That was okay, because this was the non-negotiable blueprint of his destiny; the design of which may never be understood or shared.

While Laura lay asleep, Nicolas poured himself another coffee. He sat down in his favourite chair and switched on the TV. Keeping the volume low, he waited for the latest news from Lebanon. He lit his second cigarette of the day, and sat back resting his feet up on the coffee table in front of him. Sipping slowly at his coffee, Nicolas regressed into the darker recesses of his mind, taking himself to the place where his most secret thoughts held dominion, waiting to be brought to life. In these solitary moments, he would recall what his father told him long ago;

"If you want to do something you have to first feel it; see it clearly in your mind's eye. Visualise every step until you can feel, taste and touch it; be comfortable with it to the point that when the time comes to execute your plan, you are fully prepared, and will not shy from your duty to carry it out. It must become as natural as drinking your morning coffee."

Nicolas took heed of his father's words. Every morning for years he systematically practised visualising the same scenario, resolutely and meticulously rehearsing strategies

243

until he was completely at ease; until it became second nature.

At 7.30 am Nicolas took his shower. The warm water cascading over his lean physique, released the tension incurred from his minds overworked imaginings. After vigorously towelling himself dry, Nicolas grabbed his dark blue robe from the hook on the bathroom door, and wrapped it tightly around his still slightly damp body. He shaved, and a quiet confidence prevailed as he focussed his thoughts towards the day's proceedings. Nicolas had a strong feeling his morning meetings would herald some promising business opportunities. Before dressing, he went back to the lounge to make his obligatory morning calls.

Sitting at his desk Nicolas switched on the laptop, and glanced briefly at the notes he had written. Lighting his third cigarette, he proceeded to make his calls.

At precisely 8.20 Nicolas went to the bedroom to dress. He quietly entered the room where Laura was still sleeping soundly. Discarding his robe, he carefully took his trousers from the hanger and put them on before taking a freshly pressed shirt from the wardrobe. He chose the light pink one; it was his favourite and beautifully complimented his dark Mediterranean features and olive complexion. He neatly folded the sleeves back to just below the elbow, and then tucked his shirt into his trousers fussing with it until it looked perfect.

Nicolas removed his tiny blue bible and wallet from the pocket of the shirt he had worn the day before, transferring them to the breast pocket of the one he was now wearing. Nicolas was careful not to make a sound and disturb Laura. He looked fondly at her as she slept. Before leaving he gently touched her cheek, affectionately brushing it with his fingers. Quietly and softly he closed the bedroom door behind him. Nicolas stepped out of his slippers and slid his feet into his outdoor shoes. Resting his foot on the chair in the hallway, he gave his shoes a quick brush. Nicolas never looked anything less than immaculate when leaving the house.

Pinned to the top of the front door was a small plaque with a picture of the Virgin Mary holding baby Jesus, alongside it, a picture of Saint Charbel. Bending on one knee in front of the pictures, Nicolas spent a few moments in silent prayer. He crossed himself before standing, then finally gathered together his worry beads, mobile and cigarettes. Nicolas put on his sun glasses, and left for the first meeting of the day.

As he stood at the end of the road waiting to hail a taxi cab he lit a cigarette. Moments later a taxi pulled up in front of him. Nicolas walked towards the cab. A guy appeared from out of nowhere and jumped into the back seat of the cab right in front of him. Angered by the blatant rudeness, Nicolas saw red; he was not about to let this display of disrespect go unchallenged.

Opening the taxi cab door, Nicolas politely but firmly asked the guy to remove himself from the car. The taxi driver was in agreement as it was Nicolas he had stopped for. Saying he was in a hurry the guy refused, rudely telling Nicolas there were plenty of other taxis he could take. The man was in his late twenties and from his accent Nicolas surmised he was probably of Egyptian origin. Looking daggers at him Nicolas coolly warned,

"Okay my friend; if you don't want to remove yourself from my taxi, I will do it for you."

Continuing to argue, the guy again flatly refused to get out of the cab. Without further hesitation, Nicolas grabbed him firmly by the collar, dragging him swiftly from the taxi to the pavement. Protesting loudly, the man demanded Nicolas apologise to him. Nicolas turned to the cab driver who was rather enjoying the spectacle, telling him;

"Just give me one moment."

Nicolas turned to face the man who was still objecting. They made eye to eye contact. Quietly Nicolas told him in no uncertain terms;

"If you say even one more word, I will send you to the hospital! You choose okay, you understand me?"

The man looked at Nicolas's face; he saw the fire in his

245

eyes. There was no doubting Nicolas meant it. Wisely he backed down. Only the foolish would risk a confrontation with Al Hajj.

Having appropriately dealt with the situation, Nicolas thought no more about it. He viewed the incident with cool detachment; as if he had just flicked an annoying fly from his shirt sleeve. Thankfully the rest of his work day passed without further conflict.

Laura woke around 9.30am and decided to do an hours exercise. Exercising was a necessary element of a dancer's life, and although Laura no longer danced professionally, it was one habit she had tried to keep. Nicolas usually arrived for lunch between 12.30 and 1pm, so there was enough time to fit in an hour of her dance workout before he was back.

After exercising, Laura took a shower. At 12.45pm she heard Nicolas's key in the door. That reassuring sound made her heart skip. It filled with warm relief that he was back safely. Laura was only too aware how Nicolas's hot temper might land him in trouble. Once he had changed into more comfortable attire, Laura was ready with his cold beer and a dish of nuts. He always liked to relax with a beer before eating lunch.

"How was your morning?" Laura asked.

"Not bad," he answered, and didn't elaborate further.

Nicolas preferred a sandwich at lunchtime which he always insisted on making himself. Except for Fridays, when they would have a proper cooked meal which Laura would prepare, often with his help. After finishing his lunch, Nicolas amusingly related the episode with his morning taxi. His facial expressions and mannerisms as he acted out the little skirmish were amusing and entertaining. Nicolas was a skilful actor and a very adept, well-practised story teller.

Ten o' clock the following morning, Laura woke feeling lethargic. She wasn't too keen to do her usual workout routine. After washing her face and brushing her teeth she went to the kitchen to make a much needed coffee. Still undecided about whether to exercise, Laura yawned wearily as she took her coffee to the lounge. She was suddenly startled to find Nicolas at his desk dressed casually in jeans and a T shirt. Surprised to see him there Laura asked;

"You didn't leave yet?"

He swung round in the leather chair to face her.

"I'm not going today Loulou," he told her.

"Oh, why is that?" Laura queried.

"I have nothing, no meetings today," he explained.

"Would you like a coffee?" Laura asked.

"Yeah why not, make me small one love."

Laura put her coffee down on the table, and went to the kitchen to make another for Nicky. She didn't feel guilty now about not wanting to do her workout. Nicolas being at home was a good excuse to give it a miss. She returned with his coffee, placing it on the desk beside him. As she put the coffee down Laura glanced at the laptop. What was displayed on the screen shocked her. Nicolas was studying a website showing guns and ammunition for sale. Staring incredulously at the pictures of hand guns, Laura asked;

"Why are you looking at those?"

Nicolas delivered his usual response; the one he always resorted to when he didn't care to explain himself.

"None of your business."

Laura sat down in Nicky's chair and sipped her coffee. She knew her husband's past had been wayward and not that of a choir boy; there were no illusions on that score. Before they ever met, Nicky had lived a rather chequered existence, very different to Laura's sheltered life. And later having fought through the Lebanese civil war, he was certainly no stranger to violence. Over nearly a twenty year period, the bloody conflict had all but destroyed his country. Her husband had never kept secret the fact that he had witnessed, and taken part in some ferocious battles fought between the feuding militia groups in the north. Being well acquainted with guns and other weapons, he made no bones of the fact he was not averse to using them.

Enthralled by his tales, Laura had enjoyed listening to the stories of his life during the conflict. To her they had been nothing more than stories of an existence far removed from the life he was living now. Disconcerted by his rekindled interest in fire arms, Laura realised for the first time, that although she believed his stories, they had never actually registered as being real events. Maybe Laura had been naïve in hoping Nicolas had left his old life behind. She remained silent while he browsed the selection of guns on the screen. This resurrected fascination unsettled her.

Nicolas had been as open as he could allow himself to be about his agenda. But for Laura's own sake, there were things he preferred not to share. At least not until the time was right. Sensing Laura's uneasiness, he endeavoured to play it down and lighten the mood. Smiling he asked casually;

"Loulou, you want to see my Glock?"

"You're what?"

"My Glock, it's beautiful one, the latest model. Come and look."

He said it as though he might be referring to a new shirt or kitchen appliance. Laura reluctantly got up from her seat and moved to Nicky's side. He immediately put his arm around her waist. On the screen was a picture of the Glock. Laura was familiar with the name only. When Alyssa was younger, she often played the Lara Croft Tomb Raider games on her computer. That was when Laura first heard the name. On the screen were a number of different images of the handgun. Nicky clicked to a picture displaying it worn in a shoulder holster. The face of the person wearing the holster wasn't totally visible, but there was something strangely familiar about him.

"What do you think Loulou, its good?" Nicky asked coolly; as if Laura would have even the slightest idea.

"It's a gun. I wouldn't have a clue; and why are you so interested?" she asked curtly.

"Love, it's for when I go to Lebanon," he told her. "It's normal. No man can live in Lebanon without his gun;

especially in the north."

Laura stared at him;

"But the war's over," she uttered naively.

"For now maybe, but you know how quickly things can change." Nicky rationalised. "It's the life there love."

The political state in the Middle East and its fragility was something Laura was well aware of. Of course he was absolutely right; things could literally flare up overnight, especially the Levant region, whose stability was always on a knife edge. Although he'd been honest about the need to be armed in a country with a history of political unrest, Nicolas hadn't given Laura the complete truth regarding his wanting to arm himself. She stared at the pistol.

"What's so special about this gun?" Laura asked.

In spite of knowing nothing of guns, Laura accepted they had featured heavily in her husband's life in Lebanon. Her curiosity was mildly aroused. She had never seen a gun for real. Nicolas explained the features of the pistol in detail. It was he said the latest version of a generation 4 Glock 17, featuring several devices, including an infra-red and invisible laser light. Laura had to admit she was rather fascinated.

"Good one yeah Loulou?" Nicky stated confidently. Then unexpectedly he boldly added; "I bought it. Loulou, this is my gun, this is my Glock."

Nicolas mistakenly took Laura's curiosity as a mark of approval. Laura stared wide eyed. She was speechless. It all seemed too surreal; At last she asked;

"Are you actually planning to go to Lebanon then?"

Nicolas answered flippantly;

"Maybe."

"But what about your passport and your papers; you don't have them yet?" Laura queried.

"Everything is in hand; I can pick up my passport from the court anytime I want," he said glibly.

This was news to Laura. Nicky's eyes widened as he looked at the gun on the screen, his pupils were fully dilated. Unintentionally he spoke his thoughts out loud;

"I don't need my passport for what I'm going to do," he spontaneously revealed without thinking.

"What do you mean by that?" She asked tentatively.

Fearing his answer Laura's pulse quickened. She suspected what he was referring to was something she had rather naively hoped was just talk. Now that he had let slip his intention and with the idea of his plan fully arisen in Laura's mind, Nicolas couldn't just brush it off and say nothing. With an impassioned look on his face, he continued;

"If I have to, and I'm just saying 'If' Loulou, I will go the back way; it will take me three days only; I will finish all of my problem there."

Laura sighed; her heart sank as she witnessed a look of sheer vengeful intent in his eyes. It scared her to hear him talk this way.

"What problem?" She asked, feigning innocence.

Deep down Laura already knew the answer, but hoped he would laugh and say he was just kidding with her.

"Love you know what. I told you many times. I have to kill my enemies one day."

He said it as calmly as if he were talking about making a cup of tea, but his eyes were filled with burning desire for revenge. Laura said nothing. Even after all these years, Nicolas wouldn't let the past go. He could never be at peace until he had fulfilled his vow.

"I have to take my revenge," his voice was intense. "I have to! How I can go to Lebanon? The people will say Hajj does not do what he promised; Hajj is not a man of his word. Love, everyone scared from Hajj. If I don't do it they will laugh at me. They cannot laugh to my face, but they will laugh behind my back."

Nicolas had a score to settle. Someone he loved dearly, who was his confidant and best friend, had been brutally killed, and his body left in the road near his village. The murder of his dear friend had apparently been politically motivated. Laura longed for the day when her husband would retrieve his official papers from the courts so they

250

could go forward with their lives. But part of her dreaded it; Nicolas would then have nothing to hold him back from travelling to Lebanon to deliver his vengeance.

"You are a Christian, yet you don't forgive those who wronged you," Laura protested.

It was a feeble, vain attempt to dissuade him; as if anything ever could. Nicky took Laura's hand. He knew she would never be totally convinced that when it came to his honour, he really had no choice.

"I may forgive in time," he assured. "But when I give my word, I will never go back."

This was the principle he lived by; Nicolas was a true man of honour. The kind that believes when you give your word you keep it, no matter what the cost. He pulled Laura closer explaining;

"You know love, if someone betrays you once, they will do it again. I'm not talking about making a mistake. I mean if someone makes a mistake because they don't know me, or they are stupid, I will accept it. I will be angry, but I will accept it once; but Loulou one time only."

His face softened into a smile as he looked at Laura. All this talk of revenge he knew was hard for her to digest. He wished it could be another way; but his word was his bond. This was the hard exterior he showed to the world.

Laura knew a different side, and Nicolas was grateful to have been given the chance to present another side, not just the tough guy image. He would always give to Laura the respect a man shows for his mother, and the nurturing protection of a father, and as his wife, Nicolas loved Laura as if she were the very air that he breathed.

Laura didn't mention the Glock again; she preferred not to think about it. The thought of her husband going undercover to Lebanon to dispose of his enemies, made her blood run cold. For the time being Laura would stay in denial and retreat into the safe secure little world she believed she had with Nicolas. The darker elements were deliberately and completely dismissed from her thoughts.

KOUSBAWI

Chapter 31: Tsunami

With the passing of time Nicolas and Laura's relationship reached what could aptly be described as, the epitome of harmonious familiarity. Nicolas was much more relaxed, and beginning to mellow in his attitude. The contributing factor to his more buoyant upbeat demeanour was the eventual arrival of his long awaited passport. He was still hanging on for the courts completion of his papers that would finally allow him to start a company in his name. Soon he would renew his trading license and resident's visa. Without the vital paperwork, leaving the UAE would be problematic. Doing so without the correct papers would hinder his re-entry into the country.

Nicolas had now purchased a beautiful Jeep. Having his passport back enabled him to legally drive again. The new car made an enormous difference to their lives. Things were definitely on the way up.

Reclaiming his independence meant Nicolas no longer relied on taxis or other people to ferry him around. Laura enjoyed the extra freedom it gave her too. Although he was still not keen for Laura to venture out alone, at least once a week Nicky was happy to drop her at the Maziad mall on the way to his afternoon meetings. Laura would wander around the local mall at her leisure until Nicky picked her up a few hours later. Living in a residential area had made him realise just how restrictive Laura's life had been back in the 'Cave'.

On their next trip to Mussafah's brand new Maziad mall, Nicolas pointed out familiar landmarks, telling Laura to take note of them and familiarise herself with the route. Then quite out of the blue Nicky announced;

"Maybe next week I will let you take a taxi."

Laura was astonished; she had never been permitted to take a taxi anywhere alone.

"Wow! Really?" she said in a slightly sarcastic tone. "You mean it?"

"Yeah, why not? If you're good," he said, teasingly implying she had to earn her freedom.

"You know Loulou when we get the villa, you will not want to leave the house ever."

"Why not?" she asked.

"Because it's going to be beautiful, and you will have a garden to sit and everything you need."

Anything was possible from now on; he could feel it in the air. Nicky gave her a broad confident smile; everything was finally falling into place. He was in exuberant mood today. Switching on the cars disc player, Nicky played his favourite Lady Gaga cd. He began dancing around in his seat to the music. Laura smiled at his childlike antics. Maybe now it really was safe to believe all the bad stuff was behind them. Perhaps even safe to believe everything they had talked of, planned, and hoped for, would now materialise in their lives.

Watching Nicky drive the Jeep, took Laura back. It recalled fond memories of the times he had driven her in his plush silver Mercedes when they first met. His unique driving style hadn't changed. Laura was younger then, and totally unfazed by his seemingly reckless manoeuvres. Nicky still drove like a racing driver, weaving in and out of the traffic with skill and at great speed. At times Laura felt her heart jump to her mouth; her hands gripping the side of the seat as she clung on for dear life. Nicky was an experienced driver, but as with anything he did, totally confident in his own ability. Others were not as trusting as Laura. Everyone who ever let Nicolas drive them, swore never to repeat the experience; equating it to a hair raising roller coaster ride at a theme park or fairground. Nicky didn't drive this way for thrills or to impress, it was just Nicky being Nicky. Although scary, it was very macho, and Laura found it rather sexy as he demonstrated total command of the vehicle and the road.

Around 10.30 am the following day, Laura was alone.

Nicky was at a meeting. She sat in his chair sipping her morning coffee. Outside the temperature was a very warm 29 degrees. The sun streamed in through a gap in the curtains. Laura's relaxed state was infiltrated by a sudden chill. As shivers ran up her spine she was transported back to a past memory. While they were living in the 'Cave', something disconcerting occurred by way of an extremely vivid dream.

On the day in question, Laura woke suddenly mid-morning, shaking and in a cold sweat after experiencing a frightening dream. It felt so real Laura wasn't sure if it was a dream; it was like a prophetic vision. In it, Laura found herself walking on a beach in a sheltered cove. The setting was beautifully tranquil as Laura stood on the soft white sand, gazing at a crystal blue ocean. A bright warm sun was set high in a clear blue cloudless sky. Everything felt peaceful as the waves rolled onto the sand lapping gently at her feet. In an instant the sky darkened, and the ocean froze, as though time itself had stopped. Moments later the serenity returned, but as the waves rolled back from the shore they kept going, continuing to roll back until the ocean floor was laid bare for miles. Laura became aware of her daughter's presence beside her. Alyssa was excited by the scene, suggesting they take a walk on the exposed sea bed. Struck by a deep sense of foreboding, Laura felt increasingly uneasy insisting they leave.

In a flash the scene changed, and Laura was suddenly in an apartment standing in front of a window with a view over the bay. In the distance she could hear a strange rumbling. Laura turned her head and looked back inside the apartment. The rumbling she thought may be from the washing machine going through its cycle. The sound grew progressively louder and stronger, and Laura realised the noise was coming from outside. Turning her head to the window again, Laura looked out across the bay. A gigantic towering wave thundered towards the apartment; Laura was consumed with fear at the sight. There was nowhere to run, no escape. Laura's instinct was to protect Alyssa, but death felt imminent as the noise grew to a deafening crescendo. The unstoppable Tsunami shook the building throwing them to the floor. Enveloped within the raging fury, Laura felt deep sorrow as her world was swept away. Everything then went black.

Immediately Laura woke up to find she was alone in the dark 'Cave'; her heart was still palpitating erratically. As she sat up and looked around the dimly lit bedroom, her chest felt tight and she could barely breathe, like she was drowning. Laura made her way to the kitchen with her heart pounding out of her chest. Seized by suffocating fear, Laura grabbed her mobile phone from the desk. Her hands trembled as she searched for Nicky's number. Laura desperately needed to hear his voice. When he answered she was at first unable to speak. Concerned by her silence Nicky asked;

"Loulou what is it love, are you okay?"

Eventually she managed to mumble;

"No I'm not. I don't know."

Confused and disorientated, the shaky uneasy tone in her voice was evident.

"What's the problem?" Nicky asked.

Laura tried to speak clearly but her words sounded incoherent and strange to Nicky.

"Tell me Loulou what's wrong?"

"What time are you coming?" she mumbled.

"Are you sick, are you hurt?" He asked in a worried tone.

"I had a bad dream, or something, I don't really know. It shook me up," she told him fretfully.

"Okay love. Take it easy girl I won't be long love," he reassured.

Far from being annoyed with Laura for disturbing him at work because of a dream, Nicolas's only thought was to get back to the house and comfort her. Later when Laura relayed the dream to him, he listened sympathetically. He never told her she was silly or irrational; instead Nicolas did his best to dispel her fears. Her frayed nerves soothed,

Laura was able to put the vision out of her mind.

That was until today. For some inexplicable reason, the memory quite literally flooded back, with every terrifying detail intact. It lasted only seconds, but so strong was the recollection, that Laura relived every emotion; feeling everything as intensely as when she first dreamt it. The returned harrowing vividness permeated her mind as she walked to the kitchen to make another coffee. Laura wondered why now? It was odd that the vision re-emerged at a time when she had never felt so content or happy in her life.

Laura shuddered, and tried to force her mind away from the feelings of despair and hopelessness that were unexpectedly resurrected. She endeavoured to focus on happier thoughts. But no matter how hard she tried dismissing it, that deep sense of losing everything that was dear to her became overpowering.

It haunted Laura for the rest of the day. This time she refrained from mentioning it to Nicolas. Sometime in the not too distant future, the cryptic vision might well be deciphered. Its haunting fateful message would one day irrepressibly unravel.

KOUSBAWI

Chapter 32: The Dark Side of Genius

For some time now Nicolas's ground breaking invention had been ready to be patented. Convinced 'his baby' would revolutionise the construction industry, Nicolas was waiting for the right time to market it. Until recent years the cash needed to get the prototype made up had not been available to him, but now it was, and Nicolas's childlike enthusiasm for his completed project was infectious. Laura couldn't help but be drawn into his energetic zeal.

"This year everything is coming together, we are going to be in good situation," he enthused.

Today Nicolas was on the edge of realising his long awaited glory. Laura proudly stood beside him; she could think of no one who deserved it more. His eyes shone with pride whenever he spoke of his 'baby'; a seventeen year work in progress, involving hours spent perfecting his system. For many of those hours Laura was at his side, devotedly supporting him in his passion. Excitement radiated from every pore, as Nicolas proudly pondered his achievement and the prospect of what genius he was about to eject into the world of construction.

Things had not always been easy, and for Laura, living with Nicolas was at times challenging to say the least. Impassioned and driven, he harboured deep emotions. The same drive and adrenalin that made him so brilliant, also had the power to unleash violent outbursts. The unreserved honesty of his emotions was just too overwhelming to be contained at times. Mostly he was like calm waters, but when upset would explode like a volcano erupting. Sail on his waters against him, and you may well find yourself tossed amidst a raging sea.

During their time together Laura had witnessed many such raging storms. Nicolas would let loose his fury in a startling, often destructive manner. She had on occasion observed some serious damage, caused by a few moments of uncontrollable anger. Laura had seen Nicolas trash computers, laptops, mobile phones and TV sets; whatever was the object of his fury or close to hand when the destructive beast unleashed itself. Scary as it was to witness, experience had taught Laura to discreetly leave the room, and wait for him to calm down, which he always did within minutes. The first time Laura observed such out of control behaviour, was while they were still living in the 'Cave'.

On that day, Laura was sat quietly watching television. Nicolas was endeavouring to get to grips with a brand new laptop purchased just a few days earlier. Laura felt a distinct change in the atmosphere as he began cursing in Arabic. Bewildered by his sudden irritated mood, Laura glanced away from the television to see Nicolas become increasingly agitated. As he teetered on the edge, his anger intensified, and the volatile energy was palpable. Laura had no idea why, or what was causing his agitation.

Without warning, Nicolas picked up the new laptop and flung it violently against the wall. Bingo started to meow loudly. Laura grabbed the cat and left the room. Mystified she sat on the bed. Bingo started howling at the bedroom door. Laura listened to the continuing sound of smashing and crashing coming from the next room. Naturally she feared its escalation. Suddenly everything went quiet.

Moments later Nicolas opened the bedroom door. He stood in the doorway with a slightly embarrassed look on his face. Laura nervously looked up at him as he moved towards her. Seeing the nervousness in Laura's eyes he apologised, insisting she had nothing to fear. Bingo was still meowing. Upset that he had frightened her, Nicky sat on the bed beside Laura. It was disconcertingly evident to him that Laura was shocked and shaken by his outlandish behaviour. Feeling sheepish Nicolas took her hand asking;

"Love, why you scared from me? Loulou, don't you know I will never hurt you?"

"Are you sure?" Laura questioned.

Nicolas was hurt that Laura would believe otherwise.

"Love never! Believe me; I will cut my hand before I ever hurt you. Believe me it will never happen," he vowed.

Laura looked into his dark eyes. With a pleading sincerity his eyes expressed it was important she believe him. She did, and they went back to the lounge where the remains of what was once a brand-new laptop littered the floor. Laura looked at him and asked;

"Nicky what the hell happened?"

"I smashed it," he said casually.

"I can see that, but why?" Laura asked, surveying the wreckage after the storm.

Nicolas shrugged sheepishly. "I dunno. Love my head explode sometimes." There was no malice in him, just honest rage. He was like a small boy who had just thrown a tantrum; "This is me," he quipped, as if it were a normal rational way to behave; which for Nicolas it probably was.

In contrast to his volatile moodiness, Nicky now calmly explained to Laura how the internet had persistently failed to connect. He was already having trouble getting to grips with his new apparatus, so the lost internet signal quickly exacerbated his irritation. Frustrated with being unable to fathom his new laptop system combined with the failing internet, he just lost it. Laura helped him clear up the mess. Now Nicolas was calm and saw the disastrous result of his fiery temper, he was feeling a tad repentant and foolish. But as always, his embarrassment was quickly covered by humour. Displaying a guilty grin he jested;

"Loulou, why you smash my computer, how I can do my work now?"

Laura looked at him incredulously. Then both of them started laughing.

That day Laura wasn't sure whether she had married a man or the Incredible Hulk. The frequency of Nicolas's volatile behaviour lessened over time. No matter how Nicolas behaved, Laura never criticized or judged. She understood him, and was equally accepting of the positive and negative attributes and nuances of his nature. Given the freedom to vent his emotions without fear of rejection, encouraged Nicolas to open up and gradually let go of his anger. It allowed their relationship to flourish.

Many women would have run for the hills faced with such an unpredictably explosive temperament. Laura believed the roots of his volatility stemmed from his unconventional childhood. Far from finding Nicolas too hot to handle, Laura was undeterred. Like an iceberg, Nicolas's hot temper was just the tip of what he was made of. Laura knew there was so much more to him, his anger being only one layer.

Nicolas may roar like a lion and fight like a tiger, but underneath the nervous edgy exterior, Laura discovered a purring pussy cat. She saw within him enduring love and loyalty, tenderness and compassion. Over time Nicolas allowed Laura little glimpses of his more vulnerable side, even admitting to secret phobias that haunted him. Laura was given a rare gift, a peek into a secret world; she had her very own private window to Nicolas's soul.

KOUSBAWI

Chapter 33: Storm in a Teacup

It was a very hot day in early April, and the humidity was quite oppressive. At lunchtime Nicolas arrived back to the apartment looking troubled. At first Laura put his tetchy moodiness down to the humidity which always made him irritable. She handed him a cool beer from the fridge. Nicolas had a pensive look about him; it was a look that Laura had grown accustomed to over the years. Something was on his mind, but as usual Nicolas was reluctant to discuss it. After making a couple of calls, Nicolas sat in his favourite chair and lit a cigarette. He was looking in the direction of the TV but his eyes were not focussed on the screen. Laura sat down beside him;

"Is everything okay?" she asked. "You look like you're a million miles away."

Nicolas sipped his beer and looked at Laura;

"Yeah love; it's the business." He made a circling gesture with his hand. "Many things going on in my head love."

Laura didn't push him to elaborate, if it were something she needed to know, he would tell her in his own time.

"Do you want to have lunch now?" she asked.

He placed his hand affectionately on her knee;

"Yeah Loulou I don't feel like sandwich today. What do we have?"

Laura got up from her seat and went to the kitchen. She opened the fridge;

"We have Fasulya b-zeit, (red bean stew)," she shouted from the kitchen.

"Okay bring it," Nicky shouted back.

Laura set the table, and served the Fasulya b-zeit with spring onions and Lebanese bread. Cutting a lemon into quarters she placed it in a small dish on the table. Houmus, a mixture of fresh salad leaves, baby cucumber, and fresh parsley Nicolas's favourite herb, complemented the meal.

Nicolas crossed himself and started to eat quickly. He always finished before Laura, and would immediately light a cigarette. Laura had long given up asking him not to light up whilst she was still eating; she may as well talk to the wall for all the notice he took. Apart from being an annoying habit, she worried Nicky's smoking was out of control. When confronted, Nicky insisted he would give up soon. He'd been saying the same thing to her for years. Smoking was one habit Laura had been unable to have any influence over. Nicky hated to be controlled by anyone or anything and Laura teased him saying, the little white sticks ruled him. He of course would argue, insisting he wasn't addicted but enjoyed smoking. Laura knew this particular battle was one she had no chance of winning; Nicolas knew the risks, and would give up only when he was good and ready.

Nicolas lit his cigarette, and left the table to go straight to the computer hardly giving time to digest his lunch. Laura cleared away the dishes and made herself a coffee. Nicolas wouldn't drink another coffee until after he had taken his afternoon nap. Laura sat down and watched as Nicky again scrolled through more pictures of guns and armoury. It was Thursday afternoon; Laura looked forward to the weekends and their time together. They would talk and enjoy relaxing in each other's company.

As the afternoon drew on, Laura was beginning to feel neglected. She became frustrated, as again Nicolas seemed preoccupied with this particular website. They had hardly spoken since he arrived back to the apartment. When Nicky was scrolling through pages of antiques for hours on end it could be annoying, but never bothered Laura too much; his fascination with this site on the other hand, disturbed and troubled her.

An hour and a half later and he was irritatingly on the same website. He stopped on and off to make various phone calls. Not understanding Arabic, Laura had no clue who he was speaking with. Bored and annoyed at being ignored, Laura couldn't control her irritation any longer.

"Are you going to be looking at that stuff all day?" she snapped.

"Yep, if I want," he stubbornly replied.

Already feeling dejected, Laura found his tone rather arrogant and selfish.

"What's going on with you, why are you so engrossed with looking at weapons?" Laura asked sharply.

The change in Laura's tone was immediately picked up by Nicolas. He turned his chair to face her. Laura's patient demeanour and calm expression he was more used to seeing, had given way to a look of disdain. He attempted to justify his preoccupation.

"Love, I told you. No one knows when something will happen I have to be ready," he told her.

He hoped his answer would satisfy Laura's curiosity and she would leave him be. Normally she would. Today for some reason, she was not prepared to be fobbed off and wouldn't let it go. Laura argued;

"But you have the Glock." Adding pointedly; "You're not even going to Lebanon yet."

Nicolas was un-used to being challenged by Laura. It was out of character for her to contradict him. There were things Nicolas preferred not to explain. He was becoming impatient with Laura's scornful tone and questioning of something he regarded as his business.

"Yes I have the Glock, so?" he retorted obstinately. Then as if to reinforce his authority, he defiantly added;

"I'm going to buy a machine gun too."

Laura looked at him in wide-eyed astonishment; she opened her mouth to speak. Before she could get a word out, Nicolas snapped;

"Now quiet, don't say anything, this is my business. Why you don't read a book or something," he said rather patronisingly.

He didn't mean to be condescending or speak in such a derisive tone. Nicolas hated to be questioned, especially by his wife. He was maddened she dare query his motives.

Laura would have done well to have left it there, but like a dog with a bone she wouldn't let it go. She took offence at his extremely patronizing attitude.

"Why do you need to buy weapons now?" she scowled at him. "Can't you wait until you have concrete plans to return to Lebanon? Or maybe you were planning to go without telling me?"

Laura's pointed statement and confrontational attitude hit a nerve. Nicolas lit a cigarette. He had no wish to argue about it. His eyes glowered at Laura. Nicolas could make people feel very uncomfortable with just a look. Normally that look would be a clear signal to retreat, but Laura was pushing the boundaries today. Again she challenged him, snapping contemptuously;

"You've already spent thousands on the Glock."

Nicolas felt the hackles go up, and fought to keep his cool. But Laura kept pushing;

"How much is all of this going to cost?"

Laura knew she was antagonising him, but couldn't stop herself.

"I thought we were supposed to be saving money for the villa, or had you forgotten about that?" She stated scathingly.

Her tone was more than a touch sarcastic. Miffed that Nicolas's gun obsession was taking priority, Laura was maddened by his attitude. With no immediate plans to return to Lebanon, Laura thought his insistence in buying them now selfish. Unaware of Nicolas's agenda which he was reluctant to share with her, Laura felt her criticism justified.

It wasn't so much what she said, but the way she was saying it that made him mad. Nicolas stood and walked away from the computer. He remained calm, but his anger bubbled furiously under the surface. In a bid to intimidate Laura into submission, he raised his voice several octaves;

"How many times have I told you Laura?" He always called her Laura as opposed to Loulou when he was angry.

"Don't put your nose into my business; this has nothing

to do with you."

Momentarily subdued by her husband's shouting and strong words, Laura stayed quiet. Her hurt feelings rapidly changed to anger. In a provoking argumentative fashion, Laura persisted in questioning his motives.

"But why are you buying guns now?"

"Yeah so, this is me!? This is my life; you know how I am," he replied obstinately. Much irritated, Nicolas took a cigarette from the packet of Marlborough on the desk. "You know me better than anyone Laura."

Nicolas lit his cigarette throwing his lighter angrily across the desk. It slid off onto the floor. He stormed across the room and sat in his chair. Laura bent and picked the lighter up, then followed him. He glared up at her;

"Don't be like her!" He yelled, disparagingly referring to his ex-wife Samra. "Don't lie to yourself like she did. Don't tell me you accept me, and then try and change me. I cannot change. I cannot!"

Nicolas dragged hard on his cigarette before stubbing it out. The thought of not being accepted for who he was, hit a very raw nerve; it hurt deeply and fuelled his already incensed emotions.

"This is me!" he blurted, adding coldly; "If you can't handle it Laura, maybe you should leave!"

Nicolas didn't mean for the words to come out quite as bluntly. Unaccustomed to being criticized by Laura, he felt wounded; it dragged up painful memories of Samra's persistent attempts to change him. On the surface Nicolas's manner was emotionless as he deceptively hid his hurt feelings. While he acted as though he didn't give a damn if she left or stayed, he knew it would kill him to really let Laura go.

Unfortunately his ego and stubborn pride was bigger. Not wishing to lose face by relenting, Nicolas hoped Laura would realise she had pushed him too far and back off. He would refuse to speak to her for a few hours, or maybe a day or two to teach her a lesson, and that would be the end of it.

Laura was enraged by his apparent cold indifference. She found his conduct selfish; something pushed her to be uncharacteristically quarrelsome. Instead of apologising as Nicolas was expecting, she looked daggers at him. Laura gave him the same disapproving look he had given her, openly and defiantly challenging his authority. Neither of them was ready to back down. Laura's continued defiance was unacceptable, Nicolas retaliated harshly;

"Go pack your things," he coldheartedly told her. "I will arrange your ticket tomorrow."

Refusing to be backed into a corner, Nicolas's reaction was instinctive. He became as hard as steel and cold as ice. Not even Laura, who he loved beyond words, was permitted to dictate how Nicolas should live.

Laura was speechless. The way Nicolas dismissed her and the iciness in his attitude, stunned her. Reminded of the way he had treated others in the past, Laura feared she may have fallen victim to the same unforgiving treatment. Many of Nicolas's family and friends had been subject to his closing the door on them, never to reopen it again.

Nicolas kept up his tough act, but he was bitterly torn. The moment he let the words slip from his mouth, he knew he was cutting off his nose to spite his face so to speak. If Laura left it would break his heart. How was he going to retract from this? He could never be seen to go back on his word, he never ever did that; not for anyone. Now he actually wanted Laura to fight back. If she submissively obeyed and went ahead and packed her suitcase, he would have lost. But Laura didn't disappoint; she wasn't about to give up yet. Nicolas went to the bathroom closely followed by his wife, who felt she now had nothing to lose by continuing to argue her case.

"You know I love you Nicolas, and you know you love me," she started. "Why can't you step over your pride for a moment and admit you don't really want me to leave. Can you honestly push me away and pretend I don't matter to you?"

Nicolas didn't answer, his expression softened though.

He knew Laura was right; he did love her and of course he didn't want her to go anywhere. He refrained from making direct eye contact, because Laura might see through his stony façade. Intending to carry on as normal and take his nap, Nicolas walked to the bedroom. The still impassioned Laura followed, vehemently arguing her point.

"So you're really going to cut me from your life like you do everyone who upsets or disagrees with you? After everything we've been through are you sure you're willing to let me go just like that?"

Nicolas calmly sat on the bed and reached for the alarm clock, setting it to go off at 3.50pm. His determination to take his nap as normal further enraged Laura. In truth Nicolas was desperately trying to figure a way back without it looking as though he were backing down from his ultimatum. He got into the bed without answering. Laura was far from finished though. Nicolas's nonchalant behaviour really got under her skin.

"You know one day you will have no one if you keep shutting people out of your life every time they dent your ego, or don't agree with you."

No longer afraid of his reaction to her confrontational behaviour, Laura was on fire. Nicolas knew Laura was spirited, but she had never stood up to him like this before. Despite appearing to ignore her, he was in fact listening to every word; amazed at the way her anger had surfaced to confront him so fearlessly. It sort of turned him on. But of course Laura could never know that. Taken over by sheer rage, Laura called his bluff and dropped the bombshell;

"Okay fine I'll leave. But if I go, I will never come back, and don't think I will stay alone and spend the rest of my life crying over you."

Nicolas was stunned. He buried his face into the pillow to hide his shock at her outspoken defiance. He kept up his attitude of indifference by pretending he was going to sleep. This only served to infuriate Laura yet more. She had forgotten what a good actor Nicolas was. Of course he wasn't going to sleep; he was still trying to find a way to pull their relationship out of the ever expanding hole he had inadvertently dug. He had to do it without losing face though. Nicolas couldn't be seen to back down. Laura ignored the fact he was trying to sleep (or rather was pretending to), and kept ranting;

"You may find plenty of women willing to lie with you in the bed, but you will never find one who will stay, and put up with all your moodiness and controlling ways. No woman will ever love or understand you the way I do; Not one!"

"I need to sleep," he insisted, still pretending to be unperturbed at Laura's statement.

Fuming, Laura wasn't for one minute prepared to allow him to sleep peacefully.

"Oh go on, sleep then; if you can. Act like nothing has happened," she screamed.

It was at this point Laura noticed her Teddy Bear on the pillow next to Nicolas. She had bought it years ago at the airport and given it to Nicky, jokingly telling him;

"Now you have something to cuddle when I'm not here."

Laura couldn't explain why, but just seeing the bear in the bed alongside him made her blood boil; she became incensed. Aiming to be as disturbingly clumsy as possible, Laura clambered determinedly across the bed and snatched the bear away, resolutely telling Nicky;

"And don't think that bear is going to share the bed with you anymore either."

With the teddy bear tucked firmly under her arm, Laura stormed petulantly from the bedroom, slamming the door loudly behind her. Furiously determined to be as defiant as possible, Laura decided to go for a walk. She picked up her key, but before she could leave Nicolas appeared from the bedroom.

"Couldn't sleep huh!?" Laura snapped sarcastically.

"No," he said, as he wrapped his sarong around his waist.

"Good! I'm going out," she defiantly declared.

Laura rebelliously left the apartment, again deliberately slamming the front door as she left. The heavy wood door shook; the sound of her slamming it reverberated around the apartment. Her actions signified her intention to make a clear statement; if Nicolas wanted her to go, then he could no longer dictate where she went and what she did.

As she walked away from the apartment building Laura was seething. Her heart pounded as the adrenalin raced through her. Far from feeling upset, she momentarily felt liberated. It was the first time they had ever fought this way; Laura certainly had never raised her voice to him before.

Back inside the apartment Nicolas wasn't sure what had just taken place. Many times over the years he had shouted at Laura, but not once had she ever shouted back at him. Nicolas made a coffee and sat in his chair. He turned on the TV and immediately switched it off again. How could he sit and watch TV with Laura wandering around outside, going who knows where? He hesitated to dress and go after her. If he were to follow Laura it would look as though he were caving in. He lit a cigarette and contemplated his next move. Laura's words were ringing in his ears. A smile crept across his face as he recalled what she had said about the teddy bear. He had wanted to laugh at the time, but hadn't dared.

To Nicolas's surprise he no longer felt in the least bit angry. Sure he had been angry at first, but now found it impossible to stay angry with Laura. Was he going soft? Nicolas began examining himself closely. This was new territory, would he have to climb down and backtrack on his ultimatum? For the first time in his life it didn't matter, he felt ready to do just that. He realised he didn't want Laura to leave; he hadn't wanted it even when he had said it. It was merely a ricochet reaction fuelled by pride. Nicolas looked at the clock; Laura had been gone for nearly twenty minutes. He would wait another ten, and if she wasn't back, he would drive around and look for her.

After aimlessly walking for twenty minutes in a circle

round the block, Laura had calmed considerably. The anger had subsided along with the defiance. The feeling of liberty was short lived, and had turned to a feeling of regret. Laura was suddenly struck by the painful thought that it might be over for her and Nicolas. It immediately became apparent that without Nicolas, all the freedom in the world meant nothing at all. Subdued, and with an increasingly heavy heart, Laura made her way back. She wondered how this catastrophe could have happened. It was nothing more than a storm in a teacup, but one that could spell the end of her marriage. The defiance and bravado she had fleetingly felt, now seemed silly and pointless. Nicolas was her life blood, her reason to be. What would she do without him?

Laura entered the apartment block. Her whole life with Nicolas suddenly flashed before her. They had come through many obstacles and setbacks together. To end it all this way, would be tragic. Was it too late? Had Nicolas already closed the door on their relationship? Laura was only too aware, that once it closed it would remain so.

Laura stepped into the elevator. Using her door key she pressed the button for the third floor. With that one action it suddenly dawned just how much Nicolas had influenced her. Like him, Laura had developed the same habit of not touching the lift button by her hand. The unconscious act briefly made her smile. The lift doors opened at the third level. Laura wondered if she would be able to get in. Nicolas may have locked her out and refuse to open the door to her. It was the first time she had left the building without his permission. Laura's heart and her head pounded with trepidation as to the consequences. Nicolas was bound to be angry she had openly defied him.

Contemplating her fate, Laura stepped from the lift and walked along the short passage to the door at the end. Had she burnt her bridges by storming out? Laura took a deep breath. Placing her key into the lock she nervously turned it. Resignedly she thought to herself,

"Que sera, sera, what will be, will be?"

KOUSBAWI

Chapter 34: Saved by the Bear

Laura opened the door to the apartment and warily stepped inside. She could see Nicolas sitting at the computer. He must have heard Laura come in, but he deliberately didn't turn around or speak. Laura took his silence to mean he hadn't relented from his ultimatum. She went straight to the bedroom and started taking clothes from the wardrobe.

There was so much stuff to pack; Laura began piling her things onto the bed. Two large suitcases were sitting on the top of the wardrobe. Laura would need them if she were going to pack everything. Balancing precariously on the edge of the bed, Laura leant over trying to reach one of the cases. No way was she able to pull it down; she just wasn't tall enough to reach. There was only one thing for it; Laura would have to ask for Nicolas's help. Apprehensively she walked back to the lounge. Nicolas was leaning back in his leather desk chair thinking. Calmly, and being as polite and matter of fact sounding as she could be, Laura asked for his help.

"Would you please fetch down the suitcases from the top of the wardrobe for me?"

Nicolas had heard Laura packing her things, and was in a quandary how to reverse this ridiculous state of affairs. Still being ruled by his enormous pride though, he tried his best to be indifferent and not show any emotion.

"You want them now?" he asked brusquely.

"Yes, I've lots to pack," Laura replied, also trying to remain calm and unemotional.

"I'll get them later," he told her. Nicolas needed more time to think of a way out of this dilemma.

"No, I'd rather get things done, I'm leaving tomorrow," Laura insisted.

Realising his delaying tactic was not going to work as Laura seemed determined to leave, Nicolas announced;

271

"You don't have to go tomorrow."

If he persuaded Laura to stay another day he was sure he could turn things around. Laura thought she sensed a regretful tone in Nicky's voice. She decided to test it out.

"Yes I do; you're booking my ticket aren't you?"

"I didn't book it yet. Anyway they may not have space on a flight tomorrow," he reasoned.

If Laura persisted and didn't back down, he would simply keep delaying her flight until they had sorted things. When Nicolas wanted something, he made sure he got it; and what he wanted, was for Laura to stay with him. He decided to test the water with a somewhat deliberately cheeky tactic ordering;

"Make me coffee."

Acting as if everything were normal, Nicolas said it in his usual tongue in cheek, demanding, bossy manner.

Laura was now certain he was remorseful for having told her to leave. But she would make him sweat a little.

"Make your own coffee!" She snapped, and walked to the bedroom to continue with her packing.

Slightly stunned by Laura's obstinate refusal to make him his coffee, Nicolas felt for once he didn't exactly have the upper hand. And just to confirm it Laura shouted impatiently from the bedroom;

"I really need those suitcases."

Laura was putting up a brave front. Really she was dying to make up with Nicolas. She hoped he wouldn't call her bluff and actually fetch down the cases. He may well be feeling sorry that she would really leave him, but Laura knew Nicolas wouldn't just roll over and admit he was wrong. Over the years she had never known him to back down from anything. To Laura's subsequent relief, he didn't answer her about the suitcases; instead Nicolas grudgingly went to the kitchen to make his own coffee. Laura waited a few moments before going back to the lounge to repeat her request.

They were playing silly mind games with each other. Nicolas did not want Laura to leave him, and Laura didn't want to go. But both believed the other was prepared to go to the end to prove a point. Laura went back to the lounge. Just as she entered the room, Nicolas nonchalantly leant back in his chair and began smiling to himself. Laura was amazed to catch him with a look of amusement on his face. Infuriated that he appeared to find her leaving him so entertaining, she turned around to leave the room. Nicky reached out, grabbing Laura firmly by the wrist. Stopped in her tracks, she gave him a look of bewilderment.

Intending to break the icy façade they were both putting up, Nicolas was unable to prevent a spontaneous smile as he conveyed he was rather impressed by Laura's feisty confrontation. Grinning broadly he now admitted;

"I like what you said about the bear."

"Well, he is leaving with me," Laura retorted.

Led by his heart and for once giving his big man sized ego a back seat, Nicolas decided to end this silly saga once and for all. Enforcing the message he was not prepared to let her go easily, he pulled Laura to his lap. Still gripping hold of her wrist, he struggled to hold his stern expression. Instead he gave in to a smile, telling Laura;

"You know girl sometimes you make me so angry!"

Laura knew she had broken through his proud ego and responded spiritedly,

"You can be pretty obnoxious and annoying yourself."

Nicolas laughed at her remark, and in his typically confident slightly arrogant tone he declared smugly;

"Yeah but you love me."

Laura stared at him without answering.

The smug expression disappeared as he repeated with a less self-assured look;

"You love me, right?"

Laura knew she had him wrapped around her finger now. With a flirtatious smile she confirmed;

"That was never in question."

Within moments everything was turned on its head. Nicolas began kissing Laura with the same fiery passion that had previously exuded such anger, he then avowed;

"I love you girl, but sometimes I wanna kill you."

Laura felt herself drawn helplessly into his mesmeric dark eyes. As they seared into her, she was consumed by the passion they communicated.

Nicolas's mood became unexpectedly sombre. His eyes again conveyed the intensity of his emotions. A pleading expression was reflected as he looked at Laura and asked;

"You think you can continue to live with me Loulou?"

"Well I've survived till now; I think I can manage."

"You promise you will stay with me forever?"

Laura responded with a sincere declaration;

"Until I take my very last breath."

Reassured by her assertion Nicolas smiled, telling her;

"Then Loulou let me make love to you."

With feverish passion, they expressed their love for each other intimately. As they became closer physically and emotionally, both felt they were seeing the other for the first time all over again. It was like waking up and discovering some great secret, but realising it was never really a secret; it was always there waiting to be seen.

The fear of almost losing something precious awakens you to what is really important in life. If you want to prevent a treasure slipping from your grasp, you have to at times let go of your pride; you cannot always hold on to both. Pushing each other and their relationship to the precipice, was a testing exercise for Nicolas and Laura, although neither was ever in any real danger of losing the others love, though both believed they were.

Something valuable was learned. Nicolas discovered that by putting his stubborn pride to one side, rather than lose anything, he actually gained. Laura was reminded that true unconditional love requires embracing and accepting all that a person is. Without the other, both were as flowers trying to grow in a garden devoid of sunlight and rain. Nicolas was the sunshine that brightened Laura's life, keeping her soul fed and warm. Laura was the soft rain that refreshed and awakened his desire, gently quenching the thirst of his impassioned soul.

Something as intangible, imperceptible, and elusive as love, cannot be held or lost; love just is. When you know love, you understand it is something far beyond the ever changing illusion of the physical world.

Like death, love is only truly comprehensible when you have walked in its realms.

Chapter 35: Book of Life

In early September that year Laura received some sad news. Her Aunty Joan who was her mother's only sibling, unexpectedly passed away. A few days later, Laura's own mother was suddenly admitted to hospital suffering from an extreme form of dementia. Initially treated for what doctors had believed was Parkinson's, Laura's mother had become increasingly frail and delusional. The hospital diagnosis proved Laura's earlier suspicions to be right; her mother was not suffering from Parkinson's disease at all, but rather a form of dementia, known as Lewy body. The dementia was possibly exacerbated by the unexpected death of her sister.

Laura was due to take a trip to the UK to renew her visa, and was booked on a flight in two weeks' time. Laura's sister Caralyn, said there was no urgency for Laura to return, as their mother's illness wasn't life threatening and she was being well cared for. The beginning of October Laura travelled back, and the day after her arrival went with her sister to visit their mother.

Laura was shocked at what she saw. The frail woman lying in the hospital bed bared little resemblance to the woman Laura knew as her mother; it was like looking at a stranger. Almost skeletal with her skin pulled tight over her face and body, and all her bones protruding; her mother's rapid decline was upsetting, and more noticeable to Laura who had not seen her in a while.

It was impossible to have a normal conversation with their mother, as her mind had now slipped completely into the realms of delusion. Laura doubted she even knew who they were at times. During their visit, Laura's mother spent most of the time having nonsensical conversations with an imaginary entity she referred to as John. Laura's sister said their mother had been doing this since she was brought in to the hospital. There were brief moments of lucidity when she would recognise Laura and her sister Caralyn, but the conversation would be erratic and absurd. It seemed their mother was present in two different realities. She would be lucid for a short while, and then be lost within the other world; a world only she could see and where she was absorbed in her conversations with the mystical John.

The doctor's prognosis was grim. The sisters were told their mother would require round the clock care for the rest of her life. Once she was strong enough to leave hospital, she would be admitted to a nursing home. The doctor said her condition was far too serious to allow her to return home.

Tuesday evening a couple of weeks later, after another lengthy interaction with her invisible friend John, Laura's mother turned to her two daughters and announced;

"I saw the book today."

"What book?" Laura asked.

Looking incredulously at her daughter, and with an irritated tone, Laura's mother exclaimed;

"THE BOOK!"

Laura decided to humour her;

"Okay, and what was in this book?"

"It's my book," her mother answered proudly.

Laura looked at Caralyn who just shrugged. Deciding to go along with her mother's strange imaginings, Laura asked her to elaborate on this book. In between dialogues with John, Laura's mother told them she had been asked to choose a picture for her special book. Laura was intrigued;

"What's the book about?"

Laura's mother smiled wistfully adding;

"Its a story, my story, and it ends at 2 o'clock."

"And what happens at 2 o' clock?" Laura continued to probe.

With a heavy sigh of exasperation, Laura's mother stared at them. Her expression was one of intolerance, as if thinking them stupid for not knowing. Then in a matter of fact fashion she announced;

"At 2 o'clock that's my lot."

The two sisters' exchanged incredulous glances. Laura persisted, asking her mother;

"What do you mean?"

Their mother gave another impatient huff;

"The story ends at 2'clock, that's my lot; finished," she stated emphatically, then quite unconcernedly revealed,

"I can have another hundred years if I want, but I don't have to."

After her very strange proclamation, Laura's mother immediately retreated into her invisible world, where she remained for the rest of their visit conversing solely with 'John'.

During the drive home, Laura and Caralyn discussed their mother's odd revelations. Was it just the ramblings of a woman with severe dementia, or something else? Laura's sister was dubious, but Laura wasn't so quick to dismiss it as pure fantasy. There was something about the way their mother looked when talking with 'John'; she appeared to really be seeing and interacting with another being, even if he was invisible to everyone else.

Laura believed her mother had been given access to the Akashic records, and perhaps glimpsed her own book of life; maybe even had a life review. Laura was a believer in all things spiritual.

On the following Friday, Laura was to attend an appointment for a routine check-up. Whilst she was at the hospital, she planned to visit her mother. The Thursday before, Laura spent most of the evening on Skype video with Nicolas. After talking with him for nearly four hours, she was tired. When they finally switched off the Skype, Laura decided to go straight to bed. Falling asleep quickly she experienced an unusual dream. Laura woke Friday morning clearly recalling every detail; just as with the tsunami dream, but this time her dream had more pleasant connotations.

Laura dreamt of being in a room, it felt familiar to her, although it was not a place she recognised. There were other people present who were also familiar, but again Laura couldn't say who they were. In this room Laura was overtaken by a desire to see her late Aunt, the sister of her mother who had passed away six weeks earlier. Being in Abu Dhabi at the time, Laura was unable to attend her aunt's funeral. Immediately after expressing the desire to see her aunt, a swirling white mist instantaneously rose up from the floor in front of her. As it rose higher, the mist took on a solidified form, eventually materialising into a familiar being. Straight away Laura recognised her aunty. Smiling at her, Joan conveyed to Laura telepathically that she was supremely happy in the afterlife and depicted a serene peaceful countenance. Laura was elated to see her.

A million questions filled Laura's mind; there was so much she wanted to ask. During this brief ethereal encounter, no words were spoken. Laura heard herself communicate with her aunt's spirit in her mind. She asked the obvious question, 'what it was like on the other side?' Smiling serenely and without using speech, her aunt again conveyed she was blissfully happy and at peace. They hugged, and Laura could feel her aunt's form. It was not solid in the sense that a physical body would be. Visually it appeared smooth like an alabaster statue. There was softness about the spirit's form that radiated with warmth and love. Laura found it comforting. Joan's ethereal body, although lighter than an earthly body, had substance and presence that could be felt. Laura experienced a sense of euphoria in this realm. Slowly, her aunt's form began to fade and Laura remembered there was something she wanted to ask. As the spirit melted from her view, Laura called out;

"Wait! There's something I need to know." But her aunt was gone.

Instantly Laura woke filled with an extraordinary feeling of elation. As she dressed and got ready for her hospital appointment, she couldn't stop thinking about the dream. The joyous euphoria she felt on waking stayed with her. Laura believed the vision was real, but her sceptical side needed proof. She felt compelled to exclaim out loud;

"If it was real, give me a sign."

Laura's eyes were inexplicably drawn to an old wooden music box on the dressing table. It had belonged to Laura's maternal grandmother. As children, Laura and her sister loved to hear the music box play. Their grandmother would wind it up, and they would be enthralled as it played a little tune entitled, 'I'll be loving you, always'. For nearly twenty years the music box had been broken. No matter how many times Laura wound the key or shook it, the box would not play a single note. Laura removed it from the dressing table and placed it on her bed. Again out loud she pleaded;

"If my dream was a true vision, please make the music box play."

Without touching anything else, Laura carefully opened the lid and waited. Instantly the music box started to play. Not once, but six times in succession, it played the tune all the way through perfectly, and without faltering.

Laura was beside herself; overcome with excitement and emotion. Somehow through her dream Laura had communicated with her late aunt's spirit. After the sixth rendition of the tune, the music box abruptly stopped. Laura picked it up and wound the key; nothing happened. She gently shook the box; again not a whisper. Not even an odd note. The music box was again rendered silent as it had been for twenty odd years.

All the way to the hospital Laura thought about her extraordinary dream, and the miraculous episode with the music box. She was desperate to tell someone; but who would believe it? On entering the building, Laura suddenly recalled what it was she had wanted to ask her aunt, before her spirit disappeared into the ether. Laura was curious why Joan was dressed as she was from head to foot in black, with a fine veil covering her smiling face. Joan had appeared to Laura dressed as if attending a funeral, yet she looked so radiantly joyous.

Luckily Laura's appointment was on time, and she was

in and out quickly. Just before eleven o'clock, she made her way to the ward where her mother was. It was not normal visiting time, but the nurse on duty said it would be fine for Laura to go in. Laura asked how her mother had been and was surprised to be told her mother's condition seemed to have improved. Apparently Laura's mother had eaten a hearty breakfast that morning. It was the first time she had shown any interest in food since her admittance six weeks earlier. Laura was told she could spend an hour with her mother before lunch arrived at noon.

Entering the ward, Laura was again surprised to see her mother out of bed sitting in a chair. She appeared alert, and her normally pale cheeks showed a little colour. Laura was pleased she had lost the awful pallid look. While conversing, her mother frequently made direct eye contact. Laura noticed her pale blue eyes now reflected a little light in them, something which had not been present for a while. Although she still wandered into her own world from time to time, for most of the hour they had a fairly lucid, almost normal conversation. Laura felt encouraged; perhaps her mother might regain some quality of life if she continued to improve this way; her future may not be so dismal after all. Laura's optimism grew as her mother expressed she was looking forward to lunch. Before she left, Laura told her mother she would be back later that evening with Caralyn. Her mother said,

"Tell Caralyn not to be too late."

Laura kissed her goodbye, and left the hospital to take the bus into town. It was a bright autumn day, and as Laura waited at the bus stop, a feeling of relief swept over her at the improvement her mother had shown. Laura called her friend Shelley; they had arranged to meet for coffee. Thirty minutes later, Laura was walking towards the centre of town to the café where she was to meet her friend. As she approached the coffee shop, Laura spotted Shelley waiting at the entrance. Laura waved and Shelley waved back acknowledging she had seen Laura. Just then Laura's mobile rang. It was Caralyn; she sounded frantic and upset.

"We have to go to the hospital now," Caralyn said. "It's mum."

"What do you mean?" Laura asked mystified. "I've just left her a little over an hour ago, she was fine."

"Well she's not now," said Laura's sister in a panicked tone. "The hospital just rang me."

Laura was stunned; she couldn't believe it.

"I will pick you up outside of Piccolo Mondo." Caralyn told her.

Piccolo Mondo was a little Italian restaurant that many years ago was once owned by their father. She would meet her sister there, being as it was the easiest place for Caralyn to stop on route to the hospital. Oblivious of the sudden change of plan, Shelley was still waiting at the front of the coffee shop. Laura needed to get to the restaurant at the other end of town quickly. She hurriedly apologised;

"Sorry Shelley I can't stop, Carolyn's just called. We have to go back to the hospital mum's had a turn."

Laura raced up the high street to meet her sister outside of Piccolo Mondo. At 1.30 pm Caralyn arrived looking stressed. Laura barely managed to get into the car before her sister sped away in the direction of the hospital.

"What happened?" Laura asked.

"I'm not really sure but the hospital said we had better get there soon."

Driving like a maniac Caralyn was a bag of nerves.

"Slow down!" Laura yelled at her sister. "Or we are going to have an accident."

"I can't! Look at the time." Caralyn pointed at the cars clock. "We have to be there by 2 o'clock, remember she said 2 o'clock?"

Laura remembered. Tuesday evening their mother had told them her story would end at 2 o' clock. It would take roughly twenty minutes to get there, and at this time of day the traffic was horrendous. The way her sister was driving Laura felt sure they would be stopped by the police for speeding. Eventually they arrived in one piece. Quickly parking the car Laura and Caralyn rushed into the hospital with just minutes to spare before 2 pm.

The sisters raced down the corridor to their mother's ward, but were stopped from entering. The consultant led them into a nearby room where he explained that their mother had suffered heart failure. He said the doctors were trying their best to resuscitate her. Laura glanced at the clock on the wall; it was three minutes past two. A nurse entered the room and asked if they would like to see their mother. The sisters followed her to the ward. The curtains were closed around their mother's bed.

"I'm very sorry," the nurse told them. "We couldn't save her."

Laura looked at the body lying in front of them on the hospital bed. It was just an empty shell that bared no resemblance to the person Laura been talking to less than two hours ago. Laura and Caralyn were permitted to stay with their mother's body for a few moments. The consultant said he would like to talk to them. They went back to the small room where he explained that their mother had sustained a massive heart attack. Laura asked to speak to the nurse who had been on duty at the time. The nurse told them their mother had eaten and enjoyed her lunch, and then at her request been helped into the chair next to her bed.

Since her admittance to hospital their mother had been so frail and weak, she was unable to stand upright without support. The nurse reported that today she had appeared unusually happy and relaxed. After making their mother comfortable in her chair, the nurse left her for a moment to attend to another patient.

The lady in the bed opposite revealed to the sisters that their mother had suddenly stood bolt upright completely unassisted. She had then attempted to walk, moving in a purposeful manner as if going somewhere. The lady added that Laura's mother had an expression of recognition on her face, like she was walking to meet someone she knew.

That was when she suddenly suffered massive heart failure and collapsed.

Laura asked the doctor who had tried to resuscitate her, at what time their mother had died. The doctor told her;

"2 o' clock, your mother passed at exactly 2 o' clock."

KOUSBAWI

Chapter 36: Reaching For the Stars

After the funeral Laura returned directly to Abu Dhabi. It was strange to no longer receive the regular weekly phone calls from her mother. Laura wasn't sure how she felt; she was sad of course, but had come to terms with the loss long before her mother's actual physical death. For some time Laura felt her mother was slowly slipping away. From her first visit to the hospital, Laura accepted that the woman she once knew was already gone. Her mother never fully came to terms with the death of her husband; Laura's father sadly passed away five years earlier, having lost his brave two year battle with cancer. Sometimes it's just too hard to carry on when the person who has always been there for you is suddenly gone.

Laura wondered how it would feel to lose Nicolas. The thought of facing a life without him, filled her with dread. Laura would happily die tomorrow rather than lose her beloved soul-mate. But Nicolas was indestructible; or so he believed, and he had succeeded in convincing Laura of it too. Unlike most men he would never admit to being ill or having the flu. If he did happen to catch a cold, he insisted it would not stay with him more than twenty four hours. Amazingly it never did. He would boast declaring;

"The germs will run from me; they are scared from Al Hajj."

Leading up to Christmas 2010, Nicolas again turned his attention to building a serious collection of antiques. He was determined to follow through with his plan and start an antiques business in Abu Dhabi. Impetuous as ever, he began bidding for items in online auctions. Cameras were his first point of interest, and he successfully bid for and won three items in his very first auction. He was so excited at winning, but would become frustrated and moody if he lost a bid; Nicolas hated to lose at anything.

Laura watched with interest as Nicolas excitedly bid on various items. The problem arose when he needed to pay for them. At present, Nicolas didn't have a credit card or a PayPal account. Laura had a credit card, and Alyssa had a Pay Pal account. The first five cameras' he won at auction, Alyssa purchased via her account. To assist Nicolas further in his endeavour, Laura increased the limit on her credit card and opened a Pay Pal account of her own. Whatever antiques were purchased, or won in auctions, Laura paid for. She agreed to finance the putting together of a collection until Nicolas received the money that was owed him from various projects and people he had lent money to, and from the many business's he was in partnership with. Certain individuals owed him a great deal of money. Laura's financial input kept things afloat for Nicolas while he awaited payment.

Over the coming year they worked hard at building up the antiques business. Pretty soon they had accumulated an impressive collection. Some of the smaller dealers would not ship to the UAE due to the expense and hassle, so Nicolas arranged for these items to be shipped directly to Laura's house in England. The larger more valuable antiques were delivered directly to his container in Abu Dhabi. Many filled every spare corner in the apartment until things started to get quite cramped. As he was rarely there, Tony told Nicolas to use the space in his room for storage.

On Nicolas's instructions, Laura rented a unit in the UK to store the items delivered to her house, as she had no place or room for them. Eventually the whole lot would be shipped to Abu Dhabi. Nicolas wanted to delay this until he had found a villa. The idea was to use part of the villa as a showroom. Laura would run the business from there. Nicolas was keen to ensure Laura would have something to occupy her without the need to leave the house.

When he first suggested it, Laura smiled; fully aware Nicolas was much happier knowing her whereabouts every minute of the day.

As usual Nicolas took charge; choosing which antiques to bid for and what to purchase. He made all the decisions regarding development, and marketing of the business. It made sense as he was the one with all the contacts. When it came to business, Nicolas knew what was what. He had the best ideas, and was well acquainted with how things worked in the Emirates. Already he had managed to generate a great deal of interest in their joint project. Laura had complete faith and confidence in his judgement. He assured Laura's investment would soon be fully returned to her. Laura had used her savings to fund the project, and had no qualms about letting Nicolas take the reins. She trusted him implicitly.

The local museum conveyed an interest in renting the collection for display, and there were promising deals discussed with organisers of the Emirates annual book and film festivals. Nicolas talked of hosting a fashion show where parts of the collection would be showcased.

With so many openings and opportunities, it appeared they couldn't fail. Nicolas knew exactly what he wanted and the future looked amazingly bright.

Alyssa and Nicolas spent many hours on Skype to one another. They had formed a strong bond and affectionately gave each other pet names. Nicolas wanted to spend time with her. He talked constantly of the villa he would soon acquire, and said he looked forward to Alyssa coming to stay with them in Abu Dhabi. Laura couldn't wait for this to materialise; she would no longer feel torn between two worlds.

Alyssa was helping Nicolas with setting up a website for the antiques. They were currently working on a name for it and had potentially settled on 'Kousba House Antiques'. This was after some rather amusing earlier suggestions by Nicolas. He insisted he had found the perfect name, Kousba House of Art, which sounded fine until Alyssa pointed out that the website address would read; kousba@houseofart, Alyssa didn't think that would somehow be appropriate.

Nicolas promised to buy Laura two kittens when they moved to the villa. He wanted two cats so they could play together; he had always felt sorry that Bingo never had another cat to play with. Sadly Bingo went missing while they were living in the 'Cave'. One day while Nicolas was at work and Laura was away in the UK, Bingo somehow escaped from the enclosed garden. Despite numerous attempts by Nicolas to find him, Bingo unfortunately never returned. At the time Nicolas was devastated, and refused to talk about the incident or even mention Bingo's name. He felt responsible, having failed to notice and repair a slight tear in the netting covering the garden enclosure.

As a young boy, Nicolas had a little dog called Percie with whom he had developed a similarly strong bond. Nicolas often shared his fond memories of Percie, affectionately telling how he had taught her to do tricks. Just like Bingo, Percie had been a close companion until one day she lay down and went to sleep; Percie had passed away peacefully from old age. When the unfortunate incident with Bingo occurred, Nicolas was distraught. Only recently had he felt ready to discuss getting another cat.

Keen to have a garden to sit in again, Nicolas was eager to find a villa. He was never happier than when tending the small garden back at the 'Cave'. Nicolas yearned for the normality that for so long had been denied to him. He imagined warm evenings eating dinner outside under the stars with Laura. At the weekends friends would come for barbeques, just as they had at the old house. With his soon to be acquired papers, he would establish his own company, and with his construction projects and a flourishing antiques business, they would have no money worries. It was all within his reach; in just a few months Nicolas would finally be able to give Laura the long term stability he had always promised.

Nicolas couldn't imagine a time when he would not love Laura. Often they would joke about which one of them would grow old first. Nicolas made Laura laugh by his playacting, pretending to walk with a stick like an old man, telling her she would one day be pushing him around in a chair. But he would quickly retract, insisting;

"What you think I will get old Loulou? No way, I'm still a lovely boy," he laughed. "But you Loulou will lose your mind, and not remember who I am. Who is that lovely young man you will say?" Nicolas smiled at the thought of them in old age.

Whatever the future held, he knew he and Laura would be there for one another till the end. One day while they were again light-heartedly talking on the subject, Laura asked Nicolas to make her a promise;

"Will you promise me that if you die first, when it's my turn to go, your spirit will come back and get me?"

Nicolas was adamant in his reply,

"Don't worry Loulou, it is me who will be burying you love."

"Good, that's the way I would prefer. But promise me anyway, just in case," Laura pleaded.

"Love, I'm not going to die. I have many things still to do."

"You're not immortal. Promise me you will come back for me; say it please." Laura insisted.

Nicolas was reluctant to consider his own unthinkable demise.

"Okay love, I promise I will come for you Loulou."

He laughed as he said it, and then pretended to frown at Laura saying,

"What you mean by I am not immortal? I am Al Hajj."

It seemed Nicolas really did believe on some level that he was indestructible. Laura told him;

"I promise if I die first I will come back for you."

Nicky gave Laura a feigned look of horror saying;

"You mean you will haunt me?" he kidded.

Carefree and happy they laughed, firmly believing they had many long years ahead of them before either would seriously need to contemplate the other's demise.

Finally, all their hard work was coming to fruition.

Nicolas was optimistic in reaching all his goals. Content with his lot, he felt there was so much to look forward to. He had money again, not quite the millions as before, but he was pretty comfortable.

After encountering more than his share of slippery snakes along the way, Nicolas had climbed back up the ladder, wrung by wrung. He was reaching for the stars now, and if he had his way, would take the moon as well.

KOUSBAWI

Chapter 37: One Last Summer

Summer arrived in the Emirates, and Abu Dhabi looked beautiful with its magnificent buildings shining like jewels in the hot desert sun. The parks and gardens at night were illuminated by hundreds of lights. Taking pride of place in the city centre was a large silver fountain in the shape of a cedar tree. One day while driving past Nicolas told Laura; "It is known locally as the Lebanese fountain."

With its immense wealth, Abu Dhabi exuded opulent sophistication and an extravagant lifestyle. The financial capital of the emirates was the envy of the Middle East.

There had been considerable changes since Laura's first visit in the eighties. Even more since Nicolas arrived in the late seventies to work in his father's company. With its enormous earning potential, opportunity and growth, the UAE had always been a desirable destination, especially for westerners. On the outskirts of Abu Dhabi, places like Musaffah were constantly under construction. Wide open spaces that only a few years ago Laura remembered as vast expanses of desert, were now spectacularly transformed into upmarket residential areas.

Luxury villas with perfectly manicured gardens and modern, beautifully designed shopping malls and hotels, were popping up everywhere. The excellently constructed well-lit roads stretched across the desert, uniformly lined on either side with fully grown palms. At night the parks looked like fairy grottos, lit up by hundreds of lights. Whenever Laura travelled back to the UK, everything there appeared so small, dull and dismal in comparison.

One evening Nicolas and Laura were driving back from the Abu Dhabi Mall. Laura noticed a villa that was completely covered by thousands of fairy lights. Nicky explained it was the custom whenever a wedding was taking place. Necklaces of lights were draped over the

291

entire villa making it appear as a precious jewel against the velvety inky blackness of the desert night sky.

Nicolas would often drive around the residential complexes, excitedly showing Laura the type of villa he was considering renting for them. New complexes were being constructed all the time, and Laura was thrilled that very soon they would be living in just such a place.

Their present apartment was too small and cramped, especially as it was now stuffed full of antiques. Despite its isolation, the 'Cave', did have its own special kind of charm. Nicolas had done his best to make it comfortable and beautiful inside, but Laura rarely got to step outside of the place, and would jokingly liken it to a prison.

Nicolas was now happy for Laura to take a taxi to and from the Maziad Mall in Mussafah. The very first time she did so, was unfortunately a calamitous affair.

On the day in question, Nicolas drove Laura to the Mall. On the way he carefully instructed her of the route, pointing out all the landmarks. He wanted to be sure Laura would confidently be able to direct the taxi driver. Assured that she was well acquainted with the directions and route back to the apartment, he dropped Laura at the entrance of the mall and headed off to his meeting. The condition of this rare freedom was that Laura would be back at the apartment before it got dark.

Playing it safe, Laura left the Maziad mall at 4pm while there was still a couple of hours of daylight left. She made her way to the taxi terminal. Standing with a number of other people she waited in line for a taxi. A stream of cabs were arriving, forming a long queue in front of the Maziad entrance. In no time at all Laura was at the front of the queue and happily got into the next available cab. After informing the driver of the area she wished to go, Laura sat back and took careful note, checking they were going in the same direction that Nicolas had driven. They passed all the usual landmarks he had told her to look out for, and when they reached the fourth roundabout, Laura told the driver to take the next turning on the right.

The driver was not paying attention and consequently missed the turning. Frantically Laura informed him of his mistake, but he continued driving for another mile or so, before eventually turning the car around. Laura started to panic as they were now going in the wrong direction in an area she was unfamiliar with. The driver repeatedly asked which way to go. Trying to stay calm, Laura desperately looked for the turning he had missed. Nothing was recognisable or familiar; all the roads looked the same.

Laura suddenly felt uncomfortably vulnerable, not to mention foolish for not knowing her way. Matters were made worse when she tried to explain to the cab driver where he had gone wrong. It soon became apparent he didn't speak or understand English; the little he did speak was barely legible. Laura could of course call Nicky who would immediately jump in the jeep and come to her rescue. Being as it was Laura's first journey alone; she was reluctant to call him. She wanted to prove she was capable, otherwise she feared he may never let her out alone again.

They seemed to be travelling along the same stretch of road for ever; in reality it was probably only five minutes. Nothing was ringing any bells, and Laura's state of panic heightened. Desperately she scanned the area for familiar sights and clues as to her whereabouts. But she still failed to recognise any buildings or land marks.

Suddenly in the distance Laura saw what she thought was a familiar building. Exasperated and stressed, she yelled at the driver to immediately stop the car. Laura paid him and hurriedly got out, but as the taxi drove away from her, Laura knew she was hopelessly lost.

The late afternoon sun was still very hot, and her heart raced furiously as she became increasingly more flustered. The rising humidity together with Laura's panicked state, made her slightly breathless. Pushing her now very damp hair away from her face, Laura studied her surroundings looking for any tiny hint or sign as to where she was. Not seeing any, Laura aimlessly continued walking.

She passed a mosque where a group of local men were

gathered outside, waiting for the call to evening prayer. They stared at Laura as she passed; being foreign and the only woman out in that area, she was rather conspicuous. Uncomfortable at the men's ogling; Laura quickly turned the corner into the next street. She spotted a supermarket, and started walking towards it, praying to see something she recognised. Again she was faced with a sea of men in local Islamic dress heading straight towards her. Once again as they passed, they stared as if she were an alien. The relentless heat mercilessly added to her anxiety and discomfort. Laura was becoming more and more flustered. She was beginning to wish she had stayed at home.

After walking in the intense humidity for what felt like hours, which was in actual fact around twenty minutes, Laura at last recognised something; a mobile phone shop. She gave a silent sigh of relief and quickened her pace as she headed for it. She came to a super market she knew she had definitely seen before. Gradually Laura recognised more and more buildings, until eventually she was in sight of their apartment block. The utter relief made her feel quite tearful.

Laura slowed her pace and breathed, trying to compose herself before going inside. She did not want Nicky to know she had got lost and been so panicked. He would be angry that she didn't call him. As Laura approached the building, she had never felt so happy to see the familiar blue painted window frames of their apartment block.

Once safely inside her anxiety eased immediately, but was replaced with a sudden feeling of resentment towards Nicolas. If he had allowed her more freedom to go out and get to know the area, this episode would never have arisen. Nicolas's insistence to keep Laura so isolated had left her vulnerable. Her total dependence on him felt debilitating. Infuriated, Laura contemplated whether to tell him of her unnerving predicament.

Stepping from the elevator, she wondered if he would understand that he had not done her any favours by being so over protective. The irony was Nicolas's bid to protect her, inadvertently exposed Laura to more risk.

Sometime after the event, she communicated what had occurred that day. Nicolas listened intently while Laura recalled the incident, explaining how vulnerable it made her feel. He didn't get angry, but told Laura she should have called him straight away and he would have found her. After hearing Laura confess her feelings about the unfortunate incident, Nicolas felt responsible for what had happened. Laura hoped that from now on she would have a little more liberty. On the contrary, rather than allow Laura more freedom to come and go, Nicolas tightened the reins even more. When Laura protested, he refused to budge on the subject. Instead he would pacify her by promising things would be different when they moved to a villa. Laura was frustrated, but Nicolas managed to convince her; she would just have to be patient.

Accepting Nicolas was not going to change his mind, Laura began to embrace staying home. It was easier to adapt than she thought; at least she felt nowhere near as isolated as in the 'Cave'. Funnily enough, after a time Laura began to lose interest in going out and about. Instead she cherished every moment spent at home with Nicky. He himself was quite content, and rarely felt the need for socialising. Of course there were occasional outings, but apart from his meetings and work, Nicky didn't appear to want to go out much at all. Laura thought it a little odd her husband was so reluctant to socialise. Nicolas though, had his reasons for keeping a low profile on the social scene.

That summer Nicolas and Laura were sublimely happy. The chemistry and attraction still remained as strong as when they had first met. Nicolas's fiery and passionate personality was tempered by a loving romantic streak, and cheeky sense of humour. Laura still found him irresistibly alluring. Everyday they shared much laughter. Nicolas's playful teasing was often challenged by Laura's quick wit. On a rare occasion Laura would firmly put Nicolas in his place, with humour of course; the only way she would ever get away with it.

Nicolas adored Laura, and his strong attraction was often demonstrated. He knew her intimately; physically and mentally. Beneath Laura's deceptively fragile exterior, she possessed attributes and strengths Nicolas recognised and admired. Despite coming as they did from vastly different cultures and backgrounds, they managed to strike a harmonious balance. Nicolas had never shown any real interest in dance or the arts. He enjoyed watching it occasionally, but never shared Laura's passion for the arts; except for Fairuz. An admired and respected Lebanese singer, Fairuz's passionate patriotic renditions, would fire up Nicolas's deep rooted patriotism and love for Lebanon, and he would often play Fairuz's music. Whether angered or joyfully happy, Listening to Fairuz was an outlet for his strong emotions.

Nicolas was proud for the way Laura had joined him in his venture with antiques on pure trust. Knowing nothing of antiques, Laura had not been keen initially. Faithfully following Nicolas's lead, she became devoted to making it work for him. That summer of 2011 was the best. Forging their future they continued to reach for the stars, determined to hold them firmly in their grasp.

Sadly the world news was peppered with stories of economic meltdown. Nicolas assured Laura that with its great wealth, Abu Dhabi would remain unaffected by the crisis. Over time Nicolas's inspiring self-belief rubbed off on Laura. With his nurturing and persuasion, she gained confidence in her own abilities; like a butterfly emerging from its chrysalis into full glory.

Comfortable at last in her own skin, Laura looked forward to the future. The dreams her husband had held to for so long, Laura believed were now not only possible, but finally within their reach.

"Don't allow anyone to walk on your dreams," Nicolas told Laura. "People like to smash the dreams of others."

"Why is that?" Laura asked.

"I dunno Loulou; maybe they don't have something of their own to believe in. Jealousy from others can destroy you." He continued; "Have you heard about the evil eye?"

"I've heard something, but I'm not sure what it means," Laura confessed.

"It's when a person wants or envies something about another," Nicky explained. "You've seen here many things with an eye on it, right?"

"Yes," Laura confirmed. "I've seen necklaces and key rings with a blue and white eye. I've seen them hanging in cars and in shops, and people wearing them. What are they for?" She was intrigued to know

"They are for protection against what we call here the evil eye; protection against the negative, envious or jealous thoughts of others."

Laura gave an amazed expression.

"Really, their thoughts?"

"Yes love, thoughts are powerful, people can harm you with their bad thoughts and even harm themselves without meaning to." Nicky enlightened.

It was the first time Laura had ever heard Nicolas talk this way of superstition, let alone admit to believing in it. Normally her husband would refuse to give credence to such matters; Laura was fascinated to hear him talk of it now.

"Do you believe it then?" she asked curiously.

"Yeah it happens," he admitted.

"So why don't you have one of those eyes then?" Laura enquired.

Nicolas pondered a moment, and then began to divulge a little story from his childhood;

"Love, you know when I was a kid around seven years or maybe five years; there was this lady in the village. She was nice lady, nothing bad with her. I was playing outside and she was standing near talking to my aunty. You know my aunty Hani, the one who take care of me after my mother die. They were standing near to me. The lady looked at me and said to my aunty, Oh! He's a lovely boy. I wish I had a boy just like that." Nicolas paused and lit a cigarette, then continued with his tale;

"A short time after I get sick, very sick," he dragged on his cigarette, "I was almost unconscious. My aunty called the doctor. When he came he could find no reason for my illness. He looked at my eyes and they had turned a yellow colour. The doctor told my aunty Hani it is the evil eye; someone has put their eye on the boy because they want to take something he has."

Laura listened, enthralled by the strange tale.

Nicolas gazed straight ahead and took another drag on his cigarette; he then continued with the story;

"Yeah love, this lady didn't mean me any harm but she wanted something she didn't have."

"So you're saying the doctor actually believed it was the evil eye did that to you?" Laura queried, not sure she would have reached the same conclusion. "It's like witchcraft."

"Yeah, kind of," Nicolas agreed. "But the lady meant no harm to me. Everyone does it without knowing how their thoughts have power."

Apparently the lady's fixed stares and over admiring glances at the young Nicolas, had an unconscious and unintentional malevolent impact. Laura was astonished. She stared at Nicky in disbelief.

"So you really believe this?" She asked incredulously.

"Yep, Loulou even you have done it," he told her.

"What do you mean?" Laura asked in a surprised tone.

Nicky took Laura's hand in his. Looking into her eyes he asked;

"Tell me you have never admired or envied something about someone else. Be honest Loulou."

"Yes of course, everyone does. It doesn't mean I wish to harm anyone." Laura protested.

"You don't get it." Nicky dragged hard on his cigarette. "Not everyone means harm Loulou, but it happens," he insisted. "You have to protect yourself, from your own thoughts too."

"So tell me, why you don't have one of those eyes for protection?" she argued.

Nicolas sighed, stubbing out his cigarette in a deliberate manner. Laura pressed him for an answer;

"Well?" she pushed.

Nicolas turned and pointed at the picture of the Virgin Mary on the shelf above his desk;

"I don't need it because she is taking care of me," he said. "I have my Christianity, my Jesus Christ, and most importantly I have myself." His voice carried an air of defiance. Nicky's eyes narrowed as he lit another cigarette. "Love nothing can harm me."

Nicky exhaled deeply. The smoke from his cigarette wafted in front of his face. He looked at Laura and smiled; "Got it, or got it not?" He patted her leg affectionately.

Laura smiled back saying;

"Maybe I should get one of those eyes?"

Nicolas lifted his cigarette to his lips and took another drag. Leaning forward he squeezed Laura's hand. With a mischievous twinkle in his eye he told her;

"Loulou you don't need it, you have me okay? You have Al Hajj."

Many times during the evenings Nicolas would turn off the television, and engage in conversation about his life, his deep political views, and philosophy. Laura never grew tired of listening to him. She was held spellbound by his fascinating tales, predictions, and solid words of wisdom.

The summer of 2011 was the happiest and most content Laura had ever been. She began to think and believe more like Nicolas; they were unbreakable, unstoppable.

But whether it was the hand of fate at play or the evil eye, another cruel blow was about to be dealt. One that would batter their dreams, tear them apart, and cast them mercilessly into the wind.

Chapter 38:
A shadow Over Her Shoulder

The summer turned to autumn, and the days that followed were filled with ominous news in the media of chaos and disruption around the world. Violence had escalated in northern Africa, Egypt and in Syria. With his impressive political knowledge, Nicolas had uncannily predicted these events long before they were all over the television and internet. He studied closely the unfolding events in Syria. As it bordered his homeland Lebanon, Nicolas feared his beloved country may be embroiled in another civil war not of its making. Laura found the politics of the Middle East extremely complicated and difficult to comprehend. Like Nicolas she watched with interest the escalating events, but didn't share his expertise on the subject. Laura listened to her husband's comments, and would be amazed at his uncanny ability to understand, and accurately predict the political state of play. Nicolas instinctively knew the way things were headed, foreseeing possible outcomes long before they occurred.

Although Laura had her opinions, she didn't possess a political mind. She felt it was a cultural thing. Nicolas had been born into a country where politics were a natural way of life; he had grown up with the understanding of how politics played a crucial role in the increasingly fragile stability of his homeland. Lebanon was like a tinder box, one little spark and the whole thing would blow up. It was hard for Laura to appreciate what it must be like to live so precariously, and yet accept it as a natural way of being. This unpredictability, contributed to the Lebanese people having such resilience, and determined spirit to live life to the full.

Nicolas likened his country to the mythical Phoenix; no matter what happened, Lebanon he said would always rise from the flames and ashes of destruction. Laura couldn't help thinking this same analogy could easily be applied when describing Nicolas.

People found Nicolas extremely amiable, but would soon realise if they disagreed with his views it was pointless to argue; annoyingly Nicolas had an answer for everything. He would totally dominate a conversation and had no qualms about telling people they were wrong, if that was what he believed. Either way, people couldn't help but like him, and be fascinated by his articulate and intelligent delivery when speaking. If there were ten people in a room, Nicolas would be the one holding everyone's attention; he oozed charisma from every pore.

Over the years Nicolas had amazed Laura with the way he comfortably took control of any situation. Despite loving the bones of him, there were times when she felt a little intimidated by his strong personality. The wrong side of Nicolas was not a place you would choose to be. He had high expectations of himself and equally of others, and could be very hard on those who let him down; especially if it were those he loved. Nicolas did not forgive easily, and never forgot any wrongs committed against him.

Laura learnt early on that Nicolas was quite a force to be reckoned with; to live with him successfully required adapting to his ways. Her faith in Nicolas's judgment and abilities, made Laura comfortable with this arrangement. A weaker man would never have gained Laura's respect and trust the way he had. But being a mere mortal Laura had on occasion incurred his wrath; Nicolas reacted with what he would describe as tough love.

An example of this tough love was played out a year previous. Laura had travelled back to the UK on a routine visit to see Alyssa and renew her visa. Nicolas told Laura he would book her flight to return to Abu Dhabi three weeks later. One night as they talked via skype video, Laura pushed to know the date of her return. Nicolas said he was sorting it and would let her know. The following day she asked again, and again was told he was arranging her ticket. Impatient to know the exact date, a couple of days later Laura continued to harass Nicolas for her flight times.

Laura should have known by now that when Nicolas said he would do something, he would do it; he had never let her down. Her incessant pushing was beginning to antagonise him. Her unusually tetchy mood set Laura off on a tangent, causing her to react negatively to Nicolas's rather laid back attitude over her flight. Once again she impatiently pressed him to acknowledge her request, and tell her the exact date she was travelling. Laura didn't feel it unreasonable to want to know.

That day Nicolas had been dealing with a particularly stress inducing situation. Typically playing his cards close to his chest, he had not confided his problem to Laura. He had been stressed over yet another delay and complication concerning the completion of his papers; the ones urgently required to establish a company in his own name. The last thing Nicolas needed was to be harassed by Laura over the date of her ticket. As she persisted, Nicolas gave Laura one of his silent glowering looks, signifying she should 'leave it alone'. Unwisely Laura ignored the signs and continued pushing his buttons.

Finally Nicolas snapped and began shouting angrily at her. Intimidated by his yelling, Laura acted instinctively and switched off the Skype connection; she just switched him off. The moment she had done it, Laura regretted her impulsive action; but it was too late.

Nicolas was absolutely infuriated; how dare Laura switch him off when he was in the middle of shouting at her. He decided to teach her a lesson. From that moment he refused to take her calls or answer her text messages. He stubbornly kept up the silent treatment for nearly ten days. Eventually, with barely forty-eight hours' notice, Nicolas coolly informed Laura of the time of her flight.

Needless to say, the next time Nicolas assured he was sorting something; Laura accepted he would do it, and didn't push. Of course they laughed about it afterwards, but Nicolas had successfully made his point. No one, not even Laura was totally immune to the wrath of Al Hajj. When Laura questioned why he had been so hard on her, he answered;

"Those I love most, I punish hardest. Remember if I'm hard on you Loulou it's because you are closest to me, and because I love you most."

Nicolas had high expectations of those he cared for when it came to loyalty and trust. Those he loved had the ability to hurt and disappoint him the most.

During the summer, Nicolas developed a mild stomach infection requiring him to change his diet drastically. It was nothing too serious, more of a nuisance to Nicolas who could not enjoy his favourite foods or his glass of whisky. The doctor had advised him not to drink alcohol with the medication he was taking.

It was not easy for Nicolas to refrain from eating many of his favourite foods, especially the hot spicy dishes he enjoyed so much, but he stuck rigidly to his new diet and didn't touch a drop of alcohol. He had always been on the lean wiry side, but over the years had filled out a little bit. Now he wasn't drinking, his weight dropped back to what it was in his twenties. Nicolas insisted it was nothing to do with giving up the alcohol, and put his returned boyish leanness down to being unable to eat certain foods. Laura was impressed by his willpower, and wished Nicolas could apply the same self-control to his smoking habit.

Around October of 2011 everything was just blissful. Things were falling into place, and Nicolas was ambitious for the new business. He considered renting premises close to the apartment to display, and store the antiques. It was just an idea meant as a temporary option, which would not be viable once they moved to a villa.

One evening Laura was alone preparing dinner. Nicolas called to say he would arrive back by no later than 7pm. While living in the 'Cave', Laura had often felt a little uneasy when alone, probably due to the place being so isolated. When alone in this apartment she had always felt perfectly relaxed and safe. This particular evening Laura was strangely ill at ease. The feeling was akin to being watched. It gave her shivers, like someone had walked over her grave. Laura stopped cooking for a moment. She could hear the TV on in the other room, and the familiar sounds of people coming and going outside. It was a busy area with lots of normal activity in and around the apartment block. For this reason alone, Laura preferred it so much more than living in the 'Cave'. Even when Nicolas was out Laura never felt alone or isolated.

Convinced it was her imagination, Laura tried to ignore her sudden unease but couldn't shake it off. She felt she wasn't alone in the apartment. The impression was so strong once again she paused from cooking. Cold shivers ran up and down her spine. Laura looked around. Clearly there was nobody there, but she was compelled to search each room anyway. After satisfying her mind that she was entirely alone, Laura now felt silly for actually looking. She continued preparing the evening meal without further interruption.

Several times that week Laura had the same un-nerving sensation. Sometimes Laura thought she saw a shadowy shape out of the corner of her eye. It was disconcerting. Turning around quickly Laura tried to catch a glimpse of what was lurking in her peripheral vision, only to discover there was nothing there. Feeling she was being irrational, Laura dismissed it as imagination. A week or so later the ominous feelings continued to plague her mind; emerging whenever Laura was alone in the apartment. Every so often she felt the distinct presence of a palpable energy. Laura played cd's to lighten the mood. The music helped lift the heaviness of the atmosphere, but she still sensed an unearthly manifestation. Laura wasn't afraid, as she didn't feel the energy was evil but it was unsettling.

The moment Laura heard Nicolas's key in the door she felt greatly relieved. Immediately the uneasy feeling would flee. Surely it was down to her spending so much time alone.

Laura hadn't confided in Nicolas, whom she felt sure would laugh, and say it was her overactive imagination. When the weird sensations materialised while he was in the apartment with her, it really spooked her.

It was Thursday afternoon and they were sat chatting, At the risk of being thought crazy by her husband, Laura plucked up the courage to reveal her fears to him. The response Laura received was not what she expected; but instead rather surprising. He didn't laugh or say she was crazy as she thought he might; calmly he told Laura he had felt a presence too. When Laura inquired as to what he thought it might be, Nicolas shrugged evasively, telling her simply,

"I don't know love."

This wasn't the reassurance Laura had hoped to receive from her husband. Nicolas always had an answer, and Laura was disturbed that he was not offering his usual cool rationalism. Seeing her discouraged worried expression, he quickly made light of it. Giving Laura a menacing grin Nicolas mockingly jested;

"Maybe it's the aliens or a ghost."

Laura laughed, but took little comfort from his flippant explanation. Neither of them spoke of it again, but Laura would wake in the night and feel the room heavy with an unknown energy. Although it made her fearful, she still didn't consider it evil. Whatever it was permeating the atmosphere, it did hold slightly negative vibes. Laura felt emotions of deep sadness and longing. Laura knew the energy wasn't being emitted from her or from Nicolas. It was just there, an unwelcome guest loitering on the fringes of their consciousness.

Whilst Laura was doing her ballet exercises one day, the atmosphere become heavy with the ominous presence. With everything going well in their lives, this unwelcome manifestation defied reason, and was clearly out of place. Taking positive action, Laura confronted the energy head on. Pausing from her exercise program, she looked at the pictures of Mary and Saint Charbel on the bookshelf above

Nicolas's desk for reassurance. With intent Laura said;

"Whatever you are, please go away."

Laura looked at the small statue of Jesus and all the crosses around the room then she boldly proclaimed,

"We are protected here, go in peace leave this place."

Within moments there was a change in the atmosphere. Something definitely shifted. Laura felt it leave. She was never aware of the shadows again. The presence, whatever it was, had gone and Laura erased it from her mind.

KOUSBAWI

Chapter 39: Great Expectations

As Christmas approached, Laura suggested it would be nice if Alyssa joined them for the holiday period. Nicolas was keen for his step daughter to visit, but worried about the many antiques cluttering every corner and space. Surveying the already cramped conditions, he expressed concernedly;

"But where will she sleep?"

Laura looked around; the spare bedroom was packed to the brim with boxes full of antiques. The apartment was overflowing with vintage cameras, pre-1920's movie projectors, old type writers, sewing machines and antique cash registers. Many more antiques were crammed into every corner.

"I want everything to be ready when Alyssa comes here for the first time. Better to wait Loulou," he said. "In a few months we will be in the villa, Alyssa will have her own room there."

Laura agreed; Alyssa would be more comfortable with her own room.

"Soon all my hassles will finish," Nicky continued;

"That time I will be relaxed to spend time with her."

Admittedly conditions were far from ideal, all the same Laura was disappointed; yet another Christmas would pass where the people she loved would not spend it together. Between the less than ideal living arrangements and his ongoing visa issues, Nicolas and his step daughter Alyssa, had yet to be together in the same country. Thanks to the invention of Skype video, in spite of the miles separating them, they still managed to build a relationship.

Nicolas was at his desk working on his 'Baby'. He stopped momentarily to look over at Laura. She was sitting in his chair staring into space; her expression was wistful. Nicky sensed the sadness in her. He stood and stretched telling Laura;

"Don't worry love; everything's going to be alright."

His words sounded so reassuring. Laura got up from her seat and walked over to him. Standing on tip toe, she hung her arms around his neck. His eyes were filled with great expectation and hope. Gazing into those expressive dark pools was like looking into a boundless universe of possibilities. With his strong hands gripping her tightly, Nicky told Laura;

"You know Loulou things are gonna be good now, you don't have to worry girl; it's our time. Love, this coming year is going to be our time."

Laura laid her head against him feeling the familiar, comforting warmth radiate from his body. It lifted Laura's troubled spirits. She wanted to stay there, listening to the solid beat of Nicky's heart as it drummed to the rhythm of her soul. It was like coming home; nothing in the world made her feel so safe. Laura wanted to melt into him and stay there forever. Nicolas's heart echoed the same sentiment, although he would never say it; too slushy and romantic for a man's man like Nicolas. But he didn't need to say it; Laura saw it in his eyes and sensed it in his soul.

Lightening the mood, they discussed where on earth to put the Christmas tree this year with so much clutter in the place. Laura wanted to put it where they had placed it the previous Christmas, next to the window. But that would require rearranging the furniture; frankly there was just no space available to rearrange anything.

"Don't worry about it now Loulou," Nicky told her. "Go make us two coffees; I will figure it."

As she poured out the coffee, Laura smiled contentedly to herself, feeling blessed to have a man who was totally dependable. Whatever the problem big or small, Nicky would always 'figure it'.

He was at his desk deep in thought when she took his coffee to him.

"Put it on the table I'm coming to sit," he told Laura.

Laura placed the coffee down and took a seat. Nicky

switched off the laptop. He stood and lit a cigarette, then took his favourite chair alongside Laura. Taking her hand in his, he linked his fingers tightly with hers. His hand was strong and felt protective. Laura's was small and fragile in his grasp. Nicky studied her face, Laura's expression was smiling but her eyes still reflected her sadness.

"Loulou, you want to spend the Christmas with your daughter?" he asked.

Laura sighed deeply; "What I really want is to spend Christmas with you both," she replied in a melancholic regretful tone.

Nicky's grasp tightened around her fingers.

"Soon love, soon. Let me get rid of these hassles then everything will be as you wish."

Nicolas let go of Laura's hand and picked up his coffee to take a sip. Stubbing out his cigarette he immediately lit another. Laura disapproved strongly of his chain smoking.

"You smoke too much," she told him.

For years Laura had tried to persuade him to stop, but to no avail. Nicolas would give up smoking only when he was ready. He held out his cigarette and looked at it. Then with genuine intention he stated;

"Soon, this too I will finish."

He sounded sincere, but Laura was not convinced his quitting smoking would happen anytime soon. The word 'soon' did not have the same connotations for Nicolas as it did for most people. It merely meant when he was ready. Laura teased him again about his habit;

"You know for a man who likes to be in total control of everything, I'm surprised how you allow those little white sticks to control you."

Nicky smiled at Laura's comment.

"Oh yeah, is that right?" he stated mockingly. His tone then became defensive. "They do not control me, nothing can control me," he insisted. "If I want to stop I will. But I don't want," he said defiantly.

Laura gave a look of disapproval. Staunchly defending his choice Nicolas stated;

"Loulou there is a time for everything. Everything will happen in the right moment." He dragged on his cigarette extra hard, and then looked rebelliously at Laura. "Okay Loulou?"

Laura shook her head resignedly; "If you say so."

Nicolas was irredeemably defiant; "There is a time to smoke and a time not to smoke. This is a time to smoke."

Nicolas knew his cavalier attitude would annoy Laura. He was like a rebellious child. Laura pretended not to be bothered, and changed the conversation back to the subject of Christmas.

"I could spend Christmas with Alyssa, and come back here for the New Year," Laura suggested. "What do you think?"

It had been a few years since Laura spent Christmas in the UK. Alyssa didn't particularly like Christmas, whereas Nicky loved it. Laura felt torn. She expressed her anxieties to him. Nicky predictably told her;

"Love you must be with Alyssa, she needs you."

There was no question in his mind; this year Laura would spend Christmas with Alyssa. But the thought of leaving Nicolas alone weighed heavy on Laura's heart.

"I will arrange your ticket tomorrow. You will come back after one month, okay Loulou? It will give you some time with Alyssa, and time to finish the paperwork to ship the antiques from there to here."

Nicolas remained upbeat. If in any small way he conveyed he didn't want Laura to go she would stay, and then as usual be worried all over Christmas about Alyssa. Laura's eyes glazed. She fought to suppress her tears but couldn't. Grabbing a Kleenex from the box on the table she patted her eyes.

"Hey girl it's okay," he whispered squeezing her hand. "It's not like before; we have Skype now. We will still be together. Next year Loulou things will be different," Nicky promised.

At this point, neither could possibly imagine just how prophetic those words were to become.

The days passed quickly, and much too soon Laura was preparing to leave for the UK. The bitterness of their parting was sweetened by the hopeful expectation that they would all be together in a new villa soon, and definitely would all be together for Christmas 2012.

The night before her flight, Laura lay awake for hours. She looked at Nicolas lying beside her. For once he was sleeping like a baby. Reaching out her hand Laura gently touched his arm; it felt solid and masculine, and his skin was warm to the touch. Laura desperately wanted to hug him, but was afraid he would wake up. She knew only too well that if he were disturbed, he would not easily sleep again that night. Nicolas was sleeping so peacefully now and although she ached to hold him, Laura resisted the temptation. The subtle warmth from his body and rhythmic sound of his breathing eventually lulled her to sleep.

When the morning alarm went off Laura felt sick to her stomach. She groaned; her eyes heavy from too little sleep. Nicolas reached out and switched off the alarm. He lay a few moments before getting up from the bed. Laura waited allowing him to use the bathroom before her. When she heard him go to the kitchen to make coffee, she reluctantly got up. Rarely were they up at the same time; Nicolas always rose very early.

After showering and dressing, Laura felt on edge. She paced the apartment; her stomach was in knots. Everything had been packed ready to go the day before; everything except Laura, who felt far from ready to leave. She had got up at the crack of dawn just so she could spend every last moment with Nicolas. He was sitting calmly at the computer working on something, when she entered the lounge. Nicky appeared so relaxed, Laura found it almost unbearable. She made a coffee and sat watching him work. How he could be so utterly calm while she was climbing the walls just wasn't fair. Silently she willed him to stop whatever he was doing and hold her. Laura was always nervous before a flight, but today she was way more edgy than normal. She wandered from room to room for no particular reason.

Regardless of how many times she had done it in the past, Laura hated flying alone. She longed for the day when she and Nicky would take the flight back to England together. Like Nicolas, she desperately yearned for the normality other people took for granted. She prayed he would soon have his papers and be free to leave the Emirates, without the fear of losing his rights of residence. Laura watched as Nicolas continued to work at his desk oblivious, or so she believed, of her fractured torn emotions. But Nicolas as always, was sensitively attuned to Laura's state of mind. He immediately picked up on any change in her emotions. Today was no exception, the over tense vibes emanating from her were not missed. Laura hadn't said a word, yet it was clear she was bursting with nervous anxiety. Nicolas was familiar with Laura's usual panicked state before a flight. Perceiving something other than just nervousness of flying was at play, he asked;

"Are you okay Loulou?"

Laura grasped the opportunity of having her husband's attention and forced herself onto his lap. Resting her head against his shoulder, she held to him tightly as though her life depended on it.

"Hey girl, what's going on with you today?" he asked in a concerned tone.

Laura spontaneously burst into tears. She felt intensely sad, but wasn't really sure why her emotions were running so high. "I don't want to leave you," she sobbed.

Nicolas lifted her head. Looking into her tearful eyes he told her; "It's for a few weeks only Loulou."

"I know, but I hate this. I feel as though I am constantly being cut in half."

Nicolas had never known Laura so distraught at leaving before. "You want me to call and change your ticket?" he asked.

If Laura said yes, Nicky would do it in a heartbeat. She knew it would cost more money to change the ticket at such late notice, and didn't wish to be a nuisance.

312

With tears streaming down her cheek she blurted;

"I wish you were coming with me today."

"I wish too love," he said gently wiping the tears from her cheek with his thumb. "Soon I will have all my papers, my trading license and visa in order. Everything will be different that time; I promise Loulou."

Laura managed a smile; "I can't wait," she told him.

Nicolas lifted her up from his lap. Holding her in front of him he said;

"Listen girl, you have everything ready, your passport your money, your marriage license is in your bag?"

"Yes everything is packed," she answered gloomily.

"Good, then go and make us some coffee." Laura went to the kitchen, Nicky shouted after her;

"Eat something Loulou, you have a long flight."

Laura felt hungry but was afraid anything she ate would not stay in her for long; she knew her nerves would only subside once she was aboard the plane and snuggled under a blanket.

The dreaded moment to leave for the airport arrived;

"Okay Loulou lets go."

Nicolas was ultra-calm, presenting as always a strong dependable veneer. One last time before leaving, Laura held her husband, putting her head to his chest once more. The turmoil of her emotions eased as she heard the gentle pulsing of his heartbeat; the safe feeling that sound evoked would be carried with her always.

Laura placed her suitcase in the hall near to the door. Before leaving, Nicky knelt down on one knee. Laura watched from a respectful distance, as he prayed in front of the picture of Mary holding baby Jesus that was pinned to the top of the door. She knew he would be praying for her safety on the journey. Many times she had witnessed his devotion to prayer before leaving the house and always before sleeping at night; the strength of his faith filled her with admiration. Today it touched her heart seeing him so humble. Nicolas crossed himself then stood up. Turning to Laura he advised;

"Okay Loulou? Go check you have everything and let's go."

Again Laura felt an uncomfortable heaviness enter her heart. Fighting her tears, she braved a smile and handed him her door key. It was better to leave it here, just in case he lost or mislaid his. Laura waited near the elevator, whilst her husband closed and locked the front door. Using his car keys, he pressed the button to call the lift. As they entered into the elevator, he reminded Laura to call him as soon as she cleared passport control.

Outside the brightness of the sun was intense. It made Laura swoon slightly. She put on her sunglasses. It was December, but still a very warm 28 degrees. Nicolas placed Laura's bright pink suitcase and matching hand luggage, into the back of his blue Jeep. The twenty minute drive to Abu Dhabi International airport commenced. Laura, swathed by an unexpected feeling of calm, felt a contrasting welcome relief from the torturous emotions she had felt earlier.

During the drive, everything appeared extra vibrant; the flowers in all their glory and palms lining the roads, and the people all seemed more noticeable, as though Laura were seeing them for the first time. Local men went about their business wearing crisp white Dish Dash. No matter how dusty, and there was an awful lot of dust in the Arabian Desert, they still managed to remain immaculate in their appearance. Elegant Emirati women wearing black Burkas walked slowly, appearing to almost glide about the streets. Laura felt compelled to take note of everything.

She glanced at Nicky; his hands gripping the steering wheel looked strong and so masculine. Sitting beside him Laura felt very proud he was her man. As they drove towards the airport, Laura sensed her inner voice speak to her; urging her to take it all in and to remember. Over the years they had taken this journey numerous times, but for some reason things looked and felt different. Everything was more alive; it seemed energy was oozing from every atom.

Nicolas pulled up outside of the Etihad departure entrance. A porter hurried over as they stepped from the Jeep. Nicky gave him some money. As the porter took the cases from the car and placed them onto the trolley, Nicky held Laura. She looked up at him; as usual his eyes were scanning the area to see if anyone dared to say anything. Rarely did he happily follow rules contrary to his beliefs. He would often tell Laura; "I'm a leader not a follower."

For a brief moment they stood beside the Jeep in the warm Arabian sun, hesitant to be parted; like it somehow signalled the end of something. Despite being in a public area, Nicolas held Laura a little longer than usual. Then he kissed her quickly on the lips before telling her;

"Okay hayati, have a good flight and kiss Alyssa for me when you get there."

The baggage porter waited patiently, as they embraced again and said their emotional farewells. Laura resisted the urge to burst into tears.

"I love you," she whispered.

"I love you too. Take care Loulou."

"Oh Nicky, we didn't get to decorate the Christmas tree," Laura suddenly blurted out.

"We will do it together on the Skype," he told her. "Go now; take care and call me the second you reach the duty free."

"I will, but you take care of yourself; I'm missing you already." Laura watched as Nicky walked back to the car. She called after him;

"I love you."

He waved and quickly got into the Jeep. Nicky pulled away and gave her another wave. Laura felt an irresistible compulsion to run after him. She waited, watching until the blue Jeep was out of view. She was suddenly forced to concentrate on the matter in hand, as the porter asked;

"Okay ready Madam?"

"Yes, thank you; let's go to the check in desk."

After checking in her luggage, Laura made her way to passport control. Within minutes she was through security and inside the duty free lounge. Straight away she took out her phone to call Nicky.

"Okay love, are you through?" Nicky asked.

"Yes, I just arrived in duty free. Oh I wish you were coming with me," she said mournfully.

"No problem love, soon I will. Have a good flight and call me when you reach Heathrow, okay love?"

"Okay, I love you Nicolas."

"Love you too hayati, bye love. Take care."

Laura reluctantly closed her phone; she resented having to spend so much of her time in an airport terminal, when it would be better spent with Nicolas. Fascinating as Abu Dhabi duty free was, she had no interest in looking at anything. Nicky had given her money to spend, but there was nothing she really needed. Eventually Laura bought some perfume for Alyssa and a magazine to read. The time passed slowly, until finally her flight was called. Laura made her way to the boarding gate. After presenting her boarding card at gate number 28, she took a seat in the waiting area. Her mobile rang.

"Loulou, everything okay?" Nicky asked.

"Yes I'm just about to board the plane," she told him.

"Okay love, call when you reach there. Love you girl."

"I love you too," Laura echoed back.

The next time Laura would hear his voice wouldn't be until she reached the UK more than eight hours later. Once on board and in her seat, Laura set her mobile to airplane mode and altered her watch to UK time.

Her thoughts turned to Nicky. What might he be doing? How did he feel going back to an empty apartment? Was he missing her yet? Her flight was due to leave within five minutes at 1pm; Nicolas would probably be leaving the office about now. Maybe he was already at the apartment and making his sandwich. Did he miss her not being there to fetch him his cold beer?

An hour into the flight Laura pulled her blanket tightly around her and tried to get some sleep. The airplanes air conditioning made her shiver. Not sleeping too well the night before, had left Laura feeling tired and exhausted. Emotionally drained, she drifted into the outer fringes of the dream state. As she did so, Laura's thoughts were on Nicky, visualising him taking his nap about now. Maybe they could reach out to each other via the illusive plane of the dream world.

Laura remembered the promise Nicky had made to her that morning; his words repeated in her head over and over. Next year would be different he said. Laura felt at peace with this thought. The world of dreams quickly laid claim to Laura's mind. In the innocent belief that Nicolas's undoubted fulfilment of that promise would guarantee a wonderful year ahead, Laura slept.

KOUSBAWI

Chapter 40:
Tomorrow is Never Promised

It was just after 5pm when Laura finally reached London Heathrow. After an eight hour flight with only sporadic intervals of sleep, the tiredness and exhaustion kicked in with a vengeance. The dismal grey buildings of London looked rather dejected, compared to the vibrant opulence of the country she had just left; it made her long to be back in Abu Dhabi. Laura had barely set foot on British soil, but already felt the painful pangs of separation from Nicolas.

As Laura made her way to the UK boarder control, not only her heart, but also her head were still very much in Abu Dhabi. She imagined what she would be doing at this precise moment if still there. It would be after 9pm Emirati time, and Laura would have cooked the evening dinner, and about to sit and eat with Nicolas. Visualising the scene reminded her she hadn't eaten anything. Hunger pangs too were now clawing at Laura's wearied psyche.

The journey wasn't over; it would be another hour and a half until she reached Southampton. Hundreds of people were lined up waiting to be checked through the UK boarder control. Luckily the queue for British passport holders was moving fast. Once through, Laura walked towards the baggage claim. She grabbed a trolley and headed towards carousel number three. Waiting anxiously, Laura hoped to soon catch sight of her bright pink suitcase amongst the dozens of other pieces of baggage revolving past. The area surrounding the carousel was packed with people all bustling to get their luggage from the revolving conveyor belt. Laura stood on tiptoe craning her neck to see if her case was amongst the latest pile to be dropped onto it. Her phone rang; it was Nicolas.

"Hi darling I'm waiting for my luggage," she told him while continuing to scan the baggage circling past.

"Okay love. Call me when you are in your taxi."

"I will, I love you, bye."

Laura closed her phone. She suddenly caught a glimpse of something pink making its way around on the carousel. Laura made herself ready to grab it. If she had been arriving at Abu Dhabi, there would be a porter on hand to take her bags from the carousel for her. She would only be required to point, and her suitcase would be lifted off and wheeled on a trolley to her waiting car. No such luxury here. Laura would have to jostle amongst a throng of impatient people crowded around the carousel. She needed to get into a good position to grab the case before it passed by. As it came close Laura hurled herself forward and tried to get a grip of the handle. Due to the awkward angle the case was laying, she only managed to reach one of the brightly coloured ribbons that had been tied to it for easy recognition. Being small of stature, Laura found herself suddenly dragged unceremoniously along the conveyer belt as she tussled with the suitcase. She desperately struggled to pull it from the carousel which appeared to have annoyingly picked up speed. The case wasn't close enough, and too heavy for Laura to get a firm enough grip.

Seeing Laura's struggle, a helpful young man came to her aid. He obligingly retrieved the case, and placed it onto Laura's trolley. The relieved Laura thanked him for his kind assistance. It was moments like these that made her realise how fortunate she was to be living in the UAE.

Laura wheeled her trolley through the 'nothing to declare' exit; now all she had to do was find her driver. Her eyes searched the sea of people waiting at the arrivals terminal. After a few minutes she spotted a card with her name on; 'Laura Southampton' it read. The taxi driver took her trolley, and she followed him outside to the car park. Laura shivered. The cold damp British climate was a shock to her system after the lovely warmth of Abu Dhabi. Once settled in the taxi and onto a stretch of road where she could get a signal, Laura took out her mobile to call Nicky.

She dialled the number letting it ring twice, then hung up. Nicolas insisted Laura always call this way. He rang back immediately.

"Hi love, everything okay with you?"

"Hi, yes I'm in the taxi," she told him.

"Good, now I can eat."

"You didn't eat yet?"

"No, I wanted to wait until you arrive there. Now I can relax. When first you reach your house call me," Nicolas instructed.

"Okay I will. I'm missing you too much already. Are you missing me yet?" Laura asked teasingly.

"Go, we will speak later. Okay love? Go now. I love you girl."

Nicolas rarely admitted to missing Laura; but he did, and Laura knew he did. She liked to tease him though. Laura gave a call to Alyssa to say she was on her way. By the time she finally reached her house in Southampton it was gone eight o' clock in the evening. The house was quiet as she entered. Laura could vaguely hear Alyssa in her room talking to a friend on Skype. Laura called out, but got no reply. Joey, their pet cat faithfully appeared at the top of the stairs; the fur on the top of his head was all ruffled up; he had obviously just woken up. Laura smiled, amused by how a cat could have bed head. Leaving her bags in the hallway Laura took out her mobile. In Abu Dhabi it was now well after midnight, but Nicolas would not sleep until he had spoken to Laura. Again Laura let the phone ring twice then hung up. She waited for him to return the call which he did within seconds. He sounded tired; they both were.

"You reach your house?"

"Yes just arrived," she said in an exhausted tone.

"Good, then let me sleep we will talk tomorrow. Okay Loulou? Love you girl."

Despite her extreme exhaustion, Laura wanted to keep talking just to be hearing Nicky's voice. She was aware he would rise as usual at 6.30am, regardless of what time he slept tonight. She didn't wish to keep him awake longer than necessary. Not having eaten Laura was famished, but too tired to cook; besides there wasn't much food in the house. Alyssa said she had already eaten. Laura briefly considered ordering takeout, but by the time she had unpacked her things, fatigue won over. Laura decided to sleep instead. It was after 10pm when she got into bed. That first night sleeping without Nicky beside her felt strange, but Laura was so exhausted she slept peacefully through until 9am.

After a good night's rest, Laura set about cleaning the house and making preparations for Christmas. This would be her first Christmas in the UK for some time. Normally Laura would come back around October, November time, to renew her visa and visit Alyssa. She would buy Alyssa's presents early, wrap them up, and place them under the Christmas tree, which she would put up for Alyssa before returning to Abu Dhabi to spend Christmas with Nicolas. The unexpected change of plan this year would mean a lot of last minute rushing around.

Laura had not experienced a proper traditional British Christmas for years. Nicolas preferred Lebanese cuisine, insisting it was the best. Laura kind of looked forward to a traditional Christmas dinner for a change; but would enjoy it much more if Nicolas was with her. One day she hoped to change his opinion about the British not having a real cuisine. "The British don't have a kitchen," he would insist, unlike the French or Italian and of course the Lebanese, who he boasted were the best in everything.

Within a few days Laura managed to pull it all together. The Christmas tree was up, presents bought and almost all wrapped, and the fridge and freezer were stacked with delicious Christmas goodies. Despite having so much to organise, Laura spent as much time as possible on Skype to Nicolas. Over Christmas they kept the connection open twenty four seven; it was the next best thing to actually being together.

They involved one another as best they could in their

daily activities, which wasn't so easy with a four hour time difference and over 3,000 miles of land and sea separating them. While chatting together, Nicky watched Laura wrap up presents, and she watched him decorate the Christmas tree. With all the antiques in the apartment, the only space available to put it was on the top of the dining table. Laura laughed when she saw where Nicky had placed it, jokingly commenting that it was a rather large table decoration.

"Where are the lights?" Laura asked noticing they were not on.

"You know Loulou, when I took them out they didn't work," Nicky explained.

Laura's cheery mood was suddenly overshadowed by a feeling of doom. It was only tree lights, but a sense of foreboding made her quite uneasy. The ominous feeling was reminiscent of the negative vibes, experienced at the apartment a few months back. Laura stared at the tree looking so bare and forlorn without its twinkling fairy lights. Remembering how prettily they had twinkled and sparkled the Christmas before, Laura wondered was it a bad omen the lights were not working now.

"You have to get new ones," she insisted. "Promise me you will buy new lights."

Nicolas said he would, and sure enough the following day the Christmas tree was adorned with new fairy lights; albeit rather haphazardly positioned. Laura smiled when saw them. There were areas with the lights all bunched together and huge gaps where there were no lights at all. The tree clearly missed Laura's artistic flair.

Via their Skype video calls, Laura tried to include Nicky in everything she was doing. It was frustrating if the internet signal was weak, or displayed a message saying 'Kousbawi not online'. The name Kousbawi that Nicolas previously used to identify himself in internet chat rooms was now his Skype name. Nicolas was still reluctant to reveal his identity whenever on line. He wouldn't open a Facebook account of his own, preferring instead to use Laura's to talk to his friends. When Laura questioned why he was so cagy, he was evasive. Characteristically he made light of it, jokingly telling Laura;

"I don't want my enemies to know it's me."

Despite his humorous delivery of the statement, Laura sensed an underlying truth behind his joking. Nicky was wary to the extreme of monitoring who Laura befriended on Facebook. If anyone Middle Eastern were to request friendship with her, Laura would have to run it past Nicky before accepting. He would scrutinise their profiles before giving his approval. If they were Lebanese and unknown to him, he would usually forbid her to accept. When Laura questioned his reasoning, again he would jest;

"Maybe they are my enemy."

Whether she was aware or not, Nicky's guarded actions and the restrictions he placed on Laura's movements in Abu Dhabi, were not entirely motiveless. Certain things were never discussed over the phone or over the internet. One time, Nicolas revealed his belief that his phone was tapped. Nicolas preferred to keep his whereabouts secret, hence the reason for such isolated obscurity as the 'Cave'. No one, except for those he totally trusted, was privy to the existence of their hidden dwelling; to anyone looking from the outside it was merely a warehouse.

Nicky's talk of enemies and phone tapping, was all a bit surreal for Laura, who likened it to something seen in a movie. But this was Nicolas, and to live with him required total acceptance of his over vigilant behaviour; no matter how idiosyncratic it appeared.

The day before Christmas Eve he called Laura;

"Be on," he said; then quickly hung up the phone.

Laura knew what he meant and immediately connected to Skype. A message popped up; 'Kousbawi is off line'. Laura tried to call anyway. Again the same message came up, and the connection failed. She tried several more times without success. Picking up her mobile, Laura sent him a text;

'Where are you?'

'I'm on' he texted back.

Laura stared impatiently at her computer monitor, until finally the icon changed, indicating Kousbawi was online. She waited for the familiar Skype ring tone. Moments later it was there accompanied by a flashing message on the screen that read; 'Kousbawi calling'. Laura clicked to accept the call. At last they were connected. From over 3,000 miles away, her husband's face appeared smiling in front of her.

"How are you girl?"

The line was clear as a bell, and the picture quality was good. Occasionally it would sound as though Nicky was talking from under water, or the pixels would disintegrate making him look like some sort of weird alien. Sometimes there would be a picture without sound or vice versa and Laura would hear him speaking, but have no visual. Today the connection was perfect.

"I'm exhausted," Laura told him. "I didn't realise there was so much to do. My life is much easier in Abu Dhabi." She confessed.

It hadn't taken long for Laura to become embroiled in the typical lead up to Christmas madness; something she had avoided for a number of years. Christmas with Nicky was beautifully simple and stress free. He didn't get involved with panic buying. There was always plenty of delicious food, but not piles of gifts. Nicolas chose to buy Laura gifts throughout the year because he wanted to; not because a date in the calendar told him he should. For Nicolas Christmas was about celebrating the birth of Jesus, pure and simple. Christmas Eve they would share a special celebratory dinner, usually with a guest or two. Nicky always bought champagne, and over the holiday they would relax and enjoy being together.

Laura believed Nicky had the right idea of how Christmas should be celebrated. He never panicked about anything, and his laid back attitude had a positive influence on Laura who was a natural worrier. Laura was really missing being with her husband at this special time. Without him to calm and keep her balanced, Laura was running around like a headless chicken. Bemused by her stressed out state as she rattled on hardly taking a breath between sentences, Nicky told her;

"Take it easy girl."

"You see, I can't cope without you," she laughed.

Nicolas smiled amused at Laura's confession.

"Is that right?" he laughed.

In spite of communicating via a computer monitor, Nicky's influence over Laura's mood was not in the least impeded. His relaxed cool demeanour still managed to effectively ease her over stressed mind. Within moments she was visibly serene and returned to a more tranquil disposition. Her eyes shining with love, Laura looked fondly at her husband. Both their expressions reflected a desire to climb through their computer screens and hug each other. A few seconds of silent reverie later, Laura asked;

"What are you doing Christmas Eve?"

Nicolas smiled wistfully. Skype was great, but hardly substituted having Laura there in person. Answering her question, he affectionately told her;

"I'll be right here on Skype with you love."

"Who are you having Christmas dinner with?" Laura inquired.

"With you Loulou, on the Skype."

For the past three years Nicky's cousin had joined them for their celebratory Christmas Eve dinner.

"What about your cousin Fouad? He always eats with us Christmas Eve. Won't he be coming to have dinner with you?"

"He's gone to Lebanon," Nicky revealed.

"What about Rene then?" she asked.

With a look of resigned acceptance, Nicky told her;

"Him too."

Laura was surprised and saddened. The one time she was not going to be there, Nicky would be alone. Her heart sank thinking of him alone for Christmas. He on the other hand didn't appear bothered. If he was, he would never have said so.

"No problem love, I have myself," he laughed.

Laura now felt guilty for not staying with him. Seeing her troubled expression, Nicky attempted to lift the mood. He jokingly proclaimed;

"You will have a nice Christmas with Alyssa, and I will have a nice peaceful time without you."

Nicky started laughing. His laugh was so engaging and genuine. His kidding around cheered Laura, but she wasn't fooled. His nonchalant attitude may have wished to convey he was absolutely fine, but his eyes couldn't hide the truth; they clearly transmitted the message he missed Laura being there.

Throughout the whole of Christmas, Nicky and Laura stayed connected via Skype video. Luckily the internet signal was exceptionally good. When Nicolas went for his habitual siesta on Christmas day, they left the line open; in case they were unable to reconnect. After his nap, Nicolas checked to see if Laura was there. He couldn't see her, so he sat and watched the news. Everything was flaring up in Syria, just as he had predicted. Back in the UK, Laura had just finished washing the dishes from the Christmas lunch. She looked at the computer screen to see if Nicolas was back from his nap. She could see him sat in front of the TV. Laura called out to him;

"Hi, what are you watching?"

Nicolas looked round;

"Hello Loulou, I'm watching the news," he called back.

"Anything of interest?" Laura asked.

"Big problem in Syria," he answered.

Nicolas reached for a cigarette. After lighting it he got up and walked over to the desk. He sat down in front of his laptop to chat with Laura.

"Going to be very big problem there, I believe."

"Do you think Lebanon will be affected?" She asked.

Nicolas turned his head glancing back at the television for a moment. Turning again to face Laura he pronounced;

"For sure love, I believe for sure it will." Nicolas felt it was inevitable. Changing the subject he asked;

"Loulou how was your Christmas dinner?"

Laura and Alyssa had eaten while Nicky was napping.

"It was good." Laura told him. "I wish you could have been here to enjoy it with us."

Nicolas leant back in his chair dragging on his cigarette before stubbing it out.

"Soon I will be there love," he promised.

Suddenly he sat bolt upright. Leaning in towards the camera, he looked directly at Laura telling her;

"Love, this year everything going good. What I mean, the coming year. Now many things in the pipeline; if just one of them work we will have good life."

Nicolas resumed his relaxed position. Leaning back in his chair he glanced again in the direction of the TV. After a few moments he announced;

"I'm going to fix myself one Arak." Nicolas stood up telling Laura; "Fix yourself a drink Loulou, and together we will toast the Christmas."

There was half a bottle of Moet left in the fridge, Laura poured herself a glass and sat down in front of her laptop. She could see Nicolas in the apartment kitchen fixing his Arak. He walked slowly back to the lounge glancing at the TV that was still reporting the escalating violence in Syria. He was wearing his favourite indoor attire, a white T shirt with the sleeves cut out, and his cotton sarong. Through the thin material, the light reflected the obvious outline of his naked lower half. As he walked towards the screen, Laura glimpsed the silhouette of his lithe body beneath the flimsy sarong. Nicolas was still an incredibly sexy and handsome man. Right in this moment Laura ached to be there with him. Oblivious of Laura's admiring glances and lustful thoughts, Nicolas sat down again in front of the screen. Raising his glass to the camera he said;

"Cheers Merry Christmas Loulou; I love you girl."

Laura lifted her glass to the camera;

"Cheers, I love you too, merry Christmas."

Nicolas lit another cigarette. Wishing Laura was beside

him, he stared at her fondly. Laura sipped her champagne and gazed back. Feeling sexually aroused now, Nicky held Laura's gaze intensely. No words were spoken or needed, as spontaneously they acknowledged their desire for one another, and in a moment of pure transparent intimacy they made love with their eyes. Time and distance became an illusionary dream.

After a while Nicky asked; "Where's Bunnie?"

"She's upstairs on her computer," Laura told him.

"She's okay, everything good with her?" Nicolas asked, always concerned for Alyssa's wellbeing.

Laura assured him all was okay. Not fully convinced, Nicolas gave his wife a quizzical look. Intuitively he was picking up on her angst with the situation that continued to separate him from his step daughter. He reassured Laura;

"Don't worry love, we will bring Alyssa here after for a holiday; soon everything will be fine," he promised.

Christmas passed in the blink of an eye and New Year was quickly upon them. With Abu Dhabi being four hours ahead of UK time, Laura would celebrate twice; first with Nicky via Skype, then with Alyssa and friends later. On the 31st December 2011, Nicolas and Laura spent four hours talking. Nicolas positioned his laptop so that Laura was able to see him whether he was in the lounge or in the kitchen. As they chatted, Nicky prepared and ate his dinner. Laura missed not being there to cook for him.

Midnight approached in Abu Dhabi. Nicolas had the television on, and was watching the celebrations taking place in Lebanon. Laura would normally be watching the Lebanese TV channel with him. Every year there was a psychic on the show; he was on now giving his predictions for the year of 2012. Nicolas would translate, telling Laura what was predicted. Apparently the predictions were more than 90 percent correct. Nicolas was listening intently to what the psychic foretold for the year ahead.

"What's he saying?" Laura demanded.

Nicolas waved his hand intolerantly at her, to signify he was trying to listen; "Wait a minute," he told her.

After a few moments Laura became impatient to know; "Tell me what he's saying," she pestered.

"Shoo…sh! Wait a minute Loulou I'm trying to listen," Nicky snapped.

Laura huffed impetuously, she was impatiently anxious to hear what was being predicted for the coming year.

"It's difficult to explain in English," Nicky said as he began translating. He was rather vague telling Laura; "I will tell you when you come."

Five minutes to midnight Abu Dhabi time, Nicolas poured a whisky. He told Laura to get her drink ready. She had her glass of champagne already beside her. Over the Skype Laura heard fireworks going off around Abu Dhabi. As midnight struck they raised their glasses;

"Happy New Year Loulou; love you girl."

"Happy new year, love you too," she echoed. "Here's to us."

"To us." Nicky repeated pretending to chink his glass to Laura's through the screen.

Alyssa came into the room;

"Happy new year Steppe," she said pulling a comical face directly into the camera.

Nicolas laughed; "Happy new year Bunnie."

"Wait, there's someone else who wants to wish you a happy New Year," Alyssa announced.

Alyssa bent down and picked up her cat Joey who had followed her into the room. Alyssa put Joey's face close to the camera. Nicky laughed as Joey's fluffy face filled up the screen in front of him.

"Happy new year joyeee," he said.

His mispronunciation was as usual adorably amusing.

"It's pronounced Joey." Alyssa corrected, laughing at Nicolas's distortion of the word.

"That's what I said, Joyee."

Laura and Alyssa burst out laughing as Nicolas made the same blunder again. Teasingly they mimicked the way he said it. Nicolas tried to act indignant, but couldn't keep up the pretence. He too began laughing, as Alyssa and

Laura continued to playfully ridicule his pronunciation. Wickedly, Laura and Alyssa never missed an opportunity to tease Nicky whenever he slipped up with his English.

One memorably amusing time on Skype, they had persuaded him to recite Laura's favourite childhood poem from a book Laura had added to his library. As Nicolas began reciting a poem by Edward Lear called 'The Owl and the Pussycat', Alyssa and Laura did their best to keep straight faces. But as Nicolas reached the chorus of the poem, they were both holding their stomachs doubled up with laughter. In fairness they had to give him credit, despite their wicked teasing, Nicky bravely and good-humouredly continued to recite the absurd little story right to the very end.

It was now approaching 8.45pm UK time. Laura had plans to meet up with friends for a New Year's Eve dinner at nine o' clock. Laura told Nicky she would soon have to leave for the restaurant.

"Okay love, you go. I want to watch something on the TV anyway," he told her.

"We can spend another five minutes," Laura decided, reluctant to switch off the Skype.

The restaurant was local; just a couple of minutes' walk from the house. Laura looked forward to the day she and Nicky might go there for dinner together. Before switching off the connection, Nicky sang a little rendition of the Richie Valens song;

"Tell Laura I love her, Tell Laura I need her, Tell Laura not to cry, my love for her will never die," he sang.

The song held fond memories and had become a bit of an anthem for them. Laura swooned whenever Nicky sang it to her; which he did often. She was suddenly quite emotional remembering that first time in the 'Prive'. Nicolas had continued to sing it to Laura many, many times over the years. He sung it down the phone during all the years they were apart, and still did so to this day.

"Go love, my program is starting," he told her.

Nicolas knew if he didn't take control and make the

first move, Laura would be reluctant to go and be late for the restaurant.

"I love you," she told him.

"Love you too girl. Take care of yourself we will talk tomorrow okay Loulou, Happy New Year love."

Laura waited for Nicky to switch off the Skype. Laura hated saying goodbye, and never could be the first to close their connection; she was the same with phone calls.

After dinner, everyone went back to Laura's house to see in the New Year. Laura opened a bottle of champagne and as Big Ben chimed midnight, they toasted in 2012. There were many hopes and dreams for the year ahead, and Laura and Nicky were surely about to realise theirs. But fate had a different plan; another trick card to play. In just 33 days Nicky and Laura's world would be changed; irreversibly and forever.

KOUSBAWI

Chapter 41: Thirty Three Days

Predictably, and typical of the British winter, January started out bitterly cold and miserably dreary. To begin with, Laura enjoyed the change from the incessant Middle Eastern heat. Now the novelty of the English climate was rapidly losing its allure. Like a magnet, the deliciously warm climes of Abu Dhabi were attracting her back. It was not only the attraction of sunnier climes; there was also a strong magnetic pull on Laura's heart. She ached to be back in the warm arms of her man and keenly anticipated her return.

There were some loose ends to tie up regarding the antiques in storage waiting to be shipped. The majority of their collection was already in Abu Dhabi. Everything would be orchestrated by Nicolas from there, so it was up to him to get the wheels in motion. It was agreed for the time being not to add anything more, but Nicolas's impetuous nature was unable to resist the impulse to continue visiting the live auction rooms on line. Inevitably, he would spot something he liked and start bidding. Laura warned him her funds were running low; she had already maxed out her credit card on the items he purchased before Christmas. Nicolas assured she would be reimbursed by the first week of February at the latest; Laura extended her credit to cover the cost of her husband's latest indulgences.

Laura's birthday was coming up. She hoped to be back in Abu Dhabi to spend it with Nicolas. While on Skype video, Laura teasingly asked;

"Where are you taking me for my birthday?"

Nicolas responded in his usual cheeky manner. With a saucy grin and mischievous wink, he answered;

"To the bed."

Laura raised her eyebrows;

"You're so predictable," she told him.

Smiling beguilingly Laura flirted, telling him;

"Well I guess that's a gift I don't mind receiving every year," playfully adding, "but you had better hurry up and book my flight."

Grinning, Nicky retorted; "Oh yeah, and why's that?"

Laura wittily declared;

"Because darling, I'm more than 3,000 miles away. Even the indomitable Kousbawi couldn't pull that off."

"What? What that mean?" he asked.

"Oh never mind," she told him.

"It good or bad?" he asked, giving Laura a questioning frown.

"Don't worry it's a compliment," she assured.

Laughing at her quip Nicolas responded with;

"I have my ways. Maybe I will buy a ticket to England and surprise you Loulou." A provocative glint appeared in Nicolas's eye. He was enjoying their playful banter.

Laura delighted at the tantalising thought of Nicolas suddenly appearing on her doorstep. She wished it wasn't just teasing banter, but would actually be realised. She told him wistfully;

"That would be the best birthday gift of all."

Nicolas squinted as he lit his cigarette. He then looked at Laura asking; "Is that right Loulou?" His tone was subtly mocking. Deliberately he blew smoke from his cigarette enticingly into the camera. "You know love, I don't need to call you, or to see you, or even Skype you."

Laura gave him a tentative look; "What do you mean?"

Nicolas took another slow drag on his cigarette before giving an answer. He looked directly into the camera. Switching from his playful mocking, he took on a more sincere expression, candidly replying;

"Darling, you are inside my heart, you are with me all of the time. From the time I wake up till I sleep; and even when I sleep I am dreaming about you."

Laura was speechless; she hadn't been prepared for her husband's unexpected romantic utterance; it momentarily took her breath.

This was Nicolas. He would never describe himself as a romantic in the traditional sense; he was at times though, charmingly spontaneous. He knew how to make Laura's heart race. Slightly stunned by his poetically romantic turn of phrase, Laura recollected a letter he had written her years ago; before their long awaited reunion. In the letter a similar sentiment was portrayed. Spoken tonight so eloquently, those words expressed Nicolas's feelings in an intense and emotional fashion. It was quite unexpected and it touched her heart. Looking into his eyes, Laura saw he meant every heart quickening word. She saw something else too; the reflection of her own soul mirrored back. Finding her breath to speak at last, Laura echoed the same feelings, telling him;

"Yes, I know. We are connected even when apart."

"Loulou, it's important you remember that."

He spoke warmly, but behind her husband's tender words, Laura detected an element of solemnity. Nicolas's face relaxed as he took on a half smiling expression. The potency of his passion still burned in his dark eyes; they were tinged with nostalgic longing. Even with thousands of miles separating them and across the internet, Laura felt the strength of his love. It was being etched into her soul; searing it permanently lest she should ever forget.

Laura beheld her husband's haunting gaze, and they became frozen in time. Seconds felt like many lifetimes. The impression of time itself was revealed as an illusion.

Nicolas abruptly withdrew his penetrating scrutiny, instantly breaking the spell, dropping them back into the Matrix of the fictitious reality of time. Stubbing out his cigarette he effortlessly returned to his cheeky impudence, ordering;

"Now go make me coffee Loulou."

Laura stood up and proceeded to go to the kitchen to make Nicky's coffee. It took a moment before realising she wasn't in Abu Dhabi with him. Simultaneously they burst out laughing, amused by Laura's unconscious action. It was automatic that she would go and make his coffee when told. With over exaggerated reluctance, Nicky got up from his chair declaring resignedly;

"Or I will make my own coffee."

"You see you do miss me," Laura proclaimed.

Nicolas was still laughing as he walked to the kitchen. He was so used to Laura being there at his beck and call to fetch his coffee, and cigarettes on command. He would usually just hold out an empty cup or cigarette packet, and Laura would lovingly attend to his need. Nicolas's bossy commands were very tongue in cheek though, and always displayed with affectionate humour. Laura watched him go to the kitchen, observing as he poured his coffee and took a packet of Marlborough lights from his stash on the kitchen shelf. Nicky grabbed a handful of mini bounty bars from the fridge, and then sauntered back to his desk.

"You wanna chocolate?" he asked, teasingly waving the chocolate bar at the camera. He then promptly shoved the whole bar into his mouth.

With an air of disgust Laura commented;

"Oh Nicky, that's lovely, you're so charming."

"Yep, I'm a lovely boy," he declared shamelessly.

Then purposely and over exaggerating the action, he proceeded to shove a second chocolate bar into his mouth.

"Really, do you have to do that? You are such a pig!" Laura remarked scornfully, though his deliberate childish antics, mildly amused her.

Nicky had a sweet tooth especially for chocolate, which he kept in the freezer. Early on in their relationship when first living together, Laura one time nearly broke a tooth trying to eat a chocolate bar Nicky gave to her straight from the freezer. Quickly becoming wise to his habit of putting chocolate in the freezer, Laura would move it to the fridge hoping to avoid a trip to the Orthodontist. But he would always move it back to the freezer. Eventually they compromised by putting half the chocolate in the freezer, and the other half in the fridge.

Depending on the situation, Nicolas could sometimes be very black and white in his views. But there were

335

contradictory elements to his personality, meaning he comfortably fitted into different roles. It suited to play the tough guy in business dealings. It was a role he easily fell into, especially when taking his strong political stance. Nicolas had the capacity to be nurturing, or playful and at times quite impetuous like a child.

Laura knew she was privileged. Nicolas would open up segments of himself never shared with anyone else but her. No one gained access to the real man, in the exclusive way Laura did. Yet there was a little something he kept back, even from her.

The design of Nicolas's indomitable character was as intricate as the gears and mechanics of a beautiful Swiss watch. Living with a strong, complex personality, was not without difficulties. Nicolas was like a picture or painting that you really love; you cannot remove any part and still expect it to be the same. Every piece of Nicolas's colourful character had a purpose and place; like a jigsaw puzzle. Even his unpredictable volatility was a vital component to his passionate nature; Laura would never wish to dilute even a drop of Nicolas's fiery passion. If any of his amazing attributes were changed or subtracted, an integral part of the man Laura knew and loved would be lost. Nicolas's ability to take the rough with the smooth, without deflecting from his true nature, was part of his unique persona. Whether with millions, or only the shirt on his back, and Nicolas had walked both paths, he always remained the same man.

A few days before her birthday, Laura was frustratingly still in the UK. She asked Nicolas about returning to Abu Dhabi. She believed her extended stay had been solely to organise shipping the remaining antiques to the Emirates. For the time being, it suited Nicolas to delay a little longer Laura's return. That evening as they chatted on Skype, he told Laura he had received an unexpected visit. He had not seen his step brother for a while. Up until a year ago, Nicolas and Laura were regular visitors to Freddy's villa in Dubai. Before the acquisition of the Jeep they would travel down at the weekend by taxi, and stay with Freddy and his family overnight. After acquiring the Jeep, they drove to Dubai usually on Thursday afternoon, stopping on the way to buy fresh Lebanese bread and other delicious food for the evening barbeque at his brother's villa. Over the past year they hadn't visited at all. When Laura questioned why, Nicolas made various excuses; evasively telling Laura that he didn't feel like it. Intuitively Laura sensed something was amiss.

The last time Nicolas visited his step brother, he had taken the trip alone; Laura was in the UK at the time. During that visit, something occurred to deeply upset him. Since then, whenever Freddy called to invite them, Nicolas used his stomach ailment as an excuse, saying he would be unable to eat the food or enjoy a drink. Mostly he would say he was busy with the business. He would sometimes ask Laura to take the call and say he wasn't available, so as to avoid speaking with Freddy.

The same as with answering the door, Nicolas would not allow Laura to answer his phone, and Laura would never take it upon herself to do so. So when he passed his mobile to Laura when Freddy rang one day, it was clear something was not right between them.

Laura probed her husband for the true reason behind his reluctance to visit his brother. Eventually he opened up, revealing he no longer felt welcome at his brother's house. Laura was astounded by this revelation. Nicolas confided there had been a dispute between him and his brother's wife Mollie, after which he vowed never to set foot in his brother's house again. Laura knew that for Nicolas to say something like that, a serious incident must have occurred.

Nicolas told Laura that Mollie had been provocatively unsubtle towards his feelings, regarding a subject that was of a highly sensitive nature. Whilst Nicolas was visiting and a guest at their house, Mollie invited people who were Nicolas's adversaries politically speaking. They were also Lebanese and from the north, but didn't share Nicolas's political allegiance regarding his homeland.

337

Disrespectful of his views and knowing it would wind him up, Mollie's actions and attitude were both disloyal and offensive to Nicolas. Although she never said so in actual words, Mollie's behaviour gave Nicolas the distinct impression she would rather not have him around. After that episode, Freddy's invitations for him to visit, Nicolas reckoned were made only out of obligatory courtesy and were therefore insincere. Freddy, Nicolas believed, was no longer keen to have his brother visit for fear of upsetting Mollie.

Nicolas, who had always taken care of and looked out for his younger step-brother, felt betrayed. Nicolas deemed Freddy to be like a son, and was especially generous with his money when Freddy was growing up and studying at university. Even when Nicolas had little to spare and was struggling, he would pull out all the stops to ensure his younger brother had whatever he needed. Nicolas had been equally as generous to his sisters and in later years to his step-brother's children. When Freddy unexpectedly visited Nicolas at the apartment in Mussafah, they talked things through. Not being one to beat around the bush, Nicolas made his feelings crystal clear, leaving Freddy in no doubt as to where he stood on the matter. That night on Skype he told Laura;

"I showed Freddy all what you paid for the antiques."

"Really, why did you do that?" Laura questioned.

"Just to show him," he said in a determined tone.

Nicolas lit a cigarette and leant towards the camera.

"I wanted to make it clear; you and I Loulou are equal in this marriage. I wanted him to see how much you have done to support and help me." Blowing out the smoke from his cigarette he added; "I don't want there to be any misunderstanding."

Nicolas was not one to give a damn for the opinions of others and never normally felt the need to explain his motives for anything. Purely for Laura's benefit, he felt he needed to put certain people straight about a few things. Nicolas continued;

"I believe Freddy now understands my point."

"And if he doesn't?" Laura asked.

"Then he will lose me." Nicolas was resolute in his statement.

If there was one thing Nicolas would not tolerate, it was being disrespected. If Freddy went against him it would be the ultimate betrayal. A betrayal of which there would be no coming back from.

The Sunday before her Birthday, Laura brought up the subject of her return to the Emirates. Behind the scenes Nicolas had something brewing requiring his full attention. He wasn't at liberty to discuss it, and sought to temporarily delay Laura's return, telling her;

"Love, enjoy your Birthday there with Alyssa and your friends. I will arrange your ticket for you to come in two weeks' time. Okay Loulou?"

"Why can't I come sooner?" Laura probed.

"Loulou I have business; it will take few days." Nicky explained.

Laura gave a disappointed look.

"Listen Loulou I have unfinished business to sort okay? It's nothing love, I will finish it quickly."

In the pit of her stomach Laura was uneasy; she felt something was afoot. Why would her being in Abu Dhabi while he sorted his business, suddenly be a problem?

"Once I have sorted this fucking hassle, I will be free to spend as much time as I want with you." He smiled giving a thumb's up sign to the camera. "Okay Loulou? You with me girl; you got me?"

Laura tried to force a smile, but this arrangement didn't sit easy in her mind. "What am I to do about the antiques that are here?" she asked.

"Leave it for now; we have time. There is enough here to get started with," he told her.

Curious about the unfinished business Nicolas referred to, Laura decided to ask;

"What is this unfinished business you need to sort?"

"Something," he replied.

Annoyingly her husband was displaying his usual vagueness when not wishing to illuminate further.

"Well what? Is it something to do with the antiques?" Laura persisted.

"No, no love, nothing for you to worry," he insisted. "I just need few more days."

Laura was not persuaded. Two weeks previous Nicolas had been anxious to get everything moving and was keen to ship the antiques to Abu Dhabi. Suddenly there was no rush; Laura found it bazar. Her face took on a puzzled expression reflecting her confused thoughts.

"Is there a problem? Tell me," she pleaded.

Nicolas refused to elaborate; light heartedly he brushed it off in his usual manner, telling Laura;

"None, of your business."

His unenlightening response was exasperating. Laura knew from experience he wouldn't be pushed. There was a niggling feeling in the back of her mind she couldn't shake; her husband wasn't being straight about everything. Laura's angst driven curiosity had not gone unnoticed by Nicolas. Without lying, there was nothing he could say to dispel her fears. Telling Laura the truth was not an option. Nicolas remained vague in the hope that he could deflect her worried thoughts, and avoid more awkward questions. He managed to cheer Laura's mood, successfully steering the conversation in another direction and even making her laugh a little. She smiled wistfully, telling him;

"I wish you could be here for my birthday, I can't wait for my friends to finally meet you."

"Soon they will see me," he announced.

Nicky gave a wide confident smile. Winking at Laura he added boastfully;

"They will be jealous when they see what a lovely boy you have."

Laura laughed; Nicky's self-assured opinion was so typical. Her fears allayed, Laura was quickly convinced there was nothing to worry about. In two weeks she would be in Abu Dhabi. After saying goodnight and switching off the Skype, Nicolas made a phone call. Speaking in Arabic he asked,

"You have the package ready?"

A voice on the other end of the line answered,

"Yes everything has been arranged as you asked."

"Good; give it to the guy who will come. He knows where to deliver it." Nicolas hung up.

He poured a large whisky and lit a cigarette. As he sat deep in thought, with whisky in one hand and a cigarette in the other, the TV was playing in the background. His mind elsewhere, Nicolas was neither watching nor listening.

It was the morning of Laura's Birthday and she was getting ready to go out with her friend Shelley. They had plans to visit a tea room in Lyndhurst in the New Forest, where according to Shelley they served the most delicious hot chocolate. Later that evening Laura was having a birthday dinner with Alyssa and a few close friends.

Outside the weather was bright and sunny, but being January was still bitterly cold. Laura wrapped up warmly; Shelley would be picking her up at ten. Laura glanced at the clock; it was just after 9.30 am. Nicolas would be arriving back at the apartment for lunch about now, and Laura was anxiously awaiting his call to wish her a happy birthday. Normally if she was away on her birthday he would have called by now, giving his usual rendition of 'Happy Birthday' followed by 'Tell Laura I love her', sung down the phone.

At 9.45am there was a knock at the door. Through the obscured glass Laura saw the shape of someone holding a box. She called up to her daughter thinking it must be one of Alyssa's online orders being delivered. Alyssa didn't answer, so Laura opened the door. The delivery guy asked her to sign for the package, and then handed over the large white box. Laura took it and closed the door. Without really looking at it, she carried the box upstairs calling to Alyssa that she had a delivery. Alyssa came out of her room;

"What delivery, I haven't ordered anything?"

Laura looked at the name on the box;

"Oh my God!" she screeched. "It says 'To Loulou'."

"It must be from Nicky then, he's the only one who calls you Loulou," Alyssa reasoned, and promptly went back inside her room.

Laura took the oblong shaped white box downstairs and excitedly opened it. Inside were twenty five long stemmed beautiful red roses. Laura was stunned by the unexpected surprise. Nicolas gave Laura flowers every day; wild ones that he would pick on his way back to the apartment. This was the first time he had bought Laura flowers since the bouquet he presented her with at the holiday Inn, back in the eighties. There was a card inside the box. Laura took it out and read;

'To my lovely woman Happy Birthday, with all my love, your lovely young man.'

Laura laughed; it was so typically Nicky, not too slushy with a cheeky undertone. A white china vase accompanied the roses. Laura carefully arranged the flowers into it. There were a few sharp thorns and Laura was scratched by one. As it pierced her skin, blood the colour as the roses trickled from her finger dripping onto the table. Laura wrapped a tissue around and pressed to stop the bleeding. An ominous feeling came over her. Brushing it aside, Laura continued to arrange her flowers; nothing was going to spoil her happy mood today. Picking up her mobile Laura called Nicky. She let the phone ring twice then hung up and waited for him to return the call. Seconds later he rang. Nicolas started singing down the phone,

"Happy birthday to you, happy birthday to you, happy birthday dear Laura, happy birthday to you." He then went straight into the chorus of the Richie Valens song;

"Tell Laura I love her. Tell Laura I need her. Tell Laura not to cry, my love for her will never die."

Nicky's eloquent rendition of their anthem gave Laura Goosebumps.

"Is that my lovely young man?" Laura teased.

"Yep, this is me? You get the roses, they write the

message as I say?" he asked.

"Yes they did. It was a lovely unexpected surprise."

"You are most welcome, happy birthday love. I will sleep now one hour, we will talk later tonight on Skype; okay Loulou? See you, bye love."

"I love you Nicolas," she told him still swooning over his romantic surprise.

"I love you too, take care and enjoy your birthday."

Laura couldn't wait to tell Shelley and everyone else about her roses. Alyssa took a photograph of her with them to send to Nicolas. After her trip to the New Forest with Shelley, Laura arrived home at around 3pm. She wanted to spend time on Skype with Nicolas before going out. She decided to get ready early so she could have more time with him. Around 4.30pm she switched on her computer and connected to Skype. It was showing Kousbawi was offline. Laura went downstairs to make a coffee. She was halfway up the stairs when she heard the Skype ringing tone. Laura hurried back to her computer trying not to spill her coffee. A flashing message had appeared on screen; 'Kousbawi calling'. Laura answered and within moments, the face of her 'lovely young man' smiled back at her.

Before she could speak, Nicky started singing happy birthday again; a little off key, but irresistibly endearing all the same. Laura placed her roses in front of the camera for him to see. Witnessing Laura's ecstatic mood made him happy. Nicolas remained in good humour, refusing to allow negative thoughts access to his mind; nothing was going to ruin his moments with Laura on her birthday. When it was time for Laura to leave for her birthday dinner, Nicolas wished her a lovely evening. Laura could see in his face that he longed to be there with her. Laura was optimistic that before another birthday came around, Nicolas would have his papers and finally be able to come to the UK. Despite his absence on this birthday, Laura enjoyed her evening. Proudly she showed off the photo taken of her with the roses. She drove everyone crazy going on and on about them; constantly waxing lyrical about her wonderful Nicolas.

A couple of days later, Laura spent her time chasing up a dealer who had sold her an antique printing press. Nicolas had insisted on acquiring it for their collection. Ever since September, Laura had been trying to secure its delivery to the storage unit. On numerous occasions the seller failed to follow through with delivery. While Laura was in Abu Dhabi, Alessandro had stepped in to take control of the delivery arrangements on her behalf. But he too had been unable to tie the guy down to a specific time; now Laura was beginning to lose patience. The seller had taken Laura's money, but as yet not delivered the goods. Nicolas had been aware of the situation and surprisingly he kept his cool. For the time being, he would give the guy the benefit of the doubt, suggesting he was merely unreliable. Eventually Laura managed to get hold of him and secure a definite date. Delivery was arranged for 10.00am on the 2nd February at the storage unit.

Back in Abu Dhabi Nicolas had been informed of a disturbing development. The unforeseen turn of events demanded that his planned undercover manoeuvre be immediately revised. Luckily Nicolas was used to thinking on his feet. He pulled all his resources together and with help from 'his people', swiftly restructured an intricately more complex stratagem. He wondered what to do about Laura, she was his one weakness; his Achilles heel? He spent most of the day on the phone to his contacts.

That evening as he poured his first whisky, Nicolas was on edge. He contemplated his unfortunate fate; one there would be no coming back from ever. Unable to settle his nerves or conscience, he made a call. Aware someone maybe listening in to the call, he spoke with his contact in coded phrases;

"How is the project coming, it's finished?" he enquired.

An Arabic speaking person confirmed. "Everything's ready."

Nicolas took a sip of whisky, and then asked;

"How does it look, it's good to go?"

344

"Perfect you will be happy with the arrangement. You can move anytime."

"Good, thank you my friend, someone will come to finalise everything." Nicolas hung up.

He walked slowly to the kitchen to top up his whisky, weary from the troubling thoughts circulating around his head. They swirled like a desert dust storm. Despite his fatigue, Nicolas's mental deliberations gripped at his mind tightly, like leeches gripping at flesh. Sleep would not be possible anytime soon. In silent contemplation he mentally rehearsed his strategy. Everything had to be faultlessly and meticulously executed; to the last detail. It was crucial everything worked to plan. He sat alone with his tortured thoughts; they haunted his conscience until three o' clock in the morning.

It was Monday the 30th January; Nicolas was on Skype with Laura. She told him of her renewed attempt to finally get the press from the seller and into storage.

"Good, but take someone with you to the unit, and if this fucking guy lets you down again I'm gonna break his balls."

Amused by Nicky's threat, Laura laughed. She knew he wasn't kidding; to play with Nicolas would be as foolish as playing with a loaded gun. He had absolutely no qualms about metering out his form of justice to anyone who crossed him.

Laura wore her hair loose that evening. As she sat with it hanging seductively over one shoulder, Nicolas gave her an admiring look.

"Move closer to the camera," he suggested.

"Why?" she asked.

"I want to see the colour of your hair," he told her.

"You know what colour it is," she laughed.

Laura humoured him, playfully swishing her auburn tresses at the camera. Nicolas watched mesmerised as Laura flirtatiously flicked her hair about.

"Beautiful," he said, staring adoringly.

Laura smiled; a little bemused. Nicolas's unexpected

compliment was appreciated all the same. They talked for a couple of hours, during which time Nicolas prepared and ate his dinner. They continued chatting until Nicolas said he was tired and needed to sleep.

"Okay love speak to you tomorrow, love you girl; and you love me?" He asked.

"You know I do," Laura confirmed.

She waited for Nicolas to say 'go' in his usual bossy manner, and switch off the Skype. But Nicolas didn't move; he just sat staring at Laura. He was suddenly in no hurry to leave her. Somewhat confused by his unfamiliar behaviour, Laura continued to look back at him. Nicolas was always the first to switch off at the end of a Skype conversation; it had been that way since forever. For the longest time they sat without speaking. There was a look of nostalgic yearning in Nicolas's eyes. It was so strong, Laura felt he might suddenly climb through the screen and reach for her. It appeared Nicolas was drinking in every moment, as if it were to be their last. An air of melancholy permeated the vibrational energy between them; it caused Laura to have shivers. Nicolas often gave her lingering looks, but this felt odd; different somehow. Nicolas's uncharacteristic behaviour unnerved her, but Laura didn't comment on it. Eventually he spoke;

"Okay Loulou, see you tomorrow."

"I love you," she told him.

"Love you too." He gave her another wistful look. "Bye love."

Laura waited for him to switch off the skype. Instead of disconnecting, Nicolas remained motionless and continued to stare at Laura. He smiled at her; she smiled back. He made no attempt to switch off. Several seconds passed with Nicolas smiling wistfully at Laura but not saying a word, though his thoughts at this moment were many. Laura told her husband again she loved him and then very reluctantly, switched off the connection. It felt so wrong; Nicky was always the one to close the Skype or the phone connection at the end of a call. Laura couldn't fathom what it was, but something was clearly not as it should be. And what was the thing with her hair all about, she wondered? She had been away from him longer than planned; perhaps her husband just really missed her?

The following day everything appeared back to normal. Nicolas was exuberant about the new antiques business. He was again full of ideas and Laura was relieved to see him back to his old self. He told Laura;

"In a few days I will start sending the money I owe you for the antiques Loulou. I'm collecting what they owe me in the business; I will send it after the weekend."

"Okay, that's good," she said with a relieved sigh.

Laura had ploughed her savings into Nicolas's latest venture, and was keen to put something back. On the first day of February, the day before the expected delivery of the printing press, Laura told Nicolas that Alessandro had offered to accompany her to the storage unit.

"Good," he said. "I have the money ready to send you."

"Thank you, I really need it."

"No problem, I will do it after the weekend on Sunday; okay love."

The next day, on the 2nd of February, Laura sat outside the storage unit with Alessandro, waiting for the printing press to arrive. Laura had confirmed the arrangements with the seller the night before; he had agreed to meet her with the Press at the unit at 10am. Laura looked at her watch; it was five past ten. She sent a text saying she was waiting. At 10.15am he still hadn't turned up, or replied to her text. Numerous texts and several unanswered phone calls later, Laura was beginning to fret. Glancing at her watch, Laura sighed; it was now 10.45am. They had been sitting in the car for an hour now. Laura turned to Alessandro;

"You know I don't think this guy is coming," she said.

Alessandro was looking decidedly fed up;

"I have things to do, I can't sit around here all day," he grumbled.

"Let's give him another half an hour and then we will go," Laura suggested.

Half an hour passed and there was still no sign of the press. Despite Laura's continued calling and texting, there was not a word from the seller. Having waited two hours now, Laura and Alessandro decided to call it a day. The storage duty manager told them he would call if it arrived, and keep the press in the reception holding area. Laura was furious; this seller was consistently unreliable. Alessandro pulled a face categorically stating;

"He has your money he doesn't care."

Laura was suspicious that she may have been duped, but was hopeful there would be an explanation for the no-show.

"Maybe he broke down or got lost?" she speculated. As she said it, Laura didn't really believe it.

Alessandro gave her an incredulous look, sarcastically stating; "And of course he's miles from civilisation with no phone."

Laura had to admit it didn't sound plausible.

"The guy's a crook," Alessandro said bluntly.

Laura sighed heavily; it looked as though Alessandro might well be right. By the time she got home Laura was totally stressed. Later that afternoon, she had a prearranged appointment at the salon for some waxing and a manicure. Laura decided to forgo the painful waxing; telling beauty therapist Sue all she wanted was a nice relaxing manicure. Sue began to work her magic and as she delivered some much needed pampering, Laura began to unwind. Soon she was able to laugh as she relayed to her beauty therapist friend, the calamitous events of the day.

After an hour of total relaxation, Laura returned to her house with perfectly manicured nails and feeling a whole lot calmer. She rang Nicky's mobile, letting it ring twice then hung up and waited. Within moments he rang;

"Yeah love, everything okay with you?" he asked.

"Not really," she told him mournfully. "Can we go on Skype now?"

"Okay Loulou, I'm at your service. Give me five minutes and I'll be on love."

Laura switched on her laptop and connected to Skype. While she waited for Kousbawi to be online, she made a coffee. She composed herself ready to tell him of the day's events. Five minutes later they were connected.

Nicolas was standing near his laptop. He was on his mobile talking in Arabic. As she sipped her coffee Laura waited for him to finish his call. Nicky continued talking without acknowledging her. He appeared to Laura to be somewhat agitated. The conversation seemed intense. Laura wished she understood Arabic. Watching his facial expressions she tried to get a gist of what was being said. Nicolas was very animated, appearing angry or upset with something. Laura was used to Nicolas's mannerisms and could tell without understanding the language, exactly what kind of conversation this was. Laura didn't relish having to tell him about the press. After a long and intense call, he finally came off the phone. In a concerned tone Laura asked,

"Is everything okay?"

"Yes love, just business." He didn't wish to elaborate, quickly adding; "How are you Loulou?"

Nicolas's manner was now more relaxed and vastly in contrast to the highly agitated state displayed moments earlier. He was ultra-calm as Laura tentatively explained to him, how she and Alessandro waited at the storage unit for over two hours. The guy and the press she explained, was again a no-show. Nicolas listened and lit a cigarette.

"No problem love, maybe the guy had an accident and couldn't call."

Laura hadn't thought of that. Now she felt a bit guilty for thinking him a crook.

"Don't worry love, we will sort it." Nicky reassured. He then changed his attitude and tone, adding vengefully;

"But if this guy is playing a game with you, I will buy a ticket and come there." Nicolas puffed deliberately on his cigarette; "He will not be happy to see me, and neither will his family. Okay Loulou?"

The matter of the press wasn't discussed further.

For another hour they chatted, forgetting their troubles as they engaged in more cheerful exchange. The mood and conversation was light and upbeat. There was no clue from Nicolas that anything was out of sync or unduly worrying him. On the contrary, he appeared excited for the future and confident that the business would flourish. His relaxed mood dispelled Laura's previously harboured doubts. She did wonder at his remark about buying a ticket to the UK; he sounded so determined. Had his papers come through and he had forgotten to mention it? That was unlikely Laura thought. Nicolas would be too excited not to say anything; unless perhaps he intended to surprise her. She revelled at the possibility. Nicolas said he planned to go to Rene's for lunch the following day. Laura was relieved he would have company, and in a few days she would be back in Abu Dhabi with him.

"Listen Loulou, I'm going to watch the news now," he suddenly announced. "We will talk tomorrow love?"

"Enjoy your lunch with Rene," Laura said.

"Thank you Loulou I will. Where is Bunnie (Alyssa)?" Nicky asked.

"On her computer as usual," Laura laughed.

"Okay tell her hi, and give her big kiss from me. Okay Loulou? Love you girl, take care hayati."

"I will, and you too. I love you."

Laura was confident that in a few short days she would again be telling Nicky, 'I love you' in person.

"Okay love, speak tomorrow, bye love."

Nicolas quickly switched off the Skype.

It was just after 6pm when Laura went to the local shop to buy something for dinner. It was freezing out; she hurried back to the house with her groceries. Her hands were shaking from the cold so much; she could hardly get the key in the door. Dumping the bag of groceries on the floor, Laura huddled against the radiator trying to thaw out from the numbing cold. Taking her mobile from her coat pocket she sent a text to Nicolas.

'It's freezing; I think it's going to snow. Wish you were

here to keep me warm.'

Laura took off her coat slinging it haphazardly over the bannister. Still shivering, she again huddled against the radiator trying to defrost. Her mobile rang. It was Nicolas;

"You want me to come and heat you up?"

The attractive, deep manly quality of Nicolas's voice exuded masculine virility. Laura trembled, not from the cold this time, but from his alluring sexy tones as they were transmitted to her ear.

"You want my heat Loulou?" he asked, in an enticingly suggestive manner.

Laura smiled at his sexual innuendo; she could tell he was horny.

"Yes please," she sighed. "I'm so cold here without you," she told him breathlessly; deliberately encouraging Nicolas's highly sexed libido.

"Then I will send you my heat now, can you feel it?" he asked suggestively.

Laura imagined lying beside her husband, feeling the warmth from his body radiate into her. As she visualised the beguiling scenario, the blood circulated again in her veins, quickly thawing her frozen senses.

"I feel warmer already," she whispered.

The sensual, sexually charged banter, continued for a while. Later Nicolas told Laura;

"You know in Kousba it is colder than you can believe. You will not be able to stand it," he laughed.

"Well if I'm with you, I'll be warm," she teased.

"Love if you can stand the cold in Kousba, I will give you anything you want."

Laura laughed and accepted his tantalising challenge; "It's a deal; take me to Kousba."

That evening, Laura managed to contact the guy with the printing press. He relayed some vague story, about not being able to fit the press into the van he had hired; but that was no excuse for not calling and explaining earlier, Laura thought. Delivery was rearranged for the following Monday. Laura was not going to hold her breath on that.

It was late, so she refrained from calling Nicolas to update him; he would most likely be sleeping. Instead she sent him a text. Although she was tired from the day's events, Laura needed to unwind and went to bed quite late. Planning to sleep in, she set her alarm for 10am.

The following morning she awoke quite suddenly with a start. Something made her sit up and look at the clock on the wall. It was 7.35am. Laura was perplexed as to why she had woken in such an abrupt and unnatural way. After an hour of unsuccessful attempts at trying to get back to sleep, Laura gave in. She went downstairs to make coffee. Thinking Nicky would probably be getting ready to go to Rene's Laura decided to give him a call. She let the phone ring twice then hung up. Laura waited for Nicky to return her call. Ten minutes passed by and still he hadn't called back. Laura took her shower. Maybe Nicky had been showering and couldn't answer. Laura dressed and dried her hair. Sitting in front of her dressing table, she rang Nicky's number again. Two rings then Laura hung up; she waited.

The sun glistened on the frosty rooftops of the houses opposite. Laura stood by the window and looked out. A kind of eerie quiet prevailed. There was a weird stillness all around. Picking up her mobile from the dressing table, Laura called Nicky again. This time she didn't hang up after two rings, but let it continue ringing; Nicolas still didn't answer. Laura puzzled over what he could be doing. This was not like him; Nicky always got back to her, even if he were busy. The only time he didn't, was when they had quarrelled and he was sulking.

Laura strived to convince herself there was a perfectly logical explanation for his delay in getting back to her, and tried not to worry unduly. That was easier said than done. She began envisioning all kinds of scenarios. Maybe he had been pulled over by the police on his way to Rene's house for speeding. She hoped he hadn't got into an argument or fight and been arrested. Perhaps his battery had died on his mobile; unlikely as he was always very vigilant in keeping it fully charged. Or maybe he just didn't hear his phone if he was at Rene's and they were talking. Again unlikely, as he would have seen Laura's first missed call before he left for Rene's.

Laura stared out of her bedroom window; everything was too still. Remembering that Nicolas had asked her to buy a lottery ticket, (it was a massive rollover this Friday), Laura decided to go to the shop on the corner. She would try to call Nicky again when she returned. Outside the sky was very blue and the sun was shining, but Laura knew it was bitterly cold out there. Unwilling to face the chilly wintry weather she hesitated. She was still dithering about going, when her mobile rang; it was Nicolas. At last she thought.

"Hi, where have you been?" she asked.

"How are you Laura?"

The voice that answered was not Nicolas.

"I'm fine, who is that?"

Laura thought it must be one of the friends Nicolas was having lunch with.

"It's Freddy, what are you doing Laura?" Nicolas's step brother asked.

Laura thought it a strange question.

"I'm at home, why? Where is Nicolas?" Laura asked surprised to be talking to Freddy.

"I'm sorry Laura; I have some very bad news."

Laura's heart raced, fearful of what was coming.

"Nicolas passed away today."

Laura felt her heart fall to her feet. She must have miss-heard; surely Freddy didn't say that. This is a bad joke Laura thought; they were playing a cruel joke on her.

"I don't believe you, he's there. It's not funny Freddy, put him on," Laura demanded.

"I'm so sorry Laura, Nicolas is gone; he's dead."

Laura stood silent; she froze as the blood drained from her veins. At first she felt only denial and disbelief, but as Freddy's words fully infiltrated her consciousness, like a wave washing over her, terror and panic engulfed Laura.

Just as a tsunami destroys everything in its wake, Laura's world was instantly ripped away. Collapsing to her knees, she screamed uncontrollably;

"No! No, it can't be true!!!"

Like an exploding star Laura's heart broke, shattering into a billion pieces; she physically felt it splinter and fragment within her chest. In that precise moment her life flashed before her. Nothing was registering as real; she became numb. In seconds Laura's world disintegrated. A few hours ago, she and Nicky had indulged in playful banter; that world was gone and now nothing would ever be the same. Freddy began to cry, expressing deep sorrow at the loss of his brother, but the sound was indistinguishable from laughter, and Laura clung to the hope that he might admit to playing a rather bad joke on her. But he didn't.

Laura tried to speak, her voice shaking from shock as she barely managed to ask;

"What happened?"

She was expecting to be told it was a car crash or some kind of accident.

"Heart attack, Nicolas had a heart attack Laura."

For an unknowable amount of time Laura felt frozen inside, everything stopped even her breathing. Suddenly she let out the most horrendous scream, before collapsing into a quivering heap at the side of the bed. She was still holding the phone howling like an injured animal caught in a trap.

"Calm down Laura," Freddy pleaded.

Laura couldn't stop; her emotions had gone into over-drive as felt her insides being ripped from her body by an invisible malevolent force. Hearing her mother scream so hideously, Alyssa ran into the bedroom.

"What's wrong mum?"

Alyssa was shocked to see her mother in such a state. Laura stopped screaming and looked at her daughter. She felt trance like, not really there as she heard herself say;
"He's dead, Nicolas is dead."

Alyssa couldn't take it in.

"Dead, Steppe's dead? But how?"

Laura hugged her daughter;

"Heart attack, Steppe had a heart attack." Laura's voice tailed off, fading into a barely legible whisper.

"Lay down mum, I'll get you some tea."

Alyssa hurried to the kitchen to make her mother a cup of sweet tea to help ease the shock. But this was just the beginning; the shock of Nicolas's death was to have a profound effect. Struggling to her feet, Laura grabbed the suitcase from the top of the wardrobe. Unable to think rationally, she opened up all of the cupboards and drawers, randomly throwing clothes into the case.

Alyssa returned with the sweet tea to find her mother pacing the room. Alarmed at Laura's impulsive behaviour she asked;

"What are you doing mum?"

"I have to go; I have to be with him," Laura insisted.

Alyssa told her mother to sit and drink the sweet tea. Laura's shaking hand took the tea from her daughter. Her mind whirled like a fairground ride. She felt completely hollow; like something had literally been ripped out of her. Alyssa was in shock too, but courageously held it together for her mother.

"I'll call dad," she told Laura.

Alyssa left the room to call Alessandro. Laura sipped the sweet tea. Strangely it tasted good; almost comforting. A sudden light-headedness caused Laura to feel quite detached from her body, as if barely connected by a tiny thread that may snap at any moment. This is not real, was all Laura could think. Her body felt heavy and slow, yet her mind raced with a billion thoughts, only she couldn't make sense of any one of them. She could hear Alyssa talking on the phone downstairs, the words sounded to Laura weirdly jumbled and foreign. Alyssa's voice faded away into the distance. Collapsing onto the bed, Laura felt everything slip away from her as if she were being sucked into a huge vacuum. As darkness descended all around her,

Laura wanted to scream out, but not a sound could escape through her lips, as though her vocal chords had been severed.

Thirty three days earlier, Laura and Nicky had joyfully celebrated the arrival of 2012. Looking forward to a year full of promise, that night they shared their dreams for the future. This was to be their time Nicky had confidently assured. They laughed together, making light of the world speculation about the Mayan calendar and its ominous predictions for the year of 2012. Everyone was wondering if the world would actually end. It ended for Laura thirty three days later, on the third day of February. For Laura the prophecy of 2012 was most tragically fulfilled.

KOUSBAWI

Chapter 42: Kousbawi Goes Home

After trying all evening, Alessandro managed to book
Laura and Alyssa on the next available flight out to Dubai.
At 5.00am he drove them to Heathrow. Freddy insisted
they stay with him, rather than fly directly to Abu Dhabi.
In retrospect, perhaps Laura should have made different
arrangements, but deep shock impaired her judgement and
ability to make a rational decision; she just followed along
with whatever she was told. Physically weak having not
eaten anything since Thursday, Laura was functioning on
auto pilot; barely going through the motions of what was
required. Her mind was hazy and muddled. Nothing at this
point registered as being real; as if she was playing a part
in a make believe drama. Laura felt everything inside her
become numb with grief, and a huge emotional lump stuck
solidly in her throat. The turmoil of her emotions caused
her stomach to tighten like a drum, and automatically her
mind repelled any desire to eat. This was not the journey
back to the Emirates Laura envisioned she would take. She
should be deliriously happy, excited about her reunion
with Nicolas. Instead of seeing his smiling face waiting for
her at the airport, Laura would be making arrangements to
view his corpse.

During the seven-and-a-half hour flight, Alyssa and
Laura attempted to get some sleep. Pulling her blanket
tightly around her, Laura closed her eyes and tried to shut
out the events of the last fifteen hours. Desperately she
clung to the vain hope that she would wake to find it had
been a terrible nightmare; a bad dream she would surely
soon be released from. Unfortunately this was not an
episode of Dallas; Nicolas was unlikely to miraculously
reappear from the shower, Bobby Ewing style.

Coming to terms with her husband's untimely death,
would be horrendous and difficult. Alyssa for the moment

remained strong. Laura would never get through the ordeal now facing them, without her daughter's support.

Seven and a half hours later, their plane touched down at Dubai's international airport. They were met by Mollie, who drove them straight to the villa. They were to stay at Freddy's until Nicolas's body was released, and could be flown to Kousba for burial. Freddy looked totally drained when they arrived. He had been getting together the legal paperwork required to allow Nicolas's body to be flown out of Abu Dhabi and back to Lebanon; it was proving to be a vexing task. A meal was prepared for them by Mariel, Freddy and Mollie's live in Filipino house maid. Again Laura couldn't bring herself to eat anything. Everyone was telling her she needed nourishment to keep her strength up. In an ironic twist, it was Alyssa who was now persuading Laura to eat. But Laura had no appetite. Two days now without food, left her running on pure adrenalin.

Laura expressed her wish to view Nicolas's body as soon as possible. Freddy made some phone calls and the following day, Laura and Alyssa travelled with him to Abu Dhabi. As they drove along the Dubai highway, familiar sights and sounds reminded Laura of the many times she had taken this journey with her husband.

On the way they stopped to collect a suit for Nicolas to be laid to rest in from the apartment in Mussafah. As they pulled up outside of the building, Laura's heart was heavy with grief; for the last three years this had been her home with Nicolas. Stepping from the car she looked up at the windows with their familiar blue frames, and Laura had a sudden flashback. She remembered the first time she had taken a taxi alone and been lost. The memory momentarily eclipsed her grief; how relieved she had been to see their apartment block and its blue window frames that day two years ago. Looking up at them now filled her with sorrow. An even bigger lump formed in her throat; her beloved husband had taken his last breath behind those blue framed windows. Laura's chest tightened, as if readying itself for another shattering blow to her breaking heart.

Freddy said the local police had restricted access to the apartment. Originally the place had been treated as a crime scene; Nicolas's death was at first viewed with suspicion. Their blue Jeep was still parked in front of the building. Crippling sadness gripped Laura as memories of that last journey taken with Nicolas, flashed into her mind.

Laura would give anything for the chance to once more be sat beside him in their Jeep, feeling the tension and excitement as her heart jumped to her mouth; holding her breath and clenching her knuckles as he drove, twisting and turning at speed along the highway. Laura shivered. Never again would Nicolas drive his blue Jeep as he did that day; so confident and totally fearless.

She recalled clearly the cd track playing on the stereo during that last drive to the airport with him. It was Neil Diamond's 'Sweet Caroline'. As the memories were evoked, Laura saw everything again. Imprinted still, was the way Nicolas's hands looked when holding the steering wheel, the way his foot tapped to the music while skilfully weaving in and out of the traffic, displaying his unique bravado. Every detail was vividly clear in Laura's mind just as it had appeared when she took what was ultimately her final journey in the Jeep with Nicolas.

"Let's go," Freddy said, immediately breaking the spell of this now much treasured memory.

They had a few minutes only Freddy said, in which to collect Nicolas's suit. Alyssa remained in the car while they went inside. The watchman stared at Laura as she entered the building. Laura briefly made eye contact. His eyes expressed his condolences; the words he couldn't say due to his lack of English. They stepped out of the elevator on the third floor. Laura felt suddenly chilled to the bone, as though the spectre of death itself had put his icy fingers inside her heart, freezing her soul and turning her blood to ice.

Trembling, Laura followed Freddy along the passage. He took out a key and opened the front door; the place was in total darkness. It had only been two days since Nicolas's passing, but for some unfathomable reason the electrics were switched off. A strong smell of stale cigarette smoke filled the air. Without air conditioning, the atmosphere was stifling. Laura had so many unanswered questions. She wanted to know exactly where and how Nicolas was found. But there was no time for such explanations. Freddy said they had a deadline to get to the morgue with Nicolas's burial clothes, before the mortuary staff left for the night.

Using the light from his mobile phone, Freddy lit the way to the bedroom. In spite of the lack of illumination, Laura knew exactly where to find everything. As if guided in the dark by an unseen hand, she immediately found Nicolas's white shirt, then straight away located his black suit, a dark tie, and a pair of black socks. Freddy told her shoes would not be necessary. Laura had hoped for a little reflective time alone in the apartment; the place she had shared with Nicolas since 2009. But as soon as Laura had got together her husband's burial clothes, Freddy hurried her out. Laura carefully laid Nicolas's clothes over the car seat. They then drove directly to the hospital morgue in Abu Dhabi.

On the way to the morgue, Laura quizzed Freddy about the exact circumstances of Nicolas's death. Freddy was vague on the details; Laura desperately needed to piece together exactly what happened that fateful day.

From the little she could gather, Nicolas failed to show at Rene's for lunch on Friday. When he didn't answer his phone, Rene became concerned. Along with Nicolas's cousin, Rene drove to the apartment to find Nicolas's Jeep was still parked outside. Fearing something untoward had occurred, they rushed up to the third floor and banged loudly on the door. Nicolas's phone could be heard ringing inside. With no response from him, they raised the alarm. The police arrived a while after. Laura was told Nicolas was found on the floor close to the bathroom door, having apparently suffered a heart attack. Knowing he had been alone when he passed was deeply distressing for Laura.

She couldn't get their last conversation out of her head. He was so relaxed and happy on Thursday night, while chatting on Skype. Later that Thursday evening, they had talked again on the phone. Laura remembered how Nicolas had kidded and teased her about the cold winter climate of Kousba.

Laura listened to Freddy's version of the events of Friday, but nothing made sense. People were now referring to Nicolas in the past tense; Laura wasn't ready to hear him being spoken of in this way. How was it possible? How could she associate words like death, dead, died and passed away with her Nicolas? Al Hajj was supposed to be indestructible. Hearing people refer to Nicolas as having died made Laura nauseous.

As they approached the hospital morgue, Laura's heart pounded heavily in her chest. When she stepped from the car her legs became stiff and would barley move, as if to protest their destination. Weakness from lack of food made her extremely light-headed. Laura clung tightly to Alyssa as they walked towards the morgue. A group had gathered outside. Laura recognised one or two people. Everyone expressed their condolences, but Laura just felt stunned. She shouldn't even be in such a place she thought, still struggling to accept the reality of what had happened.

Eventually, after waiting for what seemed an eternity, they were allowed inside. To Laura's dismay, everyone accompanied her into the morgue. It was disconcerting; Laura had hoped to be left alone with her husband. Again people expressed their condolences. Laura was too choked up to speak to them, and just nodded. Nicolas's body was held in an adjacent part of the morgue. Finally the doors opened. Laura looked into the room where a man's body lay on a slab dressed in the clothes she had brought from the apartment. Trembling with grief and shock, and from the mortuary's icy atmosphere, Laura peered through the doorway. Numbed to the core, she waited anxiously to be told she could go in and view her husband.

Three or four morgue attendants were milling around.

Two of them approached the body and stood one either side of it. In a rather rough manner, they grabbed the shoulders and yanked the body further up the table. Laura noticed a distinct lack of compassion on their faces. They performed the action coldly without emotion, as though handling a piece of meat on a butcher's slab. One of the attendants then hocked and spit into the corner. Laura was shocked; her blood boiled at the disrespect. She had an overpowering urge to scream at him and display her outrage, but restrained her anger. Laura fumed at the way Nicolas's body was being treated. This was her husband, not a piece of discarded meat. Laura wanted to protest, but something stopped her. Instead she remained calm, saying nothing at all.

Seconds later she found herself being ushered into the room. Laura felt all eyes upon her as she moved closer to the table where the body lay. Thankfully the other people kept a respectful distance. Laura had assumed there would be a private room in which to view her deceased husband alone. She had no wish to be ogled in her grief. Why wasn't she permitted those few moments of privacy with her late husband? In the UK things would be handled with more decorum and sensitivity.

Tears streamed from Laura's eyes. Looking down at the corpse, she tenderly touched the forehead with her fingers. It was totally frozen; she had never felt anything quite so cold ever. As Laura studied the lifeless remains, something felt wrong. Clouded by grief and tears, Laura's judgment may have been affected. Even so, the more she looked the more wrong it all felt. She glanced at the people standing around the perimeter of the room a few feet away. The tense atmosphere was palpable. Nobody spoke. Laura looked again at the body on the slab wearing Nicolas's clothes. Freddy must have handed the suit in when they arrived; Laura had been too distraught to notice. Unable to keep her thoughts to herself any longer, Laura suddenly voiced her misgivings;

"It doesn't look like Nicolas," she announced.

Glances were exchanged amongst the onlookers. Not a word was spoken in response to Laura's statement. Nicolas was relatively tall; this body Laura noted, appeared several inches shorter than her husband. Laura tried to hold his hand. It felt damp and inflexible, like a solid lump of ice. It didn't resemble Nicolas's beautiful strong masculine hand in any way. The lifeless emotionless face looked puffy and unfamiliar. Laura touched the hair. Again its appearance and texture was completely wrong. Nicky had a few grey hairs at the temples, but it was predominately still very dark. This man's hair was totally grey and much too curly. Again Laura impulsively blurted out her thoughts;

"This is not Nicolas! This is not my husband!"

Laura heard whispering in Arabic as furtive looks were exchanged amongst the group. She looked over at Alyssa's sad tearful little face; Laura desperately wanted someone to agree with her that this was not Nicolas. The body lying cold and dead in front of her was not him. Why couldn't anyone else see that? But no one seemed to share Laura's doubts. A few people left the room to congregate in the hallway outside. Laura could hear them talking quietly in Arabic. She sensed some tenseness in the atmosphere and felt she was silently being urged to leave. If this body in front of her was indeed her dear Nicolas, and Laura was not convinced it was, but if it was, then she was not ready to leave him; not ready to leave him all alone in that cold dreadful place. How could she leave him here? Suddenly she felt an arm around her shoulder. It was Elias;

"Come Laura you should leave, you need rest."

If everyone was accepting this was Nicolas, then Laura had no choice but to do the same. She gently kissed his icy forehead and told him she loved him. Lying motionless in front of her this cold frozen body was without thoughts, without a voice, and without a soul. It no longer contained even a glimmer of the warm essence of her dear husband. The brave spirit, the exuberant energy and life force that was Nicolas, no longer resided within this frozen vessel.

"Laura, you've had a terrible shock," Elias said softly.

"Please, come away now."

Elias coaxed a sobbing Laura away from the body. She was led reluctantly out of the room. On reaching the door Laura's head swooned, she felt faint and her legs buckled slightly. She was quickly helped to a nearby chair.

The drive back to Dubai was solemn. Traumatised by what she had experienced, Laura fell deeper into shock. She tried to dismiss doubts about the body she had viewed. Surely it must have been Nicolas; the grief was playing tricks with her mind. But try as she might, Laura couldn't let go of the feeling that something wasn't adding up.

Back at the villa, Freddy seemed much stressed. He was making numerous phone calls, none of which could be understood by Laura as they were spoken in Arabic. There seemed to be some urgency to get Nicolas out of the country and on a plane back to Lebanon. For whatever reasons, the Abu Dhabi authorities were reluctant to issue the paperwork authorising the release of his body. It crossed Laura's mind that perhaps they too were not entirely satisfied with the circumstances of her husband's untimely death. Laura quietly held her own suspicions.

Come Monday morning the 6th of February, there were still hassles with releasing Nicolas's body. Then abruptly, as if someone had just waved a magic wand, everything changed. Miraculously by lunchtime, the paperwork was issued and Nicolas was on a flight bound for Lebanon. His body was accompanied by his step brother Freddy, and an older cousin. Later that same evening Laura and Alyssa, along with Mollie, were themselves on a flight bound for Beirut.

The three hour flight was followed by an hour's drive by taxi into the mountains, to Kousba in the north. Beirut was cold and it was raining heavily. As they drove towards Nicolas's mountain village, there was a distinct drop in the temperature. Staring out of the window, Laura reflected on the last time she had spoken with Nicolas. Just four days ago her husband had teased her about the cold in Kousba. Laura remembered asking Nicolas to take her, to prove she could handle it. In a million years she could never imagine that her first visit to her husband's homeland would come under such shocking circumstances.

It felt strange to actually be in Lebanon; stranger still to be there without Nicolas. With the dark, and the perpetual heavy rain, Laura struggled to see anything clearly out of the car window. Tears trickled down her cheek. Falling one after the other from her eyes, they harmonised with the raindrops trickling down the window pane. Driving almost to the top of the mountain, the taxi pulled up outside of a large villa. The rain had stopped. Laura stepped from the cab and breathed the cold mountain air of Kousba for the first time. At last, Laura had arrived in the village Nicolas had spoken of so fondly and so often; the place he had dreamed of one day returning to.

Freddy came out from the villa and helped them in with their bags; his flight carrying Nicolas's body, had arrived a few hours earlier. The huge villa built over four levels was warm and cosy inside. Mollie showed Laura and Alyssa to a bedroom on the third floor. They unpacked and put out their clothes ready for the funeral the next day; Tuesday 7th February.

Everything seemed so rushed. In the UK Laura would have had longer to adjust and prepare for the event. There would have been at least a full week. But Nicolas was to be buried just four days after his death. Tomorrow was going to be a traumatic time; the worst Laura had ever endured. Never had she been gripped by such raw cutting emotions. Being present at his funeral was the last thing Laura would ever do for her dear Nicolas. Getting through it, would require every ounce of strength she had in her.

Remembering the tower of strength Nicolas had always been for her, Laura wanted to make him proud. She had to be strong; the way Nicolas had always been strong. While preparing to go to bed that night, Laura prayed to receive that strength. Somehow from somewhere a sudden wave of calmness miraculously emerged and Laura felt her prayers answered.

But both Laura and Alyssa tossed and turned the whole night, with neither of them getting the sleep they needed. Poor Alyssa, who had remained steadfastly strong, was up half the night feeling unwell and nauseous, as the shock of losing her step-dad finally took its toll on her. Laura got up at 6am, having slept barely two hours at best. She peered around the bedroom curtain. The sun was coming up over the mountains. Inside the villa it was warm, but out in the mountains surrounding Kousba, it was a different story.

After taking a shower, Laura dressed entirely in black. Alyssa had finally managed to fall asleep and Laura was reluctant to disturb her. She gently woke her daughter then left her alone to get ready. Laura wandered into the villa's third floor lounge. Sliding open the glass door, she stepped out onto the adjoining balcony. Despite the bright sun it was bitterly cold. The panoramic view of Kousba was as Nicolas had proclaimed, breath-taking and absolutely as he had described it. The cold air livened and awakened Laura; briefly lifting her from the numbness that had gripped her senses rigidly for last four and a half days. As she looked over the balcony, Laura felt a quiet peace descend; it fell upon her like a soft comforting garment, as if something or someone were protecting and watching over her.

Laura's eyes were drawn to an area towards the top of the mountain. She instantly recognised a little clump of cedar trees. Above this spot was where Nicolas said he planned to build their villa. Laura had been shown pictures on the internet of that exact area many times. Standing there surveying it for real, breathing the cool mountain air, the Kousba air Nicolas had longed to breathe again; tears welled in Laura's eyes. She felt overwhelmingly sad that Nicolas would never fulfil his dream. He so wanted to take Laura to Lebanon, his homeland. Now it was too late; they would never walk together in the village he loved so much. Looking to the sky Laura released a trembling heavy sigh. Rain clouds were forming. Laura made a pledge whispering;

"I promise you darling; I will be strong and will not fall

apart today. I love you; I want to make you proud."

At that moment a soft breeze blew, as if to scoop up her words and carry them off to heaven.

Laura had been standing out on the balcony more than fifteen minutes. She smiled; she hadn't felt the cold at all. Looking across the red tiled rooftops of Kousba, Laura softly said;

"You see Nicolas I can stand the cold in Kousba."

With a deep sigh and heavy heart, she remembered the promise Nicolas made her barely five days ago. Through tearful eyes Laura looked to the horizon and demanded he keep his side of the bargain exclaiming;

"You told me if I could stand the cold in Kousba, you would give me anything I wanted." Choking back tears Laura reinforced her demand that he fulfil his promise;

"I want you to come back to me," she pleaded.

A sudden stabbing pain pierced her heart. Broken with grief she uttered;

"Are you listening Kousbawi? You never make a promise you cannot keep. You have to come back; I can't live my life without you. I just can't!"

Laura felt her strength ebb and struggled to regain it. It wasn't until she went inside that she realised how cold she was. Alyssa came out of the bedroom holding her camera.

"I'm going to take some photos from the balcony." She told her mother. "We may never come back here again and I want pictures of Kousba, Steppe's village."

Alyssa walked onto the balcony. Laura called to her,

"It's a lovely view; don't get too cold though."

Laura watched from the warmth of the sitting room as Alyssa clicked away with her Nikon camera. She had always been a keen, talented photographer. Alyssa was deeply upset by the tragic turn of events, and was fighting her own private battle to remain strong. Within minutes she was back inside shivering.

"My fingers have gone completely numb," she said through chattering teeth; her hands red and shaking with the cold.

"Where are your gloves?" Laura asked.

"They're too thick and I can't take pictures properly with them on." Alyssa explained.

Mollie suddenly appeared to inform them they would be leaving for the church at 9 o' clock. Freddy had gone on ahead. No one had spoken of the day's proceedings or the protocol concerning funerals in Lebanon. Laura presumed it would be a formal Christian ceremony; other than that she knew very little. It was 8.35am; soon Laura would see exactly how the people of Kousba say goodbye to one of their own.

It was a five-minute drive down the mountain to the village, and the church where Nicolas lay in rest. The sky had clouded over as they stepped from the car. Laura and Alyssa followed Mollie down the wide stone steps to the church. The little streets with their pretty orange trees, and old stone buildings and archways were exactly as Laura had imagined from Nicolas's description. As they entered the large church, three very tall priests wearing traditional Orthodox black robes greeted them. The three women were directed to a room at the back. Being unfamiliar with the Orthodox traditions in Lebanon, Laura was unprepared for what awaited. They entered a room full of women dressed in black seated around, what appeared to be a low table or stand. Candles burned either end of the altar like stand. Laura was ushered closer to take a seat at the front. No one had warned her that Nicolas would be laid out on a refrigerated stand right in front of her. She imagined he would have been in a coffin. Laura gasped; suddenly being confronted by Nicolas's body almost made her keel over. Alyssa looked teary eyed at her mother; distraught seeing her 'Steppe' this way. Mollie really should have warned them. For Laura it was shock enough, but now Alyssa was really traumatised.

Quickly Laura composed herself. She and Alyssa took a seat alongside Nicolas's sisters. She stared at the body; it was a million miles away from the one viewed in the Abu Dhabi mortuary just over a day ago. Obviously it still wasn't as she remembered her Nicolas, but bore much more of a resemblance to the man she loved. The puffiness was gone from his face and his hair was black thick and straighter, styled in the way Laura was familiar with. His lower half was covered over by a large sheet with his arms over the top resting by his side. He looked peaceful, as though asleep on a bed. Overcome with emotion, Laura sobbed and knelt beside him. Gripping his hand she kissed it. It was stiff and cold, but not frozen and icy as it felt in the morgue.

"I love you Nicolas. Why did you leave me this way?" she sobbed.

Laura leant towards his face. His lips had an unnatural bluish grey tinge. Laura stared. Were these the same lips that kissed her with such passion? The lips that spoke tender words to her, and told her so many stories of Kousba, the place he loved and longed to come home to?

Now Kousbawi was home; returned to the only place he would call his home. The handsome, charismatic prince charming, Laura encountered as a girl had finally made it home. But this was not the home-coming he planned. This was all wrong! How could the undisputed King of Laura's heart be lying motionless and lifeless in front of her; cold and empty of that fiery passion? It was hard to see him this way, devoid of the warmth that had given such comfort to Laura. Many times the sound and feel of his beating heart had soothed her. It would now be forever still and silent.

Laura studied Nicolas's expressionless face. It appeared artificial; shell like and unreal as though he were wearing a death mask. In a way he was; the real Nicolas was far away. The spirit and essence of him resided elsewhere. Laura tried to be positive imagining Nicolas forever free; liberated at last from the restraints that had kept him from his homeland for so long. Now his soul would roam freely around the land and mountains of the country he loved.

Laura felt a comforting arm at her shoulder. Talia, one of Nicolas's three step-sisters helped Laura back to her seat. They had briefly met fifteen years ago in Abu Dhabi.

369

To Laura's left sat Nicolas's other sisters, Barbara and Frida. Laura was meeting them for the first time. Nicolas had spoken about his sisters, but he had unresolved issues with them, and they had been estranged for many years. Today they and his widow were united in grief.

Frida, the younger of the sisters turned to Laura telling her in a distraught tone;

"Oh, I wish that we could have met you under different circumstances," Frida sobbed, her tearstained face partially hidden under big dark glasses.

Despite his estrangement from his sisters they all wept, professing their love for their departed brother. These statuesque Middle Eastern beauties were strong, but their grief like Laura's, was overwhelming; the chance of any reconciliation with their beloved brother was gone forever. As was the tradition, all the women were separate from the men for this part of the mourning process. Female friends, relatives, and all the women of Kousba and surrounding villages, came in to give condolences to the family and pay their respects to Nicolas. The men congregated in another area.

Roughly six hours later, around 3.30pm the Orthodox priests arrived. Standing around the table where Nicolas's body lay, they began saying prayers and swinging incense over him. Minutes later men arrived carrying a solid wood coffin with a cross engraved on it. Laura wasn't sure if the coffin was made of cedar wood, but it was fittingly strong and solid just like Nicolas. As the men filed into the room, Frida explained that the women would now leave for the funeral service in the main part of the church. The priests would now place Nicolas inside his coffin. Laura became distressed; she would never see her husband's face again. She knelt beside him; one more time she kissed his cold blue lips. Through a torrent of tears Laura whispered;

"I love you Nicolas, don't forget your promise to me. Goodbye my darling, I will love you forever."

Reluctantly Laura stepped away from the table so that the priests could finish their ritual.

"Why do we have to leave?" Laura asked Frida.

"Because they don't want us to see when they put him in the coffin, the men deal with that," Frida explained.

As they moved outside, the streets were crowded with hundreds of people gathering to pay their respects. Flowers were placed at the church's entrance. Huge white bouquets lined the steps and walls. The Christian Orthodox church was packed to capacity with many hundreds of mourners overflowing onto the street outside.

Laura and Alyssa, along with Nicolas's sisters were escorted to the front of the church. Six priests carried in Nicolas's coffin, placing it on the altar directly in front of them. The service was conducted in Arabic. Frida did her best to translate what was said. There was a surprised gasp from the congregation as the priest revealed that Nicolas had anonymously sent money every month to help the less fortunate in Lebanon. This was not news to Laura who was fully aware that he had been doing this for some time. It was typical of his philanthropic nature. At the end of a very emotional service, the priests lifted the coffin above their heads.

Laura whispered her last goodbye as Nicolas's coffin was carried out of the church by the priests, with all the men following on behind. The women remained as Nicolas was taken to his final resting place. Again this was the custom. Women did not attend the burial; for fear it would be too upsetting. But Laura wanted to see where Nicolas's mortal remains were to be laid. Remarkably she managed to remain composed and strong throughout. Nicolas would have been proud of the way she held it together, despite barely having the strength to walk. Laura was frequently aided by Nicolas's sisters, who feared she may collapse. The strength of Laura's spirit belied the fragility of her body. Though exhausted with grief, Laura managed to stay calm and dignified. At least on the outside; inside she was falling apart. Laura would need to be strong a little longer; the day was not over.

Outside the crowds kept coming. Laura and the rest of

the family were directed to another large room at the rear of the church. Chairs had been placed around the perimeter of the room. A little man was walking around with a tray serving tea and coffee. Laura and Alyssa followed the rest of the family group to the back of the hall. They sat down in the seats along the back wall. The little man with the tray hurried over offering them refreshment. Laura accepted a cup of tea, adding sugar to give her some much needed energy. Suddenly everyone rose to their feet. Laura put down her tea on the little table provided. Turning to Frida she asked;

"What's happening?"

"We have to greet people who have come to pay their respects." Frida explained.

Laura looked round to see a long line of people queuing to express their condolences. One by one they shook hands with each member of Nicolas's family. Frida introduced Laura as Nicolas's wife. Some spoke to her in Arabic not realising she didn't understand. Laura followed the sisters lead, greeting and thanking the mourners sometimes in French, which is widely spoken in Lebanon. Unbelievably people were still queuing over an hour later. Laura had never seen this many people at a funeral. Irrespective of the fact Nicolas had not set foot in Lebanon for twenty five years, he was clearly well loved and respected.

At seven o' clock everyone went back to Freddy's villa where a dinner had been prepared by a local restaurant. The staff from the restaurant served everyone the delicious exquisitely presented Lebanese cuisine. Laura ate for the first time in five days. There were several more days of mourning, with the close family returning to the church to receive people who were still arriving to pay their respects. It seemed to Laura that the whole of Lebanon had turned out to mourn the death of her husband.

"Everybody loved him," Frida told Laura. "Even those who hated him loved him."

Her words may have sounded like a contradiction, but Laura totally understood Frida's meaning.

The outpouring of people was a testament to the deep respect that even Nicolas's enemies held for him. As the people filed past her, Laura wondered as to whether she may actually be shaking hands with one of Nicolas's so called enemies. Many would now sleep easily in their beds at night; those enemies who had wronged Al Hajj probably secretly rejoiced at his much too early demise.

KOUSBAWI

Chapter 43: A Very Dark Place

The day after Nicolas was laid to rest, Laura returned to the church with her late husbands close family. As was the custom in Lebanon, they were required to receive people wishing to express condolences to the grieving family. Alyssa was feeling unwell, so she stayed behind at the villa. Laura was astonished at the great number of people filing into the church hall. Mourners continued arriving throughout the day, and well into the evening. The news of Nicolas's untimely death impacted the whole community, not only in Kousba and Lebanon, but as far afield as Australia people mourned his passing. During the turmoil of the civil war, many from Kousba left to seek a safer life elsewhere. Those who had grown up with Hajj, had fond memories of a young man whose charm, appeal and larger than life personality truly was unforgettable. The huge outpouring of people paying their respects was proof that during his short lifetime, Nicolas touched many lives.

Laura requested to visit the grave of her husband before leaving Kousba. She wanted to see where Nicolas went to school, or rather didn't, the family home he grew up in, and the streets where he played as a child, and where his grandfather's shop was located. Unfortunately there was no time to visit all the places Nicolas had talked of. Freddy had already arranged their flights to return to Dubai the following day.

Nicolas had captivated Laura's imagination with stories of his notorious escapades, in and around Kousba. She would love to stay longer and absorb the atmosphere of the place that was so much a part of him. The devastating reality of Nicolas's sudden death impacted heavily, filling Laura with agonising sorrow. In a futile bid to distance herself from the soul crushing pain, Laura withdrew from her emotions. Embracing a form of denial she hovered on

374

the outskirts of grief, putting up a self-preserving shield; temporary protection against her overwhelming emotions. Laura feared the deep dark forest of irrepressible sadness, threatened to swallow her up if she dared enter its core. She believed, allowing it to permeate too deeply would surely kill her. There were moments when Laura felt death would be a welcome friend, a blessed release from the suffocating heartbreak. In spite of her reluctance to accept the nightmarish reality, Nicolas's death would sporadically hit home like a sudden thunderous bolt, leaving her frozen and crippled with grief.

On Thursday they were due to fly back to Dubai. Their flight was scheduled for later that evening. Nicolas's elder brother Jon offered to take Laura and Alyssa to Nicolas's tomb, and to the house where he grew up. At 10am they set off to visit the family mausoleum, stopping on the way at a village shop to buy candles. The mausoleum was set in a small garden. The setting was reminiscent of a scene from Romeo and Juliet; another fated love story that ended tragically.

The small crypt was sealed by a padlocked metal door behind which, Nicolas's mortal remains lay silent in his coffin. Jon lit the candles placing them in front of the stone tomb. A sudden gust of wind blew, knocking the candles over. Laura repositioned them and Jon quickly relit them with his lighter. Perhaps Nicolas's spirit was letting them know he was still very much around.

Laura silently prayed. How did this happen she asked? A tear fell onto her cheek as she knelt in front of the crypt. Laura quickly brushed it away only to have it replaced by another straight after. Just a few months ago Nicolas had light heartedly joked with Laura about how he would be the one to bury her. Laura had made him promise that if he died first, he would come back for her. Nicolas had been resolute in his belief that he would out-live Laura. He made the promise anyway. In spite of his insistence he would bury her, it was Laura standing before the tomb that held within its cold stone walls her beloved Nicolas.

The walk from the garden cemetery back to Jon's car was silent and sombre. Jon drove them to Nicolas's old family home in the village. Built in the old Lebanese style, the large house was spread over three levels. Alyssa took photos inside so Laura would have something to remember the visit by. Jon pointed out a picture on the wall of his and Nicolas's late father. Like Nicolas, he was also very handsome. In spite of having a rather strained relationship with his father, Nicolas had described him affectionately, saying he was a charismatic man with a huge personality; much less impulsive and hot tempered than his wilful rebellious son. For many years Nicolas never saw eye to eye with his father, but they reached a kind of truce in later years and became less hostile in their interactions with one another.

Back at Freddy's villa, Laura and Alyssa packed their things for the return flight to Dubai. At 4pm a taxi arrived to take them with Mollie to Beirut airport. Leaving Kousba was a wrench; Laura felt close to Nicolas there. He would now remain, leaving her to face life without him. During the journey from Kousba to the Lebanese capital Beirut, Laura tried to absorb as much as she could of the scenery and the ambiance. This was her husband's country. Laura had unfortunately only seen a tiny part.

Back in Dubai Laura tried to take stock of her situation. Everything had happened so fast. Laura needed to go back to the apartment in Abu Dhabi. She needed some closure, and to spend time in the place where her husband spent his last moments. Despite telling Laura the police had locked the apartment and were restricting entry, Freddy had a key.

Freddy stayed on in Kousba for an extra couple of days. On his return to Dubai, Laura would ask to be taken back to the apartment in Mussafah. Her belongings were there and many of the antiques she had purchased. Even with time to sit and mull things over, Laura was still in deep shock and couldn't make clear sense of anything. Many questions remained unanswered. Hoping to build a clearer picture of the events leading to Nicolas's death, she made one or two calls to her husband's close friends. It seemed no one knew what to tell her. One person commented it would not have occurred in the way it did if she had been there. What were they suggesting? It's possible she may have been able to get help in time. But that's not quite how their words came across. One person in particular was adamant. The event he said would never have happened if Laura had been with Nicolas that day. It was hard to hear, and Laura thought it an odd thing to say to her. How could she have prevented her husband's heart attack? If that's indeed what it was? Was she being given a subtle hint that perhaps things were not as cut and dried as they appeared?

Descriptions of what exactly took place on that fateful day were unbelievably vague and sketchy. Laura couldn't quite put her finger on it, but something wasn't right. She had a feeling, an intuition that there was more to the whole scenario than what she had been told; which wasn't much. The last person to speak with Nicolas and possibly the last to see him alive was probably Laura herself; or was she?

She needed access to Nicolas's iPhone to establish for sure. Freddy had taken possession of it, keeping it locked away along with the laptop, memory sticks, and some of Nicolas's private papers. Freddy wasted no time removing them from the apartment on the day of Nicolas's death. A few days later he returned from Kousba. Laura asked him to take her back to the apartment. She would prefer to go alone with Alyssa, but didn't have her key. She had given it back to Nicolas in case he lost his while she was away. Laura wished she hadn't done that.

Freddy told her the police were watching and forbidding anyone access; something else that didn't make sense. Laura wasn't just anyone she was Nicolas's wife, and Alyssa his step daughter. Why would she be restricted from entering the home they had shared for three years? Grieving heavily, Laura wasn't of clear mind. If she had been thinking clearly she would have gone to the authorities and demanded answers; found out for sure if Freddy had indeed informed them Nicolas had a wife.

At least Laura would have made her presence known as the deceased's legal spouse. In retrospect it's easy to say what you should have done; but Laura trusted Freddy and didn't feel at this point she had reason not to believe what he was telling her. Not questioning his actions more closely would be her downfall. In her defence, anyone suffering such unprecedented shock and trauma would be easily manipulated. A vulnerable trusting soul is easy prey for an unscrupulous heart.

The afternoon of the following day, Freddy agreed to take them to the apartment in Mussafah. They set off after lunch; Mollie decided she would tag along. She was annoyingly chirpy. Her ultra-upbeat mood was unbefitting, considering her husband had recently lost his brother and Laura her husband. Laura and Alyssa were in the back of the car. As Mollie happily chatted away, they looked at one another incredulously. Mollie continued to laugh and joke throughout the journey like she didn't have a care in the world. There was almost an air of excitement in her demeanour. Alyssa whispered to her mother,

"She's acting as if she's going to a party."

Laura shrugged and tried to ignore Mollie's chirpy flirtatious behaviour with Freddy right in front of them. It was inappropriate and insensitive, in view of Laura and Alyssa's broken-hearted grief. It appeared to them Mollie almost revelled in Nicolas's demise.

When they arrived at the apartment, Freddy told Laura they couldn't be long as they weren't supposed to be there. Laura's vulnerable state of mind meant she again blindly accepted without question, Freddy's absurd claims. It was utterly ridiculous; where else should Laura be other than the place that was her home with Nicolas and where all of her and her husband's personal belongings still remained. With the gift of hindsight, Laura would not have taken Freddy's word for anything.

Of course Mollie invited herself inside. Laura felt it an intrusion into what was a private affair; a time for quiet reflection. Nicolas would not appreciate Mollie's presence.

He wasn't particularly fond of her in life, and wouldn't want her poking her nose into his business after his death.

All four of them entered into the apartment. Without air conditioning for several days now, the stench of cigarette smoke infiltrated the atmosphere to quite a toxic level. In the daylight Laura was able to see the exact state of the place. It looked ransacked. The Christian artefacts Nicolas knelt before in prayer each day were unceremoniously strewn across the floor near the entrance to the lounge. Laura bent to pick them up. Why, she wondered hadn't Freddy picked them up before? They were right there in the hall, he would have to have stepped over them to walk to the lounge. It seemed he'd been more occupied with removing her husband's laptop and other more personal items. Laura should have challenged his authority to do so, but her spirit was exhausted and she was barely hanging on by a thread; she just didn't have the strength to argue.

On the dining table Laura spotted Nicolas's little blue bible; the one he kept in his shirt pocket. He would never have left it there. On closer inspection Laura noticed pages were torn from it. Laura placed it carefully inside her bag along with the picture of Mary and Jesus. She went into the bedroom. Nicolas's pink shirt, the last he would have worn, was hanging in the usual place on the wardrobe door knob.

She'd been told Nicolas was found wearing pyjamas. This was something else that didn't sit right with Laura; she had never known Nicolas own pyjamas let alone wear them. And why was his bible taken from his shirt pocket? Unless he was in the process of changing clothes it would not have been moved. The tiny bible would always remain in his shirt pocket until he exchanged that shirt for another. Transferring his bible from pocket to pocket this way was a ritual he performed every day, ensuring he never left the house without it. In the fifteen years Laura had lived with him, Nicolas never once broke his habit of dressing in this way. Her husband's wallet was missing from its regular place in a drawer in the bedroom. Like his bible, it would remain in its usual place in the drawer until Nicolas was fully dressed and ready to leave the house. Someone else must have removed that too. Again Laura suspected it wasn't Nicolas; she knew his ways and habits too well. Also he would never deliberately rip the pages of his bible; that would be sacrilege.

Laura looked around. The bed was dishevelled. Her teddy bear was sitting there. Laura picked it up. As she held it, she remembered the silly fight between her and Nicolas two years ago. The sudden flashback made her smile. Laura hugged the bear to her chest smiling wistfully as she remembered the bear's humorous role in bringing her and Nicolas to their senses that day. She heard Freddy and Mollie talking in Arabic. Laura called Freddy to help her retrieve the suitcase from the top of the wardrobe. He fetched it down and then went back to Nicolas's desk. Laura heard a crashing sound and Alyssa asking Mollie;

"What have you done?"

Laura hurried to the lounge. Alyssa looked infuriated. She turned to her mother exclaiming;

"She's broken Nicky's lamp."

While nosily going through Nicolas's things, Mollie had knocked over a lamp on the cabinet. It fell to the floor and smashed. Before Laura could say anything, Mollie defensively retorted,

"It's okay, it's nothing expensive, and anyway there's another one like it in the bedroom."

Alyssa was shocked and gave Mollie a look of utter dismay. Her callous attitude was mind boggling. The lamp Mollie had carelessly broken expensive or not, happened to be Nicolas's favourite. Clearly there was no love lost between Nicolas and his rather materialistic step-sister in law. Laura was beginning to understand why he had not wanted to visit his brother's house. Nicolas saw through the sugar-coated fake exterior of his brother's wife Mollie; now Laura was seeing through it too. Not for the first time since Nicolas's death, had Laura glimpsed another side to her.

On the morning of the day Laura visited the morgue, Mollie had driven her to the mall to purchase a black handbag for the funeral. As Mollie drove she turned up the volume on the car radio, announcing joyously;

"Oh I love this song."

In front of a grieving Laura, Mollie happily sang along to the music. Laura was stunned. In the wake of Nicolas's death less than two days earlier, Mollies behaviour was incomprehensible. Either she was incredibly insensitive, or didn't give a damn for Laura's grief. Probably both, Laura later concluded.

At the apartment Laura looked earnestly for Nicolas's wallet. It was nowhere to be found. When he dressed Nicolas would habitually put his trousers on before his shirt. If he had removed his things himself he would have been found fully dressed, not in pyjamas as Laura was told. Everything pointed to somebody else removing these items; but why? Sometime later Laura would ponder these inconsistencies.

She would also wonder as to the whereabouts of the money Nicolas told her he had collected to send to her. It should have been in his desk ready to take to the bank on Sunday, but it wasn't. Gone too was the emergency money he kept specifically for Laura's use in any emergency; it too was missing from the desk. Someone must have taken cash in excess of £12,000 from the apartment on the day Nicolas died. Laura shuddered to think of the heartlessness to take it before his body was even cold.

Laura walked into the kitchen. The red coffee mug that Nicolas would have drunk his last coffee from, was sitting on the worktop. Laura picked it up; she stared at the stain on the bottom of the cup. Nicolas loved to entertain people by reading the coffee stain pattern of an upturned cup. As Nicolas drank his coffee that fateful morning, did he have any inkling it would be his last? The shelf where Nicolas kept his stash of Marlborough was surprisingly empty. Nicolas regularly bought packs of 600 cigarettes at a time; he would never let himself run short.

As she began to connect the dots Laura felt decidedly uneasy. With the absence of clear answers, she drew her own conclusions and her suspicions were raised. What was the truth behind Nicolas's death?

Laura packed as much as she could into two suitcases. There was so much personal stuff collected over the years, it would be impossible to take it all in one day, and Laura wasn't even given a whole day. Her head spun. Laura had no wish to be packing up her life with Nicolas in this rushed way. She wanted to be left alone; given time to gather her thoughts. Why Freddy and Mollie couldn't have allowed her some space to be alone in the apartment was beyond her. Their continued presence at this difficult time was insensitive and intrusive. Laura's emotional privacy felt violated.

Near the bathroom door was where Laura was told Nicolas was found. Laura stared at his slippers still lying there. Trying to get a sense of what really happened, she willed his spirit to communicate and tell her. Laura thought about the last time she had seen him on Skype video. Replaying in her mind over and over, exactly how he looked acted and sounded. Laura couldn't draw up a single clue; nothing in his behaviour indicated anything was wrong. With one exception; the intense phone call she had witnessed. With access to his phone she could perhaps figure out who he was talking with. Was it just business hassles causing his agitation that night; or something else, something more sinister?

Despite seeing Nicolas in the morgue, and witnessing his funeral, Laura still could not, would not fully accept he was gone. He did not feel dead to her. Surely she would have felt him leave; they were so close and in love. How was it possible she didn't know? On the morning of his passing Laura had woken abruptly at 7.35 am; making it 11.35 am Abu Dhabi time. The probable time given for Nicolas's passing was between 11am and midday; this would tally with the time Laura woke up. In that moment of unexpected wakefulness Laura hadn't sensed anything to be wrong. She felt angry she didn't sense it; how could she not have felt his passing from this world? Where was the message, the warning, like the one given to her by Joan on the eve of her mother's unexpected death?

Laura was rudely jolted from her reflections by Freddy, informing they needed to leave. Things felt uncomfortably hurried. She had been expected to pack up a whole life in an hour? Laura struggled to close the crammed suitcases; she didn't have everything. There was hardly time to pack, let alone reflect on what to take or leave. Many personal mementos were left. In the weeks that followed Laura would bitterly regret leaving them. In time Laura would be consoled in the knowledge that no single memento, or any amount of memorabilia would compensate for losing Nicolas; though it would have been of great comfort to have his things close by. For example, the books they had read, the CDs they listened to together; all left behind in Mussafah.

It broke Laura's heart to leave Nicolas's precious book collection. No one would appreciate what his books meant to him; least of all people like Freddy and Mollie, who apparently only placed value on things of monetary worth. Regretfully Laura would not be able to take many of her toiletries and cosmetics or many of her clothes, due to airline restrictions on baggage. Mollie eagerly helped Laura pack them up saying she would give them to Mariel her house made. Laura remembered to take the bear; after all he had been instrumental in bringing her and Nicolas close after they fought that time. Laura wished the bear could talk now. That teddy-bear was the only witness to the actual truth. On the way out, true to form, and as if to add insult to injury, Mollie blatantly helped herself to one of Nicolas's books from his library, boldly proclaiming;

"I've been looking for a copy of this particular book for ages." Her attitude was as insensitive as ever.

Laura's things were hurriedly packed into the back of Freddy's car. Alyssa took a photo of Nicolas's blue Jeep. Freddy had acquired the keys to their Jeep as well as their apartment. Laura asked him to open it so she could remove a tape from the stereo. She was curious what Nicolas had been listening to lately. Neil Diamond's greatest hits album was still in the disc player; the same cd that was playing when he drove Laura to the airport.

Laura climbed into the passenger seat and shut the car door, determined to force a moment of privacy. She closed her eyes and drifted back to her last journey in the Jeep. Opening her now tear-filled eyes, Laura stared longingly at the empty driver's seat. Closing her eyes again, she imagined Nicolas beside her. Picturing him clearly in her mind's eye, once more she saw him driving skilfully along the highway, weaving in and out of the traffic like a racing driver, and impatiently cursing in Arabic at the other less competent drivers on the road. Her face briefly broke into a smile as she remembered his crazy fearless style. Laura wished she could stay locked inside her memories forever.

Freddy was impatient to get back to Dubai. Laura stepped from the Jeep. She felt suffocated by a wave of profound sadness as it enveloped her. She was instantly awakened to the finality of it all. Laura would never ride with Nicolas in their beautiful Jeep again. As with the apartment, the Jeep too would become a distant memory. The life shared with the man who was Laura's whole world was forever gone, shattered and broken like a mirror that slips from a careless hand. What was left was a mere remnant and hazy shadowy reflection, of a life once so full of hope and promise. In the blink of an eye it had vanished; gone forever. Laura glanced back at their apartment for the last time. Even in the bright sunlight, the little shops and businesses on the street where they lived now looked sad and forlorn. Everything was changed, an invisible heavy cloud hung over the area. As Freddy drove away, sadness gripped Laura like an unshakable virus; one she feared would infect her for the foreseeable future.

Laura and Alyssa sat in silent solemnity in the back of the car. All the way to the villa in Dubai, Mollie chatted and giggled incessantly to Freddy, coldly oblivious of the pain and heartbreak of the two back seat passengers. Laura's heart was so heavy she feared it may fall from her body. Crammed into the boot of Freddy's four wheel drive lay the soulless remains of her life; roughly packed into two suit cases and a few bags in one rushed hour. Was that time enough to pack a whole life up in; a marriage even? Laura had not been afforded a choice.

Despite the date for their flights back to the UK not being for another two weeks, Laura and Alyssa returned within a couple of days. It was Freddy's decision to change their tickets. Laura had the distinct impression he and Mollie wanted them out of the way. Laura should have insisted on staying and gone back to Abu Dhabi to seek answers, but by now she was too drained and exhausted to argue. Laura felt she was left totally helpless by Nicolas's death; caught in a whirlwind of uncertainty. As the cold reality unravelled so her suffering intensified. Despair and confusion waited.

Out of the shadows of her broken world, the demons of darkness descended like wolves circling a defenceless victim. Baring their teeth, they ripped and gnawed at her irreparably torn heart. Tortured by numbing inconsolable grief, Laura spiralled into an abyss of deep depression.

That terrible vision of the Tsunami had come to pass, realised in a huge wave of tragic loss that engulfed and overwhelmed Laura as it swept her world away, leaving her drowning in an ocean of gut wrenching sorrow.

The colossal impact of Nicolas's death was to cast a very long shadow, blocking the sun from Laura's life like a permanent eclipse. Laura's world became a very dark place.

Chapter 44: Leap of Faith

Many of Laura's personal possessions were unfortunately left with Mollie in Dubai. Laura had no desire to leave anything there, but the airline would not allow the extra baggage so she had little choice in the matter. Mollie assured Laura that her belongings would be looked after until they could be returned safely back to her. This was never going to happen of course and as it subsequently turned out, Freddy and Mollie had quite a different agenda; one that didn't include ensuring Laura receive anything that was rightfully hers.

The journey back was horrendous. Exhausted mentally and physically, for Laura and Alyssa it was most difficult. The pain of losing a dear husband and step-father, descended on them like a heavy garment. During the flight they managed to sleep intermittently as fatigue took over. For eight long hours barely a word was spoken. Tiredness combined with raw emotions, had left them drained.

The bright future Laura and Nicolas should have been destined to have, had been stolen in the cruellest twist imaginable. With her life in tatters, Laura was returning to an uncertain future. Falling into a state of denial was a convenient safety mechanism, clicking in to give temporary release from the harrowing reality.

Arrival at London Heathrow was like stepping through a time warp or doorway into another dimension; Laura felt she was in a parallel universe living someone else's tragic life. Blasted with confusion and anxiety, she was uptight and irritable. Every sound grated on her ragged nerves like a deafening pneumatic drill. The airport was teeming with people, all swarming around like bees going about their lives. To Laura it seemed everyone had a life except her. The sight of couples canoodling and chatting caused her to scream internally.

They walked outside to look for Alessandro who was meeting them. The damp, cold, drizzly climate reinforced Laura's desire to escape, to flee from a world which held neither hope nor interest. Laura was like an empty vessel without purpose or desire, a discarded shell on a desolate beach. Without Nicolas she was devoid of life.

As the days and weeks passed, Laura sank more deeply into depression. Her mood swings were manic and varied. Laura became at times hysterical which was extremely unsettling for Alyssa, who could only watch bewildered and confused as her mother visibly disintegrated in front of her. Crying for hours, Laura was inconsolable in her grief. She would flare up in anger, screaming at Nicolas for leaving her, throwing and smashing things in an uncontrollable rage that would equal any volatile outburst ever displayed by him. But this uncharacteristic volatility would ultimately end with Laura crumpled in a heap on the floor, tearful and exhausted.

At the other end of the scale, Laura would sit for hours in an almost catatonic state; unable to function or sustain any kind of normality. Nothing was normal anymore. 'Normal' was having Nicolas beside her. Normal was living in Abu Dhabi supporting her husband in his plans and schemes. Normal was cooking his dinner and making love to him each day. Normal was feeling safe in knowing she had a rock to cling to and a warm harbour to shelter her during stormy times. All this 'normal,' was ripped away the moment Nicolas took his last breath. Laura's frequent odd behaviour was her deep grief seeking release. For Alyssa it was frightening and bewildering to witness.

As for her late husband's family, there was little or no contact. It seemed to be a case of, out of sight out of mind. Laura received no emotional support from them; only Frida kept up any real contact, but that too was short lived. Freddy made even less of an effort. If he communicated anything, it was to tell Laura how stressed he was and how he was practically bankrupt. It never occurred to inquire how his brothers grieving widow was coping.

Laura felt so isolated. With the exception of Alyssa, none of her friends or family knew or ever met Nicolas. There was no one close Laura could talk to, or share fond memories with. Alyssa was unapproachable on the subject; she was suffering her own grief and couldn't deal with her mother's as well.

While Laura was in Dubai, Freddy promised to do all he could to ensure she benefitted from her husband's estate. Now he was quickly backtracking on that promise. Freddy blamed everything on Nicolas's estranged daughter in America, saying she was putting pressure on him, and making all sorts of demands on her father's estate. Due to the vengeful actions of his ex-wife Samra, Nicolas had never known his daughter. Now a grown woman, she could have tracked down her father long before his demise if she had any interest in knowing him. Nicolas would wish Laura to have a fair share of his estate, not for it to be handed to someone who was basically a stranger to him, leaving his wife who he dearly loved and who depended on him with nothing.

Laura was not sure what to believe, she had been told by other sources that Nicolas's estranged daughter never made any claims on his estate. Whether she had or not, she wasn't entitled to everything. Somebody was clearly lying.

Some years back, Nicolas set aside something to secure Laura financially in the event of anything happening to him. Laura suspected there were papers and evidence of such a provision in his desk or on the laptop. Nicolas also left instructions with someone he trusted to take care of things. Freddy was quick to remove personal papers, along with Nicolas's iPhone, laptop and memory sticks on the day of his death, all of which he flatly refused to hand over, preventing Laura access to anything that might help her. Whatever Nicolas left in trust, the person who knew about it failed to come forward; at least not to Laura.

Two weeks before his death perhaps unwisely, Nicolas had shown Freddy everything Laura had paid for the antiques. Freddy would have seen all the paperwork, and after Nicolas's death known exactly where to look for private documents. He would have been well aware that Nicolas still owed Laura a great deal of money. Without being appointed as the legal executer of the estate and Nicolas's much younger half-brother, Freddy had no real rights over Laura who was Nicolas's legal wife and next of kin. When she questioned his actions, Freddy coldly told Laura if she wished to dispute anything she should get a lawyer. Freddy knew only too well that Laura was left penniless after putting her money into helping Nicolas build the antiques business. Left with no means of support, Laura didn't have the thousands of pounds required to hire an expensive Abu Dhabi lawyer. A British lawyer would only work in conjunction with a lawyer in the UAE, which would mean paying two different lawyers. Laura was stuck, most conveniently for some, between a rock and a hard place. Just like Mollie, Freddy's mask had quickly slipped. His true nature and many different faces were revealed. Laura had fallen victim to the proverbial snake in the grass.

Grieving, vulnerable, and without support emotionally or financially, Laura was alone; heartlessly dismissed and purposely kept out of the loop. The fact she was Nicolas's wife and his widow, seemed irrelevant in certain quarters. Instead of helping her, they had literally thrown her to the wolves. Nicolas would be appalled by their less than charitable attitude. This generous hearted man, who sent his money to help the less fortunate in Lebanon, would never leave his wife without means of support. Nicolas would judge harshly the actions of those who claimed to love him, yet were unwilling to assist his widow in the wake of his demise.

Exactly forty nine days after Nicolas's passing, Laura experienced a mystifying encounter. She dreamt she was standing in a high place or mountain top. Below her, a mass of fluffy pure white clouds stretched to the horizon. Laura was aware of a presence standing at her left. The strange entity, which Laura perceived as male, was dressed in robes similar to those worn by a monk. As with the encounter with her aunt Joan, no words were exchanged. Communication with this entity was telepathic.

Far in the distance, Laura saw something emerging from beneath the white cloudy mass. She could make out a figure of a man. Laura recognised him immediately. It was Nicolas climbing up through the white mist. Laura called to him. He stood with his back to her and didn't appear to hear Laura. She called out again, louder;

"Nicky wait!"

Nicolas was dressed in blue jeans and his favourite pink shirt. He stood motionless, totally oblivious of her. Laura sensed the being to her left watching intently. The snowy white clouds began separating, revealing a darkness filled with a thick swirling mass. Laura looked across the void. Nicolas was floating away from her as the gap between them widened. Laura sensed her thoughts being read as the entity telepathically urged caution but at the same time, conveyed she had complete free will to follow her heart. Without a glimmer of hesitation Laura leapt, flying across the swirling abyss as it opened up beneath her. She landed a short distance from Nicolas. Immediately the clouds separated again, widening further the void between them. Again Laura called out;

"Nicolas I'm coming; wait for me!"

Laura felt a desperate urgency to reach Nicolas before it was too late. Beneath her, the swirling abyss rapidly grew. Laura would have to leap again. As the quagmire of darkness expanded, Nicolas floated further and further away. If she failed to reach him in this final leap, she knew she risked being lost forever in the darkness below. Laura determined to jump, regardless of the consequences. She was not going to lose Nicolas a second time. She looked to the entity for reassurance. Telepathically he told her the choice had to be hers alone; neither approving nor disapproving of her decision. Undeterred, Laura leapt. Her unyielding faith in the power of her love for Nicolas lifted her. As soon as she made the choice to leap the entity left.

Effortlessly she flew over the void. Safely beside him, Laura took Nicolas's hand. He looked at her but didn't speak, appearing confused by her presence. The dark abyss completely disappeared. Together they climbed back down through the clouds by way of some sort of white ladder.

They had only gone a little way down when the ladder transformed into stone steps. The steps led to a courtyard and garden. Holding tight to Nicolas's hand Laura asked,

"Where are we?"

Nicolas spoke for the first time, answering he didn't know. Laura thought he was unusually subdued, as if in shock. Laura commented,

"I think we might be dead." To which Nicolas replied,

"I think you're right."

The garden scene quickly transformed and they found themselves in some sort of holding area, on what looked very much like a train station platform. Tall blond people, both male and female dressed in blue uniforms, scurried about the platform. They were preoccupied, busily making preparations for something and seemed unconcerned by the presence of two strangers in their midst. Laura noticed a ticket kiosk at the end of the platform. Overcome by a sense of urgency, Laura suggested they should hurry and get a ticket.

Hand in hand they walked to the kiosk. Nearby a girl with very long hair was loading packages onto a trolley. Through an opening Laura could see outside, it was extremely bright but no sun was visible. In what appeared to be a ships dock, a huge cruise liner was berthed. Nicolas was given two gold tickets at the kiosk. Walking back along the platform Laura clung tightly to him. Nicolas remained unusually quiet. Laura was aware there were no others like her in this place. An older fair-haired man was walking up and down talking on what looked like a mobile phone. Laura had the impression the people in the blue uniforms were waiting for the arrival of something.

A phone started to ring on the platform. The ringing tone became progressively louder. Laura saw the older man answer it. Suddenly he looked directly at Laura as if only just noticing her. Laura panicked, telling Nicolas she believed someone had called to say she shouldn't be there. In the distance a train was arriving. Laura willed it to get there quickly so she could board with Nicolas. Alarms were going off all around the platform. Laura instinctively knew everyone had been alerted to her presence. The older man stopped talking on the phone. He looked shocked and somewhat annoyed by her presence. Moving towards her, he put out his hand.

Instantly Laura woke up in her bed with a heavy thud, feeling as if she had been dropped from a great height. The alarm on her mobile was ringing. Laura reached over and turned it off. She stared up at the ceiling; her heart still palpitating rapidly from the sensation of falling. Laura had an uncomfortable feeling of heaviness. Being in her body felt claustrophobic, as if hopelessly trapped inside a vessel she no longer cared to be a part of. Laura believed that for a brief moment she pierced the veil separating her from Nicolas. Her deep love for him carried her spirit beyond the illusion of death to where he was; still alive.

Whether or not Laura had glimpsed an alternate reality, another dimension or realm where Nicolas was alive, no one can say. Maybe it was just her imagination, fuelled by a deep longing to be reunited with the man she loved. Either way it didn't matter. Whatever the experience was, it gave Laura a glimmer of hope. In the darkest moments of her depression, something inside Laura's soul was ignited. Her dream had given a revelation. Something told Laura that her story with Nicolas was far from finished. She didn't know where, why, or even how, but Laura knew their journey together wasn't over but would go on. The bond of love was strong. Somewhere, somehow she would be reunited with Nicolas. One day, as her dream implied no matter how unknown the outcome, Laura would take a huge leap of faith.

KOUSBAWI

Chapter 45: Betrayal and Laura's Dark Night of the Soul

The days and weeks that followed were lonely and dark as Laura struggled to establish some form of normality from her crumbling world. With Alessandro's help, her antiques were removed from storage. With no income, she could no longer afford the monthly storage fees. Laura never did receive the printing press. It turned out the guy who sold it to her was a crook after all. But he was just one, in a queue of people who couldn't wait to pounce and exploit her vulnerable situation. Without her husband to protect her, Laura was an easy target for the unscrupulous of this world. The UK was now in recession and try as she might to salvage something from her investment, no one was interested in buying antiques. Laura may as well take them to the local dump for all the interest they aroused. The cream of the collection was still languishing somewhere in Abu Dhabi, or Dubai. Freddy held the key to exactly where. What Nicolas predicted to be a thriving business, was now a source of financial loss and a burden to Laura. Just looking at the antiques was a painful reminder of what should have been. Whichever way Laura turned, doors remained closed. Holding on to any small resemblance of a life had become a dispiriting endeavour.

The slippery slope intent on dragging Laura further into the mire of depression was never very far away. On the brink of crashing emotionally, she couldn't get a firm grip on reality. Uprooted overnight from the life she knew, Laura felt she had been dropped into a parallel universe or entered an alien world. It was like walking through a hall of mirrors, where everything reflected back appears unreal and distorted. Nothing made sense. Whichever life she was living, Laura felt it wasn't hers. Without Nicolas, her life had lost meaning and direction.

Veering dangerously off course emotionally, Laura balanced on a razors edge; hovering precariously between life and death. She wasn't ready to be a widow; Nicolas promised he would never leave her. She should have died first, that was the deal. And if by chance he did happen to go before her, it was supposed to be many years in the future when they were both quite old. Laura's next attempt to move forward with her life was a short-lived solution; a sticking plaster placed over a gaping wound. Rather than indulge her grief she took a job. For a while it served its purpose in providing a place to hide, and escape from the rawness of her emotions. Leaving the house before 8am and not arriving home most nights till after 9pm, left Laura exhausted, but with little time to dwell on the reality of her changed world.

Throwing herself whole heartedly into this new, albeit unwelcome phase, Laura tried her best to stay strong. In spite of her good intentions to make it work, it wasn't to last. How could it? Laura was lying to herself in thinking she could ignore her grief. Most days she felt like a caged rat on a treadmill; dispassionately going round and round with the same tedious routine. This passionless existence was a million miles from her old life. Every night Laura cried herself to sleep, praying to be spared the agony of waking and face another day without Nicolas. But she did wake, and would be filled with despair that her prayers were not answered. Just to survive another twenty four hours, Laura forcibly and deliberately pushed the grief aside.

On top of everything she was already dealing with, it soon became apparent Freddy was not going to keep his promise to help her claim her rights to Nicolas's estate. Astounded by his change of heart, Laura thought his U-turn a cowardly move and she felt betrayed. Nicolas would never go back on his word. But as Laura was to discover, men like Nicolas were thin on the ground. She had hoped, perhaps naively so, that her husband's step-brother would display a little backbone in carrying out what would surely have been the wishes of Nicolas.

Soon after Freddy delivered another blow, telling Laura he was withdrawing his offer of storage for the antiques and Nicolas's things; including his book collection. Laura was bitterly disappointed in Freddy's attitude. Nicolas had always looked out for his brother, but in the wake of his death his widow would not be afforded that same loyalty. Freddy's actions were a double betrayal, of both Laura and Nicolas. It brought to Laura's mind something Nicolas had once said;

"If someone betrays you once they will do it again. And you know family is not blood only. Family are those who won't betray you behind your back. Even when things get tough for them, the good people will stick by you when you have nothing to give but yourself. Loulou, you are my family now. You stayed with me through all the bad, and loved me when I had nothing to give you."

Now Laura was quickly finding out how greed gets the better of people. Far from doing what is morally right; they will take all they can for themselves. Such self-serving greed is motivated out of fear. Nicolas feared nothing. There were times in his life when he had very little, but would give even that, if someone else was in need. Clearly Nicolas and Freddy were like chalk and cheese; cut from very different cloths.

Things became increasingly difficult as Christmas approached; it was to be Laura's first without Nicolas. She wished she had spent the Christmas of 2011 with him. If only she had known it would be their last. The signs were there, had she connected the dots she might have read them. The ominous shadows and strange feelings in the apartment, her reluctance to leave on the day of her flight, the Christmas tree lights not working; Laura knew that was a bad omen. If just one thing was done differently would it have changed the fatal outcome? Fate had robbed Laura once again of precious time with Nicolas.

This Christmas there was to be no tree, no presents, and no celebrations; none of the joy this time of year normally evoked. Laura just felt empty. During all the years they were apart, Nicolas called her every Christmas Eve, proclaiming his love. She had taken solace in knowing that even though they were far apart, he was out there under the desert sky looking up at the same stars she was. But now he wasn't there, he wasn't anywhere and Laura would no longer hear him profess his love to her at Christmas or anytime. But she could still hear him speak to her via the tape recording.

The precious tape Laura played incessantly. Being able to hear Nicolas's voice was of some comfort. But Laura would be wracked with inconsolable grief every time she listened to Nicolas talk of his hopes and dreams for their future life together; it was heart-breaking. What a terrible waste; all that passionate energy and hope gone. What was the point Laura wondered, of making plans or having hope for anything? Surely hope must be the luxury of those unburdened by fate.

Fearing the tape may be damaged from over-use; Laura locked it away in a red box tied up with a red satin ribbon. There it would remain with Nicolas's painstakingly written love letters to her; these things were now a precious and irreplaceable treasure.

The advent of New Year was worse still. Laura was becoming progressively more depressed as she recalled the eve of 2012. Nicolas had talked of accomplishing much in the coming year of 2012. The memory left Laura bereft; those many dreams of his would never be realised. The repetitious cycle of barely surviving from one moment to the next went on. As her birthday came around, Laura's mood was contrastingly different from a year ago. When she received those beautiful roses, Laura was blissfully ignorant that her beloved Nicolas had only ten days left.

The sticking plaster used to cover Laura's emotional wounds was losing its adhesive quality; it wasn't going to hold indefinitely. In her bid to escape the pain, Laura pushed herself to run before she was ready to walk again, deceiving herself that she was conquering her grief. Not surprisingly it backfired.

The anniversary of Nicolas's passing was days away, and it was just a matter of time before Laura imploded from within. Ignoring her grief made the darkness grow, until it consumed her entirely, heralding the onset of a total collapse of mind and body. Laura began to feel unwell. Wracked by a sudden virus, Laura was bedridden for a month. The grief she had tried to push aside demanded attention. What Laura was desperate to keep at bay rose to the surface, ravaging her body and mind mercilessly as it fought to be acknowledged and recognised. Weakened physically, she was driven deeper into depression. Laura was forced to give up her job.

Days passed, and then weeks. Laura couldn't summon the strength or enthusiasm to rise from her bed most days. If everything were to catch fire around her, she wouldn't have the will to drag herself to safety. Now Reclusive and withdrawn, Laura rarely left the house. Irrational phobias never previously encountered, jumped on the bandwagon exacerbating her doom and gloom. The intense emotions she was now forced to acknowledge, saw Laura helplessly freefalling through her life. She had no idea or even cared if she would be smashed on the rocks, or caught by a well-placed safety net. Absence of a reason to remain in this pointless existence, led Laura to examine the darkest recesses of her fractured mind and soul. Believing there was no point in fighting, she immersed herself in the darkness, allowing it run freely through her and flow from every pore.

Dominant in Laura's mind was her desire to be reunited with Nicolas. Suicidal feelings were never far from her tortured thoughts, beckoning her ever more closely toward the longed for release death would bring. Oddly, having opened the door to it there was comfort to be found in the darkness. With no will to fight anymore, Laura chose to give up the battle. Relinquishing her battered armour, she surrendered; submitting her soul to the inevitable fate that waited within that dark abyss.

KOUSBAWI

Chapter 46: A Stranger Calls

Laura felt little remorse or guilt at wanting to end her life. When Nicolas died she felt part of her had died too, so in effect, she considered she was already half way there. The only thing guaranteed to cure Laura's malaise would be for Nicolas to return. She figured that wasn't going to happen. It appeared the price of great love, is great misery when one of you dies.

It was late spring and as the summer approached, Laura was emotionally at her lowest ebb. As if suddenly struck blind, she stumbled from one moment to the next trying to keep a balance and hold it together. But with her mind flooded by grief, there was little room for rational thinking and Laura found it impossible to fully concentrate on the simplest of tasks. Falling deeper inward, she cut herself off from the outside world in an almost reclusive way. On the rare occasions she ventured outside, Laura walked as if wearing blinkers, hurrying on past people in a bid to avoid unwelcome conversation and side-step seeing others go about their lives. To see people happy and participating in activities she once took for granted, was to rub salt into an already-gaping wound.

People appeared irritatingly oblivious of her suffering. It cut like a knife to see elderly couples walking together. Not long ago, Laura had envisaged that would be her and Nicolas in their later years. But he had been robbed of his old age and Laura robbed of ending her days beside the man she loved. Engaging in conversation was at times unavoidable. Laura politely listened to people drone on about inconsequentialities, silently longing to have those trivial matters; instead of the drama she'd been dealt. She would scream internally and be overtaken by an irresistible urge to run away. Laura wanted to retreat into a cocoon of denial and stay there, where she felt comfortable and safe.

Instead of running, Laura faked a smile and just faded out. She would see lips move but all she would hear was a white noise, thundering inside her head. She soon became rather adept at masking her true feelings. To have Nicolas back even for a moment, Laura would give her last breath. To hear him laugh, shout in anger, or have one of his volatile destructive outbursts, smashing and throwing things. It didn't matter what he did as long as he was there.

Embroiled in a tunnel of darkness which offered no guiding light at the end, Laura's thoughts of ending her life were prevalent. She teetered dangerously on the edge. It was all so wearisome. Why carry on? Betrayed and lied to, forgotten and discarded like yesterday's news; robbed of everything she held dear, Laura hit rock bottom. Her relationship with Alyssa became increasingly strained. Nicolas's untimely death had driven a wedge between them; each being a constant reminder to the other of what could and should have been.

One evening in late summer, Laura was sat as usual in self-imposed solitude. Curled up in the arm-chair clutching a blanket, she stared at Nicolas's picture. Every night since his death she had lit a candle next to it. Light from the flickering flame reflected on his face. Nicolas's dark eyes shone and sparkled in the candle light. He looked happy and alive. Laura remembered clearly the night she took that picture at the Prive. Nicolas had been unwilling as usual to have his photo taken, and Laura sneakily caught him off guard. Close by was another photo of the two of them; also taken at a time when they thought they had the world at their feet.

Laura stared at the now well-worn pictures. Maybe if she stared long enough she might propel herself into them. Laura closed her eyes and wished. Desperately she tried to wish herself out of existence, but when she opened her eyes she was still there, still feeling the same inconsolable sorrow clenching at her broken soul. Her heart became ever more tightly compressed with unrelenting grief. The grief exhausted her. Her eyes were heavy, tired and sore from a never-ending river of tears. For months depression had clouded her mind like a dense impenetrable fog, obliterating memories of ever feeling happy.

As Laura surrendered to her moroseness, something unexpected happened. Like the sun breaking through the clouds, she had a sudden flash of clarity. The depressive fog momentarily lifted, clearing the gloom and muddy debris from her fractured mind. As if injected by some outside force, a surge of adrenalin energised her like the recharging of a long dead battery. A force outside of her was at work. Laura felt it push into her jaded fading spirit, compelling her to seek answers to the mystery surrounding the day Nicolas died.

The official description of the probable circumstances of his passing had always failed to satisfy. The clue was in the word probable. Nothing was conclusive. Laura craved to take up the quest for truth; to know exactly what happened that fateful day. Whether a sixth sense or mere intuition, whatever was driving her, Laura was convinced there was something peculiar about the whole affair. There were too many inconsistencies and things that didn't tally. With her head suddenly clearer, these inconsistencies were rushing forth begging to be re-examined. A natural death no longer convinced her as being the legitimate cause for Nicolas's untimely and sudden passing. Laura considered a much darker possibility.

What if her husband's so called heart attack had been deliberately induced? Had something more sinister been covered up? The police in Abu Dhabi originally suspected foul play. The first questions asked by the police of his friends and step-brother, was did Nicolas have enemies? Of course they told the police he did not. Had Laura been asked the same question she may well have given a different answer. Laura now feared Nicolas may have been deliberately targeted.

He died on a Friday the Islamic holy day, which left two days for the circumstances to be examined. Two day's was not enough time for a thorough investigation. Initially there were delays in acquiring the official paper-work to release his body. Suddenly within hours, he was on a flight out of the country before any further investigation could be carried out. There were discrepancies in Nicolas's death certificate. His age, marital status, and occupation were all incorrectly noted. Nicolas was accidentally registered as Muslim. Freddy said it was a clerical error, and had it changed. He failed to correct the other mistakes though; namely his brother's marital status, of which he was well aware. Keeping the fact Nicolas had a legal wife from the authorities probably suited him. With Laura out of the picture, it would be so much easier to rob her of her legal entitlement.

If there was the slightest doubt surrounding Nicolas's death, Laura felt she had a duty to uncover it, no matter how long it took or how much time had passed by. Laura was on a mission to uncover the truth and seek retribution. Meticulously she went over what she knew of his activities in the hours and days leading up to his death. Freddy had the iPhone containing Nicolas's contacts and accounts of his last calls, but Laura still had one or two numbers to hand. These were people with no hidden agenda or any reason to lie. It transpired none of them had spoken with Nicolas on the morning of his death. Without his mobile to hand, Laura was unable to ascertain who he did speak to last. If anyone visited in those final hours, they most likely would have called him first.

Laura tried to retrace her husband's activities in the days before his demise. Nothing stuck out as unusual, with one exception. Nicolas's step-brother paid an unexpected visit days prior to his death; did he know more than he was saying? Laura remembered the infamous Glock. The gun was purchased in Lebanon on Nicolas's behalf. The person who acquired it was known to Laura. She recognised him from pictures he emailed to Nicolas showing him wearing the Glock in a shoulder holster. Laura had a hunch Nabil may know something.

She didn't hesitate to contact him and her hunch proved

correct because what Nabil disclosed, was illuminating. To Laura's astonishment two weeks prior to his death, Nicolas had sent for his gun. He instructed Nabil to hand the Glock over to someone who was to deliver it to an undisclosed destination. The identity of the source Nicolas appointed to collect the Glock was not known to Nabil. He told Laura; "Hajj appeared to be in a hurry."

For nearly eighteen months Laura was too heartbroken to comprehend what had happened; let alone be in any fit state to examine the facts, or lack of them. From day one at the morgue, Laura had a nagging feeling things were not right. Now those same suspicions were reinforced. Perhaps Laura was clutching at straws in a desperate bid to find answers to a situation she found intolerably unacceptable. Only time would tell. But with the bit firmly between her teeth, Laura held rigidly to the old adage and belief that if something felt wrong, then it probably was.

Laura deliberated who may have had a motive to kill Nicolas? Many times he spoke of his enemies; he never hid that actuality. Nicolas kept a hit list with several names on. Laura had been aware of its existence, but had never told anyone. Freddy claimed to have seen it. If Freddy was aware his brother had enemies, then why didn't he tell the police when asked? Unless Nicolas had shown it to him, Freddy would only have been privy to such a list by going through his brother's private papers after his death.

Alternatively, Nicolas could have shown Freddy his list on the day he visited him at the apartment; but why would Nicolas do that? Maybe there was a name on the list he wished to bring to Freddy's attention; meant perhaps as a warning?

Her imagination in overdrive, Laura envisaged the fatal scenario; the last moments of Nicolas's life. Did he willingly open the door to someone he knew and trusted, allowing them into the apartment; someone who wished him harm? Evil is always more dangerous when wearing the cloak of familiarity.

Nicolas was more than capable of handling himself;

overpowering Al Hajj would not be an easy task even if he was taken by surprise, and even then it would be difficult to do. No, no one could physically get the better of Hajj; the perpetrator was probably more underhand and sneaky.

Laura recollected how the religious icons, pictures of Mary and Saint Charbel, were lying scattered inside the hallway. Originally she was told the door was forced open by the police, which would have caused them to fall to the floor. Later a different version of events was relayed to her. The friends Nicolas planned to have lunch with that day, claimed they had broken the door open after failing to get a response from Nicolas inside the apartment. These were relatively small inconsistencies, but inconsistencies all the same. Sometimes the biggest clue to solving a puzzle lies within the smallest of discrepancies.

Laura figured another motive could have been robbery. If Nicolas had opened the door to a person or persons with malicious intent, they would have left the apartment the same way they had entered; quietly and most probably unobserved. Money is always a motive for committing crime, and large amounts were definitely missing. But who would have known Nicolas had money inside; maybe an opportunist had struck? If simply a robbery, no doubt the laptop and Nicolas's latest model iPhone would have gone too. Freddy had taken these. Now he was extremely keen, to ensure Laura didn't have access to either her husband's mobile, laptop or memory sticks; but why? What was being kept hidden from her? If Nicolas was unlawfully killed, in Laura's mind no one was above suspicion.

The unacceptable inconsistencies led Laura to spend time searching the internet, anxious to discover if it were possible her husband's supposed heart attack, may have been deliberately induced. Astonishingly, Laura learned it was not difficult to kill a person and pass it off as a heart attack. She found there were many ways to use substances that would induce and mimic heart failure. With a little knowledge of what was needed and how to administer it, anyone with the will to commit such a crime could do so.

Laura discovered these substances were easily available in the Middle East, and undetectable under autopsy unless specifically looked for by the coroner. Even then it would mean performing the autopsy within hours of death, as the substances would dissipate quickly. Nicolas was not found for some time. Through her research, Laura learned that a heart stopping drug could be administered in liquid form, for example dropped into a drink, or injected by syringe. Many heart attack inducing substances are naturally made by the human body; foul play would therefore not be entirely provable. Performing autopsies is forbidden under Islamic law unless there is concrete evidence a crime has been committed. Laura established no time was allowed to gather evidence for an investigation of that kind.

Plagued with endless probabilities, Laura was tortured by the thought that her husband may not have left his life as naturally as she had been led to believe. Every one fell under the umbrella of suspicion without exception; no one was exempt. Personal experience had shown Laura how self-serving people can be where money is involved.

Even if it were possible to ascertain the perpetrators, it was unlikely to be provable that a crime was committed. Laura's allegations would be written off as the ramblings of a grieving widow denied proper closure. On a brighter note, the upside of Laura's playing 'Miss Marple' had given her a respite from her grief. Sadly that respite was as fleeting as spring blossom. Confusion and despondency soon crept back in.

Beset once more by crippling sadness heightened by thoughts that Nicolas may have been unlawfully killed, Laura was again despondent. One day she randomly sent a text message to Nicolas's phone. He was unlikely to answer, but Laura had never been able to bring herself to erase his number from her phone contacts. After typing her message, Laura pressed the send button fully expecting to see 'message failed'. She was surprised when the text was delivered as normal. Did this mean his number was still live?

Nicolas had two mobiles, the iPhone Freddy had taken and another kept in the house. Laura wondered what had happened to that phone, she didn't recall seeing it at the apartment. Just for the hell of it Laura sent another text, this time to the other mobile. Again the text was delivered. The following day Laura made enquiries with the Etisalat phone company in the UAE. She was told the number would have been discontinued after her husband's death, but had been kept active and paid for; unfortunately they couldn't tell her by whom. Who would keep his phone active and why? Intrigued by this mystery Laura called the number. An Arabic-sounding man answered.

Laura was shocked; someone was in possession of Nicolas's other mobile.

"Who are you?" Laura demanded.

The man immediately hung up. Laura sent a text;

'Who are you and why do you have my husband's phone?' A text came back asking, 'Who are you?'

Laura texted again; 'I am Hajj's wife; my husband is the owner of this number.'

A couple of minutes later Laura's mobile rang. A male voice with a distinct Middle Eastern accent spoke. Laura repeated her question,

"Who are you?"

There was silence for a moment, and then the stranger said; "This is the wrong number."

"It's not the wrong number," Laura insisted. "Who are you and why do you have my husband's phone number?"

He hung up. Undeterred Laura sent another text, 'Tell me who you are?' Again Laura received a text back, but this time it came via a different mobile number.

'Who is Hajj?' The text read. Laura texted back to Nicolas's number; 'Hajj is my husband and you appear to have his phone.' Laura's mobile rang again;

"Who is this Hajj?" the stranger asked.

"If you don't know Hajj, why do you have his mobile number?" Laura asked; her heart was pounding heavily. There was a brief silence. Laura could hear male Arabic sounding voices in the background. Then the same person said hesitantly;

"I don't know Hajj. I don't speak English please you have wrong number." In spite of their claim not to speak English, they weren't having much trouble conversing in or understanding it. Laura thought they were behaving in a cagey manner and hiding something.

"Where are you from?" the stranger suddenly asked.

Laura hesitated before answering. She didn't know who she was talking to, or if they were connected to Nicolas. Airing on the side of caution, she answered that she was from Abu Dhabi.

"Are you living in Abu Dhabi now?" he asked.

Laura said she was not, and inquired where he was.

"I am in Al Ain," he told her.

Laura had heard of Al Ain, Nicolas had talked of it and done business there in the past. Located near the Omani town of Buraimi, Nicolas said Al Ain was commonly known as the garden city of the Emirates. He also said it was famous for its camel Souk. Typical of her husband's humour, Nicolas once told Laura he was going to take her to Al Ain remarking;

"Yeah love, there I will swap you for a camel." Remembering his cheeky comment, Laura smiled; she missed Nicolas's humorous quips and jovial banter.

Laura refused to give information to this stranger who persistently tried to persuade her. She just as persistently, continued to badger him as to how he came to acquire her husband's number. Refusing to give a straight answer, the man abruptly hung up. Laura didn't send any more texts. The whole episode made her uneasy. She was no closer to the truth. If this Arab guy holding Nicolas's phone number was guilty of anything, Laura had at best ruffled a few feathers; but that was all. After this her imagination took off; Laura was convinced there had been a huge cover up. Imagination aside, this kind of thing was not entirely unheard of in the Middle East.

Time may have passed, but with its passing Laura's

love for Nicolas had not lessened or diminished; on the contrary, she felt her bond with him grow. Writing poems and laments dedicated to his memory was a therapeutic and cathartic exercise she indulged in, helping to release her grief. Pouring out her feelings in a creative manner dispersed some negativity, but Laura would never recover from her loss.

Laura believed strongly in the continuation of life after physical death and when alone would talk to Nicolas, relaying her thoughts and feelings to him just as she had when he was alive; on occasion even expressing anger. She would shout at him for having the audacity to leave her. She felt Nicolas was alive, albeit in another realm of existence. She may no longer see, touch or hear him, but that didn't mean he ceased to exist. Often she would feel his love and know he was close. If to others Laura's belief seemed absurd, it was an effective coping mechanism that may have saved her sanity on more than one occasion.

One morning late August, Laura woke up early and for once summoned the will to get up; a very rare occurrence. Deciding to make the most of it, she set about cleaning and tidying the house. Laura's mobile rang. She stopped what she was doing and picked up her phone. Noticing the number was blocked Laura answered hesitantly. A male voice with an accent she couldn't place asked,

"May I speak with Laura Quinn Chehade?"

Not many people knew her married name.

"Who's calling?" Laura cautiously asked.

"Is that Laura?" The voice sounded innocent enough. Laura became a little less guarded.

"Yes, who is this?"

"Listen carefully; I have something to tell you."

The words took her back; it was a phrase Nicolas used. Whenever he wanted to tell her of something important he would start with the words 'listen carefully'. Although this clearly wasn't Nicolas, Laura would grasp at anything that brought back precious memories. She asked again;

"Who is this please?"

"I am calling to pass a message," the stranger said.

Laura was reticent but her curiosity was aroused.

"Okay, what's this message?" she asked assertively.

"Laura, what I am about to say to you will sound a little strange, but please don't hang up."

"Yes, okay I won't," she assured.

"Are you alone in the house?"

This question slightly unnerved her. Airing on the side of caution she told him;

"No I'm not."

"Can you be overheard?"

"I don't think so." She confirmed.

"Good, don't speak just listen. I know this will seem mysterious but all will become clear."

Laura listened intently as the stranger told her to expect a delivery; a package would be sent to her via a private courier. The courier would call in a couple of days' prior to delivering. When she received the couriers call, Laura was to be ready with a form of identification. It was important the package be handed only to her. The stranger assured Laura there was nothing to fear, but said it was imperative she open the package in private. Inside she would find a letter. She must not show the package or its contents to anyone else.

"This is very important Laura?" the stranger said. "You have nothing to fear. Believe me; something of interest to you will be gained. Everything will be revealed soon, but you must keep it secret. You understand Laura?"

Laura wasn't sure what she understood, or believed; but answered yes regardless. The caller wished her well then hung up. Bemused Laura stared at her phone. What the hell was that all about? Could her life get anymore surreal?

Laura's head spun with a million questions, all circling like birds at twilight. Was there any point in even trying to make sense of the strange call, or anything else in her life? Perhaps it was a hoax; somebody having a laugh? Laura could think of no one who would do such a thing. If and when this mysterious package came, she would hopefully have an answer. Laura was on her nerves anticipating its arrival. Despite the caller's assurances, Laura knew the world was full of weirdo's. Exactly thirty six hours later her mobile rang. Laura picked it up; again the number was blocked. Nervously she answered. A deep male voice with a foreign accent Laura again couldn't place said,

"I have a delivery for Laura Quinn Chehade."

He hung up before Laura could speak. She ran to the window; there was no one in sight. Remembering she had been told to be ready with identification, Laura went into the hallway and took her passport from her bag. She sat on the stairs and waited. Laura stared apprehensively through the obscured glass of the front door. She saw the outline of a dark figure approach and was gripped by a mixture of trepidation and excitement. The imposing figure stepped inside the porch. He then banged purposefully on the glass. Startled, Laura jumped. She rose to her feet and nervously walked to the door. The tall male figure was wearing some sort of helmet; his reflection looked like an alien through the obscured glass. Standing motionless on the other side of the door he waited. Hesitantly, Laura turned the key in the lock and peered round the door. Dressed from head to foot in black motorbike leathers, the man was wearing a crash helmet with the visa down. No part of his face was visible. His appearance was intimidating. He spoke only once;

"Laura Quinn Chehade?" The foreign sounding voice was as mysterious as his look.

"Yes that's me," Laura answered, flashing her passport in front of him.

The enigmatic stranger scrutinised the document for a moment. Without speaking he held out a black leather clad hand. Warily Laura took the package he was holding. For a few seconds he stood silently staring. The mysterious stranger suddenly turned and briskly walked away. Laura watched as he mounted his motorbike and sped off. Laura looked at the package in her hand. Hurriedly stepping back inside, she closed the door. Running upstairs Laura went inside her bedroom and locked the door.

With her heart racing ten to the dozen and her mouth as dry as the Arabian Desert, Laura placed the package on the bed. It looked harmless enough. Laura paced backwards and forwards deliberating as to whether or not she should even open it. Deciding her life couldn't get any crazier, Laura recklessly tore open the seal. Alyssa called out;

"Mum, are you in there?"

Disturbed by the sudden interruption, Laura quickly pushed the package under her pillow.

"Just wait a minute Alyssa."

"What are you doing, why is the door locked?" Alyssa asked suspiciously as her mother opened the door.

"I was sorting some things, I didn't realise I'd locked the door," she lied.

Alyssa looked unconvinced.

"Who was at the door?"

"Oh, er…umm no one. Someone selling something or other, probably." She lied again very unconvincingly.

Alyssa gave her mother a quizzical look proclaiming,

"You're weird."

Alyssa hastily went back to her computer. Grabbing the package, Laura quickly took it to the bathroom where she could lock the door without arousing suspicion. Sitting on the edge of the bath, Laura tentatively opened it. Inside were two envelopes. On one were written the words; 'For the attention of Laura Quinn Chehade'. Laura opened it and found a typed letter inside. Before reading it, she opened the second envelope. It contained a first class return ticket to Bucharest. The date of the flight was for the following Sunday at 10.30 in the morning from Heathrow, via the Alitalia airline. Laura was mystified as to who would have sent her this. She didn't know anyone in Romania. Laura unfolded the letter and started reading.

Dear Laura,

If you do decide to go on this journey, call the number at the bottom of the page within 24 hours of receipt.'

Laura looked at the number; she didn't recognise it as

being a UK number. She continued reading;

'You will hear a voice asking for a password. This is the code you must give; **11 15 21 19 2 1 23 9,** Repeat the numbers and wait for the code to be confirmed, then hang up. Once you have made the call and confirmed this password, a car will be arranged to collect you from your house at precisely 6.15am on Sunday. You will then be driven to Heathrow to meet your flight. On arrival at Baneasa airport Bucharest, you will be met by a driver. He will be holding a card with your name on, **LAURA** is all it will say. You will be driven to the Radisson Blu Hotel. Once you have checked into your room further instructions will follow.'

Laura's heart palpitated as she continued reading;

'Leave a note saying you need to get away for a bit and are taking a break. Don't say where, or give details of your trip to anyone. Do not check in any baggage at the airport, take carry-on hand luggage only. Take this letter with you. Be sure to leave nothing that will give any clue about your trip. All will be revealed in due course. I wish you well on your journey. Remember, if you decide not to go, you **MUST** destroy this letter along with its contents, leave no trace. If you decide to go, all will become clear very soon.'

There was no name or address; no clue as to where the letter had come from. Laura sat silently staring at it. Of course she could choose to ignore it completely. But then she would never solve the curious mystery. It seemed all very cloak-and-dagger; Laura didn't know what to make of it. Curiosity was pushing her to go ahead and see exactly where it might lead. But fear of the unknown was having an influence too on the decision Laura would soon be required to make. Twenty four hours was all the time she had to decide whether or not to make that call.

Did Laura really want to be confounded with another confusing episode? She had dealt with so much recently. On the other hand, she was promised answers. What waited in Bucharest? Laura was completely baffled and bewildered. She put the letter back inside the envelope with the plane ticket and resealed it. Laura thought where to hide it. Alyssa rarely came into her room, so Laura stuffed it back under her pillow. With just over twenty-three hours in which to make her decision Laura was on her nerves. Outside the weather was hot. The bedroom windows were open wide. Laura sat on the edge of the bed and stared out at the cloudless sky. Her eyes were drawn to Nicolas's worry beads on the dressing table in front of her. Laura picked them up. Clutching them tightly to her chest she whispered;

"Nicky help me decide what to do? What do you want me to do?" Laura was looking for inspiration; a sign of some kind.

The clock on the wall behind her ticked conspicuously louder than normal, as if to emphasize the fact Laura needed to make a decision. She turned to look at it; uncannily the time was exactly 11.11am. If deciding to go ahead with this mysterious journey, Laura had until 10.30 the following morning to make the call. Holding Nicolas's beads to her heart, Laura walked to the window. Looking out she quietly asked;

"I don't know what to do Nicky give me a sign; guide me?"

The sky was blue and completely clear of clouds, there was no breeze either and the trees lining the avenue were motionless in the bright sun, casting dappled shadows onto the pavement below. Laura paced the floor. She hated to make quick decisions, especially one as absurd as this. Life had been far from straightforward, or anywhere near normal for as long as she could remember. Perhaps it was just her fate that it should be so consistently bizarre.

Laura felt anxious as she struggled to make a decision. Should she go, take a risk and find out who or what was in Bucharest? Or should she just destroy the contents of the package and never discover the mystery? As if her mind were unconsciously made up, Laura pulled her flight cabin case down from the top of the wardrobe. Was this some kind of intuition telling her to go ahead? Her heart again palpitated with apprehension. Taking the package from under her pillow, Laura placed it in the side pocket of the little case. Again Laura picked up Nicolas's worry beads. She looked out of the window as if expecting to see some sort of sign. Right above her, in the middle of an otherwise completely clear sky, was a white cross. It had appeared quite literally out of the blue. Laura knew it was probably contrails from a plane, but wondered why with everything so still and quiet and with the windows wide open, she had not heard the plane go over? Laura took it to be a sign;

"So is this your sign Nicky?" Laura asked, staring up at the cross shape in the sky. "You want me to go?"

A sudden breeze blew, eerily rustling the leaves on the tree in front of the house. Instantly everything was still again. That was it. It was all that was needed to convince Laura that Nicolas wished her to take this journey. Before she had time to dwell on her decision and change her mind, Laura set about packing the items she would need for her mysterious adventure. She couldn't fit much into the tiny case, so decided not to pack any toiletries; she would buy them at the airport in duty free. That would free up space for more clothes and an extra pair of shoes. Laura felt some relief at actually coming to a decision. Now all she had to do was call and confirm the code she had been given. Pushing all doubt and fear to the back of her mind Laura squeezed as much as she could into the small cabin case.

Despite her incredible apprehension, an inner voice was willing Laura on. She looked at her screen saver photo of Nicolas on her mobile. She gazed longingly at his face. She told herself he was giving his approval, saying she had made the right choice. Laura could almost hear him say;

"Go Loulou, I'm with you girl."

Laura took out the letter from the pocket of her case. Picking up her mobile she dialled the number and waited. After just three rings a recorded voice asked for her to say the password. Laura repeated the numbers of the code;

"11- 15- 21- 19- 2- 1- 23- 9"

A few seconds later the automated voice said,
"Your code is confirmed."

The line went dead. There she'd done it; taken a plunge into the unknown. Her instincts told her it was risky, but was a risk she must take. Nothing is ever accomplished in life without risk. If you continue to follow the same safe path, nothing ever changes; the scenery will always be the same. Laura couldn't remain in this stagnant existence; it would kill her to remain as she was. Laura remembered the words of the enigmatic message;

"Soon all will become clear."

KOUSBAWI

Chapter 47: The Journey

After a restless night, of sleep disturbing tossing and turning, Laura woke early. Preparations needed to be made before her imminent departure on this mysterious Quest. Laura shopped, stocking up on food for Alyssa, and Joey. After filling the fridge, freezer and cupboards with as much as she could afford to buy, Laura cleaned and tidied the house. In spite of her decision to proceed with this secret endeavour, Laura was now having second thoughts. With no idea what awaited her in Bucharest, she was more than a little fearful and anxious. But as they say, nothing ventured, nothing gained. Laura pushed her fears to one side, focussing her energies on the positive aspects; if there were any. Just as her dream prophesised, Laura was about to take that giant leap of faith.

On the eve of her departure, Laura retired early, setting her alarm for 4.30am. Clutching Nicolas's worry beads tightly to her heart, she said a prayer asking his spirit to watch over her. In the face of her imminent leap into the unknown, Laura slept surprisingly peacefully. As dawn broke, she was awakened by the shrill of the alarm. Laura opened the bedroom shutters and peered out. With the exception of an occasional car carrying people home after a late night on the town, it was quiet. Most people were tucked up in their beds, and would be for a few hours yet. Laura tiptoed down the stairs to the kitchen; she did not want to wake Alyssa. Explanations as to her leaving needed to be avoided; if Laura was forced to consider her actions too closely, she may well back out.

After drinking a glass of warm water and lemon to refresh her, she made a coffee. Joey followed Laura from room to room, rubbing around her legs and purring. Laura picked up her cat. Holding Joey in her arms she looked into the grey tabbies soulful green eyes. They exchanged a knowing look. Being the sentient creature he was, Joey understood Laura was leaving. Whispering softly to the perceptive feline, she told him;

"Take care of Alyssa while I'm away Jojo. I love you both so much."

Fearing the repercussions from her impetuous decision, Laura had mixed feelings. Leaving without explanation tugged hard at her conscience. It was eased by the fact she had a return ticket; had it been one way only, Laura would never consider embarking on such a clandestine mission.

As the sun rose, Laura dressed and checked she had her passport and flight details safely packed. She placed the note she had written for her daughter on top of the wooden ottoman in the landing. Laura took one last look around. Walking quietly downstairs carrying her cabin case, she felt the emotion rise. Until now she had remained strong about her strange assignation with fate. The torn feelings now eating away at her conscience were uncomfortably familiar. Laura had felt them many times in the past; they tore at her heart just as deeply as ever.

Laura placed her luggage in the hallway near the door. Determined not to allow her emotions to overwhelm her, she tried to brush off and ignore a strong sudden impulse to go back up to her room. The urge refused to be brushed aside, so Laura quickly went back upstairs. As she entered the room, her eyes were immediately drawn to Nicolas's pink shirt. Since his death, it had hung on the outside of her wardrobe. It was the last shirt he had worn and the sleeves were still neatly folded back. Comfortingly, it still smelt of Nicky and often Laura would put her face against the pale pink cotton, close her eyes and imagine him there. She took the little bible from the pocket, and picked up his worry beads from the dressing table. Laura placed these now precious items inside her handbag; they would be her talisman for the journey. She was about to leave the room, when again she stopped. Impulsively she went back and grabbed Nicolas's shirt from the hanger and took it with her downstairs. Laura lifted it to her face and breathed the scent of him. Then carefully folding it, she placed the shirt into the pocket of her case. A small photo of Alyssa with Joey was on the hall table. Laura picked it up. A twinge of sadness gripped her heart as she looked at it, then it too was placed into the case with Nicky's shirt.

Just to test the water, a few days ago Laura tentatively mentioned to Alyssa she was considering taking a break away somewhere. Alyssa responded to her mother's plan in her typical dry witted manner, saying;

"Whatever, at least I'll get rid of you for a while."

Alyssa's slightly mocking retort, made Laura smile. It reminded her of Nicolas's sharp, witty humour. If Alyssa had asked too many questions or been overly concerned, it would be impossible for Laura to go ahead. Alyssa's cool unruffled attitude made Laura's decision more bearable.

Laura glanced at the large Parisian clock on the wall in the hallway. It was just before 6.15am. Laura gave Joey another cuddle before leaving him on the armchair in the lounge. She was desperate to hug her daughter and tell her how much she loved her, but Laura dare not wake Alyssa. Secretly in the back of her mind, she had decided that if by chance Alyssa were to wake before she left, it would be taken as a sign to call the whole thing off.

Right on the dot of 6.15am there was a gentle knock at the door; this would be her driver. Joey looked up. A look was exchanged between Laura and her perceptive feline friend; it was a look that echoed deep within Laura's heart. Joey's insightful expression conveyed an unspoken truth; ones destiny must be fulfilled wherever it may lead.

This is it Laura thought, trembling with apprehension. Taking a deep breath she quietly opened the door. Alyssa continued to sleep soundly. It appeared therefore Laura must go through with this strange rendezvous with destiny. As she opened the door, the figure standing in the porch was not what she had been expecting. An older gentleman roughly five feet nine inches tall, of slim build and with gentle bluish-grey eyes that twinkled asked,

"Miss Laura?"

The unassuming driver, wearing a chauffeur's uniform greeted her with a kind, friendly smile. Laura felt a sense of relief. She had assumed her driver was going to be more mysterious, in keeping with the nature of the clandestine journey she was about to take. Laura expected to see someone similar to the enigmatic courier who delivered the package.

"Yes I'm Laura," she confirmed.

"Good morning madam. May I take your bag?"

He was softly spoken and looked harmless she thought. Laura felt more at ease as she handed him her trolley case.

"I've been instructed to give you this Miss Laura."

He handed over an envelope, and then briskly took her case to the car. Laura peered inside. It contained £500 in crisp new twenty-pound notes. There was a note attached; "Leave this for your daughter," it read.

Laura quietly tiptoed upstairs. As she placed the money inside the envelope along with the note she had written for Alyssa, the emotion welled up again. Pushing the envelope gently under Alyssa's bedroom door, Laura whispered;

"I love you."

Fighting back tears, she sneaked downstairs. Before leaving, Laura poked her head around the lounge door. A sleepy Joey was on the chair purring softly with his paws tucked under his fluffy tummy. He blinked slowly at her. With a heavy sigh, Laura picked up her handbag. Slowly and quietly, she closed the front door and walked down the path to a waiting black Mercedes. The chauffeur opened the door for her. Laura took a last look back at the house before climbing into the back seat. The chauffeur closed the door then walked to the driver's side and got in.

"Are you ready Miss Laura?" he asked.

"Yes let's go," she answered quickly.

Laura sighed as she considered with trepidation what she was doing. Was it sheer madness fuelling her desire to embark on this covert, risky and possibly dangerous venture? Staring back at her house as they drove along the Avenue, Laura had a feeling of deja-vu. Genuine doubt in her sanity persistently gnawed at her conscience.

The morning sun was starting to rise above the grey slate rooftops. The smart black Mercedes was very plush and comfortable. Laura tried to relax and reconcile her decision with her uneasy conscience. They cruised along the motorway so smoothly; it was only when Laura looked out of the car window she realised how fast they were travelling. The speedometer was easily topping ninety miles an hour. With hardly any other traffic on the road they would reach Heathrow easily in under an hour.

Several miles down the motorway Laura's bravado all but dissipated. Gripped by uncertainty and the fear she may be making a terrible mistake, Laura panicked. Her heart palpitated so erratically it seemed it was preparing to jump right out of her chest. There was a strong compulsion to scream at the driver to stop the car, turn around and take her back. Laura looked anxiously into the rear view mirror. The driver lifted his eyes to look at her.

"Are you alright madam?" Her driver asked. "Only, you seem a little on edge."

He must have seen the anxiety in Laura's face. On the brink of having one very serious panic attack, she asked if they could perhaps stop at the next available services for a breather.

"Of course madam; there's one close. We will reach it in less than five minutes," he reassured, smiling at his nervous passenger.

"Thank you," Laura said in a relieved tone, trying to breathe normally.

"You know many people have a fear of flying, it's very common." Her driver assured.

If only it were just a fear of flying plaguing Laura's mind with insecurities. Still she would let him believe that was the case. Laura decided to fish for information;

"Who exactly are you?" she asked.

He looked at her in the mirror with a slightly puzzled expression.

"I'm your driver madam, who do you think I am?" he

softly chuckled. The question amused him.

"Yes, I know sorry. What I meant to say was who booked you?" Laura was trying to glean an insight as to who might be behind this mystery.

"The agency acquisitioned me the job; I am booked to drive people wherever they need to go. I have no idea as to who booked the car with the agency. I presumed it was you or the airline madam."

Laura felt a little foolish. Perhaps he was after all, just a driver and not some underworld spy. Laura's imagination had a habit of occasionally working overtime; in fact most of the time. Having regained some composure from her panicked state, she tried to relax. Moments later they were pulling into a service station.

"Here we are madam; you look like you could do with a nice cup of tea."

Plenty of people were at the services which gave Laura a renewed sense of security. They entered the café and the driver asked what she would like to drink. Laura said she would like tea.

"You take a seat Miss Laura and I will bring it over," he told her.

Laura found a seat near the window. She was starting to feel more at ease. She watched as her driver ordered and paid for two teas, which he then brought over on a tray.

"The tea's not too bad here," he commented putting the tray down on the table.

Laura took some money from her purse;

"How much do I owe you for the tea?"

"Oh no madam it's all part of the service," he said with a smile.

"Really I didn't realise?"

"Oh yes, all expenses are included in my driver's fee. If you want to have a cooked breakfast, you can have that too; it's all been very nicely taken care of," he laughed.

"Oh I think I'll pass, but thank you."

Laura smiled for the first time. Her driver did appear to be a genuinely nice person. All the same Laura decided to try and find out a little more about him;

"If you don't mind me asking, what is your name?"

"My name, my name is Harry?" He smiled, "I suppose I should have introduced myself earlier, but people aren't normally interested in knowing anything about me. They require me just to drive them; most rarely bother even speaking."

Laura sipped her tea; she was feeling a lot calmer;

"Are you married Harry?"

"No Miss Laura, I'm a widower."

Harry took a sip of his tea staring wistfully out of the window. Laura noticed a misty faraway look in his eye, as if he were remembering his late wife. Laura could totally relate to that wistful look. Then Harry chirped up, adding;

"I have two grown up sons living in London, and three lovely grandchildren." His face lit up like a sunny day, as he spoke fondly of his family.

"So you live in London Harry?" Laura inquired.

"No, I have a little place in Hertfordshire."

Laura decided not to quiz Harry further, she could tell he really didn't know anything; she was just another client to him. Anyway she couldn't exactly talk about herself; she had agreed to keep the details of her trip a secret.

They finished their tea and Laura said she needed to visit the ladies restroom before continuing. Harry said he would wait for her by the newspaper stand. While washing her hands Laura stared at her reflection in the mirror. What was she doing, was she crazy to go on with this charade? If she decided to tell Harry to turn around and go back home, no one would stop her. It was a tempting objective, but one that would leave her with an unanswered conundrum. To turn back would be pointless; Laura felt that her life since Nicolas's death was quite pointless enough. Come what may, she would stick to her guns and face her fears. Laura would see this through regardless of where it might lead. Who knows, perhaps by some miracle her luck would be changed and something good may actually be at the end of it. Besides, the worse that could happen already had. With renewed intent Laura determined to carry on.

Harry was waiting by the newspaper stand reading a Sunday paper. Laura took a deep breath, stood up straight and put her shoulders firmly back. Placing a confident albeit forced smile on her face, Laura walked assertively over to the news stand. Harry looked up from his paper as she approached. He smiled and asked;

"Okay Miss Laura shall we continue with the journey?"

"Yes let's go." Laura answered positively.

She was now feeling optimistic about the whole affair. They walked back to the car and Harry held the door open as she got in. Laura fastened her seat belt, and consciously made the decision to relax and enjoy the rest of the journey in the comfortable Mercedes.

"How long until we reach Heathrow?" she asked.

"Not long now, around twenty to thirty minutes. We've plenty of time as you're travelling first class you will be checked in straight away so you don't need to be there so early."

"How did you know I have a first class ticket?" Laura asked suspiciously.

Harry smiled at her in the mirror answering jovially; "Because I would not have been booked to drive you Miss Laura if you didn't."

"Oh right, yes of course."

Laura felt silly for not realising that. Harry went on to explain;

"Airlines often book cars for their first class travellers. Most of my customers are company executives, politicians or even celebrities. What about you Miss Laura? Are you a celebrity?" Harry light-heartedly inquired.

"No I'm not," Laura laughingly admitted.

Harry smiled; again looking at Laura in the rear view mirror he responded warmly stating;

"Well I'm sure you are very special all the same."

Laura smiled back. She found Harry extremely genial. A while later they pulled into Terminal four at Heathrow. Harry parked the car and opened the door for Laura. After taking her luggage from the boot, he escorted her to the Alitalia first class check in desk. After she had checked in, Harry took an envelope from his breast pocket. He handed it to Laura.

"What's this?" She asked taking the envelope.

"I was instructed to give it to you after you had checked in." Harry told her.

Laura opened the envelope inside of which was £500 in crisp £50 and £20 notes.

"What's it for?" Laura asked Harry.

"I assume it is for you to spend in duty free."

Harry seemed amused by Laura's obvious surprise and innocent lack of knowledge about her journey. He told her cordially;

"I must take my leave of you now Miss Laura. I wish you a very pleasant trip, and I hope you continue to have lots more nice surprises."

"Thank you Harry."

Harry then turned to walk away but Laura instinctively stopped him;

"Wait a minute Harry, what exactly do you know about my trip and other surprises?"

"Nothing Miss Laura, it's none of my business. I was assigned to get you here safely. Have a good flight and a lovely time Miss Laura; I'm sure you must be very special to someone." Harry smiled tipping his hat to Laura like a real old fashioned gentleman.

"Good bye Harry and thank you."

Harry turned and walked away out of sight. Laura was sorry to see him leave; she had felt at ease in his company. Harry had that sort of familiar looking face you think you know, or have seen before somewhere.

After purchasing a few toiletry and cosmetic essentials, Laura made her way to the first class lounge, where she found a seat and was immediately offered refreshment. She ordered a pot of mint tea and a bottle of un-chilled still water. Laura had bought a large bottle of 'Angel' perfume from duty free. She took it from her bag and sprayed some onto her neck and wrist. Nicolas loved this fragrance on her; in remembrance of him Laura wouldn't wear anything else. On a whim, she had also purchased his favourite men's cologne; she didn't know why, but just felt the urge to buy it. In the past Laura had always bought Chanel for Nicolas whenever at an airport. Over the years she would give him various different fragrances to try, but the Chanel was his firm favourite. Even though he was no longer with her physically, at least she could be reminded of his smell.

At precisely 9.55am, first class passengers were invited to board. Laura's nerves had calmed quite a bit, although she was understandably very apprehensive as to what would happen when she arrived in Bucharest. Laura made a last minute trip to the ladies bathroom. On her return to the lounge, a stewardess was waiting for her.

"Mrs Laura Quinn Chehade?"

Laura nodded.

"Would you please allow me to accompany you aboard your flight?"

Laura picked up her bottle of water and quickly stuffed it into the large shopping bag she purchased to hold her duty free items. She followed the stewardess to the first class boarding desk where she was given a boarding card. Laura was then led straight onto the plane. As she boarded first class, she was greeted by name and shown to her seat by an immaculate and smiling, member of the Italian cabin crew. No sooner had Laura settled in her seat, when she was offered a glass of champagne. Laura accepted and almost immediately they were taxiing along the runway. As the plane gathered speed, Laura gripped tightly to the side of her seat. The take-off was always the worst part. Holding her breath, Laura clenched her knuckles as the plane gradually climbed higher. Once it had gained height and levelled off, Laura could relax and breathe normally. Soon the seat belt sign was turned off, and the Italian captain welcomed everyone aboard. He said they were expected to arrive in Bucharest on schedule at 3.30pm local time.

Laura re-set her watch to local time in Romania. She looked around the plush first class compartment. Apart from herself, there was only one other first class passenger, an elderly gentleman seated on the other side of the aisle behind her. He nodded and wished her good morning. Laura smiled and returned the greeting. Laura was then handed a menu by the flight attendant. She wasn't particularly hungry, but decided to indulge anyway, ordering rocket salad with spinach and ricotta pasta, followed by fresh fruit. After eating her early lunch, Laura relaxed. Surprisingly she actually began to enjoy the flight.

Before landing Laura freshened up in the first class toilet, brushing her teeth and hair. After tying her long hair into a high pony tail she twisted it into a bun and secured it with two squiggle pins, (corkscrew shaped hairpins that you twist clockwise to secure and anti-clockwise to take out). Laura applied moisturiser to her face to combat the planes dehydrating air conditioning, and sprayed on some more 'Angel' perfume. When she returned to the cabin, the seat belt sign came on. The captain announced that they would soon be landing at Baneasa airport. He said the estimated arrival time was 3.35pm and that the weather in Bucharest was warm and sunny with temperatures around 27 degrees.

As the plane started its descent, Laura held Nicolas's worry beads tightly against her chest. For once it was not the landing worrying Laura, but rather what waited for her in Bucharest. At least she had a return ticket. If things did go pear shaped she would simply take the next available flight back to London. Laura resolved to try and remain positive until given reason to think otherwise. Knowing she had the choice to turn back at any time, helped ease the uncertainty. She was booked into a five star hotel in the centre of Bucharest, not exactly the middle of nowhere. So long as she kept her wits about her what could honestly go wrong?

The planes wheels were down and the captain asked the cabin crew to take their seats in preparation for landing.

There was a slight bump and screech of the planes wheels as they hit the tarmac at speed. Gradually slowing along the runway the plane finally came to a stop. Laura took her sunglasses from her bag and placed them on the top of her head. Gathering up her belongings Laura checked that she had everything before leaving the aircraft. As Laura exited the plane, the cabin crew wished her a lovely stay in Bucharest.

Being a first class passenger, Laura moved quickly through the passport checks into the arrivals terminal. The terminal area was pretty crowded, and Laura struggled to see anyone who looked as though they were waiting for her. A fluttering of nervous butterflies was felt and Laura's anxiety heightened as she fervently scanned the people with cards. She could see no one holding a card with Laura written on it. Slowly she walked towards the terminal exit, continuing to keep a keen eye out for a card displaying her name. On reaching the exit Laura still hadn't met with her driver.

Walking through the automatic glass exit doors, Laura stepped out into the warm sunshine. Although it bared no resemblance, Laura was instantly reminded of the times she arrived at Abu Dhabi to be met by a smiling Nicolas. The memory of those sweet moments made her heart ache. What she wouldn't give to see Nicolas standing here now. Laura felt a solitary tear sneak from her eye and land on her cheek. She pulled her sunglasses down over her eyes and looked at her watch. She was glad she remembered to set it to Romanian time whilst on the plane. It was now 4.10pm. She would wait until 4.30 then make enquiries as to the next available flight back to London.

Part of her secretly hoped the driver wouldn't show, so that she could return home. Five minutes later there was a tap on her shoulder. Laura jumped. A tallish slim man in his late twenties to early thirties and wearing sunglasses, was suddenly at her side holding a card with her name on.

"Oh you startled me." She exclaimed.

"I'm sorry, are you Laura Quinn Chehade?"

"Yes I am."

"Please, I'm Marcello; I'm to drive you to the Radisson Blu Hotel. Please come this way Miss Laura."

He had the most delectable accent. Laura followed the dark haired rather handsome young man to the waiting car; a classic style silver Mercedes. Laura's heart flipped when she saw the car; it was almost identical to the one Nicolas drove in Abu Dhabi back in the eighties. Marcello took her bags and placed them into the boot. He held the door open and Laura climbed into the back seat. As they drove away from the airport, Marcello apologised for his tardiness in picking her up.

"The traffic was unbelievable," he told her.

Laura decided to engage in conversation;

"Are you Italian?" She asked the handsome stranger.

"No, you think I look Italian?" He laughed, "I speak Italian but I am Romanian."

His accent was so appealing, but then Laura did have a penchant for men with sexy foreign accents.

"Do you speak Italian Miss Laura?" he asked.

Marcello was openly friendly in an almost cheeky way. Laura felt strangely at ease in his company.

"Yes I speak Italian," she told him. "How long is it till we reach the hotel?"

"Not long, maybe twenty minutes, the traffic is not so bad now."

Laura looked out of the window taking in the sights of Bucharest while Marcello continued to chat away.

"So you are speaking Italian Miss Laura? But a part of your name, Quinn it is Spanish no? I am right?"

Marcello's voice was so attractive. The confident way he talked reminded Laura of a young Nicolas. It stirred up nostalgic memories; memories long buried because they were just too painful to acknowledge.

"Yes I have Spanish blood on my father's side," Laura confirmed.

"Then you also speak Spanish," Marcello assumed.

"No not really, maybe a little."

"Me I'm speaking five languages," Marcello boasted, "Romanian, English, Italian Arabic and German."

Laura wished she had learned to speak Arabic. It was down to Nicolas that she didn't. Whenever she tried to learn, Nicolas had been less than encouraging, insisting on speaking only English with her. Laura had the impression there were things he didn't want her to understand. When she jokingly challenged him on the subject, he had been evasive, insisting that he needed to perfect his English. Laura often wished she had learnt the language without Nicolas's knowledge, but there was never the opportunity.

Roughly twenty minutes or so later, the silver Mercedes pulled up in front of the Radisson Blu hotel. Immediately a porter opened the car door for Laura. Marcello exchanged a few words in Romanian with him.

"I wish you a very good stay in Bucharest Miss Laura," Marcello said as he handed Laura's bags over to the porter. Laura thanked Marcello who then got back into the silver Mercedes and drove away.

"Follow me please." The porter said, in much too perfectly spoken English.

Laura followed him to the hotel reception where she was asked for her passport. The receptionist looked at it and then looked back at Laura;

"Welcome to Bucharest and the Radisson Blu Hotel." She handed Laura back her passport.

"I hope you will have a very enjoyable stay with us."

The receptionist said something in Romanian to the porter and handed him a room key. The porter directed Laura to the lift. They got out on the fourth floor where Laura followed him along a corridor stopping outside of room 110. Laura stared at the door number; uncannily it was the same as Nicolas's room number at the Holiday Inn hotel Abu Dhabi, where he was staying when she met him. Laura marvelled at the synchronicity of both the room numbers and of the silver Mercedes. She felt more than a twinge of nostalgic sadness. After unlocking the door the porter placed Laura's bags inside. The room was beautiful with a large king-sized bed, en-suite bath and shower, and a balcony. Laura thanked the porter who wished her a nice evening and left.

Laura opened the balcony doors and stepped out into the late afternoon sun. It was still pleasantly warm and a gentle breeze was blowing. For a while Laura managed to completely forget she was on a mysterious quest. Feeling relaxed she breathed in the view of the beautiful gardens and pool. She was almost taken in by her own fantasy that she was on vacation. A sudden knock at the door startled her, abruptly bringing Laura back to the cold reality that she was not on a real holiday. Laura went back inside and cautiously approached the door. She hesitated and was startled again by a second even louder knock.

"Who is it?" She asked tentatively.

A male voice answered;

"I have a delivery for you Miss Laura."

Laura opened the door and took the package the porter was holding. This must be the further instructions she was told to expect she thought, quickly closing the door. Laura ripped open the package. It again contained two envelopes. The first was another typed letter, and the second envelope contained money in local currency. Laura put the envelope with the cash to one side, and sat down on the bed to read the letter.

'Dear Laura,

I trust you had a good flight and like your room at the Radisson Blu. You are of course free to come and go as you please. May I suggest you have a nice relaxing dinner in one of the excellent hotel restaurants, or if you prefer take advantage of the room service. You do not need to pay for anything as it has all been taken care of. You will find 5,115 Romanian Leu; one thousand in sterling in the second envelope. This is for you to spend as you wish. Tomorrow at 11.30am a car will arrive to take you on to another destination. I cannot reveal where, but have faith that everything will become clear very soon. Tomorrow you will have an answer to your questions, and I promise you will not regret embarking on this journey. Be sure you take your entire luggage with you tomorrow. Have a nice evening Laura, and a good night's rest.'

The letter was unsigned leaving no clue as to whom it was from. Laura's head started spinning. This journey was becoming ever more intriguing by the moment; every step pulling Laura further into a cryptic puzzle. Laura paced the floor. Suddenly stricken with a thumping headache she felt nauseous. Pretending to be on vacation had been a short lived affair. Laura had been expecting further instructions, but their arrival served to reinforce the fact that she really was on a journey into the unknown. It was both scary and exciting at the same time. The letter promised answers by tomorrow. She wondered what truths would be uncovered.

Her head pounded; it felt like a whole percussion orchestra was warming up inside of it. Laura flopped onto the large bed. A million thoughts ran through her brain simultaneously. She had in her purse a return ticket; what was to stop her from taking a taxi to the airport and flying back home? Nothing, absolutely nothing, except for her unquenchable curiosity, which amazingly was stronger than her fear; she couldn't leave now and never know what might have been.

Laura unpacked her case then took a shower. The water felt soft; unlike the hard water of southern England. As it fell over her face and shoulders gently caressing her tired body, Laura felt all her anxieties briefly washed away. She stayed under the shower for a full ten minutes, enjoying the relaxation the soft warm water brought to her highly stressed mind and body.

Turning off the shower, Laura grabbed a large fluffy white towel from the rail wrapping it around like a sarong. She used a smaller one to wrap turban style around her wet hair. Laura sat in front of the dressing table and stared at her reflection in the large oval mirror. She felt as though she had been on this journey for days, but it was less than twenty four hours since leaving her house.

Combing through her wet hair, Laura contemplated the

events of the day so far. Again anxious feelings arose, and the awakened butterflies in her tummy felt as though they were doing a version of the River Dance. Laura's thoughts turned to Alyssa. Was she okay? What did she think when she found the letter Laura had left for her? Laura felt her eyes become heavy with tears. If Laura intended to see this mystery through to whatever conclusion awaited, then she would need to take firm control of her emotions. Alyssa was quite independent; she had managed perfectly well when Laura was living in Abu Dhabi. It was Laura who couldn't cope with the separation. She brushed the tears from her face, mentally brushing away any doubt that she had made a mistake in following this quest for answers.

Laura ordered a pot of tea. While waiting for it to arrive she made herself a promise; from now on she would have no regrets about anything. Ten minutes later there was another knock at the door and the hotel porter brought in the tea. He placed the tray down on the table and asked if there was anything else she needed. Laura thanked him and took a couple of notes from the envelope containing the Romanian Leu, handing them to the young man. Laura had no idea how much money she had given him, but he looked pleased enough.

While sipping her tea, Laura browsed the restaurant menus that had been left on the tray. At 7.55pm she left her room to investigate the location of the restaurants. There were four to choose from. Laura couldn't decide between Café Citta, which was Italian and Shakia, which funnily enough was Middle Eastern. Laura followed the signs to Café Citta on the ground floor, passing by Shakia on the way. The Italian looked nice but was pretty busy, with most of the tables occupied by families and couples. Laura felt a little conspicuous being alone and hesitated to go in. She walked back to where Shakia was situated. It was less busy and the ambiance appealed. Laura decided to eat there.

The waiter showed her to a nice table near the window overlooking the gardens. The atmosphere was relaxed and friendly; Laura felt perfectly comfortable dining alone here. She ordered a meze of houmus, grilled vegetables, taboule, grilled haloumi, and olives stuffed with almonds all served with warm Arabic bread. The waiter asked if she would like a drink. Laura ordered still mineral water. After serving Laura her dinner, the waiter suggested that she might enjoy a glass of champagne. Laura said she would, and he poured her a glass of chilled Moet Chandon.

The evening was warm and balmy with a soft delicate breeze blowing through the open window. It blew a strand of Laura's hair onto her face which she tucked behind her ear. Water could be heard trickling in a nearby fountain and as she sipped her champagne, Laura felt a serenity she hadn't felt in quite some time. The champagne bubbles tingled around her lips, reminding Laura of the last time she and Nicolas had drunk champagne together. With the fond memory clinging to her mind, great sadness suddenly invaded her heart and Laura's tranquil serene mood was all too soon disturbed. Her eyes glistened as tears threatened to stream from them at any moment. Just in time the waiter arrived to top up her glass of champagne, forcing Laura to regain her composure.

"Would you like to take your champagne out onto the terrace?" he diplomatically suggested. "It's a beautiful evening."

Laura agreed it would be nice and the waiter carried her drink to a table. He brought the rest of the champagne out to her in an ice bucket for Laura to help herself. It was a peaceful spot, softly lit with fairy lights and lots of pretty lanterns hanging from the trees. Laura was thankful for the solitude and privacy this little oasis afforded her. Sitting out under the stars on this warm balmy summer evening, Laura wondered what secrets tomorrow would reveal.

That night, as she climbed wearily into the sumptuous king-sized bed, Laura's thoughts and feelings were many. But all slipped effortlessly away as she drifted into sleep.

KOUSBAWI

Chapter 48: The Revelation

"Ask and it will be given to you;
Seek and you will find.
Knock and the door will be opened to you;
For everyone who asks receives;
He who seeks finds;
And to him who knocks,
The door will be opened.
Mathew 7; 7-8

Laura woke the following morning feeling refreshed and a little more optimistic as to what the day ahead may herald. At 7.15am she opened the balcony doors and breathed in the cool morning air. A cloudless blue sky greeted her as she stepped out onto the veranda. Squinting in the bright sun, Laura lifted her hand to shield her eyes and surveyed the pretty view. Her balcony looked over the hotel's old historic gardens. Despite feeling cool in the early morning freshness, the sun was subtly pushing through to gently warm her pale skin. It promised to be another gloriously warm sunny day.

Laura stepped back inside leaving the balcony doors open, allowing a gentle breeze to waft around the room. The white muslin curtains billowed softly as if dancing in the morning sun. Laura sat back onto the bed and sipped a glass of water embracing the quiet tranquillity. The brief serenity felt the night before whilst dining, returned like a long lost friend. Laura's mesmerised calm was again short lived, as the peaceful ambiance was rudely interrupted by the ringing of the hotel room phone beside her. Curious as to who would be calling at this time, Laura reached over and apprehensively picked up the receiver;

"Hello," she said.

A female voice answered her,

"Good morning Mrs Chehade. This is reception with your wake up call."

Laura didn't remember asking for a morning call.

"Would you like to have an English newspaper?" asked the receptionist.

"Err, no thank you," Laura told her.

"Would you like breakfast brought to your room or will you eat in the restaurant Madam?" the woman asked.

Laura hadn't given breakfast a thought. She picked up the breakfast menu from the bedside table.

"Can I have breakfast in my room please?"

"Of course madam what would you like?"

Laura glanced at the menu quickly making her choice; ordering poached eggs, toast, preserves and a pot of tea.

"What time would you like to have breakfast?" The woman asked.

Laura looked at the clock; it was 7.25am.

"Eight o' clock please."

"Very well madam, at eight o' clock your breakfast will be brought to your room."

Laura went into the bathroom to take a quick shower. After dressing casually in jeans and T shirt, she picked up her 'Angel' fragrance. A feeling of sudden euphoria came over Laura as she sprayed the perfume into the air and playfully danced through the scented mist. Eight o' clock sharp, a knock at the door signalled breakfast had arrived. Laura opened the door and a porter wheeled in a trolley.

"Would you like to take breakfast out on the balcony?" he asked.

Laura told him she would, and her breakfast was laid out on the balcony table. Laura took some money from her purse and handed it to the porter.

"Thank you madam, thank you very much," he said cheerfully, taking the notes from her hand.

"Enjoy your breakfast, and have a lovely day." He left smiling broadly.

Laura thought she really must find out about the local currency exchange rate. Putting on her sunglasses Laura sat at the table on the balcony to eat her breakfast. A single flower had been placed in a tiny vase on the breakfast tray. It reminded Laura of the first breakfast Nicky had made her on their first long awaited reunion; he too had placed a single flower on the tray for her.

Sitting on the veranda in the warm morning sun felt so peaceful. Laura couldn't remember the last time she had been this relaxed. However the day panned out, Laura resolved to enjoy this blissful moment and embrace the notion she was on holiday; even if it was only pretend. Whatever happened next, nothing could top the perpetual heartache suffered every day since Nicolas's death.

For too long Laura had lived in a continuous waking nightmare. In a way the pain and grief had become a part of her; it was there when she went to sleep at night and there to greet her when she woke, and all the hours' in-between. Tranquillity and peace were rare, so Laura was determined to be fully present in this moment and enjoy the precious fleeting interlude, while it lasted. Freedom from your thoughts and incessant chattering of the mind, is true liberation. Soon enough the peace would fly away to become a distant moment in time; returning Laura to the sorrow that gripped her so tightly at times she could hardly breathe.

As predicted and right on cue, her troubled thoughts intervened stealing her peace away; flooding her mind with anxiety once again. Instantly Laura's serene state fled, evaporating into the ether. Vainly Laura tried holding on to it just a moment longer, but all too soon it faded into the background; like a dream disappearing from your memory as you wake.

She glanced at her watch; it was 9.10am. A car would be collecting her at 11.30am. In a couple of hours Laura would be on her way to discovering what was behind this mysterious journey. Laura went back inside the room and started getting her things together wondering what lay in wait. Distracted for a moment from her anxious thoughts, Laura couldn't decide whether or not to change, or stay casual in comfy jeans and T-shirt. She sat in front of the dressing table mirror and stared at the fragile reflection. Laura no longer knew who she was. This ghost of a person looking back was like a stranger. Without Nicolas she just wasn't the same Laura. It wasn't that Nicolas defined her as a person; on the contrary, he had always encouraged Laura to explore her strengths and discover her own worth. But his death hit hard, resulting in Laura's sense of self-worth, confidence and belief in her own abilities, being brutally knocked out of her.

Laura felt like a rag doll with no real substance to hold her up. Like a leaf carried helplessly on the breeze as it falls from a tree, Laura was at the mercy of fate. Rather than feel she had any influence over where life took her, life became something that just happened to her. The sparkle was gone; not only from her eyes but from her soul. Laura quietly asked of the pale sombre reflection;

"What is to become of you, where will you end up?"

It would be another hour and a half until the car arrived to drive her to who knows where? Taking her makeup case from her bag, Laura applied some colour to her pale skin. She took her time. Whatever lay-in-wait, she may as well look her best to greet fates next manoeuvre. After tying her long auburn hair into a high ponytail, she paused. Nicolas loved for Laura to wear her hair this way. She smiled remembering how his compliments would influence the way she presented herself. She knew he had been subtly moulding her to do things the way he liked.

Finally happy with the finished result, Laura decided after all to change from her casual attire. She put on pale blue Capri pants and pretty, pale lavender top. Gathering up her bags, sun glasses and light denim jacket, Laura was ready to face the next stage of this mystery.

It was now 11.25am. Laura checked the room to make sure nothing was left behind. She considered whether or not to go on down to reception, rather than wait in her room. Before Laura had a chance to answer that dilemma, a loud knock at the door startled and made her jump.

It didn't take much to startle Laura. Nicolas had often found it amusing to sneak up on her and scare her half to death. He would tease her about her jumpiness, especially when they were watching a creepy movie together. Of course nothing ever made him jump.

Laura opened the door to the same hotel porter who had shown her to her room when she first arrived.

"Good morning madam, you are checking out today at 11.30 yes?" he said, offering to take her luggage on down.

Laura took a last look around then followed him to the lift. Inside the elevator, the porter asked if she had enjoyed her stay. Laura told him she had. He asked if the service had been satisfactory.

"Yes thank you, very much so," she told him.

"But it was a very short stay for you? I hope you will come back to the Radisson again," he said.

Laura took a couple of notes from her purse. As they stepped from the lift on the ground floor, she handed them to the young man.

"Thank you madam, enjoy the rest of your holiday in beautiful Romania," he told her.

Holiday she thought, if only he knew. Laura took a seat in the hotel lobby and waited nervously. Again she looked at her watch. It was now 11.40am and the tardiness of the driver was making her anxious. Facing the hotel entrance Laura watched the people come and go. She felt envious of those arriving who were on real vacations. Laura wished her life were more normal and less dramatic; but normality for Laura continued to be elusive.

Nervous impatience was making her fidgety. Deciding to wait outside in the sun, Laura bent to pick up her bags. It was then she heard a familiar voice.

"Good morning Miss Laura."

She turned to see the tall handsome figure of Marcello.

"I'm so sorry to have kept you waiting," he apologised. "The traffic was a little heavy."

"Oh, I didn't know it was going to be you," Laura said, surprised but relieved to see the familiar face of the driver who had collected her from the airport.

"I hope you are not too disappointed," he said, smiling flirtatiously at her.

She coyly smiled back. His flirty vibes made Laura feel a little awkward. Marcello was an attractive young man; his self-assured attitude reminded her of Nicolas. Marcello picked up Laura's bags and she followed him out to the silver Mercedes. He opened the boot and put her bags inside. Holding the car door open, he was less than subtle in deliberately eyeing her up as she climbed into the back. Laura felt conscious of Marcello's eyes on her, aware he was checking her out; he could not have made it more obvious. Taking his mobile from the car Marcello walked a short distance away from the Mercedes. When he was sure he was out of earshot, he called someone. Laura watched him but couldn't hear what was being said from inside the car. She tried to wind down her window to listen but it was locked. Laura strained her ears but couldn't even make out which language Marcello was speaking; it could have been any one of five. A moment later he was back and getting into the driver's seat.

"Are you ready Miss Laura?" he asked turning around to face her.

Laura nodded;

"I guess so," she told him rather resignedly.

Marcello smiled, and pulled away from the Radisson onto the main road. Several times as he drove along the highway, Laura caught him looking at her in his mirror. Their eyes accidently met; self-consciously Laura looked away.

"You look very pretty today Laura, can I call you Laura?" Marcello asked, rather cheekily Laura thought. Just the same he was charmingly brazen, so she agreed he could dispense with the 'Miss' and just call her Laura. Marcello was extremely handsome, but when confronted with it, his openly flirtatious manner did make Laura feel awkwardly shy. She had no desire or wish to seek flattery, or attention from another man; that particular page in her book of life belonged to Nicolas and would she believed, never be rewritten.

As they drove out of Bucharest Laura took note of the sign posts. They seemed to be heading in the direction of somewhere called Targovista. Laura asked Marcello where they were going.

"We are going into the mountains," he told her.

"The mountains?" She repeated in a shocked tone.

"Yes Laura, the Carpathian Mountains to be exact. We will pass near to the authentic Dracula's castle."

Lifting his eyes to look at Laura in the mirror, Marcello added teasingly;

"Do you believe in vampires Laura?"

He smiled wickedly. She smiled back telling him;

"I'm not sure, but I have certainly come across a few blood-suckers."

Marcello laughed at her quip;

"You are funny Laura," he told her.

Marcello turned on the radio. An Italian music station was playing. It amused Laura the way he sang along to all the songs he knew. It certainly helped lighten the mood, and ease the awkward tension Laura was feeling. Two and a half hours and one hundred and ninety one kilometres later, plus several Italian serenades' from Marcello, they finally arrived in Targovista. Marcello pulled up outside of a small hotel. He turned around to Laura and asked;

"Are you hungry Laura, we can get something to eat and drink here?"

It was nearly 3pm; Laura hadn't eaten since breakfast. That was six hours ago. Marcello got out and opened her door. She stepped from the car and together they walked towards the small hotel. The sun was still hot, with the temperature around 29 degrees. Marcello had kept the air conditioning on in the car and the sudden heat felt good, warming up Laura's chilled skin. She liked the heat and after many years living in Abu Dhabi, was used to much hotter temperatures.

The small hotel was very gothic looking in style; Laura

thought it could easily have come straight out of a Dracula movie. Stepping inside from the bright sunlight, it fittingly appeared a little dark and eerie inside. A tall skinny hotel receptionist with very long black hair, who could easily have passed for a member of the Adams family, greeted and directed them towards the bar and restaurant. The little restaurant opened out on to a terrace with a small shaded garden.

"Do you want to sit out there?" Marcello asked Laura.

"Yes it's nice." She said walking towards the garden.

Laura looked around the enclosed area, before deciding to take a seat at a table shaded by an enormous umbrella. A warm soft breeze tickled her skin and made the umbrella stand creak and sway. It was very restful. Laura could hear Marcello talking to the barman. A moment later, the tall skinny dark haired woman came out and handed Laura a menu. Laura ordered grilled mixed vegetables, a salad with feta cheese, olives and Rye bread. Marcello brought out a bottle of still mineral water from the bar for her, then went back inside and continued chatting to the barmen.

Within ten to fifteen minutes the food arrived; it looked most appetising. The delicious rye bread was warm, and studded with pumpkin seeds. Marcello left Laura in peace to eat alone, while he stayed at the bar and tucked into a traditional Romanian dish. Laura noticed Marcello was drinking red wine with his meal, and wondered about the Romanian laws regarding drinking and driving. Luckily he stopped at one, but after his meal did partake in a shot of something that Laura presumed to be alcoholic.

At 3.45pm Marcello said they should leave soon, as he wanted to reach their destination before nightfall. Laura quickly used the ladies to freshen up, and then walked with him back to the car. Marcello held Laura's door open for her. Once she was inside, he again walked a little distance away from the car just out of earshot. After he had spoken to someone on his mobile, he returned and got into the car. Marcello adjusted his rear view mirror before starting up the engine. Laura felt inclined to ask him who he had been talking with, but didn't. Remembering she had not paid for her lunch, Laura asked how much she owed. Marcello told her she owed nothing; it was included in his expenses. He turned around and smiled at her. He had such a lovely engaging smile, just like Nicolas's Laura thought. Before setting off Marcello removed his sunglasses.

"Are you ready to go Laura?" Marcello asked leaning towards the back seat. They made eye contact. Laura was enthralled at how beautiful Marcello's dark eyes were; she hadn't noticed before. Probably because it was the first time she had seen him this close up without his sunglasses.

"Where exactly are we going?" she asked.

"I told you Laura; to the mountains," he answered without elaborating further.

"Is that all you are going to tell me?" she pushed.

Marcello just smiled teasingly at her in the mirror. The secret of their mysterious destination was staying a secret for now. Marcello clearly was not going to reveal anything more, so Laura tried to relax and enjoy the view of the beautiful Romanian countryside.

The sun was just beginning to set as they drove further into the Carpathian Mountains. Now they had entered the much cooler mountain air Marcello turned off the cars air conditioning. Laura took her jacket from her shopping bag and wrapped it around her shoulders. Marcello asked if she was warm enough. She told him she was but he obligingly put the car heater on anyway. At 5.30pm they entered into a long winding driveway. Marcello pulled up outside of a secluded three storey mountain chalet, overlooking a small lake. Laura noticed cable cars in the far distance going up and down the snow-capped mountain.

"We must be near a ski resort," Laura said stepping from the car.

"You like to ski Laura?" Marcello asked as he took her bags.

"No I've never tried, well not on real snow anyway." Laura confessed.

Marcello laughed; "What other kind of snow is there?

441

Everyone ski's here. I am an excellent skier," he boasted.

Laura didn't doubt he was, but his total lack of modesty amused her. She shivered as the cool mountain air whisked around her bare arms and ankles. She pulled her jacket tightly around her shoulders. Marcello carried her bags and she followed him towards the chalet. Laura looked up to see smoke billowing from the chimney. The chalet looked eerily beautiful with the sun just beginning to set behind the rooftop. But it was lonely and a little too quiet Laura thought, as she followed Marcello up the path to the front door.

"Well this is it." Marcello announced as he unlocked the door, placing Laura's bags inside.

Laura stepped into the chalet. It felt surprisingly warm and cosy. Marcello put the key down on the table in the hallway, then announced;

"This is as far as I take you Laura. Sadly I must leave now."

Laura stared at him; "What that's it! You mean you are just going to leave me here alone?"

"Those were my instructions, to bring you safely here. I really must go. It will be dark soon." Marcello seemed suddenly in a hurry. "Take care Laura, and good luck."

With that Marcello left, leaving Laura all alone in the chalet. Hearing the Mercedes drive away, Laura was filled with a sense of panic and defenceless vulnerability. She felt compelled to run after it and beg Marcello to take her back to the hotel in Bucharest. But he was gone and Laura was alone in this extremely isolated location. A crackling sound could be heard coming from the room to her left. Gingerly Laura walked into the large room. In an open stone fire place a log fire crackled and burned. There were armchairs either side, each with a small table beside it. To the left of the room, was a large dining table and over to the right, a comfortable looking sofa. In spite of the scary isolation, the setting and décor was invitingly cosy. Even so, Laura was confused as to what she was doing here. Over on the table something caught her eye.

A bottle of Moet Chandon champagne was sitting in an ice filled bucket. Two champagne flutes were beside it. Laura touched the bottle; it was still very chilled and the ice hadn't melted, so it couldn't have been there very long. Might there actually be someone else in the chalet? The thought gave her shivers. Laura decided to be brave and investigate. There was a staircase to the left of the hall and to the right an archway leading to an open plan kitchen and breakfast room with a log burner. Laura walked through the archway. In a spontaneous action she opened the fridge, which she found to be packed full of food including fresh vegetables, salads and cheeses, a large selection of fruit, quite a few large bars of Swiss chocolate, and a bowl of ripe strawberries.

"Well if I'm marooned here, at least I won't starve." Laura said to herself.

She wondered who the second champagne glass was intended for; would somebody soon be joining her? Just as the thought materialised, a knock at the door caused Laura to be rooted to the spot; maybe she was about to discover the identity of her mysterious companion? Hesitantly she called out;

"Who is it?" A male voice answered;

"I have a delivery for Laura."

"Oh here we go again," she thought.

No doubt this would be some more cryptic instructions. Laura walked boldly to the door. On opening it she found not a person with a package, but a bouquet of red roses on the door step. She cagily stuck her head outside to see who had left them. There was no one in sight. Warily scanning her surroundings, Laura bent down to pick up the flowers. Feeling an eerie chill, she quickly took the flowers inside. She looked for a note but there was nothing accompanying the roses. A large crystal vase was conveniently placed on the table in the hall. Laura filled it with water, and hastily arranged the two dozen blood-red roses into it. Placing the crystal vase now holding the roses back on the hall table, Laura decided it was time to explore the rest of the chalet.

Tentatively climbing the stairs to the next level, she discovered two large double bedrooms; both with an en-suite bath and shower. The larger of the two rooms had a balcony. Situated on the third level at the top of the chalet was an attic bedroom, with a separate toilet and shower room. Laura went back down to the main master bedroom. She still had no clue where this mystery was leading. Whoever was behind it had good taste Laura thought; the chalet was beautifully decorated. It was exactly the sort of place she and Nicolas had once talked of holidaying in. Nicolas would have loved it, Laura thought wistfully; he preferred seclusion and liked cosy surroundings.

Laura opened the balcony's French doors. Slowly she stepped outside. She stood a little while looking over the picturesque lake and mountains. The scenery and setting was lonely, but absolutely breath-taking. A chilly breeze swept in, making Laura shiver and she hurried back inside. Being dusk the mountain air was rather cold now. Laura sat wearily down on the bed and switched on the bedside lamp. Lying back onto the large pillows, the bed felt soft and warm. Laura began to drift off; nervous tension had totally exhausted her.

A sudden noise from the floor below made her sit up with a start. With her heart pounding Laura got up and quietly walked to the door. She peered out onto the dark landing. Someone else was definitely in the chalet. With trembling jelly-like legs Laura slowly crept down-stairs, wishing she had thought to turn some lights on earlier. She turned left making her way to the lounge. The log fire crackled in the stone fire place throwing out a warm glow.

Cautiously she scanned every corner. The soft glow from the fire enabled Laura to see a little better. The room appeared to be empty, but Laura was shocked to see two glasses of champagne had been poured. She was definitely not alone here. Stricken with fear, Laura moved guardedly nearer to the fireplace. She had spotted a heavy iron poker, which could be handy if needed.

Laura stared at the champagne glasses. Her attention

was drawn to a note surreptitiously placed next to the bottle of Moet Chandon. Laura reached for it and then quickly stepped back closer to the fireside. Holding the note to the light she read the following words;

Tell Laura I love her.
Tell Laura I need her.
Tell Laura not to cry,
My love for her will never die.

Laura's heart all but stopped. Was this some kind of cruel joke? Who was doing this to her? Something in the handwriting was familiar. Laura held the note closer to the light of the fire. She dismissed her next thought as insane, not to mention impossible. But insanity aside; she knew this hand writing. Those famous song lyrics held special meaning. Laura felt the presence of someone else. She grabbed the iron poker and stepped away from the fire, dropping the note into the grate. Whoever was there they were hidden from her view in the shadows, where as she would be easily visible in the fire light. Laura strained her eyes to see who was hiding from her in the darkness. Her voice trembling and sounding like a squeaky mouse, Laura nervously asked;

"Who's there?"

There was a noise in the doorway and a shadowy figure moved slowly across the room towards her. Laura gripped the iron poker. She was so afraid she clearly heard her own heartbeat thumping in her chest. As the silhouette of a tall male moved slowly closer to her, Laura thought she smelt cigarette smoke. Rigid with fear she pleaded;

"Who are you?"

A voice she knew only too well answered;

"Who do you want me to be?"

This was not possible. Surely she was hallucinating. The man's face caught the light from the fire. Laura's heart froze inside her chest. Her head swooned and she became faint, loosening her grip on the iron poker. It slipped from her hand clanging loudly, as it hit the tiled floor. Weak with shock Laura's legs buckled beneath her. She fell into unconsciousness and crumpled to the floor. The man rushed to her side. Leaning over Laura's limp body, he lifted her up into his arms and carried her to the sofa. Slowly Laura opened her eyes. She felt a warm hand smooth her brow. As her eyes tried to focus, they met with those of the concerned figure leaning over her, and he smiled the most radiant smile.

Had she died? Was she perhaps in heaven and this was an angels face she saw? Marcello must have crashed the Mercedes, or maybe the plane had crashed. She must have died or be dreaming? Struggling to comprehend, Laura again tried to focus her still blurry vision.

"It's okay you're safe. I'm here Loulou."

The familiarity in his voice with its strong masculine tone, made Laura doubt the reality of everything that had happened. No one called her Loulou except him; the one who had been her world, her night and day, owning her heart and in whose absence, life became meaningless. Was she now dead too? Laura supposed she must be. He came back for her as promised. How else could he be holding her in his arms? The light from the fires flickering flames lit up his face and his eyes twinkled like stars. Laura tried to sit up.

"Take it easy you're still in shock," he told her.

Laura's head spun like a fairground waltzer. Millions of thoughts and questions flooded her already fragile mind.

"But how, I don't understand? How can you be here?"

"Take it easy and I will tell you everything; but slowly when you are ready."

He stood and switched on the lamp. The light now fully revealed the face of the man she thought was lost forever; her Nicolas. Laura watched him walk towards the kitchen, still unsure if she were dreaming or hallucinating. In a moment he was back and handing Laura a glass of water.

"Here drink this," he said.

Laura took the glass from a very real flesh and blood hand. This was no phantom or figment of her imagination. He was back, Nicolas was back. Laura drank the water and stared at him as he sat beside her on the couch.

"You want me to get you some more?" He asked taking the empty glass from her shaking hand.

"No. Pass the champagne I need a drink," she told him determinedly.

Nicolas laughed. Taking the two Champagne flutes from the table he passed one to Laura who downed it in one go, then grabbed his and drank that one too.

"Hey! Slowly, since when did you drink like this?"

"Since my husband decided to reappear from the dead," she quipped.

He laughed and poured out another two glasses. He sat beside her and chinked his glass to hers;

"I love you girl. I've missed you Loulou. Tomorrow we will talk and I will explain everything. But tonight we are going to drink the champagne and we will make love like never before. Okay hayati?" He stood and picked up the champagne bottle. Taking hold of Laura's hand he said;

"Come love, we will have this night together without any questions being asked or answers given. Just be with me Loulou and I will make you forget all the bad."

Nicolas led her upstairs. Laura's head was spinning like a top. She wasn't sure if it was the champagne she had drunk too quickly causing her feelings of disorientation, or more likely, the fact that her husband had miraculously returned from beyond the grave. Laura was desperate to know exactly how he had returned, but for tonight the only words spoken would be by their hearts.

Nicolas eagerly removed Laura's top. His heartbeat quickened as she slipped out of the rest of her clothes, throwing them with abandon to the floor and pulling loose her pony tail allowing her hair to tousle seductively over her shoulders. Laura stood vision like before him. Feasting on her nakedness, Nicolas's eyes darkened; his pupils fully dilated as he savoured her delicately pale flesh.

447

Laura's hands trembled with anticipation as she undid his shirt buttons, impatiently ripping them open to reveal his golden toned, well defined torso. Within seconds he too was naked. Their eyes locked, as he placed his hands tightly around her tiny waist, persuasively pulling her to the bed. Hungry for her love he penetrated her quickly as they kissed passionately. Laura sighed with pleasure as Nicolas took her to heights of unparalleled bliss. Their burning carnal passions intensified, and raw savage desire took over. With a fevered intensity, they pleasured each other; kissing, licking and sucking as both bodies trembled with orgasmic delight at the others much longed for touch. Like starved Tigers released from captivity, each devoured the other with hungry passion.

Laura's fully awakened desire voraciously reclaimed its territory, avidly encouraged by Nicolas's erotic moans. He breathlessly whispered his sexually explicit yearnings into her ear. Laura responded, surrendering to his primal need. Freely and uninhibited, their bodies merged. Obsessively exploring every imaginable position, they indulged in pure sensual love making, which would put the Karma Sutra to shame.

Nicolas's pulsating moves made Laura vibrate with delirious pleasure. Lost in the moment she revelled in his familiar touch as it rhythmically re-awakened the sensual woman inside of her; a part of her she thought was destined to sleep forever. Overcome with emotion he could no longer refrain from climaxing. For a moment longer he sustained his energy, ensuring they came together. It was a skill that would be the envy of any man. What Nicolas was blessed with between his firm thighs would make Laura the envy of every woman.

With their lustful desires satisfied, they lay exhausted in an afterglow of ecstatic bliss. A silent dialogue passed between them, no words were capable of expressing such rapturous emotion. Laura traced her fingers gently over Nicolas's warm damp torso, and then placed her hand over his heart to check it really was still beating.

Nicolas smiled warmly but stayed silent. His thoughts were many, but he kept them locked in the back of his mind, allowing him to dwell longer in this revelry of utter contentment. Euphorically entranced, Laura looked into the eyes of the man she had mourned for nearly two years. All she would ever want or need was seen, as it reflected from his soul through those expressive dark eyes. Nicolas put his arm protectively around her, and Laura gently laid her head against his chest listening to the drumming of his heart, feeling its beat strong and clear. It was to her, the reassuring sound of home. Laura closed her eyes. She felt light years away from the person she was less than twenty four hours ago.

Embarking on this journey had taken courage; requiring Laura to face her fears and suspend her scepticism. The reward of her determined faith was being finally released from her perpetual suffering. Nicolas had returned to her from the land of the dead. Laura was reborn, as she felt her spirit evolve through him to become whole again. She didn't know how, but Kousbawi was back.

Safe in his arms Laura vowed never to let him go, or ever take for granted the treasure of his love. Nothing in the whole of creation would ever separate them again. Nicolas had been restored to her; resurrected and reborn like the mythical Phoenix of legend.

KOUSBAWI

Chapter 49: A Secret to Keep

Even the sweetest, truest, most rapturous love, can come with a bitter pill to swallow. Nicolas and Laura's night of unbridled passion, was nothing but a short reprise. Soon they would be returned to the unfortunate reality of their unusual situation, and forced to discover how bitter a pill it would really be. After the miraculous reunion, Laura woke from the deepest sleep she'd had in months. For the first time in what seemed like forever, she didn't wake with her heart feeling broken and heavy with grief; a feeling Laura had become so accustomed to, she wore it like a second skin.

So many times Laura had wished her life away, praying to be released from her sadness. For months she had lived amongst the dead; her soul wondering precariously within the darkness of the void, between this world and the next. Now feeling suddenly alive again, she was joyous; filled with renewed energy and zest. Her whole being shone, overflowing with joie de vivre and gratitude for life. Free from the heavy overcoat of depression, Laura felt light and reborn as she stretched her limbs. Not only her face, but her whole body smiled with innate happiness. She turned on her side fully expecting to see Nicolas beside her. She was startled to find herself alone in the bed.

"Please God don't let this be another dream. Tell me it did happen, please let him be alive."

Feeling panicked, Laura sat up and looked frantically around the room for signs of Nicolas. Not for the first time in the last twenty four hours, she seriously began to doubt her sanity. All the good her peaceful night's sleep had delivered, was now being rapidly erased.

"Hey sleepy girl, you want something to eat?"

Laura jumped; startled by Nicolas's sudden appearance in the doorway.

"Oh thank God. You are here. I thought for a moment I had dreamt it," Laura cried in relief.

"No not a dream love, I am here." Nicolas laughed at Laura's look of alleviation on seeing him, adding saucily, "Tell me truthfully Loulou; you have dreams about what we did last night?"

Laura's relieved expression, turned to one of self-consciousness. Giggling with embarrassment at Nicolas's saucy insinuation, she answered;

"No that was way beyond even my wildest dreams."

"Good, now move your ass from the bed and come and eat breakfast with me." He ordered. "And hurry, we have much to discuss Loulou."

Laura smiled. She had missed Nicolas's domineering bossy temperament; during his absence it appeared he had lost none of it. His thoughtfulness was also still intact. Nicolas had brought Laura's case and her things upstairs. As well as picking up her lustfully discarded clothes from the floor, he had lovingly placed them neatly over the back of the chair. Laura took her robe from the case and slipped it on. She quickly washed her face, brushed her teeth and hair, then hurried on down to the kitchen where Nicolas waited, contemplating his next move. Laura's heart danced with joy at the sight of him. He was sitting with his back to her, puffing on a cigarette. Seeing Nicolas smoking again strangely made her feel happy. The corners of her mouth rose in an expression of subtle amusement as she pondered the irony. He turned quickly around;

"Loulou, how are you? Fix your coffee love and come."

While making her coffee, Laura decided that from this moment on whatever Nicolas did, she would not complain about it.

"Come love sit, bring your coffee," he told her.

Laura sat down at the table opposite him. Nicky gave her a lingering look, and then asked;

"I made you happy last night?"

Laura looked into his eyes. Words could never express how much she had longed to gaze into them again.

"Yes," she told him, "you made me very happy."

Nicolas gave Laura a beguiling smile. With a familiar mischievous glint in his eyes he laughed, unashamedly declaring;

"And you remembered to be how I like it in the bed."

Laura blushed like a shy teenager, as Nicolas continued with his colourfully explicit sex talk; normally confined to the bedroom not the breakfast table. He laughed again. He was wickedly aware his outspoken, rather choice, sexually orientated vocabulary, embarrassed her.

"Nicky please!" Laura exclaimed, in a bashful tone.

"What?" he said, feigning innocence. "Who can hear? No one else is here, and Loulou don't pretend you don't like it. Right? I know what you like."

Laura lowered her eyes in shy reticence, and sipped her coffee. She felt a little silly at her embarrassed reaction and sudden reserve around her husband, especially after their carnal exploits of a few hours ago. When it came to sex, Nicolas had no inhibitions. Laura's coyness amused him. In spite of her blushes, she couldn't help smiling at the unsubtlety of his words. Nicolas had a way of saying things that could make even the most vulgar and obscene sound funny and inoffensive. Admittedly, she did find the way he delivered his sexual dialogue arousing.

Nicolas watched fondly as Laura sipped her coffee. He felt emotional; he couldn't take his eyes away. The past eighteen months had been as much of a hell for him as they had been for Laura. He too had endured moments of despair, exacerbated by the constant pressure that he may be betrayed and his secret uncovered. His deep desire to be reunited with Laura plagued him like an unquenchable thirst. Being unable to deny his heart indefinitely, Nicolas sought to bring her back to him, risking everything.

Despite how it might appear, he had not easily let her go. Now she sat in front of him, wearing the smile that for so long he could only imagine. Laura looked up and caught him studying her. Nicolas saw behind her big green eyes, the innocence and vulnerability; all he had originally fallen in love with remained untarnished by the fall-out of his deception. This slightly eased his conscience. Nicolas wouldn't blame Laura if she were to be angry at being so deceived.

In retrospect he may have chosen to handle things very differently. When backed into a corner, Nicolas as always acted impulsively. At the time he feared the repercussions may endanger Laura. Better to risk his own liberty, than subject her to his unpredictable fate. Samra's accidental shooting by one of his enemies, had caused him to be rigidly protective of Laura.

Eighteen months ago Nicolas's original agenda was hastily revised at the eleventh hour, pushing him into this clandestine existence. Afforded the luxury of a less impetuous nature and time to think, he may have been swayed from fulfilling his mission in quite the way he did. The consequences of hesitation, he believed at the time would have put him and possibly Laura, fatally at risk. The magnitude of his deception and the implications it carried, would soon have to be explained to her. But for a while longer, Nicolas would enjoy being with the woman whose love he could not forsake, before forced to upset their harmonious reunion.

Laura couldn't be angry with Nicolas for his deception. Just as the father of the prodigal son hurt by his offspring's wayward actions, could only celebrate when his son finally returned home, Laura felt only rapturous joy at the return of her husband. Nicolas searched for the words to explain the irreversible fallout of events that took place eighteen months ago, and which had brought him here.

Nicolas switched from his light-hearted demeanour, substituting it for moody solemnity. With a pained intense expression, he stared mournfully into space. The look signified distinct unease with whatever he was obliged to divulge. His reticence wasn't without good reason. He had displayed nerves of steel and supreme bravado in carrying out a dangerous risky charade, and in the face of it hadn't blinked once.

Contrastingly, revealing the inescapable aftermath of his bold but headstrong actions to Laura was troubling. Nicolas's big secret was a haunting burden, a burden which he would no longer carry alone. Leaning forward he reached for Laura's hand across the table.

"Loulou you know I love you, right?"

"Of course I know," Laura assured, gripping his hand tightly. Nicolas was uncharacteristically unsure of himself, and his dithering hesitant behaviour continued.

"Make me coffee and we will sit and talk."

Nicolas lit a cigarette and walked to the lounge. Laura made two coffees and followed him. He seated himself in a chair near the fireplace. Laura set the coffees down on the small table beside him. Sitting in the chair opposite she waited. She had a feeling Nicolas's imminent disclosure was not going to be easy to digest; but since when had anything in their fateful relationship ever been easy? Laura braced herself.

"Loulou listen, listen to me carefully," he started. Then stalling once again, stubbed out his cigarette immediately lighting another. Under normal circumstances Laura would have berated him for chain smoking, but she said nothing.

"I dunno love how to tell you," he began. His voice faltered, stumbling over his words which fractured with emotion as he spoke. The constant long pauses were not Nicolas's usual deliberate playfulness. His approach was notably uncertain and guarded. Laura felt chills as she readied herself for the bombshell about to drop.

"Just tell me," she pleaded.

It was warm and cosy in front of the fire. But Laura shivered; her body temperature dropped with trepidation of what she clearly detected wouldn't be welcome news. Exhaling the smoke from his lungs Nicolas stubbed out his cigarette and continued;

"I don't know Loulou where to begin. You know love, I'm not a selfish person, but I feel I've been selfish." Nicolas looked at Laura's worried face. He was unable to hide the emotion in his eyes as they became moist with the tears that were forming; but he didn't let them flow. This was not a look Laura had seen often in him. He looked remorseful; regret was another emotion Laura had rarely seen him portray. Nicolas was always so self-assured with any decision taken. This unprecedented challenge to the wisdom of his judgement was as much a shock for him to experience, as it was for Laura to witness. He began again;

"Maybe I made a mistake. It would have been better if I had not brought you here."

Laura felt a lump form in her throat. Hearing him say he had made a mistake by reuniting with her, was painful. But her husband wasn't finished, Nicolas continued;

"Better you believe I'm dead, better for you I mean. It was selfish of me to turn your world upside down again, to place this on your head after what you already faced."

Staring disbelievingly into Nicolas's tear moistened eyes, Laura wanted to scream at him; how dare he presume she would be better off still believing him dead! Raising her voice Laura exclaimed;

"Are you crazy? Do you know how close to the edge I've been?" Like Nicolas's, Laura's tears were waiting in line ready to be expelled. Repressed by the anger now fuelling her enraged emotions, they held back as Laura continued to rave at a stunned Nicolas;

"Since the day I was told you had died I've been living in a never ending bad dream. I don't know if I could have survived much longer. My life has been hell. You left me with nothing and I had no one! You were everything to me, without you my world disintegrated."

Nicolas felt every fibre of Laura's pain pierce his soul. It echoed and reverberated around his subconscious as if it was his pain; in a way it was. During their separation, he had mirrored every emotion Laura experienced. Nicolas had been mourning the loss of a great love too. With her anger released, Laura's tears were now free to burst forth, which they did; flooding out like a river bursting its banks. Nicolas moved out of his chair to hold her.

"Let it out, let it all out," he soothingly encouraged, as

Laura sobbed hysterically in his arms.

It was disturbing to see her this fragile. He now took solace in the knowledge that what he considered a mistake, clearly wasn't. It took time for Laura to calm. Eventually she did. Nicolas had just witnessed first-hand, how hard his death had affected her; it shook him to his core. Laura was strong, but how much more she could handle he didn't know. With more revelations to endure, Laura would need to find strength again. Nicolas wondered did she have it; was there any fight left in her?

"This has been too hard Loulou I know; believe me I didn't want to put you through any of it." He kissed her gently on the forehead. "Hayati I know you didn't receive proper support or help, or your rights as my wife. Love, I would never have left you with nothing believe me. People have behaved very badly. Believe me Loulou, one day they will face Al Hajj; they will answer to me."

Nicolas reached for his cigarettes. Laura passed him the packet of Marlborough lights. He took out a cigarette. After lighting it he continued talking;

"What they did it made me so angry. Love I swear to you, nothing will go unpunished." Nicolas had a steely unyielding look, the one he projected when planning to exact retribution.

Witnessing his determined expression, Laura smiled. For once she whole heartedly agreed; some people need to learn the hard way. Whether believing him alive or dead, there are lines you do not cross with Al Hajj. In this world or the next he will never let it go. Nicolas's eyes softened again and he continued;

"But you know Loulou, I am not surprised; people are selfish, too greedy. But Loulou I know how strong you are. You're a fighter like me." Taking a tissue from the box on the table he handed it to Laura. She patted her tear stained face and looked at him; plainly Nicolas had suffered too. Instantly Laura forgave him everything.

"I wasn't always strong," Laura confessed, "there were many times I almost broke completely."

Laura admitted reaching untold depths of despair where she had even contemplated taking her own life, finding it too unbearable to continue living without him. After such a confession Laura reluctantly met Nicolas's gaze. She was waiting for him to shout and tell her she was stupid. He didn't. Instead Nicolas held her close, hugging her tight like a protective father.

"What if I hadn't made it? What if in a moment of unbearable grief I ended my life?"

"But love, you didn't."

"What if I had? You couldn't be sure; I wasn't sure."

Nicolas became visibly disturbed. The thought of Laura not surviving to be with him now, was unthinkable. He looked deep into her eyes.

"To play a game with your life was not my intention. If anything happen to you I would feel responsible. Loulou it would be as if by my hand. I would not accept it."

Nicolas looked away unable to reconcile his conscience with such a grave thought. Laura felt a twinge of guilt at telling him. He picked up his coffee. It was cold but he drank it anyway. Determined to lighten their rather morbid conversation Nicolas added in a more light-hearted tone;

"Because Loulou, do you know why? Why I would not accept it?" he gave a husky chuckle. "Because love, you were not on my list." He laughed again in a deliberate bid to lift the repressed mood. Nicolas's dark humour worked bringing a smile to Laura's sombre face. Then totally changing the subject he exclaimed;

"Loulou we didn't eat yet and I am hungry. How about you love, you want to eat something?"

"Yes I am hungry. But you must have much more to tell me surely?" She queried.

Nicolas moved Laura away from his arms. Standing up he told her;

"Slowly love. First of all we will eat. And second of all, you know what? I'm ravenous." Nicolas laughed proudly proclaiming, "You see Loulou how my English is good now."

He walked towards the kitchen telling her;

"After, I begin my story. I don't want to put too much on your head in one time. First girl, we eat something."

Laura smiled and got up to follow him. Nicolas opened the fridge and began taking food out. He felt Laura was still fragile; too many shocks at once he believed could have a devastating effect. Nicolas may have gone on to tell Laura everything if she hadn't broken down. He intended to tread more carefully; the last eighteen months had taken an enormous toll.

"What would you like me to make?" Laura asked.

Nicolas had his head in the fridge mooching for ideas of what to eat. He took more food out telling Laura;

"You Loulou will make nothing. Today I am going to make for you."

"You're going to cook?" Laura gave a surprised look.

"Yep!" He proclaimed assertively. "Remember Loulou when I used to cook for you?"

Remembering those times filled her with a warm fuzzy glow. Back in the 'Cave', it had been the highlight of Laura's day eating the delicious meals he would serve up.

"But you don't enjoy cooking," she reminded him.

"I don't mind. I want you to relax, and let me take care of you," he insisted.

Laura sat at the table. It felt like taking a step back in time as she watched her husband prepare her a meal. She was his princess again. In time the emotional wounds would heal. Slowly Laura would regain her energy and strength. She was going to need a lot of strength to cope with what Nicolas would soon be asking of her.

After eating they decided to sleep for a short while. No matter where he was, Nicolas didn't break habits easily; he still enjoyed his afternoon siesta. Laura snuggled up close holding him tight for fear he may suddenly disappear into the ether. Nicolas became aroused at her touch.

"Loulou what are you doing? You didn't have enough last night?" he laughed naughtily.

Laura tenderly kissed his shoulder telling him;

"I can never have enough of you."

Now fully aroused, Nicolas turned to face her and they made love. Not quite as energetically as the night before, but slow passionate and tender. A day ago, Laura could only dream of having another moment of intimacy with her husband. His warm touch felt like heaven. The deep longing in her heart was again satisfied as they intimately caressed. The question of exactly how Nicolas had cheated death was on hold; Laura was yet to be enlightened to the answer. For now all that mattered was, he was alive. As Nicolas slept Laura lay content beside him, hypnotised by the rhythm of his breathing. How precious it was to hear, how precious to know his heart was beating strong inside his chest. Laura smiled as she lay there, amused at the irony of him reappearing in Transylvania. Of all the places Nicolas could have chosen to come back to her. Like the vampires of legend, he had risen from the dead. Laura's eyes grew heavy. Soon she joined her resurrected husband in restful sleep.

The sound of running water gently lifted Laura from her peaceful slumber. She glanced at the clock on the bedside table. It was 4pm; Laura had slept for an hour and a half. Nicolas was taking a shower. Laura crept to the bathroom and silently watched him. Everything he did mesmerised her; his pure masculinity held her spellbound. The passage of time had not lessoned their attraction; the chemistry felt on that first encounter remained undiluted. Laura's eyes were exotically transfixed as soap bubbles cascaded over his lithe torso. Rinsing the soap suds from his face, Nicolas shook his head and opened his eyes to see Laura standing there. He stretched out his hand to her;

"Come Loulou."

Laura took Nicolas's hand and joined him under the warm soft water. It felt good on her skin as did the feel of his strong hands massaging shower gel into her shoulders and back. Moving his hands over her smooth wet skin, Nicolas became absorbed in Laura's sensual femininity. How easily she managed to arouse him.

He felt the blood coarse to his lower regions. His heart rate gathered speed and before he could help himself he was inside her. Laura moaned with pleasure as he kissed the back of her neck. His hands tightened their grip around her narrow hips as his penetration deepened. The warm water stimulated as it cascaded over them exciting their arousal, causing them to climax quickly.

"Yeah….yeah, was good Loulou?"

Laura smiled in agreement as Nicolas stepped from the shower wrapping a towel around him. He grinned saucily telling her;

"I like to fuck you this way. If you stay with me Loulou I am going to fuck you like this more often."

He started drying himself vigorously. Laura turned off the shower and Nicolas passed her a clean towel.

"What do you mean if I stay with you?" she questioned, wondering why he might think she wouldn't.

Nicolas was evasive telling her;

"Love, dry yourself quickly before you catch cold; after we will talk."

He walked quickly from the bathroom and down the stairs, wearing only the large white towel around his waist. Laura dried herself and hurriedly looked for something to wear. Remembering Nicolas's shirt was in the pocket of her case; Laura took it out and slipped it on, then hastily followed him downstairs.

Nicolas attended to the smouldering remains of the fire. He fed it another log immediately reviving its dying embers. Gradually the flames built, throwing out a rush of welcome heat into the room. Being high up in the mountains it was chilly outside. The chalet was cosily warm, with a log burner in the kitchen as well as the open fire in the lounge. Nicolas sat in the chair next to the fire and lit a cigarette. He didn't have much time to collect his thoughts before Laura was sitting in the chair opposite.

Tucking her legs underneath her, Laura clutched tightly to a large cushion. Her expression was one of questioning as she looked at Nicolas. Her eyes wide, Laura implored answers from him. Nicolas felt under pressure to start explaining. His train of thought was suddenly interrupted. Nicolas's face broke into a broad smile. His whole being lit up, radiating with the same bright intensity as the flames from the fire. Like an excited child he exclaimed;

"My shirt! I love that shirt."

"I have your bible and your worry beads too," Laura told him.

"I love you girl." He gave Laura an adoring look. "But before I can tell you the whole story you have to decide."

Laura watched as he walked to the fridge to get some ice. After putting five cubes into a glass, he walked over to the side cabinet and poured a large whisky, sipping it as he walked back and took his place again by the fire. Nicolas gave Laura a long quizzical look. Laura returned a similar expression, her inquiring eyes pushing him to continue.

"What I am going to ask will be hard for you." Nicolas took another sip from his whisky. "If you accept, I swear I will do everything to make you happy."

Laura remained silent; she didn't dare wonder what he was going to say. Nicolas once again was visibly on edge. He was risking everything and about to ask Laura to make a huge sacrifice. He hesitated to do so;

"But maybe it's too much? Loulou I will understand if you refuse."

Laura didn't say a word. Her uncharacteristic silence worried him, but at the same time he was thankful that for once she wasn't interrupting; something Laura was prone to do whenever he was talking.

"Hayati I love you and I want you with me forever. But I love you enough to let you go if I have to."

Laura was confused. She had just got him back; what could he possibly ask to make her consider leaving him? Anxious to get it over with, Laura pleaded with him;

"Tell me Nicky, please just tell me,"

"Love I'm sorry. If there was another way, believe me. One day maybe when some time pass, but not yet." He dragged hard on his cigarette.

"I'm sorry love it has to be this way for now."

Her imagination was going wild; Laura wanted him to put her out of her misery.

"Nicky you have to say it."

"Loulou if you want to be with me, to stay with me, you have to stay from now."

Laura had an idea what Nicolas was implying. If she was right, it explained his reluctance. Her heart fell heavy; she uttered not a word but listened as her husband revealed the sacrifice their being together would require.

"If I tell you everything Loulou and you still wanna stay, you cannot go back to your old life and be with me. It would be too risky." Nicolas had searched for a way to break this gently; there was no easy way, so he just said it; "Love, you cannot come and go like before. Someone may put two and two together. You stay now, or you go and forget everything." He quickly lit another cigarette.

It was a mere distraction to avoid seeing the anguish in Laura's eyes. Laura remained silent trying to comprehend the implications of what he was asking. Nicolas needed to ensure his secret remained secret. He had come too far, risked too much to slip up now.

"To stay with me you must leave everything without looking back. Laura you will become dead as I have. I need you to trust me. You understand Loulou? To stay with me, to be with me, Laura you must disappear."

Nicolas couldn't allow his emotions to get in the way. If Laura was unable to accept the sacrifice it would be better she leave; and the sooner the better. Nicolas loved his wife and would in a heartbeat give his life for her. Unfortunately he couldn't turn back the clock and undo what had already been set in stone. To the world Nicolas was dead; if Laura chose to stay she must now embrace a similar fate.

There was nothing Laura would regret leaving, but for Alyssa. Why did it have to come back to this? Why was she always torn, forced to choose between the people she loved? What effect would her sudden disappearance have?

462

How could she gamble with Alyssa's life, to be with the man who was her life? For twenty four hours Laura had been cocooned in a bubble of joyful bliss. Finding Nicolas again, she had come home; she was whole again. That secure happy bubble rapidly began deflating, as the reality and consequences of his deception pierced Laura's blissful state, causing it to evaporate all around her.

"If you cannot accept, I will understand hayati."

Laura wanted to cry but for once the tears wouldn't come. Maybe she was all cried out? Nicolas continued; "It's okay love. You will return to Bucharest and fly back to London. I will arrange for money to be sent to you. If this is what you choosing I will arrange it today."

Laura detected Nicolas's tone had hardened slightly and become matter of fact. It was a front, he was preparing for Laura's choice to be other than what he wished her to make. For many months Nicolas agonised hour upon hour, debating whether it was right to let Laura know he was alive. Reuniting with her had not been a rash decision, he had taken it with his eyes open to the possibility it may not turn out as he hoped. Laura could easily have chosen not to travel to Bucharest. Nicolas was a gambler by heart; risk taking was part of his make-up. If Laura chose to walk away now, it would break his heart. At least he would have given it his best shot. Now it was up to her.

"Love listen, if you go we cannot have any contact. No one must know the truth. Do you understand Laura?"

Laura was rendered speechless at the impossible choice. Nicolas felt bad for putting this pressure on her. Letting Laura in on his secret had perhaps been a selfish move. Nicolas's manner remained serious. He lit another cigarette and looked at Laura; she felt his eyes penetrate her soul. Laura contemplated their doomed fate. The blood drained from her veins; sucked out of her as if by Dracula himself. Nicolas looked at his wife's pale face. The pain in her eyes was evident; it made his heart bleed with remorse. Nicolas softened his manner.

"Are you okay Loulou? I'm sorry, if I could make it

another way, but I cannot come back to you the way you wish it, I cannot live that life." Laura's continued silence bothered him. "Listen, Loulou you don't need to decide right now. Love, take some time."

Laura was still clutching the cushion, she felt numb as her mind wondered back over the horrendous events of the last couple of years. Nicolas moved to her side taking her hand. It felt cold as he wrapped his fingers tightly around it. To be the cause of her torment disturbed him. Knowing her husband was alive had changed everything for Laura. Whichever route she now chose, knowing he lived brought tremendous solace.

"You know love; perhaps it would be better for you to have never met me," he stated remorsefully.

His statement shook Laura from her silence;

"What? Why would you say that?"

"I mean, for you it would be better. Love I was fucking trouble maker. But I swear I never wanted to hurt you. I'm sorry, I'm sorry I did this to you. Forgive me Loulou."

Laura stood up from her seat dropping the cushion she had been clutching. She walked across the room. Putting her hands to her head she grappled with her conscience. Turning quickly back she looked her husband in the eye;

"I have made my decision," she announced suddenly.

Surprised by the speed of her answer he told her;

"Love, there's no rush to decide, take your time."

"I don't need more time." She told him assertively. "I don't regret a moment of knowing you, loving you and even losing you; and if you had not come back to me now, I still wouldn't change anything; not even to avoid the pain I went through. Nothing would be as bad as never having you in my life."

Nicolas listened as his wife poured out her soul;

"You taught me so much, and gave so much. You made me a woman. Because of you I came to know myself. You showed me how to be myself. I am more myself when I'm with you than without you. Loving you completes me."

Nicolas felt his eyes become misty with tears as Laura

further confessed her love.

"My love for you is limitless with no boundaries. I love my daughter desperately, she is everything to me, but she's strong and will survive without me, but Nicky I cannot survive another day without you."

Nicolas brushed the tears from his eyes and embraced Laura. Holding to each other tightly they sobbed. Through his tears Nicolas made Laura a firm promise;

"I swear to you Loulou I will find a way to reunite you with Alyssa. Just give me time to figure it. One day the three of us will be together as we planned. Believe me hayati I will make everything be okay. Just give me little time."

Laura smiled;

"I know you will make it okay, I trust you with all my heart. That is why I am staying." She hugged him closer.

"Hayati, you know I love Alyssa. I will arrange for her to have money. After all she is my daughter, and this hurts me too. One day we will be together; all of us."

Taking hold of Laura's left hand Nicolas undid her gold bracelet.

"What are you doing?" Laura asked confused by his action. Nicolas put the bracelet on the table.

"Loulou I told you, you have to leave everything."

Laura was astonished;

"But my bracelet," she protested. "It was your wedding gift to me. I never take it off."

Nicolas gave his wife a stern look;

"Laura if you cannot lose even your bracelet how you can tell me you are ready to give up everything?"

This was a test? Nicolas needed to be sure Laura knew what was at stake. He became vexed. His serious manner returned;

"Maybe you should forget this and return to London. I don't want you to make a decision you cannot live with."

Laura was taken aback by his sudden change of tone; it was clearly meant as a reminder that this was no game.

Nicolas turned his back. Lighting a cigarette he walked

away from Laura. Even with his back turned away from her, Laura detected the tension in his demeanour. Pain lay beneath his anger. Nicolas was not angry with Laura, but with the situation he had knowingly imposed upon them; however difficult this was for her, it was equally so for him to reconcile. Laura moved over to him. Placing her arms around his waist, she hugged him tightly from behind refusing to loosen her grip, until she felt his tension ease. No matter what the situation Nicolas had to be the man. He hated to show weakness; even to Laura whom he loved beyond measure. But at times he felt like a wounded soldier; one who had fought too many battles. Eventually Nicolas's tension ebbed. Laura felt his angered frustration subside as his attitude gradually softened.

"I don't need a bracelet," Laura assured. "I have you, and that is all I will ever need," she told him sincerely.

Nicolas still had his back to Laura so she didn't see his face break into a broad relieved smile. He stubbed out the cigarette he'd been smoking in the silver ashtray on the dining table in front of him. Turning around to face Laura he deliberately let the towel slip from his waist. Gripping her by the shoulders he vowed;

"I'm going to make you happy; Loulou I promise you won't regret your decision to stay with me."

Sliding his hands under the shirt Laura was wearing, he eagerly explored her naked flesh beneath it. Gently he pushed her to her knees. Laura followed his lead, keen to encourage his growing passion. For the third time that day they made love.

The flames from the fire flickered, dancing seductively as if mimicking the lover's passionate moves. But even with its provocative flames, the fire paled in the presence of their burning desire, as the inseparable couple generated their own fiery heat. With its unprecedented difficulties, their love affair defied logic. Yet it survived to become stronger than ever. In a manner of speaking their love had conquered death itself.

KOUSBAWI

Chapter 50: Masquerade

Over the next few days Nicolas revealed the extraordinary tale surrounding his miraculous return. Totally enthralled, Laura listened as he explained an incredulous story to her, outlining the events that led him to fake his own death.

Three weeks prior to his 'death', he received an ominous warning from his contacts in Lebanon. A name from his hit list, an enemy designated as a problem to be eliminated in due course, had learned that Nicolas now had access to his passport and was free to travel outside of the Emirates.

Believing Al Hajj would now seek his sworn revenge; this old adversary decided to act first; arranging an assassin to travel to Abu Dhabi. The intent was to dispose of Al Hajj before Al Hajj came looking for him. Inadvertently, but luckily for Nicolas, this enemy let slip his fatal intentions.

Leaked details of the deadly plot were picked up by the ears of those holding allegiance to Al Hajj. Alerted to this most recent attempt on his life, Nicolas was quick to act.

With help from his 'people', the lethal plan was intercepted and prevented from being accomplished.

Laura never knew who his 'people' were, but Nicolas had alluded to them many times over the years. She presumed they would be some clandestine underworld network; Nicolas had connections everywhere.

Before this latest assassination attempt, Nicolas had an agenda of his own in place. Planning to travel undercover and using the element of surprise, Nicolas would go to Lebanon and dispose of his problems (enemies), in one fell swoop; fulfilling his long standing vow of vengeance.

With yet another attempt on his life, returning to Lebanon with Laura would be troublesome, while his enemies lived. Nicolas's notoriety (especially in Kousba), meant he had an image to live up to. In the past he had wielded a certain amount of power and control. Al Hajj did not wish to lose face, or the respect he had grown accustomed to by failing to fulfil his solemn oath to take revenge. Not doing so would send the wrong message to his enemies; Al Hajj had gone soft and was no longer to be feared.

Nicolas believed he would not only be subject to ridicule, but would put himself and those close to him at risk. Nicolas intended to keep Laura in the UK out of harm's way, while he carried out his secret mission. His original plan was to tell her he had business requiring him to go to the desert, under the pretext he was investigating possible construction sites. Nicolas would exact his long awaited revenge without Laura needing to know anything. Once the deed was accomplished she would return to Abu Dhabi none the wiser.

A look of sudden realisation came across Laura's face as she began connecting the dots. Nicolas's procrastination over the antiques and her return to Abu Dhabi, suddenly made sense as the real reason for his stalling emerged.

"So that is why you were dragging your feet?"

"I didn't want you to worry. I was going to finish my 'problem' in quick time; three days only, and I would have finished everything."

Laura sat silent and wide-eyed, amazed at his shocking disclosure. Undaunted by his own mortality, her intrepid husband had constantly been readying himself to one day face off his enemies. He would half-jokingly raise the subject many times; even openly admitting his intent to Laura in the recording he had sent her. She had hoped, somewhat naively perhaps, it was light-hearted bravado. Unfortunately that was just wishful thinking on Laura's part. For Nicolas, seeking his sworn revenge was a serious aspiration. He would sooner risk death than break his vow of honour; his honour was everything.

Nicolas paused from his extraordinary narrative. He got up and poured another whisky before divulging any more facts. Whisky in hand, Nicolas sat down. After getting comfortable, he went on to tell Laura how the unexpected turn of events had forced him to take a more drastic line of action. With his enemies alerted to his new found liberty, everything changed; Nicolas had lost that crucial element of surprise.

The success of his original agenda hinged on catching his targets unprepared. Being forewarned of his freedom to travel, they would now be expecting the inevitable return of Al Hajj; making Nicolas's mission more perilous. With help from a few trusted allies, he formulated his felonious deception at the eleventh hour. Nicolas surmised no one would accuse a dead man for the death of his enemies. The decision to follow through with this dangerous ruse was instinctively driven by his natural headstrong tendencies. Despite the huge sacrifice on Nicolas's part, he felt time was slipping by, and he could never truly be at peace until he had upheld his sworn vow. Either that, or for the rest of his life be looking over his shoulder. Al Hajj's enemies wanted the threat of him gone. While Nicolas was unable to leave Abu Dhabi, they slept easy in their beds.

With everyone believing him dead, Nicolas was able to sneak into Lebanon via the back door. His enemies had let down their guard and like a thief in the night, Al Hajj caught them unaware. Finally he eliminated the names from his infamous hit list. Exact details were not disclosed to Laura and she didn't ask. But you could be sure Al Hajj would have been unyielding and relentless in his methods.

The guaranteed closed mouthedness of those in on the deception was pivotal; they were carefully chosen. Crucial to successfully pulling off this daring masquerade, was a qualified medic who would officially pronounce Nicolas dead at the apartment. Another was engaged to distract people, insuring no one got too close to his body. Once the scene was set, the alarm was raised. Of course Nicolas was merely comatose, having ingested a carefully formulated solution of a herb and morphine based drug. This was prepared with help from his underworld medically trained co-conspirator. The drug would lower Nicolas's heart rate just enough to convincingly mimic death, and temporarily render him unconscious.

This bold charade was not without great risk. Nicolas's body was swiftly removed from the apartment and taken to a commissioned ambulance. Safely inside the ambulance, the hired medic worked quickly to rouse Nicolas from his self-induced coma. After being roused, Nicolas put on a paramedic's uniform. With the authorities alerted to a 'death', a substitute body was required. So a man working for them on the inside at the hospital ensured they were able to perform their next task, without arousing suspicion. With the insiders help, a switch was made with the body of a man of similar height, build and appearance; a temporary substitute for the supposedly deceased Nicolas. This would have been the body Laura viewed at the mortuary. Nicolas had been kept informed of everything whilst remaining under-cover. He told Laura;

"Yeah, you bloody my people were worried. You were saying it wasn't looking like your husband," he laughed.

"They were there?" she asked.

"Two of them; but Loulou you were not supposed to be at the morgue. No one was supposed to see that body; we needed it for paperwork only. When everyone turned up at the morgue, it was fucking scary time; believe me we were on our nerves. But thanks' the God, only you Loulou was suspicious."

Nicolas laughed as he recollected the intensely nerve wracking moment when he was informed that Laura along with umpteen others, had gathered at the morgue.

"I was right. I knew that wasn't you. But everyone else accepted it was, and I was so in shock I just went along with what I was told. Something felt wrong though, I just couldn't put my finger on it."

Laura became pensive as her mind drifted back to that awful day, recalling how she had heard whispering and felt a distinct tension as she viewed the body, insisting it didn't look like Nicolas.

"You know for quite a while I did believe you had been killed, assassinated," she told him.

"And you know Loulou if it hadn't been for my people

470

alerting me, who knows? Maybe I would be."

Nicolas stared into space; his dark eyes widened. They shone in the firelight and he looked momentarily wistful. Suddenly a wry smile crept across his face;

"But no one can kill me," he began laughing; "Because I am Al Hajj, right Loulou?"

Nicolas clasped Laura's hand, grinning proudly as he recalled his astonishing masquerade. He couldn't resist indulging in a little conceited amazement at his own daring genius. But the arrogance soon gave way to an expression of pensive melancholy. With a long drawn out breath, he gave a deep melancholic sigh, declaring;

"You know Loulou? I have done many things in this fucking life, some good, some bad and some very bad. But I would do them all again if I had to," he said resolutely, his attitude was uncompromising. He instinctively reached for the packet of Marlborough while continuing with his reflective thoughts. After lighting it, he puffed hard on his cigarette giving a little cough as he exhaled the smoke. He then forcibly cleared his throat. It was dry from all the talking. He relieved it with a swig of whisky, before continuing in a somewhat raspy tone; "But love, I regret nothing; not even this. And Loulou you know I cannot go back," he confessed.

There was a hint of nostalgic longing in his expression and tone. Nicolas smiled but remained pensive. Again he stared blankly into space as though momentarily stunned; perhaps for the very first time he was fully realising the ramifications of his reckless actions.

Behind that enigmatic smile lay a world of complex emotions. Maybe only Laura really understood him. Once she asked him what he feared most. Nicolas had answered her without reservation, telling Laura;

"Nothing scares me Loulou; except one thing, myself."

Nicolas knew he was headstrong and often acted too impulsively. But he had fire in his soul and when fuelled by his intense passions, the fire inside him would rage and fulminate; when ignited it would blaze quicker than a spark can set fire to a tinder dry forest. Nicolas would never apologise to anyone for being who he was.

Perhaps Laura saw him differently to others? To her he was a brave individualist; a true maverick. Nicolas was in her eyes the stuff of heroes and legends. He was Laura's enchanting Prince Charming and her Rhett Butler. Merge those characteristics with the dark tortured passions of Emily Bronte's Heathcliff, and the brave warrior spirit of Hector, (the Trojan hero from Homers Iliad), and there you have Nicolas. But none of these characters on their own could adequately sum him up; he was bits of them all and more. Not averse to allowing those darker tendencies to surface, especially when honour was at stake, Nicolas was a self-confessed bad boy, a non-conformist and a rebel.

Darkness though dwells in us all; but for most, the need or even the courage to act on it, rarely arises. Nicolas was only too aware of the reputation he carried. There was kudos to be gained for anyone claiming to have taken out Al Hajj. It made him and those close, a target. This reality was nearly fatally realised with the fortuitous shooting of his first wife Samra.

A long subdued silence prevailed, abruptly interrupted when Laura suddenly asked,

"Why choose to die from a heart attack? Would it not have been easier and less risky to stage an accident?"

Nicolas didn't answer straight away. Instead he took another cigarette from the packet of Marlborough lights on the table beside him. After lighting it, he looked intently at Laura before giving her his answer. Putting his cigarette to his lips and narrowing his eyes as he inhaled, he told her;

"Because love, this way only the God has taken me, and no one of my enemies can say they killed Al Hajj."

Laura smiled; even in death Nicolas would not allow his enemies to get the better of him. He poured another large whisky. Laura watched as he walked to the kitchen to get some ice. He moved with such a confident swagger. Laura found it sexy.

Nicolas could drink heavily, but in all the years they

472

had been together, never had Laura known Nicolas to look, sound, or act drunk. Nicolas would handle his booze like a man; to be seen drunk, was another unacceptable weakness he would not allow. As she watched him, Laura silently contemplated the far reaching consequences of Nicolas's irreversible and drastic actions.

Their eyes met as he walked back from the kitchen,

"You know Loulou," he said as he came towards her. "As I said, I have done many things. But no one time did I do anything bad to anyone, who didn't deserve it."

In his heart he wished things could be otherwise; but he felt vindicated. Nicolas sat down in the chair and studied Laura's expression. His piercing gaze gave her tingles.

"You believe me Loulou?" he asked. "You understand I had to do it, I gave my word."

"Yes, but no one knows Nicky; no one except you and I will ever know you kept your vow."

Expressing a look of contented gratification, Nicolas smiled. Referring to his now extinguished enemies, he proudly told Laura;

"They knew Loulou, believe me they knew."

When Al Hajj exacted his long awaited revenge, his enemies knew he had finally come for them.

Surprisingly, Laura had few qualms pertaining to his extreme form of justice. Quite the contrary, knowing the objectives behind his thirst for revenge, rightly or wrongly Laura regarded it as highly defensible. Nicolas leant back in his chair resting one foot up on the small table. Puffing nonchalantly on his cigarette, he expressed a look of indulgent satisfaction. Laura could feel his relief at finally fulfilling his pledge.

Predictably and as always, when one problem is solved another pops up in its place. Ironically, Al Hajj could now never return to his homeland. Nicolas was okay with this; the Lebanon he craved was the old Lebanon, not the one it had become in the quarter century he had been absent. His Lebanon, the one he grew up in and remembered with such fondness was gone, but would remain forever in his heart.

473

Considering the ingenuity of his incredulous deception, Laura revelled at the unfair irony.

Watching Laura's confused expression as she struggled to digest his shocking revelations, Nicolas smiled. Her thoughts were so readable; he could practically see them forming in her mind. As she began processing everything, Laura's next realisation was rather predictable.

"Hang on a minute," she started, "I sat with your body in the church in Kousba and it looked exactly like you."

"You mean I look like a corpse?" He kidded trying to look insulted.

"No, you know what I mean, how did you do it?" She asked mystified.

Laura waited with bated breath, intent on knowing all the details. Just how exactly, did Nicolas manage to pull off his elaborate masquerade? Giving Laura another one of his lingering determined looks, Nicolas slowly stubbed out his cigarette. He smiled teasingly at Laura's face, which was a picture. She looked totally awe-struck, like a child waiting to hear the end of an exciting fairy-tale. He loved to play with her. Taking another sip of his whisky, he deliberately dragged out the suspense.

"Well?" she said impatiently.

"Wait a minute!" he playfully snapped.

Nicolas lit his cigarette very slowly, purposely teasing and cruelly keeping Laura in suspense a little while longer. Finally he began divulging another fascinating sequence. Laura sat in silence, spell-bound as Nicolas talked.

He described how an artist was commissioned to make him a mask. First a caste was made of his face, and from the mould a latex mask was constructed which perfectly depicted his bone structure and features. These features were then enhanced by careful painting, to add the very recognisable markings of Nicolas's own face; including the darker pigmentation of the four large freckles on his cheek. Because of the shape they formed, Nicolas always referred to these flat moles as, his mark of the cross.

The completed mask was then taken to Lebanon and

given to a bribed mortician, to be placed over the face of the chosen replacement for Nicolas's body. Finally, with the morticians cleverly applied makeup techniques and the right hair styling, the finished result gave a convincing likeness, which easily passed for the deceased Nicolas.

"So when did all this happen? Whose body was used?" Laura asked hungry for every last detail.

"Love you always have to know everything?" he joked, adding, "But if I tell you everything Loulou, I will have to kill you." Seeing the sceptical look in Laura's eyes he laughed wickedly; "What you think I would kill you?" He laughed again proclaiming; "But love, I cannot kill you; you are not on my list." Still jesting he added wickedly; "Maybe one day, but not today. Okay Loulou?"

Continuing with his tale, Nicolas went on to illustrate how an unclaimed body from a morgue in Lebanon was used for his funeral. Nicolas continued, telling Laura that the obliging mortician worked the whole night to create the perfect illusion.

"And this mortician won't talk?" Laura asked

"No love, no way! He has a family and was paid very good. He would go to jail. But even if he talks, my people will catch him and kill him."

"And the body in Abu Dhabi, what happened with it?" Laura asked.

"I dunno love; I believe he was buried by his family. But not till after we take my suit." Nicolas laughed again; his tone remained humorous and darkly irreverent. "We just borrow him, so you would have a body to see. You cause me big problem Loulou," he joked, laughing at Laura's bewildered expression. Nicolas playfully tapped her cheek as she tried to absorb what she was hearing.

"So the coffin flown from Abu Dhabi to Lebanon, was it empty?"

"Not empty," Nicolas admitted, then he wittily added, "But I was not inside." He winked mischievously.

"What was in it?" Laura curiously enquired.

"Don't ask. Questions, questions, Loulou fetch me a

whisky. Maybe then I will tell you something more," he continued, still teasing.

Nicolas was obviously delighting in being able to talk freely about the affair for the first time since it happened. Laura fetched his whisky, and then sat at his feet in front of the fire. Her eyes displayed a look of incredulous awe as she gazed up at him.

"You are amazing Nicky. It's like something from a Bond movie. I can hardly believe you did it."

"That's me, Al Hajj. Did I tell you Loulou they used to call me Simon Templar? Yeah love; when I was young the people used to say I look like that guy. Loulou I was a bloody good looking boy those days." He smiled amused by his blatant lack of modesty. "But you know love, nobody in Kousba had seen me for many years; it was easy to fool them." He took another swig of whisky. "But you love; I was worried when I heard you came to the funeral."

"Of course I would go to your funeral, what did you expect? I wouldn't go?"

In a darkly weird way it amused Laura to be discussing the events of her husband's funeral, while he was seated next to her. On a more serious note Nicolas added,

"And love, what about Bunnie? You know it hurt me what you was both going through."

"It was hell," Laura told him. "I still don't know how I managed. Alyssa was strong, but cried a lot."

"You were both strong, you made me so proud."

Nicolas lent forward planting a gentle kiss on the top of Laura's head. Talk of Alyssa re-awakened Laura to the dilemma they faced. She had total faith that Nicolas would do everything in his power; go to the ends of the earth if necessary to keep his promise to her. If anyone could make it happen Nicolas could. It would be child's play after what he had already pulled off. For Laura this was a consoling concept. However long it took, he would find a way to reunite them. If his secret were to get out, Nicolas would become a fugitive and so would Laura; he would fight equally as hard to prevent that from happening.

With her imagination fired up, Laura pushed him for more revelations. Eagerly, she waited to hear exactly how he had fled from Abu Dhabi and got into Lebanon, without arousing suspicion. Nicolas said there was an urgency to act very quickly; his 'death-mask' was made in just two days. The artist commissioned for the job was told it was needed for a theatre production. Believing Nicolas to be an actor, the artist happily obliged. At the time Nicolas said he felt he was acting. The only way to get his head around the absurd charade was to pretend he was playing a role.

When he was in his twenties, Nicolas was friendly with a well-known American movie director, who told him he possessed excellent acting skills. He was invited to go to Hollywood for a screen test. Despite his friend's insistence that he had talent and could become a star, Nicolas never followed up on the invitation. Laura was convinced if Nicolas had taken that route, he would no doubt have been a big movie star. The saga continued;

On the night of his 'death', Nicolas was smuggled outside of Abu Dhabi armed with his new identity. Two nights later (Sunday night), one of the accomplices flew to Beirut taking the mask and Nicolas's burial suit with him, which he delivered to the bribed mortician. Nicolas then travelled by road into Jordan, where he boarded a private boat bound for Lebanon. He arrived at the port of Jounieh sometime later, to be met by one of his people who drove him to the mountains. Here he remained incognito, while all of Kousba mourned his passing.

When the time was right, Al Hajj carried out his deadly mission. He looked deep into the eyes of his enemies and as they breathed their last, they were in no doubt as to the true identity of their assassin. His long awaited retribution accomplished, Al Hajj retreated again to the mountains. Still incognito, he finally made his escape; sailing from Tripoli north of Lebanon to Greece. Nicolas then travelled across Greece towards the Black sea. From there he went to Bulgaria; finally making his way to Romania.

Laura listened, paying attention to every incredulous

word. She had heard Nicolas tell some crazy stories in the past, but this one really took the biscuit. Laura felt she was listening to a story too unbelievably crazy to be true. Yet here he was, alive and breathing and it mattered not how, or even what had taken place. Her husband was alive and now Laura could live again too.

"Did you always plan to come back to me?" she asked.

"No!" he answered honestly. Sighing deeply Nicolas added; "I did it all believing I would leave everything. Family, friends, anything connecting me to my old life would be gone. Leaving you was the hardest, believe me."

Saddened by his candid words, Laura lowered her eyes. Although she understood his motive, it hurt to hear him confess to undertaking such a drastic decision fully aware of what it entailed. Hearing Nicolas's frank admission made Laura very despondent. He lifted Laura's chin gently with his hand, turning her face towards him. Then intently fixing his eyes on hers he declared;

"Love, I never wanted to leave you; never. Believe me I cried."

Laura lowered her eyes again. In an effort to convince her, Nicolas compelled her to look at him. His eyes were pleading.

"You believe me Loulou don't you?" he implored.

Tears formed in Laura's eyes and began to fall. Pulling her from the floor to his side Nicolas asked;

"Hey! What's this? I'm here aren't I? I'm with you? And Loulou whatever happens I will always love you."

His sincerity was not in question. Laura could see how much he must have agonised over his decision.

"But you know love I couldn't be sure how everything was going to work. I didn't know if I would have money to bring you or even if I would survive. Maybe something goes wrong, and one of my enemies kills me?" Nicolas took another sip of whisky and lit a cigarette; he paused again before continuing. His rueful look implied it had just dawned on him, exactly what he had sacrificed. "I knew if I survived I would find a way. You are my love, hayati I

478

told you long ago, you are on my path, on my road. As long as I live, I would find a way to be with you hayati." Nicolas held Laura so tight she could feel his heart beating against hers; "Hayati eyouni, not one day passed when I didn't think about you, and pray for you and Alyssa to be okay."

The atmosphere was heavy. Permeated by a rainbow of emotions, it was overwhelmingly joyful and painful at the same time. It seemed an age passed by as they embraced one another in the firelight, wrapped in the ethereal silence of their deep thoughts. After an un-knowable amount of time, Nicolas abruptly broke their silent reverie;

"Loulou, fetch me another whisky and get one drink for yourself."

Laura took his empty glass and went to the kitchen. She put five ice cubes into the glass and poured a large whisky. Taking the Chablis from the fridge, Laura poured a generous sized glass. Elated as she was to have Nicolas back, Laura was with good reason fearful of what kind of future lay ahead. She could never live without him again, but was also acutely aware of the sacrifice she would be making by staying. The tremendous implications scared her. Laura's mind was in turmoil. As she handed Nicolas his drink, her eyes reflected the agony of her conflicting emotions. He could read her so well. Laura's deliberate lack of eye contact told him she was worried at her choice.

"Hey Loulou, it's gonna be okay love."

Laura stared blankly ahead. Nicky probed her thoughts;

"Tell me hayati, what are you thinking about?"

Laura's demeanour became subdued as she stared into the fire.

"I was thinking about what will happen," she answered.

"What happens? Loulou if you staying with me, and I want you to stay with me, we have to make for you a new identity. Do you think you are you ready to leave your old life?" he asked earnestly. "Or you want to go back and be as before?"

"Yes," she whispered without lifting her eyes from the

flickering flames.

"Yes what? You stay or you go? Laura, look at me!" he demanded.

Laura reluctantly turned her head to face him. Nicolas asked again in a tone that was suddenly serious.

"Laura; are you ready for all this? Don't lie to yourself! You cannot change your mind. If you have any doubt, you must say it now; you understand?"

Unable to meet Nicolas's penetrating gaze, Laura looked down. Again he lifted her chin, forcing her to make eye contact. It was imperative he read the thoughts behind her words. Laura found his relentless scrutiny intimidating and uncomfortable. Nicolas needed to be sure, no matter how painful the situation, any weakness of heart at this point was unacceptable; too great was the risk of his deception being exposed. Once her decision was made, there would be no turning back. Laura now knew his secret; their future life depended on her staying strong and discreet.

Nicolas would have no qualms about letting Laura go, if he felt she wouldn't cope; as much as it would kill him, he would always be the epitome of strength. His true identity had to remain undiscovered. Nicolas would take whatever measures necessary to keep it that way. There could be no slip ups. Once he made a decision, he would carry it through to the bitter end; there was no room for regrets or reservation.

Laura knew she could never fool him. The only choice open to her was total honesty. Her eyes reluctantly met the intensity of his questioning gaze, and as she bared her soul Nicolas listened. All her fears and reservations poured out of her heart. Laura felt excruciatingly torn. Through a torrent of relentless tears she explained to him whichever way she decided, stay and leave Alyssa behind, or go back and never see her husband, both would be unbearable to live with; either would bring unimaginable heartbreak.

Nicolas lowered himself from his chair to the floor next to Laura. Putting his arms tightly around her, he gently rocked her as she sobbed her heart out.

"I know love, I know. It's okay love." He hugged her so tight Laura feared her ribs may crack. "This is what I was expecting. It's too much; love it's too much pressure to put on you."

Laura wiped her tears with a tissue, and tried to calm herself. Searching his mind for another solution, Nicolas lit a cigarette. If it came down to the wire, he was strong enough to let Laura go back to be with Alyssa. He would hate his life without her, but he would survive. Laura on the other hand would most likely fall apart. As long as he could give her hope, she would be okay. Nicolas found himself giving his word to Laura and making a promise he could not guarantee. Whichever way the dice was thrown, it appeared their love was doomed. However the cards were dealt and whichever way that dice landed, one thing could be guaranteed; Nicky and Laura would love each other till both took their last breath, and beyond.

"Listen Loulou; I will figure something. Love, don't be worried."

Once things settled they would devise a plan. Nicolas promised Laura she would be reunited with Alyssa. He would find a way to do it without arousing suspicion.

"Alyssa can keep a secret right?" he said.

Laura nodded in agreement.

"I know we can trust her, she doesn't have a big mouth like her mother."

Nicolas's joke made Laura laugh, lightening the mood considerably.

Laura agreed; if Alyssa was told anything in confidence she would never reveal it.

"Good, as I said we will make a new identity, I have many contacts here and after some time, when we feel it's safe, we will, or you will reunite with Alyssa. We will explain everything to her. If she wishes to come with us, then we will arrange it. Okay Loulou?"

Laura hugged him.

"Meanwhile," he continued. "We have to keep a low

profile, not to attract attention. Okay Loulou? And Alyssa she has Alessandro and the house and Joyie."

Laughing at his pronunciation, Laura corrected him;

"It's pronounced Joey!"

"Joheeey." He repeated deliberately over exaggerating the pronunciation.

"Alyssa will be okay love; I will see she has money to be comfortable."

"Who will send it?" Laura asked.

"I will arrange a lawyer to send it, and write her a letter explaining," he said. "I know one good crook lawyer who will do it without asking questions."

Laura laughed;

"Just the one, I thought they were all crooks?"

"You're right," he laughed. "But on this occasion it's good for us."

Laura smiled and snuggled closer. His strong arms made her feel safe. Anything felt possible with Nicolas. It was a feeling she had missed.

"Thank you," Laura kissed his cheek. "I love you so much; I know you will figure something."

"Alyssa's the only daughter I have ever known. I have to take care of her. You know I love her and I have missed her too much."

"When will we reveal our secret to her?" Laura asked eagerly.

"Love, I don't know. A year, few months, maybe next week; I don't know love the time needs to be right, okay."

Laura relaxed, happy in the belief that staying with her husband would not mean a permanent separation from her daughter.

"You trust me darling?" he asked kissing the top of her head.

"I trust you more than anyone else in the universe," she told him.

"Good! You have to trust me with this and do whatever I ask. No questions no regrets; okay Loulou? We will stay here for some time it's nice, and then we will make our move okay, you with me hundred per cent hayati?"

Laura nodded in agreement. Nicolas turned her round to face him.

"Say it! I wanna hear you say the words," he insisted.

"I'm with you one billion per cent," Laura assured him.

"Good, that's my Loulou," he said in a satisfied tone.

Nicolas threw another log on to the fire. As the flames grew bigger the heat warmed their skin. Stretching his arm out Nicolas grabbed a small box from the table.

"What's that?" Laura asked.

Nicolas took her gold bracelet from it and fastened it securely around her left wrist.

"But I thought you needed it to be found as evidence of my death?" she questioned, puzzled by his action.

"No love. That was just a test. If you could not leave this one connection to your old life, then you are not ready for this." His tone was pragmatic, further illustrating the seriousness of Laura's decision to stay with him.

Relieved to be keeping her precious bracelet, Laura's face lit up. Nicolas kissed her hand;

"It will stay with you as long as you live, but my love will stay with you forever."

For a moment they sat motionless and silent.

"You haven't told me your new identity and I guess we have to decide what mine will be." Laura whispered.

Nicolas was deep in thought. He lit his cigarette and didn't even blink as the smoke wafted in front of his face; he just stared into oblivion. Laura turned to look at him;

"Well, what is your new name? You didn't say. What do I call you now?" She repeated.

Nicolas looked at Laura as if she had just broken his train of thought. Suddenly jolted back to this world from elsewhere, he smoothed her hair, lovingly tucking a loose strand behind her ear.

"For now love relax; enjoy things as they are. While we are here we are Loulou and Hajj, Nicky and Laura. Loulou let's enjoy this time before we have to change anything."

True to form Nicolas would only reveal what he wanted

to reveal, when he wanted to reveal it. Laura put her head on his shoulder and whispered;

"Okay, whatever you say you're the boss."

"Yep I'm the boss, good you remembered." He smiled and kissed Laura tenderly. "Hayati, eyouni everything's gonna be okay."

Nicolas's relaxed demeanour and light hearted tone hid his tormented thoughts. Staring pensively into the flames, he began figuring his next move. The carefree confident smile gave way to a look of reflective self-examination. Nicolas was hard headed yes, but he was not always so pragmatic in his decisions. In the relentless pursuit of his desire, he had risked even his liberty. Nicolas would argue that freedom of the body is not enough when your soul is chained to a dream of what could have been; if only you had taken the risk.

Nicolas was confident of rebuilding his world, stone by stone if necessary; there would always be new mountains to climb and new dreams to dream. Together he and Laura would build those dreams again. One dream salvaged intact from his old life, was his ingenious invention, his 'baby'. For now it remained safely locked inside his head. When the timing was right, Nicolas would unleash his 'baby' on the world as he always planned. It would secure them financially and give back to him a little more power over what till now, had been a rather unfortunate destiny.

But as with every silver lining, there was a dark cloud hovering on this new horizon. Now they both would carry the burden of his deception. Keeping his secret safe was easier while alone; now he would need to keep Laura safe too. Silently Nicolas made a vow; whatever was required he would not shy from it.

Safe in his arms, Laura remained unaware of the many tortured thoughts haunting her lovers mind. She didn't see the solitary tear slowly creep from the corner of his eye and trickle onto his cheek, as he embraced her.

Whether written in the stars or in the choices we make, either way, fate must be accepted before it can be changed.

Some fates are more challenging than others; perhaps only the strongest among us are given the heaviest burdens to carry. Before time unfolded another year, Nicolas would lay down a new path for them; one clear of obstructions.

No matter how faithfully followed, their old path had been littered with stumbling blocks. From day one their old adversary fate, had mercilessly placed hindrances in front of every step they had taken. From now on, Nicolas would walk one step ahead of fate; nothing would obstruct what he believed was his true destiny. This time around he would fulfil his dreams, all of them.

Materialistically, he wanted his power to be as before. Nicolas was on his way, but he knew the greatest and strongest power was of a more spiritual nature. Through his many trials and tribulations he had come to realise, the hearts most sought after treasure, cannot be found in materialism. Nicolas was fortunate in having found his everlasting love. For some love can be as transitory as a snowflake melting in your hand. Life for Nicolas needed to be lived on the edge to be fully experienced; the same with love. A heart broken by the pain of love is a heart that knows how to love. Life and love should be lived and felt to the point of tears.

A man's ability to love cannot be calculated; it is often unpredictable. Like the wind, love is a force whose power can be witnessed, but to know its true elemental nature, it has to be felt. Loves strength can lift the strongest man off his feet, or drive him to his knees. A man of great passion will likely kill for love. The force of his passions can drive him to kill for the love of his country, his faith and beliefs, or the love of his woman. Always at the route of every passion and driving force, is the love of something.

KOUSBAWI

Chapter 51: Conclusion: The Rose

Sometime later, a news report revealed a woman had gone missing from the UK. It was believed she had travelled to Romania and boarded a ferry off the coast of Constanta. It appeared she had not returned from that trip. The missing woman was named as Laura Quinn. Although no body was ever recovered, a gold bracelet had been found, which was identified by the woman's daughter as belonging to her missing mother. The report disclosed Laura Quinn was heavily depressed following the death of her husband two years ago. Witnesses later recalled, seeing a woman fitting Laura's description board the ferry with a man. Despite numerous requests for him to do so, he has never come forward. It was feared Laura may have accidentally fallen overboard and drowned. The report stated suicide had not been ruled out. As for the identity of the man seen with Miss Quinn, well that remains a mystery.

Many years later an immaculately dressed, strikingly handsome man of an indiscernible age, stands on a clifftop in the distance. If you looked closely you would see that his dark eyes had a wistful faraway look in them. He holds something in his hands; twelve long stemmed blood red roses. One by one, the man tosses eleven of the roses into the sea below. The twelfth rose he keeps and slowly walks away, leaving eleven roses floating and drifting delicately out to sea.

This mysterious stranger is often seen at different times performing the same sad ritual. Nobody knows who he is, but there was once talk in the village amongst the locals who told stories, saying he had lost something precious to him; perhaps a great love? In the past, people had tried unsuccessfully to make conversation with the stranger. They were always met with silence and a defiant steely gaze, which intimidated them enough to leave him alone.

Today he is there again, standing alone staring out over the horizon of the Black Sea near Constanta. A beautiful young girl barely seventeen years old is walking nearby. She stops and watches spellbound, as the man tosses roses onto the water below. Intrigued by the act, and possessing a wilful curious nature, the young girl is determined to find out why he is doing this. Of course she had heard the local stories and rumours saying he was unapproachable, but being an adventurous confident young woman, she took it upon herself to try and engage in conversation with the stranger. For whatever reason he fascinated her, and she felt compelled to know his story.

Quietly she approached. As she came close she sensed a deep sadness about him. There was a feeling of loss emanating from the stranger. The young woman held back briefly, not wishing to intrude too quickly into what was clearly a very private moment. Part of her felt she should perhaps leave him alone and not interfere; after all it was none of her business.

Blessed with a disposition of unrelenting curiosity, not to mention a hopeless romantic, she naturally ignored her reservations. Inquisitively driven to be bold and speak with him, the girl moved closer still. At first he didn't seem to notice her presence as she warily stood at his side. With her curiosity awakened and in the hope of discovering something about the fascinating stranger, the young girl bravely asked why he was tossing roses into the sea. The man turned his head to see who had dared to interrupt him, giving her the same steely gaze he gave to everyone. As he looked at her, she noticed his dark eyes were moist from silent tears. Far from being intimidated, her interest was aroused further. In a gesture of friendship, she held out her hand to him;

"My name is Marie-Elena", she said. "I'm sorry if I disturbed you," she apologised, quickly pulling her hand back; he clearly was not going to shake it.

The stranger just stared at the audacious young woman. Something about her felt familiar. At five feet four inches tall and as slender as a reed, she had waist length auburn coloured hair. It flowed down over her shoulders waving gently in the soft late summer breeze. Her large striking green eyes flashed at him with inquisitive innocence.

The tantalisingly pretty Marie-Elena, felt the strangers dark eyes burn into her, as if reading her somehow. It was a little unsettling. But the intrepid young woman held her nerve, determinedly meeting his penetrating gaze. Maybe this was not the best idea after all she thought, she should leave him be. As the girl was about to make herself scarce, the stranger suddenly spoke;

"Marie-Elena you said? That's a pretty name."

He spoke with an accent, which she didn't recognise as being of local origin.

"Thank you," she said. "What's yours?"

The stranger deliberately ignored her question. Turning his head away he continued to look out to sea. For a while they stood in silence looking across the horizon. Although he remained silent, Marie-Elena felt a strong charismatic aura. It was powerful; she believed if he were to walk into a room, everyone would take notice. Being in his presence was mesmerising. Without warning the stranger suddenly spoke again;

"May I ask you something?"

The unexpectedness of his utterance, made Marie-Elena jump; her startled reaction appeared to amuse him. His expression automatically changed into a broad smile that lit up his entire face, wiping away in an instant the sad melancholic look he was wearing a moment ago. The girl thought he had the most charismatically beguiling smile.

"Tell me Marie-Elena, do you believe in true love?" The stranger asked.

Being a sucker for romance, Marie-Elena delighted at this unexpected question;

"Oh yes, I absolutely do," she told him.

Pleased by her response he smiled again and continued;

"I mean, the kind of love that neither time nor distance will ever fade. A love without boundaries and with no end, a love you would gladly kill or die for."

Marie-Elena was astounded by his passionate, poetic style of speech. His words held a profound truth, revealing he was a man who had loved very deeply and probably sacrificed much for the sake of it. He took a packet of cigarettes from his pocket and lit one.

"You do know that's no good for you," she boldly told him, referring to his smoking.

He gave a little laugh then retorted;

"People have been telling me that for years, one person in particular."

Shaking his head he smiled wistfully, adding;

"But you know we don't always do what is good for us do we; am I right Marie-Elena?"

Nodding in agreement the young girl smiled coyly at him. Immediately she warmed to the enigmatic stranger. A moment of connectedness transpired between them. Like kindred spirits, they understood each other. An impossible, yet distinct déjà vu was felt by both. Familiarity reflected in their eyes and a deafening eerie silence prevailed, as they gazed at one another. Marie-Elena then spoke;

"To answer your question, yes I do believe in love, true love," she said. "But I haven't found it yet."

The mesmeric stranger took one last drawn out puff on his cigarette, then flicked it over the cliff. Turning to the girl he smiled. She couldn't help but notice how his dark eyes twinkled like stars in a night sky; she felt drawn into them. How beautiful he must have been as a young man, she thought.

"Well Marie-Elena, you are still very young, there is no rush. But if you are ever fortunate enough to find love, I mean real love; never let it go, never let it slip from your grasp. Because you will have found the greatest treasure this world has to offer."

Marie-Elena looked at him quizzically.

"How will I know when I have found true love?"

"Oh you will know," he answered. Then he told her;

"But with anything worth having, it comes at a price."

"What kind of price?" she asked.

He looked into her young questioning eyes, so innocent so full of hope. He could have told her that true love would require her to give her soul. That love would grip hold of it so tightly she would not be able to imagine life without it. And if one day she was without her love, then a piece of her soul would be missing; her world would become meaningless and empty. She would walk through life half dreaming, continually searching for that elusive part of herself. She would wake every morning, longing for the day when she would at last be reunited with her one true love; only then would she feel whole again. He could have said that, but instead he told her;

"If true love knocks on your door one day Marie-Elena, don't run from it. Embrace it with all that you are, because whatever the price, the prize is greater. Love will set your heart ablaze; smouldering at first, then whoosh and it's got you. And if its true love, you will be lost in its fiery flames forever."

There was a wistful longing in his eyes as he spoke, and a fierce hunger for days gone by. As he stood there fondly remembering his great love, Marie-Elena felt an aura of glowing warmth radiate all around him. She knew that whoever this woman was who had taken hold of his heart so completely, he must have loved her very deeply, and clearly he still did. Impetuously she asked;

"You found your true love then?"

He gave Marie-Elena another penetrative look.

"You remind me of somebody," he told her, "always asking questions."

The stranger again stared out across the horizon. His eyes shone with so many untold secrets. He looked to be a million miles away as he revealed;

"Oh yes Marie-Elena, I found her."

His mood immediately lifted. The melancholy was now replaced by sweet memories. Again he was lost in thought, as they stood in silence on the cliff top; the roses were still bobbing on the water below.

"You didn't tell me your name," she blurted suddenly breaking his pensive reverie.

"You don't give up do you? Pushy like somebody else I know."

With a wry smile and a mischievous glint in his eye, he handed her the rose he was holding. Reaching into his coat pocket, he took out a silver pen and a small piece of paper. He started to write something down. Folding the paper in half he held it out to Marie-Elena. She took the paper from his hand. The stranger turned away and began to walk back down the cliff path. Marie-Elena unfolded the paper; mystified she stared at it. Confused by what he had written she called after him;

"Wait! What's this!? I don't understand."

He had written a sequence of numbers;

11-15-21-19-2-1-23-9

"You asked me who I was." He replied without looking back, and continuing down the cliff.

"Wait!" she ran after him "These are just numbers, is it some sort of code?"

The stranger stopped walking and slowly turned round; her puzzled expression caused him to smile.

"You're a smart girl, I'm sure you will figure it out," he told her, turning away again.

"No wait!" she insisted, following him down the cliff. "You forgot your rose."

The stranger stopped again and looked at the rose she was holding out to him.

"Keep it, it's yours," he said.

"Thank you, it's lovely." Marie-Elena stared at the rose's delicate beauty.

"You're most welcome Marie-Elena. I don't need it, where I'm going the most beautiful rose of all is waiting."

With a pensive look, the mysterious stranger continued on his way. Marie-Elena clasped the rose tightly breathing in its alluring perfume;

"OUCH!!" she cried out suddenly, having pricked her finger on a sharp thorn.

The stranger stopped, and looked round at her. A small amount of blood trickled from the girl's hand. It matched the deep red colour of the rose. The stranger told her;

"You see Marie-Elena, even the beautiful things in life will bring you pain, but the reward of love is worth the risk of pain; remember that!"

Marie-Elena quickly sucked the blood from her finger.

"Really, that's so poignant," she declared. "You seem to know a lot about love and roses."

Smiling enigmatically at her, the stranger responded, proclaiming,

"Let me tell you something, when you first see the rose you are trapped by its beauty. You may be cut by its sharp thorns, but as much as you continue to bleed, you will still want to embrace the sweet fragrance. Even the rose itself, needs both the sun and the rain in order to fully blossom."

Marie-Elena could tell this stranger was well-read and really very cultured. His turn of phrase was so poetic and philosophical. He gave a prolonged sigh before turning back down the hill. She watched for a moment as the stranger took the long walk down the cliff path.

Marie-Elena glanced briefly at the rose in her hand. She quickly looked back towards the stranger. To her amazement he had disappeared out of sight. Looking in all directions into the distance her eyes searched earnestly for him. The stranger was absolutely nowhere to be seen. Marie-Elena was puzzled; he couldn't possibly have got down the hill that quickly. She scoured the cliff for any sign; but to no avail, it was as though he had evaporated into the ether.

Marie-Elena never saw the charismatic stranger again. But she never forgot him, and often when she was out walking, she would look expectantly to the cliffs to see if by chance he was there. But the enigmatic foreigner never returned to that spot. Marie-Elena wished she could have known him, he fascinated her. She wanted to hear the story of his life, and about the woman he loved with such passion. She imagined he would have many stories to tell.

Some weeks later while sorting through her purse, Marie-Elena came across the folded piece of paper with the numbers the stranger had written down. Curious as to their significance, she decided to try and solve the cryptic puzzle. After spending a few moments trying to figure out the mysterious conundrum, frustrated Marie-Elena gave up impatiently throwing the paper to one side. It was then she was struck by a sudden flash of inspiration. Matching each number to a corresponding letter of the alphabet a strange name was revealed.

KOUSBAWI

The End

Laura's Laments:

Heroes Never Die

Above the snow-capped mountains,
You fly so high and free.
Your soul descends upon the land,
Where your heart yearns to be.
You left this place so long ago,
For other lands to roam.
But Lebanon will always be,
Your one and only home.
High in the mountains of the north,
Your beloved Kousba lies.
Unseen unheard you'll walk beneath,
Those Middle Eastern skies.
To go away was not your choice,
Your plan was to return.
Back to the land you held so dear,
Your heart for Kousba yearned.
Sweet forests of cedar scent the air,
Their perfumed trees grow strong.
With roots deep like the cedar tree,
To Lebanon you belong.
Beirut's iridescent beauty
Will enchant your soul at night.
This jewel of the east at dusk reflects
The shimmering neon lights.
You see your loved ones left behind,
Their eyes are sad with pain.
Can they not see you did not die?
One day you'll meet again?
In time the truth they too shall find,
You're near they must not cry.
If only they could understand,
That heroes' never die.

Loulou

Laura's Laments

Love Has No End

He's walking towards me, surrounded with light.
I see him smile, such a beautiful sight.
Our days together were happy and long.
But now he's not here it's hard to be strong.
I talk to him often, I call out his name.
When he does not answer I'm broken with pain.
My tears keep on falling as I lay in my bed.
But then I remember the words he once said.
Nothing can kill me, for I am Al Hajj.
I love you hayati so please don't be sad.
So strong and so brave, for you death held no fear.
But you left me alone, and I miss you Hajj dear.
Through tears I will smile remembering our love.
I'm sure you are watching from heaven above.
Though my heart may be broken, I know you're not gone.
I feel you so close when they're playing our song.
Our love is eternal, and it fills me with joy.
To know you still love me, my sweet dark eyed boy.
So Nicolas my darling rest peacefully now.
Till I can be with you I'll get through somehow.
At last I will see you surrounded by light.
To your arms I will run and hold you so tight.
So God bless my teacher, my lover, my friend.
You'll always be with me our love has no end.

Loulou

Laura's Laments

Whisper of the heart

The whisper of my heart,
Speaks words I can't ignore.
It guides me through in troubled times,
And will sail me safe to shore.
You were everything I dreamt you'd be,
I bless the day we met.
Burning bright within my soul,
You're the love I can't forget.
A gentle echo within my heart,
Tells me you never died.
You must know that I love you still,
Just count the tears I've cried.
It took a while to realise,
You're alive within my heart.
You whisper everything's okay,
We are really not apart.
You wish to guide and comfort me,
To soothe my grief and sorrow.
Each moment spent without you hurts,
I'll grieve much more tomorrow.
So darling, please keep whispering,
Your words eternal and true.
Poured into my heart with every beat,
Until the day I return to you.

Loulou

Laura's Laments

The Day You Couldn't Stay

Time slips by it goes so fast, a new year soon is dawning.
I didn't know it wouldn't last, fate never gave a warning.
That day you left me all alone, death took your soul away.
The saddest day I've ever known, the day you couldn't
stay.
I know we chose it long ago, this life we'd live together.
Winds of change set to blow, and dreams are gone forever.
This mortal body I too shall leave, when the time is right.
To this earthly plane I will not cleave, while eternity's in
sight.
One day my soul to you will fly, in loving arms I'll be.
Tears of joy I know I'll cry, as your smile again I see.
Beneath my pain I know it's true, you never left my side.
It hurts too much this missing you, return to your grieving
bride.
Too short our time together was, upon this mortal plain.
Eternity is ours because, love's truth will forever reign.
How much longer must I wait, I feel so lost and alone.
I know you stand at Heaven's gate, just waiting to call me
home.

Loulou

A collection of Poems by Lynda Chehade

And ever has it been known that love knows not
its own depth, until the hour of separation.
Kahlil Gibran.

Lightning Source UK Ltd.
Milton Keynes UK
UKOW04f1838141115

262720UK00001B/1/P

9 781785 074394